PENG

Murder at Mistletoe Manor

Flic Everett lives in rural Scotland with her husband, two spaniels and one black cat, in a very small cottage between a forest and a loch. As well as being an author of fiction and non-fiction, including her cosy mystery series *Edie York*, Flic has experience working as a journalist, broadcaster, agony aunt, vintage shop owner and as a tarot reader.

Flic's favourite things are reading, animals, very hot baths, cooking and buying clothes that are hopelessly unsuitable for her life. She also has a never-ending appetite for rummaging in charity shops.

Murder at Mistletoe Manor

F. L. EVERETT

PENGUIN BOOKS

PENGUIN BOOKS

UK | USA | Canada | Ireland | Australia
India | New Zealand | South Africa

Penguin Books is part of the Penguin Random House group of companies
whose addresses can be found at global.penguinrandomhouse.com

Penguin Random House UK,
One Embassy Gardens, 8 Viaduct Gardens, London SW11 7BW

penguin.co.uk
global.penguinrandomhouse.com

Penguin
Random House
UK

Published in Penguin Books 2025
001

Typeset in 11.88/15 pt Fournier MT Std by Six Red Marbles UK, Thetford, Norfolk
Printed and bound in Great Britain by Clays Ltd, Elcograf S.p.A.

The authorised representative in the EEA is Penguin Random House Ireland,
Morrison Chambers, 32 Nassau Street, Dublin D02 YH68

A CIP catalogue record for this book is available from the British Library

ISBN: 978-1-804-95452-2

In loving memory of Vera Preger, who taught
me all I know about crime.

Trapped at Mistletoe Manor

Nick Caldwell, 36, journalist
Lorraine Pinner, 56, mum to Jade, 29
Alan Pinner, 58, Lorraine's husband; business-owner and stepdad
Destiny, 29, yoga teacher
Violet Evans, 30, works in PR
Branson Mitchell, 50, American and rich
Penelope Mitchell, his wife, 51, worked in publishing
David Foley, 45, GP
Emily Foley, 8, his daughter
Matilda Mannering, 80, widow, retired
Colt Alfred, 24, hotel chef
Donal Walsh, 28, hotel manager
Jingle, 4, black and white cat
Gaia, 2, miniature French bulldog

1

December. Somewhere in the Yorkshire Moors

Five days till Christmas Eve

Everything is white. The road markings have vanished in a blur of whirling snow; the windscreen is so encrusted with ice, he's peering through a gap the size of his hand; and the wipers have died. Soon, he won't be able to see anything at all and the fog lights are no use because all they're doing is illuminating the vast, feathery flakes that have been falling since before he left Middlesbrough, three hours ago.

'Sure you won't stay the night?' asked Nick's photographer, Fletch, as they surveyed the weather. Nick was briefly tempted by the thought of deconstructing their dying newspaper industry over a takeaway curry, but shook his head.

'Not fair on Harriet. I've been away nearly a week already and she's been on her own with Cara.'

His wife's last message read, *Still in dressing gown at 4pm. Luckily, Cara is thrilled with life regardless. Just found some toast in my bra. Hurry back x.*

Nick smiled at the thought of his three-month-old daughter.

He couldn't wait to see her gummy pink grin, and earnestly accept whatever damp toy she wanted to wave at him. If he was honest, though, his assignment for the *Daily Globe*, where he was still clinging to his 'Long Reads' reporter job, had come at a good time. He and Harriet were both exhausted, bickering and competing for who had it worst – ticking off every thirty-something new-parent cliché on the list. They needed a break from each other, and while researching an in-depth piece on Middlesbrough's ageing homeless population in mid-December was admittedly bleak, it ensured Harriet had no reason to envy him.

Nick hopes the enforced separation has done them both good. He's missed her as well as Cara, though they've spoken regularly, and his long drive back to London through the snow was, he'd thought, a price worth paying to be home in time for a glass of wine with his weary wife before bed.

Now, after a series of horn-honking tailbacks, overturned lorries and complex diversions, that seems unlikely. Some distance down the hedge-bound country lane where the malfunctioning satnav has sent him, his engine cuts out with an asthmatic wheeze and the car skids slowly to a halt on the verge. Nick checks his phone. He may as well have time-slipped back to Victorian times for all the signal he's got. He wouldn't be surprised if a carriage rolled past, its top-hatted coachman cracking a whip. In fact, the sight would be a relief – at least he could beg for a lift. As it is, there's nothing out there but the snow, an endless white murmuration against the ink-dark sky. Luckily, he's not the panicking type. He's more of a 'make a list, work your way through, then failing that, make another list' man. It drives Harriet mad.

'Be spontaneous!' she often says, and he always gives her his standard dad-joke reply:

'I'll need to plan for that.'

Nick assesses the situation. He can't walk far in this. Before the engine gave up, the dashboard display claimed the temperature was minus two. It's after six and pitch-black but for the eerie gleam of the drifting snow. He hasn't seen any other drivers down this lane, and is beginning to think he took a wrong turn at the crossroads almost six miles back.

He can either stay put and hope someone comes past before he dies of hypothermia, or he can go for a recce and see if there are any houses nearby where he can shelter and await the AA. Admittedly, most weary home-owners enjoying a post-work drink aren't going to be thrilled by the sight of a six-foot bloke with shoulders like hams and a cauliflower ear from his rugby days pitching up in a snowstorm. Then again, Nick's old editor would have said, 'You won't get the story if you don't knock on the bloody door, Nicholas.'

He gathers his phone, wallet and overnight bag, pulls on his beanie and climbs out into the blizzard. He'll give it fifteen minutes, then if he has no luck, he'll return to the safety of the car and wait for a fellow driver.

Nick doesn't remember snow ever being this thick. It's spinning around him like a swarm of angry bees, and immediately, he loses all sense of direction. Maps won't load on his phone and, like all millennials, he didn't even consider packing a paper map. Why would he? The torch function still works, a feeble shaft of light in a monochrome kaleidoscope, and he thinks he's identified the centre of the road. Nick shuffles along like an old man, straining to spot a gate in the endless hedgerow. Perhaps he'll find a farm where he can shelter in the cowshed.

He's no idea how far he's gone, but he can't feel his fingers and his nose is entirely numb. He's going to have to return to the car – perhaps he can have a look at the engine. Nick almost laughs. Car maintenance is not his forte. His dad was a Latin teacher in a boys' school. Nick could tell you how ancient Romans got around the empire but he'd be hard-pressed to explain the function of a carburettor. Besides, the phone's battery is now on 9 per cent. He's not going to have a torch for long.

Nick stops. On his right, just visible through the dizzying flakes, the dark bulk of the hedge appears to be higher than it was. There's a tree, perhaps an oak, its bare branches laden with snow. Nick trudges towards it, feeling an icy trickle enter his left boot, and is rewarded – the tree marks the entrance to a concealed driveway. On the other side of the gap is a dark rhododendron bush, twice his height, and beneath it, faintly illuminated by the beam from his ailing phone, is a wooden sign. Nick crouches and uses his sleeve to brush away the snow clinging to the old-fashioned, faded words:

MISTLETOE MANOR HOTEL

Beneath, a painted feathered arrow directs guests up the drive, with no suggestion of how far it might be to the house. Nevertheless, he feels greatly relieved. Even if the hotel has closed for the winter, or shut down altogether, there might be a caretaker – worst-case scenario, he'll break in and use the telephone to call Harriet and the AA, and find a bed for the night.

It beats a cowshed. He sets off, trying to ignore the mirage of the blazing fire and glowing brandy decanters that glimmers before him, knowing it's probably going to be a locked door and a painful scramble through broken glass into a freezing utility room. Worse, the place might have burned to the ground years ago, and he'll find himself in a field, surrounded by charred beams.

It's hard to see where he's going – the drive seems to twist and turn as if it follows the curves of a river, and he blunders painfully into a hawthorn bush, badly scratching his face and snagging the wool of his hat. This will be a funny anecdote when he gets home, he tells himself firmly. He imagines a dinner table, laughing friends, someone topping up his glass – *Oh my God, Nick, tell us about that time when you* . . . Although it's a long time since they've had anyone round, apart from Harriet's mother. 'It's too hard with Cara,' she says, and he knows what she means. Just tidying the kitchen is like undertaking the kind of home renovation that requires living in a caravan for the winter.

Nick has no idea how long he's been walking up the drive, but it feels like hours. He's beginning to worry about frostbite and hypothermia, afraid that if he doesn't reach shelter soon, he'll begin to hallucinate; then he'll simply lie down in the snow and die of exposure. He forces Cara's little face to mind, and he carries on, round another bend, a stumble into a concealed ditch and – finally – he sees the light.

Somewhere up ahead, beyond the black, looming trees and the seething snowflakes, a window glows the colour of clear honey, and he's fairly sure he can make out the shapes of people inside.

Elation gives him a burst of speed. He's approaching a huge, pale, Georgian manor house with a pillared porch, the window of the drawing room lit up like a glittering Christmas-card illustration. For a second, he thinks he can hear music, but it's his mind playing tricks – there's nothing but the muf-fled squeak of his footsteps as he makes his way past an ornate, iced-over fountain towards the wide stone steps.

The panelled front door is painted a glossy black, with tar-nished brass fittings illuminated by the porch light. A Victorian boot-scraper stands by the step, and snow-crusted ivy writhes up the walls beside the pillars. Nick ignores the bell; lifting the heavy knocker in the shape of a lion's head with numb fingers, he bangs it twice. Almost immediately, he hears the turning of a key and the door swings open on to a wide hall leading to a flight of red-carpeted stairs.

A young man stands in the doorway. He's wearing black trousers, a white shirt and a padded navy gilet. He's in his late twenties, with a thin, clever face and black hair swept back from his forehead.

'Good evening, sir,' he says. 'Can I help you?' There's a hint of a Dublin accent.

'I hope so. I'm afraid my engine's died, and I've been lucky enough to find you – I wondered if I could call the AA and wait here for them?'

The young man looks startled. 'You can, of course,' he says. 'Come on in, you must be frozen. The guests we have with us are all in the drawing room, there's a good fire in there, so you can warm up. Where are you headed?'

'London,' Nick says, stepping inside. 'I think I took a wrong turn.'

The young man laughs. 'I should say you did, sir. We're not exactly easy to find. But have you not heard the weather report?'

'Well, I know it's snowing.'

'They're saying it's the worst blizzard to hit the east coast in decades. Climate change, probably.' He shrugs. 'I heard a guy on Radio Four earlier saying they don't expect it to stop – they're advising everyone to stay put with candles and torches, in case it brings down the power lines. There's no trains running and the police have shut the motorway.' He pauses. 'I think you might be staying with us overnight.'

2

Nick knows it's inevitable, but still, his heart sinks. He thinks of Harriet's anticipation of his imminent return, Cara asleep in her cot, the mobile twirling soft, coloured lights across her face, their battered blue linen sofa, and a bottle of red wine open on the coffee table . . .

'Do you have a room available?'

'Absolutely. I'm afraid we're a skeleton staff in the run-up to Christmas, a few headed home before the snowstorm, but we'll do our best to make you comfortable. I'm Donal Walsh – I'm the . . . well, the manager, receptionist, juggler-in-chief and, if required, Irish dancer. Junior champion, Cork, 2011.'

'Nicholas Caldwell. Can't Irish dance to save my life.' Nick smiles at him, and takes a seat at the reception desk.

'Let me just see where I can put you . . .' Donal opens a large green ledger and runs a finger down the columns. Nick realises what's missing from the mahogany desk with its stand of tourist leaflets and old brass bell.

'No computer?'

'Ah, the owner isn't keen. Likes things done the old-fashioned way. To be fair, we've only the twelve rooms, so it's easy enough.'

'How do you deal with bookings coming in?'

Donal grins. 'Between you and me, I've an app on my phone.'

Nick looks around him while Donal studies the book. The entrance hall is large, draughty and was once immensely elegant. The crimson walls are hung with gloomy oil paintings of seascapes and furious-looking bewhiskered ancestors, there's a large, tea-coloured water stain on the moulded ceiling, and the parquet floor has been scuffed by generations of feet. A marble fireplace the shade of raw mince contains nothing but an empty brass grate, and although there's a huge Christmas tree in a pot by the stairs, some of its needles have already dropped and its decoration is sparse – a few dull, silver baubles that look decades old, some sagging paper chains and a single string of flickering fairy lights. Where there should be a star or an angel on the very top, there's nothing but a bare branch.

He thinks of the bushy little Christmas tree at home, laden with home-made decorations, shiny, multi-coloured baubles, all the fairy lights they could fit on it. Nick always loved decorating the tree as a child. He hopes it will become a tradition for Cara too, when she's a bit older and he can lift her up to place a glittering star on the top . . .

'Ah, here we are.' Donal lifts his head and smiles. 'I'll put you in Hawthorn. It overlooks the front gardens, and it's got an en-suite. It's not as big as some of the others, but it's quite warm, and I think you'll be comfortable.'

Nick experiences a wave of gratitude. The feeling is beginning to return to his tingling fingers, and he has his overnight bag, with a change of clothes. A call home, a hot shower and some food . . . this may yet turn from the most stressful evening of his life into a pleasant diversion.

'Is there a Wi-Fi password? I need to let my wife know where I am.'

'It's "mistletoebough", all lower-case,' says Donal. 'Though I must warn you, signal can be intermittent. Let me show you to your room, then when you've warmed up a bit, come down for drinks. There's just nine of you this evening, and Chef and I thought you might all prefer to eat together.'

Nick suspects Chef and Donal thought serving one table would be easier than rushing between several when they're so short-staffed, but who can blame them?

'Of course.'

Donal hands Nick a large, brass key with a handwritten tag: 'Hawthorn' – the tree that scratched his face on the long trek up the drive. In the relative warmth and light of the manor, his walk through the blizzard is beginning to feel like something he once dreamed, long ago. Nick follows Donal up the shallow stairs with their waxed mahogany bannister and round the sweeping curve to the left, past a brocade-curtained window. The wide landing is parquet too and he wonders whether guests ever object to the noise of footsteps passing to and fro. The air smells of woodsmoke and beeswax.

'Here we are.' Donal stops halfway down and indicates a large wooden door. 'I'll leave you to it. The drawing room's just opposite reception.'

Nick thanks him, and lets himself in, flicking the light switch by the door. Hawthorn is exactly as described, with dark green walls, a moth-eaten Persian rug on the wooden floor and, to his relief, an old-fashioned iron radiator. It's off and the air is icy, but he turns the dial and hears encouraging clanking noises echoing from deep within its chambers. The double bed with its polished walnut frame looks Victorian, and there's a matching chest of drawers and small desk with a free-standing mirror, as well as a fold-out luggage rack. In fact, there's altogether too much furniture, and he closes the rack against the wall to make more space. He might feel trapped in a BBC period drama if it weren't for the electric lamps on either side of the bed, and the white cotton duvet and neatly tucked green chenille throw. Over the bed is a large, gilt-framed oil painting of a hawthorn tree – and wound through its branches, he realises as he looks more closely, is mistletoe, its white berries shining from the darkness.

Nick sits on the creaking bed to remove his wet boots, plugs in his phone to charge, and types the password. Nothing. He tries Mistletoebough, MistletoeBough, and mistletoe_bough. There's no connection. He'll have to use a landline. He feels as though he's had a crucial organ removed. Nick's a journalist, he doesn't function without the small, rectangular comfort-object in his hand, as essential to his well-being as Cara's fluffy musical zebra is to hers. Perhaps the snow has already damaged the local phone mast, or he misheard Donal.

He sets the phone aside and tries the door opposite, which leads to a black-and-white-tiled bathroom, with a small enamel tub and overhead shower and an ancient-looking loo with a wooden seat and wall-mounted cistern. There's a round mirror above the cracked basin, and he recoils as he catches a glimpse of his face. Blood has dried in streaks from where the thorns pierced his skin, and his bloodshot blue eyes stare unnervingly from under his unravelling hat. He looks exactly like one of the homeless men he's spent the week interviewing. *How quickly life can change,* Nick thinks. A bit of bad luck and we can all go from a carefully curated professional façade to chaos, in a frighteningly short time.

*

After a hot shower he dresses in fresh clothes and pulls his damp boots back on. The room is warming up – by the time he returns it should be pleasant enough. Nick pulls aside the curtain. Snow is still falling, thick and soft as goose-down, piling on the windowsill in drifts. He can't call the AA out now – they must be inundated, and besides, it's not safe for any driver out there. He'll have to wait until morning. The next, crucial thing is to find a telephone that works and ring Harriet. He locks the door behind him and heads back down the stairs. The sound of voices is drifting up from the drawing room; Nick's not feeling at his most sociable, but he can make an effort – getting along with all kinds of people comes with the job.

Donal is back at the desk, and sitting in front of him, licking a paw, is a large black-and-white cat with a bell around its neck.

'Evening. This is Jingle,' says Donal. 'He's very friendly, I hope you're not allergic.'

'Nope. I love cats.' Nick wanders over to stroke his silky head. Jingle pushes against his hand, and stretches a paw to pat his sleeve for more.

'Does he live here?'

'Yep,' says Donal. 'He belongs to the hotel and everyone in it. The bell is because he's a terrible one for catching birds and bringing them in as gifts. At least this way, they get fair warning. Everyone's down already,' he adds. 'I'll be bringing whisky cocktails shortly. Unless you don't drink, of course?'

'No, I drink,' Nick tells him. 'Not many teetotal journalists out there.'

'Oh, you're a journalist! Better be careful what I say.'

Donal must be the three-thousandth person to have said that in the course of Nick's career.

'My phone's not working,' Nick tells him. 'Is there a landline?'

Donal pulls a face. 'The Wi-Fi does seem to be down. I apologise. If you can bear to wait, I'll track down the old-school phone – the handset seems to have vanished. A previous guest must have left it somewhere.'

'That's fine,' says Nick. It isn't, but what choice does he have? He smiles politely and raises a hand, making his way to the open door of the drawing room.

Inside, it's much warmer. The walls are a dull gold, hung with more portraits, and a long sideboard holds bottles and glasses, with a small sign reading 'Honesty Bar'. The gold brocade curtains are now firmly closed, and people are grouped on old velvet sofas and sitting in wing-backed armchairs around an enormous marble fireplace, where logs burn invitingly in the grate.

Nick feels the tension leaving his body like smoke curling up the chimney. Harriet isn't expecting him for hours; it wouldn't hurt to have a drink before he calls. He makes his way to the group by the fire, seeing now that one is a little girl of about eight.

'Evening. May I join you? I'm Nick Caldwell.'

'Blimey.' A balding man in his fifties wearing a navy blazer and chinos stands up and offers his hand. 'Where did you come from, mate? I thought the roads were impassable.'

'Well, clearly they weren't, Alan,' says the woman sitting alongside him. She's around the same age, with white-blonde, straightened hair and a stretchy red dress that reveals a scoop of leathery, tanned cleavage.

'My car broke down,' Nick explains. 'I found this place by accident.'

'Good job you did,' says the woman. 'You'd have died of exposure out there. I'm Lorraine Pinner, and this is my husband, Alan. We're meant to be at our daughter Jade's for Christmas, but somebody' – she glares at Alan – 'forgot the present bag for the kiddies and we had to turn back. By the time we got past Durham it was snowing cats and dogs and we've had to stop.'

'It's "raining cats and dogs", not snowing—' Alan begins, but Lorraine speaks over him.

'Anyway, nice to meet you, Rick. Always fun to have a good-looking man joining proceedings.'

Nick has no idea how to respond, given the implied insult to her husband. Fortunately, another guest touches his arm. She's a tall, slim young woman with long, shining brown hair and the wistful prettiness of a seventies perfume advert. She's wearing a beautifully cut blue silk dress, there's a diamond on a chain round her neck, and at her feet is a Gucci bag. He wonders why someone with money has chosen to stay at this slightly dilapidated hotel.

'Violet,' she says. Her accent is upper-middle-class. 'Nice to meet you. Have a seat – I'll introduce you. None of us knew each other until about half an hour ago.'

'Well, everyone seems to be getting along famously,' Nick says, aware that he's slipping seamlessly into professional 'bland small-talk' mode. There's a rattle behind them. Donal is pushing a drinks trolley laden with crystal glasses holding amber liquid.

'Ooh, cocktails!' says Violet, clapping her hands. There's a general murmur of satisfaction as he begins to hand them out. Nick swigs his and almost chokes – it's alarmingly strong for a

14

pre-dinner drink. Or maybe he's just lost his touch, now he can barely manage a glass of Merlot without falling asleep.

'This is Penelope and Branson,' says Violet, indicating a couple perched on the adjacent sofa, who smile slightly and lift their hands in greeting. She's what the women's desk at the *Globe* would call 'well-preserved', with a sharp black bob and, Nick suspects, a great deal of Botox maintaining a brow so smooth it gleams in the firelight. She has hazel eyes, neat, dark eyebrows and she's dressed in a cashmere jumper, smart jeans and brown leather knee-boots – the safe 'casual evening' uniform of the upper middle class. Her husband, Branson, has the handsome, dissolute features and sculpted hair of a news anchor gone to seed and wears a grey suit and blue tie.

'Good to meet you.' He has an American accent and pumps Nick's hand as if he's jacking up a car.

'Are you over from the States for Christmas?'

'Sort of, yes.' Penelope has a Home Counties tone, redolent of beloved spaniels and boarding-school hockey. 'Actually, we were rather lucky. We won a competition for a few days' stay here before Christmas, and thought we'd combine it with a trip to Devon, to see my grown-up son.'

'Didn't count on the English winter weather though!' Branson chuckles. 'Looks like we might be stuck here a while.'

'Oh, don't say that!' Penelope turns to him, a flash of dread in her eyes. 'I'm not sure how many times we can play Scrabble in the library.'

'Well, not if you're gonna insist on the English spellings . . .' Branson catches Nick's eye, humorously seeking support. He suspects the American is the sort of man who constantly seeks the validation of other men.

'There are plenty of other board games, I believe.'

The speaker is a much older woman, who has been hidden by the wing of the armchair by the fire. Now, she leans forward and smiles at Nick. She must be in her late seventies at least, but she's beautifully dressed in a smart, ivy-green woollen frock, a sparkling brooch pinned to her shoulder. Her white hair is clipped into a feathered bob, and her large blue eyes and winged cheekbones recall the beauty she must once have been.

'I'm Matilda,' she says. 'Mattie, if you prefer. Did you have far to go this evening?'

Nick feels as though he's talking to the late Queen. 'I was heading home to West London,' he tells her. The whisky cocktail is blazing a warm path through his body, flooding him with contentment. 'My wife and baby daughter are waiting for me, so I need to call home. Donal's trying to find the phone for me.'

'I'm sure there must be a telephone here somewhere,' says Matilda comfortably. 'How lovely to have a baby daughter. I don't have much family left these days, so I usually come to Mistletoe Manor for Christmas. I stay till New Year, then I toddle off home.'

'Where is home?'

'Oh, not far away from here,' Matilda says. 'Not as far as London. Now, have you met David and Emily?'

The man on the sofa breaks off from the conversation he's holding with the little girl, and leans in, smiling.

'Welcome to our motley crew,' he says. 'Appalling weather, though of course this one loves snow.'

Emily, who has long, dark curls and is wearing a Fair Isle jumper and pink dungarees, smiles. 'I do *so* love snow,' she agrees. 'Maybe we can play in it tomorrow?'

David puts his arm around her. 'We'll have to see, sweetheart,' he says. 'It might be too deep by then.'

'So we'll build an igloo.'

Matilda laughs. 'The endless inventiveness of eight-year-olds,' she says. 'We'll all get frostbite in there, Emily. Still, if we do, I believe your daddy is a doctor and he can fix us.'

'Are you?'

Nick doesn't know why he's so surprised, but David looks like any tired middle manager in his forties. He's wearing a navy jumper and jeans, and his thinning, sandy hair is brushed over to hide a bald patch.

'I am.' He raises his glass. 'GP, single dad, absolute demon at Jenga.'

'Perhaps that's what we should play instead of Scrabble,' observes Penelope.

'No, wait!' Lorraine bangs her empty glass on to the table. 'I know what we should all play – charades! It's nearly Christmas: let's have some fun!'

She gazes round at the assembled guests. 'We all know the rules, right?'

There's some doubtful murmuring, and Matilda says, 'Well, yes, but I'm not sure . . .'

'Oh, come on,' says Lorraine. 'I'm up for a bit of fun. At Jade's, we'd be doing a conga round the tree by now.'

'*You* would,' mutters Alan.

Penelope looks horrified. 'Well, rather charades than a conga, perhaps,' she says. 'I suppose it'll fill the time before dinner.'

Five minutes later, Donal reappears. 'I'll look for the phone now,' he murmurs to Nick. 'Been a bit busy.'

Nick feels a spike of irritation – he needs to speak to his wife, before she's left wondering if he's dead in a snowdrift. But Donal has also delivered a second round of cocktails – Nick vaguely wonders what this will add to his bill, but they're now going down very easily – and they've all written down a book, film or song, screwed up the bits of paper and thrown them into the empty glass proffered by Lorraine.

'We'll go from the left.' She looks flushed and excited. 'You first, David!'

He picks out a twist of paper, grimaces as he reads it, and stands up.

'Book and film,' they all chant. 'Five words. First word . . .'

David is clutching his neck, and writhing.

'Choking!' shouts Lorraine.

'What film title starts with "choking"?' demands Alan and she shoots him a contemptuous glance.

'Death,' Nick says, and David makes a 'carry on, try harder' gesture.

'Killing . . . illness . . .'

Nick glances at Emily, who is watching her father's grim pantomime, wide-eyed. He's now miming stabbing himself in the chest. Nick hopes it will end soon, to avoid the little girl having nightmares.

'Murder!' cries Violet, and David almost collapses with relief, pointing dumbly at her.

It's swiftly established, thanks to his enthusiastic impression of a train, that David is attempting to mime *Murder on the Orient Express*.

Alan goes next, and does a fair job of *Death of a Salesman*.

Nobody guesses Lorraine's ('*Mean Girls*?' asks Matilda, puzzled. 'Whatever's that?') and now it's Nick's turn.

He opens the paper and reads *Tinker, Tailor, Soldier, Spy*.

'Sewing!' calls Penelope, as he attempts 'Tailor'.

'Waddle!' shouts Alan while he marches on the spot to indicate 'Soldier'. As he stomps and swings his arms, Nick has a brief moment of lucidity, despite the cocktails. An hour ago, he was driving home to his family. Now he's drunk and humiliating himself in front of strangers with no chance of escape for at least twenty-four hours. He makes his hands into binoculars and creeps to the back of the couch, scanning the faces of the other guests.

'*Tinker, Tailor, Soldier, Spy*,' says Matilda. 'You're a spy!'

Nick opens his mouth to congratulate her, when a noise cuts through the air. It's the doorbell, jangling and clashing; by the sound of it, someone is leaning on it, hard.

'Who the hell . . .' begins Alan, and Lorraine adds:

'In this weather!'

The group falls silent, craning their necks to watch Donal unlocking the great door and pulling it open. A strong wind gusts into the hall, bringing a flurry of snow, and he steps back.

'My goodness, you'd better come in . . .' Donal begins; then he cries out as the figure on the doorstep stumbles, clutches at him – and before any of them can reach the hall, collapses heavily to the floor.

3

Nick gets there first as Donal struggles to slam the door on the wild blizzard. It's a woman, wearing dark clothes now sodden with melting snow. Her long hair is a tangle of wet rope, she has no hat, and as Nick gently turns her over to take her pulse, he realises she's not clutching a baby, his first, horrified thought, but a small dog, which wriggles from her arms, revealing itself to be a miniature French bulldog.

'Can you hear me?' Donal is kneeling at her other side, gently patting her damp, frozen cheek.

'We should get her to the fire,' says Nick. 'It's very cold in this hall.'

'Lift her with me?' But as they prepare to carry the slight woman to the drawing room, she stirs and opens her eyes.

'Gaia?' She half sits and her voice rises in panic. 'Where's Gaia?'

'Your dog?' Nick scoops the little creature up and passes it to the woman, who clutches it to her.

'Oh, thank Goddess,' she murmurs. 'I thought she'd gone . . .'

Between them, they support her into the drawing room. 'Oh my goodness, you poor thing!' exclaims Matilda. 'Here, have my chair by the fire.' She rises with surprising alacrity and moves to the long sofa to sit beside Violet.

'What on earth happened?' Lorraine asks, her eyes gleaming with curiosity. 'Did you break down, like Nick here?'

'No, I just couldn't see anything. It wasn't safe to go on.' The woman gives a little hiccuping laugh and a paroxysm of shuddering passes through her. She has a low voice and a gentle Yorkshire accent. 'Before I found you, I thought I was going to fall in the river, or die of hypothermia.'

There's a murmur of concern, and Nick now sees the woman is wearing small, fabric ballet shoes, which are soaked through. Her feet are grey-blue with cold and her teeth are chattering.

'Get those wet clothes off immediately,' says Penelope briskly. 'You can borrow some of mine, come up to my room . . . I'm so sorry, what's your name?'

'Destiny.'

There's a momentary silence.

'*Destiny?*' repeats Matilda blankly. 'What an . . . unusual name.'

'I was born Deborah, but when I became enlightened, my soul name, Destiny, was gifted to me during a meditation.'

Nick suppresses a snort.

'If you can manage the stairs now, you can have a hot shower too, and join us for dinner,' says Penelope kindly. 'What a ghastly experience you've had.'

'That's very nice of you,' murmurs Destiny, 'but I've no money on me – I can't pay for food or anything – I was on my way to the yoga class I teach.' She stands up, still clutching Gaia.

'Here,' Violet says. 'Give me the dog. We can look after him while you change.'

21

'She's a she,' says Destiny. 'Or at least, that's her biological sex. It's hard to tell how she identifies, but I've been told she sees herself as much bigger than she really is.'

'I'm sorry?' Lorraine says. 'Told by who, love?'

'Gaia. Shared meditation is vital if you live with a companion animal. I ask her telepathically what's wrong, and she puts pictures in my mind.'

'Pictures of her lunatic owner,' Alan whispers to Nick.

Penelope appears to be losing patience. 'Come on,' she says. 'You'll go into cold shock if we don't get you warmed up fast. Chop, chop.'

Destiny reluctantly hands Gaia to Violet, who happily fusses the little dog, and follows Penelope upstairs.

Nick hears her saying, 'But the money . . .' and Penelope replying, 'For goodness' sake, we're hardly going to throw you into the snow and leave you to die,' as they head up.

Matilda looks unnerved, perhaps by the stranger's sudden arrival, or her peculiar take on the world. She sips the remains of her whisky cocktail, staring into the fire.

'I wonder why she doesn't have a phone?' Lorraine says. 'Everyone has one. Our Jade can't get her Brett and Kyle off theirs. Snapbang this, Insta that, they're on it at all hours. It's no wonder they're always tired.'

Donal returns, and clears his throat. 'Once everyone's ready,' he says, 'dinner will be served in the dining room, down the corridor across the main hall. Our chef, Colt, wasn't expecting quite so many for dinner but we'll do our best!' He laughs awkwardly. Nick feels sorry for the younger man – he's been thrust into a situation that's tricky both logistically and financially, with the arrival of two unexpected refugees from the storm. He hopes the owner won't object to Donal giving Destiny food and a room for the night – it would be inhuman to refuse her. He thinks about the wild snow, the gale slamming into the hall like a violent intruder. Sending her out there again would be akin to murder.

In the dining room, there's a log fire in the grate of the marble fireplace and a long, white-clothed table with ten carved wooden chairs set in the centre of the large room. The panelled Georgian shutters are closed against the storm, the walls are painted a soft, sky blue, and huge, gilded mirrors reflect the light from the central silver candelabra, which gleams on the polished glass and china.

Nick thinks of what Roly Barrington, food critic of the *Globe*, would write about what he'd probably call:

. . . this charmingly shabby Yorkshire bolthole, with its pretensions to grandeur reminiscent of a duchess fallen upon hard times. The historic décor is an *hommage* to the establishment's long-flown past, yet the contemporary menu is anything but, albeit that our much-anticipated Gordal olives (£5) were a meagre offering indeed . . .

Sometimes, he and Harriet describe their pesto pasta eaten in front of Netflix in Roly's florid style to amuse themselves. Nick is struck by a pang of homesickness.

He and Harriet have been married for five years, together for eight. He fell in love with her when he pulled a muscle during a game of rugby, and she was his assigned physiotherapist. She came into the blue-curtained cubicle with her cloud of dark hair and eyes the soft silver of a Scottish loch in winter, and he thought, *Oh, it's you.*

Harriet grew up in the West End of Glasgow, 'the posh bit', as she calls it, and she takes no nonsense from anybody – least of all Nick. He looks at the tapered candles on the dining table now, and thinks of their winter wedding at the journalists' church, St Bride's. Harriet wore a red velvet dress, and carried ivy and white hydrangeas. It snowed as they came out of the church, spinning flakes mingling with the white rose petals thrown by the guests. Nick had been filled with joy.

Now, other guests, people he doesn't know at all, are seating themselves along the table, faces shadowed in the candlelight, and there's a small commotion as Penelope and Destiny appear in the doorway and Gaia leaps from Violet's grasp, scratching her arm in her enthusiasm to reach her owner. 'My angel,' croons Destiny, who is now wearing a burgundy cashmere jumper, skinny jeans that are almost billowing on her tiny frame, and running trainers. Her long, dark hair is combed back and her cheeks are no longer deathly pale. She has a beautiful face, Nick realises as he sees Alan and Branson politely and subtly vying to sit beside her. She reminds him of a deer, with her slight body and huge brown eyes. She looks as though she could bolt away at any moment, as she murmurs, 'I'm actually vegan,' to Donal, who disguises his horror with a professional nod.

Nick's seated between Penelope and Lorraine, opposite Branson. He notes the guests have naturally arranged themselves with couples parted to sit beside strangers and the traditional man-woman seating order – even young Emily is sitting next to David, and opposite Violet. Nick wonders where her mother is. Perhaps they're divorced, and it's David's turn to have his daughter for Christmas. He shudders inwardly at the idea of sharing Cara with Harriet, living in a soulless rented flat close to the office, taking her on trips to McDonald's and museums, straining for conversation once a fortnight with a child who's growing up and away from him. He resolves never to let it happen. As soon as he gets home, he's going to make more effort, take more of the burden from Harriet. Stop moaning about how exhausted he is when she's had Cara all day.

'Penny for them,' booms Branson across the table, raising his glass of dark wine. Nick wonders if they could hold an entire conversation in clichés without Branson realising, but thinks better of it.

'Just wondering how long until the snow stops and I can drive back to London,' says Nick. 'My baby daughter . . .'

'Oh, you have a daughter!' Branson nods as if they have something profound in common. 'Penelope's son Peter's down south and we're intending to visit for the holidays. Now I'm wondering how safe it will be to drive on your roads. You don't have the monster snowplough trucks we do in the States.' He laughs sympathetically at the sorry state of England's roads. 'Of course, it'll be me doing the ice-road driving,' he adds. 'Penny always prefers to be the passenger, don't you, honey?'

Penelope ignores his barb, and leans towards Nick. 'What is it that you do for a living, Nicholas?'

'Call me Nick,' he says. 'Only my boss calls me Nicholas.'

'When he gives you a rocket, huh?' Branson chuckles. Nick smiles, already weary.

'I write features for a newspaper.'

'Better be careful what I say!' Branson looks delighted with his joke.

'That must be interesting,' says Penelope. 'Is that what you were doing when your car broke down?'

Grateful for normal conversation, Nick tells her about his week with the homeless, and she nods politely.

Donal returns, pushing a trolley laden with rattling soup bowls, which squeaks as he wheels it to the table. Again, Nick thinks of how Harriet would nudge him and murmur, 'Two soups?' – referencing the Julie Walters sketch. It occurs to Nick that there's often nothing so lonely as being trapped amongst polite strangers.

'Lentil and tomato,' Donal announces, delivering soup to each place, and laying a bread basket of warm rolls in the centre. The scent is enough to make Nick feel weak with longing. For a moment, the bread, the reaching hands, the soft light at the long table remind him of Da Vinci's painting of *The Last Supper*. He and Harriet went to see it on a trip to Milan early on in their relationship, and, he remembers, she turned to him in the cool space of the old convent and said, 'Imagine knowing it was your last. How could you eat?'

There are no such qualms here. Even Emily is carefully spooning up her soup, as David butters a roll for her. He seems to be a very attentive dad, thinks Nick. But perhaps a little lonely.

Nick finds himself talking to Lorraine about his plans for Christmas.

'Just the three of us . . . quiet, really,' he says, his heart yearning to be home as he thinks of it.

'Ooh, that's no fun. We're the opposite,' says Lorraine.

'Our Jade always has a houseful. Big roast, all the trimmings, massive pork pie buffet and kitchen disco on Boxing Day, all the kiddies running round . . . one big happy family!'

'Well, let's hope we all get to where we're going in good time,' says Penelope. 'I'm not a great fan of snow at the best of times, and it shows no sign of stopping.'

There's a lull in the conversation and Emily hears her. 'Can I look?' she asks David and he nods. The group watches indulgently as Emily runs to the long shutters and unhooks them, folding one back to see outside. There's a security light fixed to the back of the manor, and in its stark beam, huge flakes are still falling with hypnotic speed.

'It's up to the windowsill!' she calls breathlessly. 'Look!'

'Oh now, don't exaggerate, poppet . . .' begins David, rising to join her. 'I doubt it's that high – Oh!' He turns back to the table. 'She's right, it really is.'

He helps Emily rehook the shutters and they return to their seats.

'Thing is, Nick,' David says quietly, 'it really doesn't look as if it's stopping. I'm not sure when you'll be able to get away.' He takes his phone from his pocket and jabs at the weather app. 'Not loading.' He tries another app, then gives up. 'Maybe there's a TV and we can see the weather on the ten o'clock news. Anyway, it could be that we'll all have to bed in for a couple of days.'

Nick's heart sinks. He's never been good with feeling trapped, not a fan of caves or tight spaces. Being stuck in a manor house with food and wine on tap might sound more than acceptable on paper, but Harriet's already climbing the walls, Cara must surely be missing his presence in her life, and his boss is expecting him back tomorrow for the big New Year features meeting. He'll run out of small talk within hours. Still, he reassures himself, by morning the blizzard will surely be over. Once the snowploughs have been, he'll be back on the road, and he'll never have to think about these people again.

4

Donal returns with plates of chicken wrapped in Parma ham and roast potatoes. In front of Destiny, he places a bowl of steaming chickpeas. 'Colt – Chef made you this,' he says.

She studies the dry pulses. 'Is there any dressing?'

'I'll ask.' Donal hurries away.

The meal limps on. Nick speaks to Matilda about Cara for a while and, when Donal has collected the plates (Destiny did not receive dressing), to Penelope about the extreme weather. 'I certainly don't believe it's climate change,' she says sharply. 'I well remember building a snowman as a child, and the snow was easily up to my knees back then.' Nick refrains from pointing out that children's knees tend to be lower down than adults'.

'It's bad, at any rate,' he says. 'David was saying we might be stuck here for a while.'

'Oh dear God.' Penelope shakes her head irritably. 'Surely not. Peter's expecting us in Ilfracombe, he's doing a PhD at UCL and he's gone down there early to stay with my parents. We can't possibly expect them to manage, they're over eighty!'

'So am I,' says Matilda steadily. 'And I'm not quite dead yet.'

'No, I didn't mean . . .' Penelope is embarrassed. 'But they're much feebler than you are: my mother had a fall in the autumn and my father's quite frail.'

'Perhaps Peter can help them out, then,' says Matilda. 'He sounds very clever.'

'Oh, he is.' Penelope nods. 'He's doing wonderfully well, though of course he's benefited enormously from our support.'

Matilda smiles. 'Such a great help, to have generous parents.'

'Do you have children?' Penelope asks.

'Daughters,' Matilda tells her. 'Quite far away these days, sadly.'

Donal returns to ask if cheese is required. 'I'm afraid Colt hasn't had time to make a pudding,' he adds, and Alan groans stagily.

Cheese is brought, more wine is drunk, and David stands. 'Right,' he announces cheerily. 'Time to get this one up to bed. It's long past time.'

'Oh, Daddy, no, don't make me,' says Emily. 'I want to watch the snow.'

'There'll be plenty of it tomorrow,' says David, holding out a hand to her. Gaia emerges from beneath the table and sniffs at the little girl's ankles.

'Oh, it must be cos of Jingle,' she says, 'I smell of cat! Density, can Gaia come up to bed with me?'

'Destiny is my name,' she corrects Emily, seriously, as everyone laughs. 'I'm afraid not, Emily, I need her with me. She's my emotional support dog.'

Nick looks away. It feels cruel to mock when Destiny is clearly not gifted with a sense of humour.

The adults wave goodnight to Emily in avuncular fashion, and Branson stands up, yawning hugely. 'Better turn in ourselves,' he announces. 'Looks like we might be digging our way out tomorrow, guys. We'll need a good night's sleep.'

The others push back their chairs, throw down napkins, swig the dregs from their glasses.

Donal is in the hall again, waiting to bid them goodnight. There's now a large, unlit log in the fireplace, Nick notices.

'The Yule log,' says Donal, following his gaze. 'Not to be lit until Christmas Eve – an old Mistletoe Manor tradition.'

It occurs to Nick that a break with tradition might mean a warmer hall, but Donal adds, 'Breakfast is at eight,' and turns away. Nick wonders whether to mention the Wi-Fi problem, but already his fellow guests are sweeping him along towards the stairs, and the moment passes. With horror, he realises he hasn't yet rung Harriet.

'Donal!' he calls, urgently. 'Did you find the phone? I can't get a signal.'

'I did, it was in the library.' Donal gestures to a plug-in hands-free telephone behind the desk. 'You're welcome to use it.'

Sagging with relief, Nick dials Harriet's mobile. It goes straight to voicemail.

'Hey, it's me . . .' he begins, aware that Branson is standing a couple of feet away, apparently waiting his turn. 'The snow's terrible, the car broke down, and I've found a hotel in York-shire to stay in overnight, it's called—' There's a click on the line and the connection disappears. Nick shakes the handset as if it's a broken toy.

'It's gone.' He turns to Donal and Branson. 'It's stopped working.'

Branson grabs the receiver and listens, as if he needs proof that Nick's not lying.

He thrusts it at Donal. 'You better get this fixed pronto, son, we need to let Pete know the deal.'

'I think it's the telegraph wires,' says Donal. 'If the lines are down because of the snow, I'm not sure I . . .'

Nick's optimism withers away. He can only hope that Harriet will hear enough of his message to understand he's safe, and let his boss know what's happened. A pang of homesickness grips him, thinking of Harriet lighting the red tapered candles to welcome him home, and waiting in vain for the sound of the car engine. As for Cara . . . he longs to feel the soft little weight of her in his arms, and kiss her fuzzy head. He has to get home tomorrow, no matter what.

As they head upstairs, Nick wonders once again how he's found himself in this peculiar hotel with its motley collection of guests – and quite how quickly he might be able to dig his way out in the morning.

It's too hot in the bedroom. Nick wakes at four from a hectic dream, sweat pouring from him under the tightly tucked covers, and staggers to the radiator. It's pumping out heat; the room feels like the tropical pavilion at London Zoo. He feels deep regret over the extra glass of red wine he drank with the cheese – his entire body is a dehydrated husk. He turns the old-fashioned metal wheel on the radiator, and is relieved to hear ticking and clanking from within. Wide awake now, he crosses to the window. Nick unhooks the panelled wooden shutter and peers out to see thick snow still falling. The ground seems higher, somehow, the window lower . . . it's the snow, he realises. It's now drifting halfway up the front door, and almost covering the ground-floor window below his room. There's no chance he'll escape tomorrow if it doesn't stop soon. Maybe not even then. He'll miss the meeting, Harriet will be worried and annoyed, he won't see Cara . . . Nick gulps water from the bathroom tap, though the taste is unpleasantly ferrous, returns to bed, kicks off the covers and lies, wakeful. By five, he's drifting back into sleep, and he isn't sure if he hears a noise – the rattle of a door, perhaps, or just the old pipes banging somewhere else in the house. *Maybe it's Jingle,* he thinks hazily, comforting himself with the thought of a contented cat going about his nocturnal business. Two hours later, he wakes again, crosses to the window, and finds it's still snowing.

5

Four days till Christmas Eve

The guests are tired at breakfast, and Destiny is wearing a white towelling dressing gown, the style of which Nick recognises from his own wardrobe. It looked thin and scratchy and he didn't put it on after his shower. There's a cold buffet laid out on the long sideboard with miniature packs of cereal, yoghurts, rolls, sliced cheese and cold meats.

'You'd think a hotel like this could lay on a cooked breakfast,' mutters Alan, resentfully piling his plate with cheese.

'Oh, shush,' says Lorraine. 'When we get to Jade's, it'll be fry-ups all the way. Anyway, this is better for your heart.' Looking at Alan's groaning cheese plate, Nick feels less convinced.

Destiny is at the table, wan and beautiful, with a small plate of the tomato slices that were laid out to accompany the cheese.

'Do you think any dairy has touched our plates?' she asks Alan worriedly. He laughs.

'If it hasn't, I'm suing under the Trades Descriptions Act,' he says, indicating his toppling selection of European cheeses.

'Oh no.' She puts her knife down. 'I can't eat next to that, I'm vegan.'

Alan pantomimes an eye roll at the others. 'Our Jade went vegan when she was fifteen,' he says. 'Lasted all of three days, till Lorri made her a bacon butty.'

Polite laughter ripples down the table, and Destiny looks furious.

'Do you think these gentle beasts give of their burden willingly?' she demands. 'Or do you not realise that dairy cows are kept in a constant state of debilitating and unwanted pregnancy, then killed the moment their reproductive organs are too weak to sustain another foetus?'

Alan swallows. 'Well, we're each of us entitled to our opinion,' he says. 'England's a free country, thank God, and I haven't been arrested yet for my Sunday roast. Though with the bloody wokerati on the rise, it can only be a matter of time!'

Branson chortles appreciatively and Lorraine says vaguely, 'Well, I suppose it's an issue of respect, really . . .' as the conversational waters close over again.

Matilda is fully coiffed and dressed, today in navy blue with a sapphire brooch in the shape of a snowflake pinned to her cardigan. She raises an elegant hand to David as he and Emily come into the dining room.

'Coffee, Destiny?' asks Branson, proffering a cup. 'Might be the only thing that gets you through the day at this rate.' He guffaws, and she half smiles and shakes her head.

'I don't drink caffeine.'

'Of course you don't,' mutters Alan, performatively swigging from his own cup. Destiny shrugs.

'I learned to appreciate the vessel that houses my soul,' she says. 'You don't trash a precious temple, so why would you do the same to the human equivalent?'

'My precious temple was trashed long ago,' says Violet, over-hearing, and Lorraine shrieks with laughter. Branson glances irritably at her and David checks to see if Emily is listening, but she's gazing out of the window.

'I want to play in the snow!' she says excitedly, but David looks worried.

'It's too deep, poppet,' he tells her. 'You can't build a snow-man: it's up to the windowsills.'

She runs across to the window, but in contrast to last night's excitement, she's downcast to see the whiteness pressing against the glass.

'Is all that white stuff snow?'

'I'm afraid so,' David tells her. 'It snowed very, very hard during the night.'

'And it's still coming down,' adds Matilda. Emily seems to be on the verge of tears, and Matilda adds, 'If you like, you can come to my room later and look through my photograph albums.'

Emily smiles tentatively and Matilda twinkles back at her.

'I take them everywhere with me,' she adds to Nick. 'Nice to have a memory of happy times. Much better than silly little snapshots on a phone.'

Matilda is clearly not the iCloud type, he thinks, and Destiny looks up, interested. 'I don't have a mobile phone either,' she says. 'People have no idea what they're doing to their brains. The 5G roll-out killed all the birdlife in its path and the government has suppressed the findings, so imagine what it's doing to us.'

David exchanges a glance with Nick – one that clearly says, 'It's not worth arguing, mate,' and Nick agrees. It's too early.

He fills a roll with cheese and takes a seat beside Matilda. Violet glances around the table. 'Where's Penelope?'

Branson shrugs. 'She'll be down soon, for sure. She was up late last night, watching the damn snow, worrying about getting out today.'

'It's not looking likely, is it?' says Alan. 'Us blokes should do a recce, see if we can find some spades, start digging.'

'Perhaps the police . . .' begins Matilda, and Alan barks a laugh.

'They'll be dealing with stranded motorists with hypothermia and ambulances stuck in drifts. They won't be fretting about a luxury hotel miles from anywhere, trust me.'

Nick silently agrees.

'It's so *boring*,' sighs Emily. David smiles at her.

'Perhaps we can think of a game to play indoors.'

Emily studies the bread roll on her plate for a moment. 'I've had a good thought!' she announces. 'I've got a Christmas game we can play!'

'Oh please, no more charades,' says Violet wearily.

'Twister?' asks Alan hopefully, to a quelling look from Lorraine.

'No!' Emily makes them wait, like a reality contest host announcing the loser. 'Secret Santa!'

There's a pause. 'We only have presents for our family with us,' says Lorraine to David frostily. 'Why would we have brought them for strangers? I've got a mango-scented Yankee Candle in the boot for gifting emergencies, and that's it.'

'No, no,' he says. 'You explain, Emily.'

'We find things, all around the house. And we wrap them and give them to each other.'

'I don't think . . .' Donal begins.

'Oh, we don't have to *keep* them,' David says quickly. 'It's just for fun. Like a treasure hunt, to see what catches our eye and lets us match the gift to the recipient!'

'I think it sounds quite a laugh,' says Lorraine unexpectedly, and Destiny agrees.

'Yes, why not? Gaia loves finding things.'

'Well, I'd ask you to keep out of the staff rooms . . .' says Donal uneasily, and Lorraine laughs.

'Of course we will! It's not as if there'd be anything interesting in there anyway. It'll be fun, love,' she adds to Emily, surveying the less than enthusiastic faces around the breakfast table. 'What are the rules?'

'We all choose a person to give something to, then you get half an hour to find something you can wrap up, then we all open them and find out why you've chosen the present you have for the person,' says Emily, smooth as a radio announcer. Clearly, this is something she's done before.

Convoluted games make Nick's head hurt. They remind him of endless hours playing Trivial Pursuit on dreaded festive visits to his grandparents' house, with questions written before he was born about people and places he'd never heard of. 'Come on,' his exacting, geography-teacher grandfather used to snap, 'you must know this!' The mantelpiece carriage clock would tick loudly into the silence as they waited. Nick once heard a single pine needle drop from the Christmas tree as he racked his brain for the word 'Zambezi'.

Now, he smiles weakly. He'll just wrap up a tooth mug or something – what else are they going to find?

'We don't have any wrapping paper,' he points out, feeling a sliver of hope that the idea might be abandoned.

Donal has come back, with a fresh pot of tea. Nick wonders if he ever sleeps.

'No problem,' says Donal, 'we've got plenty in the back store-room; people have left it behind over the years. I'll fetch some.'

'Yay!' says Lorraine, and claps her hands. Emily looks marginally happier, and Nick feels guilty for being so joyless. But right now, he should be pitching all his New Year Long Read ideas to the features meeting, back at the *Globe*'s shiny London office that overlooks the Thames. Instead, Maya Hudi, the 25-year-old wunderkind who recently joined from *The Times*, will be presenting hers, to general delight and enthusiasm. Sometimes, Nick feels very old.

Back in the drawing room after breakfast, the shutters are open, but snow has blown against the window, and the light inside is cold and flat, despite the fire Donal has lit. He's placed a drift of differently coloured wrapping paper on the vast oak coffee table and, helpfully, several rolls of Sellotape.

'On your marks . . .' says Lorraine, who has clearly appointed herself Mistress of Ceremonies, alongside Emily. 'Pick a name from the jar – they will be your recipient – take the wrapping paper and some tape to your bedrooms, then you've got half an hour to find and wrap your Secret Santa present. Ready . . . steady . . . Go, ho, ho!'

Lorraine snatches up paper and gallops off in a blur of white trousers and sequinned sweatshirt. Alan, today in a zip-up Fair Isle cardigan, follows, and David encourages Emily to choose some paper decorated with snowmen. For himself, he takes a dull tartan.

'What about Penelope?' Nick asks Branson as they trudge towards the stairs. 'Does she enjoy games?' Even as he asks, he can't imagine it and Branson shakes his head.

'Nope. She prefers to read. Booker Prize, literary fiction . . . if it's got a miserable-looking woman on the cover, she'll read it. She's probably in bed reading right now. I'll leave her to it.'

Nick puts the wrapping paper on the desk in his room, which is freezing again. Outside, fat goose feathers of snow are still spinning down. His boots haven't quite dried out, and his jeans retain a hint of damp. Nick removes the unused tooth-mug from the basin, then, struck by a thought, heads to the wardrobe. He slung his wet jacket in and closed the door last night, but now, just as he'd hoped, he sees there's a small fridge behind the other door. Inside is a selection of miniatures, a can of white wine and a Toblerone. He experiences a moment of happiness almost on a par with Cara's birth. Nick's not a big drinker, but knowing he can hide in his room with booze and chocolate makes everything infinitely better.

Feeling generous, he takes a brandy from the shelf, puts the little bottle in the tooth mug and wraps them both in plain red paper. He writes 'BRANSON' on the parcel, and spends the next twenty minutes trying and failing to find a phone signal.

The guests gather downstairs again as the gold mantel clock chimes nine thirty. It's still early and, as yet, there's no sign of Penelope. Perhaps she's avoiding them all, thinks Nick – and could anyone blame her? Not everyone enjoys manufactured fun at breakfast time. In fact, hardly anyone does. But Emily is cheerfully gathering their small, badly wrapped parcels and heaping them on to the low table in front of the crackling fire. The air smells of woodsmoke and coffee, and for a moment, despite everything, Nick feels almost festive.

'Well done, all,' Lorraine calls as they seat themselves. Nick notices that everyone has chosen the same position they sat in last night. Amazing how quickly people learn a routine. Perhaps there's a feature in that . . .

'Nick,' Emily says, 'first present for you!'

He makes a show of excitement, because she's watching, her eyes alight. It's from David, judging by the tartan paper. Nick unwraps it to find a smart black ballpen. He recognises it as the pen Donal used to check him in.

'Fabulous!' says Nick. 'You know me well.'

'So who was it?' beams Lorraine. 'Own up!'

'Me,' says David shyly. 'I thought, with Nick being a journalist . . .'

Nick feels oddly touched by the gesture.

Matilda opens a small pocket mirror from Lorraine. 'Because you're so well put together,' Lorraine explains. 'I thought, for little touch-ups on the run . . . It's mine,' she adds, 'so no need to give it back.'

'Well, thank you, Lorraine, dear,' says Matilda. 'I shall treasure it.'

Violet receives a lemon from Branson and shoots him a confused glance.

Branson shrugs. 'You like G & T,' he says.

Nick wonders when she said so – as far as he remembers, last night she was drinking whisky cocktails and wine, like everyone else.

41

There's a convivial atmosphere building. David receives a Victorian book on household ailments from Destiny, and seems genuinely thrilled. 'I found it in the library,' she says, and smiling, she opens Emily's present, a little compass which Nick remembers seeing on Donal's desk – 'Because you couldn't get to your yoga and this will help!' – while Alan is gifted a small plastic ball containing a bell. He regards it, puzzled.

'I thought you could practise golf with it!' calls Violet. 'Jingle said I could borrow it.'

To general laughter, Branson opens Nick's present. 'You're a gentleman and a scholar, sir,' he shouts, opening the brandy and making a show of slugging it into the tooth mug. Matilda looks disapproving.

Lorraine opens a small, expensive shower gel. 'This is already mine,' she says blankly.

'Well, as usual, I didn't know what to get you,' says Alan, and they all shriek as Donal comes in to pour more coffee.

Emily is last. Her face shining with excitement, she opens a dog lead from Matilda. 'Destiny might let you take Gaia for a walk when the snow stops,' she says, and Emily looks thrilled.

'I mean, sure, if I can come too,' says Destiny, cuddling the dog to her. 'It's just she's my emotional support—'

'What can happen to you if an eight-year-old girl takes her for a walk?' asks Matilda, quite kindly. 'Surely you can manage your unruly emotions for ten minutes, Deborah.'

'Destiny,' she mutters as Nick tries not to smile.

'Oh!' Violet leans over from her seat on the sofa and lifts a parcel. 'There's another one, look.'

She holds up a shining, flat, gold-wrapped parcel, the size of her hand. There is no name written on the paper.

'Own up!' she calls expectantly. 'Who did an extra one?'

'Maybe it's for Gaia!' says Emily, but there's general head-shaking.

'Finding one present was hard enough,' murmurs Branson.

'Donal? Is it from you?' Nick asks.

'Not me. I was with Colt, sorting out the lunch menu. We're a bit low on rolls; we'll need to defrost some for lunch.'

'Go on then, Violet,' cries Lorraine. 'Don't keep us in suspenders, open it!'

'I love a good mystery!' says Violet, using a long, manicured nail to slit the paper.

She pulls out a gold metal star with five sharp points, and holds it up to show everyone. 'The Christmas star!' she says. 'We must put it on top of the—'

Lorraine screams. Heads turn in shock.

'What on earth—' begins Matilda; then she sees what Lorraine is looking at.

6

One of the star's points isn't gold. It's a dull crimson, as though it's been dipped in paint. But as they stare, it becomes clear that it's not paint at all.

'That's . . . is it . . .?' Lorraine manages, and Violet turns the star round to examine, immediately dropping it as it smears her hand.

'Oh my God!' She holds her hand away from her body in horror. 'Is this a joke? Does someone here think this is funny?'

David is on his feet, shepherding Emily from the room.

'What? What is it, Daddy?' she asks, craning her neck to see.

'I think I heard mewing. We need to find Jingle. Come on . . .' David urges her away.

Nick wonders if he'll be the same kind of dad to Cara – alert, kind, protective. He hopes so.

In the drawing room, there's uproar. Branson is shouting, 'What the hell kind of gift is that?'

Violet looks as though she's about to pass out, and Alan has his arm around a shuddering Lorraine. 'Can't stand the sight of blood,' he mouths.

'My goodness,' says Matilda to Nick. 'Someone's got a peculiar sense of humour.'

Alan reaches to pick up the fallen star.

'Don't,' says Nick. 'Fingerprints.'

The others stare at him, aghast, and Violet gives a strange, high giggle.

'You think this is a *crime*?' she demands. 'Come on! It's just a horrible joke.'

But Nick is looking at Branson. The handsome older man is pale, his forehead is clammy, and he's gazing fixedly at the stairs.

'If none of us is injured . . .' he says. '*Penny.*'

Donal extends a hand to Branson. 'Give me your room key.'

'I don't . . .' Branson pats his pockets. 'I musta left it up there.'

'I've got mine,' says Donal, patting his pocket. He runs to the hall then takes the stairs two at a time. Nick follows, with Branson and Alan. The others gather in the hall.

'Would you like a hug?' Destiny asks Lorraine, and she nods tearfully. The two women cling together as Matilda and Violet stand rigid and fearful by the drooping Christmas tree.

There was no star on its top branch yesterday, Nick realises, but there's no time to think about what that means. Donal has drawn to a halt by a panelled door in the corridor on the other side of the stairs from Nick's room.

He knocks, tentatively.

'Hello? Mrs Mitchell?' There is silence behind the door.

'Could be she's put her earplugs in and gone back to sleep,' says Branson. 'She sleeps like the dead with those things.'

Nick glances at him, and the older man's bravado drains away. Branson closes his eyes, bracing himself.

'Go on,' Nick tells Donal. 'Or do you want me to do it?'

He pictures Penelope sitting up, still half asleep, shocked at the intrusion.

Donal shakes his head. He fits the key into the lock and turns it, pushing the door open. The room is dark, the shutters closed, but the vanity light shining from the bathroom illuminates a human shape in the double bed.

'Penny!' Branson shouts. 'Wake up, honey!'

She doesn't stir.

Nick moves towards the bed. 'Let me check,' he says. He's thinking about the time he did a first aid course, that if Penelope's really hurt, he knows how to make a tourniquet, he can staunch the blood, he can . . .

Donal folds back the shutters and grey light spills into the room. Now, the men can see that Penny is lying on her back. Her left arm is flung out as if in greeting, her right hand a claw on the pillow. Her eyes are open, her mouth a rictus of fear – and in her neck there's a wound so deep, Nick involuntarily turns away, but not before he sees the blood soaking into the pillow, the spatters across the bedspread. She has clearly been dead for several hours.

'Branson, Alan, out of the room,' he says urgently. 'Don't come any closer, go and find David right now. We need a doctor.'

'She's my wife!' storms Branson. 'I need to see what's . . .' He steps nearer and sees the damp red pillow, the spray of arterial blood.

'Oh God, no,' he whispers. He collapses against the wall. 'Penny, no.'

'Come on, mate,' Alan half lifts him and pulls him from the room.

A woman's voice floats from below. 'What's happening? Is she OK?'

Nick takes charge. 'Donal, could you go and break the news to the others, please? Alan, can you ask someone to look after Branson downstairs, then find David, and I'll stay with the bo—with Penelope.'

Donal nods as he heads for the door, and Nick feels profoundly grateful for the young man's swift grasp of the situation.

'We need to try and find a way to call the police,' Nick adds. The scene is surreal: the old-fashioned bedroom, the red blood, the falling snow. He should be at the office near Blackfriars Bridge right now, eating a festive Tesco meal deal, typing up his notes, thinking about last-minute presents for Harriet.

'I'll ask everyone to try their phones again,' says Donal. 'The landline's dead, and the Wi-Fi seems to be out.'

'Yes, it wasn't working last night when I arrived,' says Nick. 'Could you maybe have a look at the box, just to make sure a wire hasn't come loose?'

'Sure,' says Donal, already on his way out. 'But I think it's the snow. There's a mast up on the moors, it's probably been damaged in the blizzard.'

Nick knows he's right. He's just finding it hard to believe that in a world where basically everything runs on Wi-Fi, AI and tech, they can't get an urgent message to the police.

Somebody is wailing downstairs. Nick can hear gasps of horror, the sound of a woman sobbing. Donal has done his duty, then. Perhaps Nick should have taken on that horrible task, but the truth is, he doesn't know who to trust and someone needs to stay with the body and ensure it's not moved.

Clues, he thinks. Forensics. Nick scans the room. The shutters were closed when they came in, but the curtains were open – that may mean nothing, of course. On Branson's side of the bed, there's a mobile phone, clearly out of battery, and a half-empty glass of water. Nick bends to sniff it, and inhales that ferric tang he recognises from his own bathroom tap. He straightens up, feeling foolish. It's not as if she was poisoned – it's perfectly clear how she died.

On Penelope's bedside table, there's a lamp, switched off, and a book – *The Testaments* by Margaret Atwood. She doesn't seem to have got far with it, judging by the bookmark placement. Nick feels a sharp pang of sorrow that now she'll never finish it. Beside it is a lavender-silk eye-mask – why wasn't she wearing it? Did she rip it off when she heard a noise? Nick looks more closely at the polished surface. There's an almost invisible trail of fine, white dust.

Surely not drugs. Neither Penelope nor Branson seems the type. Some kind of vitamin powder? It suddenly strikes him why it looks familiar – it's the dust that comes from ripping open a thick envelope. He sees their sunny kitchen last summer, Harriet tearing open a thick cream envelope, scanning a wedding invitation. His heart sinking, knowing he'd need a new suit, they'd need to buy a present . . . the ripped envelope made just that kind of fine dust on the worktop.

Nick crosses to the metal waste bin, under the desk. He shouldn't touch anything . . . he creates a makeshift mitten from the bottom of his T-shirt and gently pulls it out. There's the envelope – thick, white, torn open, a single P in black ink on the front. And beside it, next to an apple core and a crumpled information leaflet about Castle Howard, there's a leaf of plain white paper, screwed into a ball. Nick pinches it by the corner, holding it through his T-shirt, and pulls it out, unfolding the creases. These five words, too, are in black pen, printed in neat capitals:

I KNOW WHAT YOU DID.

7

David knocks.

'Come in,' says Nick. 'I'm afraid it's not pleasant.' He's relieved to see that Emily isn't with her father, and hopes Donal was tactful in his explanations.

'Emily's with Lorraine and Matilda,' says David, as if in answer to Nick's thought. He looks over at the body, rigid in the bed.

'God almighty.' David shakes his head. For a moment, he can't speak. 'Poor woman,' he says eventually. 'Do you think her husband . . .?'

'If so, he's a superb actor,' says Nick. 'But where was he when it happened? Why wasn't Branson in the bedroom with her this morning? And if it was him, wouldn't you make sure you had an alibi?'

'Crime of passion? A row, then a heat-of-the-moment thing?'

'The star as a murder weapon looks planned,' says Nick. 'It wasn't on the tree when I arrived yesterday, I noticed. And wrapping it up . . . that's evidence of a deeply sick mind. Emily could have unwrapped it.'

David blanches. 'Heaven forbid,' he murmurs. 'I've told her it was just a silly joke someone played on Violet, and she seems to believe me. But God knows how long I can keep her from all of this.'

Nick offers the crumpled note to David. 'There was this, too. In the bin. Best not touch it,' he warns as David reaches out a hand. The doctor scans the note and looks up.

'It doesn't seem as though Branson did it, then,' he says. 'Unless it's a double bluff, of course.'

'We need to know where he was last night,' says Nick. 'Until we can contact the police, we have to find out by ourselves who did this. It may have been targeted at Penelope – but until we know for sure, we're all at risk.'

He crosses to the window, studies the closed catch.

'Could someone have broken in? An intruder?' Even as Nick says it, he realises that's impossible. Nobody could have made it through last night's snow to the manor. Which means the killer is amongst them.

'David, we could try to—'

David looks pale. 'I have to protect Emily,' he interrupts fiercely. 'I can't be creeping about sleuthing, putting myself in the murderer's path – I'm all she's got.'

'Understood. Perhaps I can ask a few questions. I've done a few courses in interviewing techniques. Mostly D-list celebrities, but . . .' Nick tries for lightness, but the circumstances are too grim, their awareness of the nearby body too leaden.

'I think you should.' David nods. 'I'll take a look at the body, but I must get back to Emily before she finds out the truth about what's happened.'

He crosses to the bed, puts on a pair of reading glasses, and peers at the corpse, using a finger and thumb to examine Penelope's staring eyes more closely. Thankfully, when he's ascertained what he needs to know, David gently closes them.

'Ideally, I need a thermometer,' he says. 'I'd estimate she's been dead for at least four to six hours. I'd say she was killed sometime between the early hours and six a.m.'

Nick remembers the noise in the night – a door, a murmur? Or perhaps, as he thought, just the heating or the cat. Penelope and Branson's room is on a different corridor; he may not have heard anything suspicious at all.

'I can find Donal and see if there's a first aid kit here,' Nick says.

'Bit late for that.'

'For a thermometer, I mean.'

David half smiles. 'My awful GP humour, sorry. I'll stay here with her while you find him.'

Downstairs, as he glances into the drawing room, Nick sees that everyone is huddled round the fire, now silent with shock. Someone has fetched the brandy decanter and several of the party are sipping medicinal measures. Lorraine has her arm round Branson's heaving shoulders, and Violet is weeping quietly. Destiny stares into the flickering fire, while Alan sits awkwardly alone, clutching a tumbler of brandy. Matilda, presumably, has taken Emily somewhere else – wisely, thinks Nick. He finds Donal in the dining room, rather shakily clearing the remains of breakfast. He looks shell-shocked.

Donal straightens up, clutching a coffee pot. 'Any word on what happened?'

Nick sighs. 'I'm afraid not.'

'Did someone really . . . I mean . . .'

'We think she probably died in the early hours.' Nick

wonders at the automatic softening of his words. He's a journalist, he deals in facts – of course Penelope was murdered. But stating the bald truth out loud seems too brutal for this elegant room and this shocked young man.

'Jesus. I mean . . . who?' Donal puts the pot down on the table, and leans heavily on the back of a carver chair. 'She seems – *seemed* a nice enough woman. She helped Destiny with her clothes. Why would anyone . . .' He stops. 'Was it Branson?'

It's always the husband. Words drummed into Nick by a cynical news editor fifteen years ago, when he was a naïve cub reporter. 'Doesn't matter how grief-stricken he looks – assume he did it,' Ray O'Connell said over his third lunchtime pint. 'Never believe a sobbing spouse.'

Nick pauses. 'I don't know. If so . . .' He wonders whether to tell Donal about the note, but the young man seems both intelligent and trustworthy. He takes the risk. 'This was in her waste basket,' he says, laying the note on the table. 'Best not touch it.'

Donal studies it. 'Somebody hated her,' he says flatly. 'They must have planned it. Maybe they followed her here to the hotel, do you think?'

'Maybe.' But Destiny, like himself, surely arrived by accident, Matilda comes every year . . . Lorraine and Alan? Violet? David and his little daughter . . . the idea is ridiculous. All of it seems ridiculous. He'll have to speak to them all, Nick realises. And that means they'll have to trust him. Perhaps those D-list celebrity interview techniques will be more useful than he ever imagined.

Nick dispatches Donal to find the hotel's first aid kit,

and wonders what they'll do with the body. It will begin to decompose within a day or so, even with the heating turned off. They'll have to put her out in the snow . . . Nick swallows. He consciously fills his mind with images of Cara, fairy lights, candy canes on the tree . . . but he can't see past the blood-covered star on the top.

'Here.' Donal is holding up a thermometer. 'Shall I take it up?'

'It's OK, I'll go,' Nick says, thinking that the younger man doesn't need to witness Penelope's rictus grimace a second time. 'Maybe you could check on the others.' A thought strikes him. 'Where's the chef – Colt? I don't think any of us have met him.'

'He was in the kitchen a bit ago,' says Donal. A look of concern crosses his face. 'He lives on-site; his room's up the back stairs.'

'Where are the back stairs?'

'Down the corridor from Penelope and Branson's room, behind a door . . .' Donal trails off.

The sound of a door shutting, just before 5 a.m . . . 'Perhaps I could have a word with him shortly.'

Donal nods. 'You're in charge, then? The Poirot of the situation?'

Nick smiles uneasily. 'I wouldn't lay claim to that. But I'm a journalist – a nosy bugger, you might say. I can have a chat with everyone, preserve any evidence, try and work out what might have happened so we can tell the police as soon as we're able to contact them.' He doesn't say that focusing on the details is the only thing that will get him through this. That deep down, he's afraid for his own life; of leaving Harriet without a husband

and, worse still, Cara without a father. She's far too young to have any memory of him at all. He has to find out who killed Penelope, and ensure his own survival, along with everyone else's. And of course, he reminds himself, bring the murderer to justice before Christmas.

Donal is looking at him, a glint that almost looks like amusement in his bright blue eyes. 'The thing is, Nick,' he says, 'how do we know *you* didn't kill her?'

'You don't. None of us know each other. None of us can trust one another.' He shrugs. 'But I can show you a photo of my three-month-old daughter, and you can ask yourself why I'd risk her entire future to kill a woman I've never met.'

Donal shrugs. 'I can show you a photo of my fiancée, Aisling,' he says. 'She's working as a chalet girl over Christmas, tending to the whims of rich families in Courchevel. We're saving up to get a place together. I'm pretty sure any of us could find a picture of someone we love. But one of us did it.'

Back in the cold room, David is waiting by the bed.

'I'll try not to disturb the body,' he says. 'I've taken a few photos of her position to show the police, and some close-ups of her face. They'll be time-stamped.'

David is studying the thermometer. 'Pretty cold,' he says. 'This is a bloody chilly room, but looking at this, I'd say around three to five a.m. It's only a rough estimate, of course.'

Surely Branson couldn't have done this, then slept beside his wife's blood-soaked body for hours, Nick thinks. Even a psychopath . . .

'David, I'm going to ask Donal if there's any way we can get her outside,' says Nick. 'I suggest the sooner the better . . .'

'I think the snowdrifts are too high,' says David. 'Unless we throw her out of the window into one.'

'What do you—'

'Joking again. Sorry. I'm afraid dark humour comes with the job. I suppose it's a way of managing the worst horrors.'

'Comes with being a journalist too,' says Nick. 'Shall we join the others?'

'I think I'll find Emily now, perhaps ask Destiny if she can take the dog for a walk round the hotel. Anything to distract her.'

'Sure.' Nick picks up the note again, with his hand wrapped in his T-shirt. 'I'll take this to my room, and then I'll go and find Donal. Have a chat with a few people, see what they might know.'

'Good luck.' David pauses in the doorway. 'Sorry you were the one who found her.'

As Nick descends the stairs, Donal comes into the hall.

'Can I get you anything? A drink?'

Nick shakes his head, a hand on the bannister. He finds he doesn't want to look at the tree.

'Listen, Donal, what did you know about the Mitchell booking? Did you speak on the phone?'

'No, I'd have remembered they were coming from America. It must have been via the online system I use on my phone. It's all done remotely: I just get a name and the payment goes to the hotel.'

'Can you access the payment system?'

Donal shakes his head. 'It's through a bigger company. I don't even know who the owner is. Some business, I assume. My payslips say "Mistletoe Manor".'

Nick sighs. 'Had you ever met the Mitchells before yesterday?'

'Never. I've a good memory for faces. I'd know if they'd stayed here before.'

'Did you recognise the writing on the note?'

'Hardly. It's not mine, and Colt writes his shopping lists like a drunken spider. Let's just say spelling's not his strong suit.'

Could Branson have brought the note with him, or written it himself while Penelope helped Destiny? Nick dismisses the idea. They lived alone together. If he'd wanted to kill his wife, he had ample opportunity to do it at home.

'If anything occurs to you . . .' he says weakly, and Donal nods.

'Of course.'

'Listen, Donal, can you help me move Penelope outside? Is there anywhere we can access?'

'Yes. I've been thinking about it. There's an outhouse that backs on to the kitchen where Colt keeps bulk supplies. I'd say it's big enough to . . . you know. There's a door that leads to it, and it's not heated.'

'Perfect.' Nick sounds too enthusiastic, he thinks. People-pleasing is baked in, but he'll have to let that go if he wants to find a murderer. Ask tough questions, refuse to hand over his trust to a single one of them – except, of course, for Emily. That poor kid. What a Christmas for her. Surely today, the snow will stop, someone will mend the phone mast on the moors, this ludicrous isolation will end. The idea of being here for much longer with a killer in their midst is unbearable. He thinks of *Lord of the Flies*; he did it for English GCSE. And they were just kids stranded on an island, not adults trapped in fear of their lives. How long will it be before they all turn on one another, hurling barbs of rage and blame? There is a coldness inside him, he realises, an icy, grief-shaped hole that he can't acknowledge, because his job is to stay calm and gather facts. But fact number one is that an innocent woman has been killed horribly in her bed, and her killer enjoyed wrapping the blood-soaked weapon and presenting it as a gift while an excited child watched.

8

Downstairs, the others are sitting silently, frozen with shock as flames leap in the drawing-room hearth. Alan is staring at his phone. He has punched in 999, Nick notes, but the call won't connect. His schooner of brandy has been significantly topped up.

Branson is now slumped in a wing chair by the fire, his hands over his face, and Lorraine is crouched alongside him. The star, Nick realises, is still on the floor where it fell.

'It's horrific,' she's saying. 'An absolute nightmare. We're all here for you, Branston, anything you need, just say.'

'Branston is the pickle,' says Alan irritably. 'He's called Branson.'

Lorraine shoots her husband a look of vicious contempt. 'His wife's just died, Alan! As if it matters!'

Nick glances at Emily, who is on the floor by the window, playing with Jingle, rolling the little cat ball to and fro. She appears to be in a world of her own.

'Listen . . .' Nick begins quietly. One of them is the murderer, he's sure, but the more people who know the details, the more likely they are to find the killer, he reasons.

Pale faces turn to him.

'There was a note.' He holds it by the corner and places it on the table. 'Don't touch it!' he adds sharply as Matilda cranes forward and Lorraine fumbles for her reading glasses.

'"I know what you did",' reads Violet, puzzled. 'What who did?'

'It was in Penelope's waste bin in her room.' Nick finds himself gazing at Branson. 'Did you know about this?'

The older man looks grey and clammy. Nick mentally runs through the signs of heart failure. That's all they need.

Nick explains: 'It was crumpled up at the bottom of the bin.'

'I don't . . . What? No! I've never seen—'

'There was a P on the envelope.'

'She musta opened it when I was showering,' Branson says. 'Last night, we got back to the room after dinner, she said she was going to read in bed, I went to the bathroom – but when I came out, she was still dressed, looking out at the snow. She seemed tense, stressed – I assumed she was upset about the weather, worrying about her family in Devon.'

'Did she close the shutters?'

'I think so. And then she got ready for bed, but she didn't read, she just pulled on that eye-mask thing she always wears – wore.' He takes a heavy breath. 'And you know what happened after that.'

'Who knew you were coming here?' asks Destiny. 'Could someone have planned it in advance?'

Branson shrugs. 'Just the hotel knew. So I guess whoever takes bookings . . . Donal?'

'I asked,' says Nick. 'He doesn't seem to know anything beyond the guest names.'

'I have to ask, Bran,' Lorraine says confidingly. 'What *did* Penny do?'

Nick's relieved someone else has asked.

Branson shakes his head violently, like a wet dog. 'Nothing. She never did anything wrong. She was a good mom, a great wife, a caring daughter . . . she did *nothing*!'

'Branson, we urgently need to find out who did this,' Nick tells him. 'Are you up to it?'

Wearily, Branson nods. 'Believe me, I want whichever bastard did this caught. Knowing it's someone here . . . it makes me sick to my stomach.'

'You poor love,' murmurs Lorraine. 'Oh, and Penny's son . . .'

'I'll need to call Pete,' Branson says hoarsely. 'He has to know; he's expecting us – and oh, hell, her parents. How am I going to . . .' Tears once again flood his cheeks.

'I'm so sorry,' Nick offers inadequately. *Imagine if it had been Harriet* . . . the sensation of icy horror inside him intensifies and he places a hand on Branson's arm. 'I wish I didn't have to ask you anything at all, but we have to find out who did this, as soon as we can.'

Branson swallows and nods, wiping his sleeve over his eyes. 'Rest assured, my friend, when we find out, I'll kill him myself.'

'You think it was a man?'

'Of course I do. What woman could . . .' Branson glances at the faces surrounding him. 'Lorraine, Matilda, Violet, Destiny. *Emily*. You honestly think any of them could have done that?'

'I can assure you I didn't,' says Destiny.

'It must have been a man,' says Lorraine with certainty. 'No woman could murder another lady.'

'Could have been you, Branson,' says Violet. It's the first time she's spoken. 'Husbands and their wives . . .'

He shoots her a look so vicious, it feels physical.

'I'd never harm her,' he says, 'But you might.'

'Me?' Violet clutches her hands to her chest. 'Why the hell—'

'Oh, come now!' murmurs Matilda.

'Stop!' David chimes in, his voice reedy with shock. 'We mustn't turn on each other like this! If one of us is the killer, or it's Donal or the chef, we need to be methodical. Look at the facts, not hurl accusations.'

'David's right,' says Nick, and Alan nods soberly.

'Fine. What do you suggest?'

'We look at the facts,' says Violet irritably. 'Obviously.'

Branson wipes a hand across his brow, and Nick sees his crested gold signet ring – clearly, he comes from money. He wonders if debt could have played a part. Life insurance? But surely then he'd have staged an accident – Penelope's death is quite obviously a murder; a tableau designed to be discovered, the Christmas star a brutal message – *I know what you did*.

He glances around at the men. David, Alan, Branson himself, Donal, and then there's Colt – the one inhabitant he hasn't yet met, whose bedroom is just up the stairs close to Penelope's room.

Branson lights a cigarette and takes a shaky gulp of sugared coffee. Nick loathes cigarette smoke, but the man's just been bereaved.

'Really?' mutters Destiny, flapping a hand.

'Disgusting,' says Lorraine. 'It'll kill him, you know. I made Alan give up when we met; he hasn't touched one since. On our first date, straight up, I went, "Alan, if you think I'm going to snog somebody who tastes like an upended ashtray . . ."'

'Oh, let him, this once,' murmurs Violet. 'He's just been bereaved.'

'He won't be long for this world either, if he carries on with that filthy habit,' Destiny mutters.

'Calm down!' Violet turns. 'He's trying to give up!'

Nick pushes a saucer towards Branson to serve as an ashtray, and hopes Mistletoe Manor isn't sophisticated enough to have a sprinkler system.

'Where were you in the early hours of this morning?' he asks.

'Good point,' puts in Alan. 'Where indeed?'

Nick hopes Alan isn't going to behave as a Greek chorus, the unwelcome Watson to his Holmes.

'I know it seems a little crazy.' Branson sits upright and sucks hard on his cigarette. 'Look, it's kind of embarrassing. I just . . . well, the truth is, I snore. Real bad, actually. I have a deviated septum, it means I don't breathe well lying down.'

Nick sympathises, having been forced to the spare room on several occasions when he's gone heavy on the red wine. 'You sound like a *bloody* gaggle of *geese*,' Harriet once hissed, wild with sleepless rage.

'Alan snores,' puts in Lorraine sympathetically.

'Because I have allergies, Lorraine!' snaps Alan.

Destiny asks, 'Have you tried nettle-leaf extract?'

'Go on, Branson.' Nick wonders if Poirot ever felt as though he was herding bad-tempered cats.

'So,' Branson sighs. 'We'd had a long flight, breathing in recycled air, I'd had something to drink, I'm a smoker . . . she was desperate to sleep. At home, we often sleep in separate bedrooms.'

Nick nods. He's beginning to understand. 'We had . . . not

a fight,' Branson says, closing his eyes. 'But she wasn't happy. She kept elbowing me, waking me up . . . in the end, I got up and left the room, with my stuff, and I tried a couple of doors and found an empty room. And that's where I slept. If I'd only stayed . . . or even checked on her this morning . . .' The words peter out, guilt and grief cracking his voice.

'It's not your fault,' Matilda says. Nick wonders if that's true. Branson could easily have killed Penelope, then crept out and fashioned his story. But the star, he thinks. That was the act of a vengeful lunatic, not of a violent man suddenly enraged with his wife. It must have some meaning.

'Do you know what time you left?' Nick asks.

'Around midnight. No later than that, as I looked at my cell to see if there was any signal. I can't recall exactly, but it was eleven-something. Forty, fifty.'

'How would the murderer know you were going to leave, though?' Nick asks. 'Seems oddly convenient.'

Branson shakes his head. 'Maybe they'd have killed me too, if I'd been there. You know, Nick, I'll never forgive myself. If I hadn't snored . . .'

'You can't blame yourself for that.'

'Oh, I can.' Branson looks crushed by grief. 'I do.'

Nick takes a long drink of coffee, eats a biscuit, waits a few beats for Branson to rejoin the conversation.

'How long have you been married?'

'Five years.'

Nick's surprised. He had thought they were a long-married couple with grown children.

'Pete's not mine – didn't I say before?' Branson says. 'He's Penelope's son from her first marriage, to some prick named

Sebastian. We met when I was over here on business, at someone's dinner party. She was divorced, I asked her out; we got along. Still do. Did.'

'No affairs, then, or . . .'

Branson shakes his head quickly. 'We were yin and yang. I see that on the surface it looks a little strange: rich, brash American guy; reserved English rose. But we brought the good stuff outta each other. We had a lot of fun.'

Violet puts her cup down with a loud crack. 'Sorry,' she murmurs. 'Just tense.'

Nick nods. 'What brought you here?' He wonders why a rich couple who could go anywhere in the world would choose genteelly declining Mistletoe Manor.

Branson takes another sip of coffee; his hand is steadier this time.

'Penny was in a Facebook group, something to do with growing up in Yorkshire. She was born in Harrogate. A few weeks ago she got a message via the group to say she'd won a prize draw for a two-night stay at a "classic Yorkshire hotel". We checked it out and it was all legit – we thought it'd be a fun way to begin the trip.' He takes a shuddering breath. 'It was snowing hard when our plane landed, and by the time we got here . . . well, you know yourself.'

'Who owns the hotel?' asks Alan. 'Could it be them?'

'Just some business, Donal thinks,' Nick tells him.

'It was a real Facebook group,' Branson adds. 'I checked. I took screenshots – Penny could be a little too trusting.'

'Was there anyone Penelope had issues with?' Nick presses on. 'Maybe someone in England – in her family, perhaps, or a business contact?'

Branson stares into the fireplace, tears still standing in his blue eyes.

'Nobody,' he says. 'Penny worked in publishing before we got married. It was all expensive lunches with middle-aged lady authors, and literary festivals in tents with warm white wine. She'd never fallen out with anyone in her life, as far as I know.'

'And her family?' Nick feels horrible for pressing on.

'Pete and her parents – they are her family. She was an only child. She was everything to them.'

'Any problems with money? Could she have got into debt?'

'No! And if she had, all she'd have to do is tell me, I'd have fixed it for her. She wasn't a gambler or a drinker – a couple of glasses of wine at parties, that was all she ever drank. And barely anything since she moved across the pond. It's less of a drinking culture there. She liked the health-kick aspects of LA life – yoga and juicing and long walks on the beach.'

Branson smiles sadly. 'We have a house at the shore. It's beautiful. Penny hates winter weather.' He shakes his head. 'As soon as I saw the snow falling at the airport, we should have forgotten the whole damn plan. Then she'd still be here.'

He falls silent, and Nick lifts the coffee pot, a question. Branson shakes his head.

'I gotta go,' he says. 'I'm gonna try calling the police again. Then I'm gonna find the guy who did this, and listen, I like you all but I swear to almighty God, if it was any one of you, I will kill you with my bare hands, and I will happily do the time for it.'

9

There's a silence as Branson departs. Lorraine clears her throat.

'Can I have a word, Nick?' she asks. 'In private?'

He's surprised. 'Sure. Where?'

'Don't see why you can't say it to all of us,' huffs Alan.

'Yes, if you have suspicions, we should all know,' agrees Violet.

'It's not . . . it won't take a minute. I'll explain later.'

Lorraine glances round and Nick sees Donal pushing in the tea trolley, on his everlasting round of serving and clearing.

Has he already moved Penelope's body? Nick shudders inwardly. Donal's hands are pale and clean on the trolley handle, his nails gleaming.

'How do we know Nick's not the killer?' Alan asks suddenly.

'I don't,' Lorraine says. 'But I feel like he's not.'

'Gaia likes him,' says Destiny as the little dog snuffles at Nick's trousers. 'She's never wrong.'

'For God's sake—' Alan begins.

'We'll chat in the library,' Lorraine says. 'It's just by the dining room; anyone can come and check I'm alive if they want.'

Nick follows her as the others turn to watch them leave.

*

The library immediately becomes Nick's favourite room in the hotel. While the others are a little shabby but striving for elegance, here the worn furniture and moth-eaten rugs only enhance the old-fashioned, peaceful atmosphere. Nick battles a powerful urge to lock the door and remain in here until rescue arrives, surrounded by the comfort of books.

Three of the walls are fitted with tall, glass-fronted mahogany cupboards holding huge sets of Victorian encyclopaedias, a blue, cloth-bound set of Anthony Trollope novels, several feet of long-forgotten tomes on botany and country pursuits, and a whole section of travel books from the days when 'travel' meant a creaking wooden ship and an iron-studded steamer trunk. By the fire, which is unlit, there's a table set up with a game of chess, several blue, velvet-upholstered wing-backed chairs, their arms worn to a shine, and, in the corner, a shelf holding a stack of battered jigsaws and board games: Monopoly, Scrabble, Cluedo. Nick almost smiles at the irony, but he feels too sick at heart.

The long window's damask curtains are open, and the snow is now almost halfway up the frame. Still it comes down, as though a curse has fallen on the hotel and everyone within it.

Lorraine is wearing her sequinned sweatshirt, and looks like the queen of the office party but for her expression, which hovers somewhere between horror and anxiety.

'Have a seat,' Nick says, indicating one of the wing-backed chairs. 'What's on your mind?'

Lorraine narrows her large blue eyes. 'What I wanted to say, Nick, is – have you thought it might be Donal? He's always *there*, isn't he? Creeping about, pushing his little trolley. Listening.'

'He seems pretty trustworthy,' Nick says. 'He works here, so it's unlikely he'd have known Penelope in any context other than as a guest. Why would he?'

'*I* don't know!' Lorraine says irritably. She fiddles with her hair. Her eyes remain fixed on Nick. 'You're the detective, apparently. I'm just saying. For all we know, Penelope's his long-lost mother and she abandoned him at birth.'

'Well, Donal's from Dublin, so I don't . . .'

'I'm just saying we don't *know*,' insists Lorraine. 'There was a thriller on ITV, one of those ones with a massive glass house and a woman in a silky dressing gown drinking wine out of a giant fishbowl. She got herself murdered by some guy who turned out to be the friend she'd turned down at university, and he became a property developer, purely to . . .'

Nick feels he's losing control of the conversation.

'Lorraine, am I right in thinking that you and Alan didn't know Branson and Penelope before last night?'

'Do we seem like we'd be mates?' Lorraine rolls her eyes. 'Yank millionaire and his posh wife, hanging out with Lorraine and Alan from Gateshead?'

He almost laughs at her tone of outrage. 'Did she tell you anything last night? Anything that might have shed any light at all on why someone might have a grudge?'

Lorraine takes a deep breath and closes her eyes, like a medium entering a trance.

'She said she was looking forward to Devon . . . she's not keen on Newport Pagnell services . . . I had a horrible cheese toastie there once, and I mentioned it, that's why it came up in conversation.' Nick tries not to let his impatience show. 'And I asked her why she'd moved to America and she said there'd been a bit of an unhappy time in England before that, and she wanted to make a new start.'

Nick looks up. 'That's interesting. Did she say why it was unhappy?'

Lorraine shrugs. 'I assumed her divorce. We've all had unhappy times, haven't we? I certainly have.'

He nods. 'Did you hear anything at all, during the night?'

'Only Alan, grinding his teeth. He always does it when he's stressed. Sounds like a bloody galleon at anchor, creaking away.'

'But no doors opening, screams, anything like that?'

Lorraine shakes her head. 'If I'd heard a scream, I might have mentioned it before now, Nick.'

'Sorry.'

She sighs, and plays with the chunky pink glass ring on her finger, spinning it and twisting the stone. He waits.

'Everyone seems nice, don't they?' she says eventually. 'It's hard to believe any one of us would have killed her. I mean, some are a bit nuts, like Destiny – I think of her as Density now, in my head,' she adds.

Nick smiles.

'But not killers. Except for Donal. You know what, Nick, I have a sixth sense about people. Not a woo-woo one, like Miss Yoga out there, just . . . a feeling. He's almost *too* helpful, isn't he? Always there when you need something, always knows where everyone is. I'd keep an eye on that one.'

'I'll have a chat with him.'

'I would. Though I don't doubt he'll be very convincing in his innocence.'

'Has he said anything – done something, even – that's made you suspicious?'

'Not as such. He's just one of those people who sets me on edge. Too smooth. Nothing's ever too much trouble. It makes me uneasy. And,' she added, 'he's got keys to all the doors. He knows what room everyone's in. He knows when we go to bed and get up. He probably knows our inside leg measurement and the name of our cousin's first cat. He knows this hotel so well he could find a particular room with his eyes closed and get back to his own before he opens them. And he'd have access to the Christmas decorations.'

'But this is all speculation,' Nick says. She shrugs.

'Isn't what you're doing speculation too? Asking us all probing questions, and hoping we don't lie through our teeth?'

'Yes, I suppose it is.'

'Well, then.' Lorraine stands. 'I'm going, before my hubby comes looking for me. He may not show it, but he worries.'

After her departure, the library settles into silence. It's as though a flock of tropical birds has flown from a tree.

Nick stands, promising himself he'll come back for a proper look at the books later. He wants to ask Donal a few questions – and he needs to meet Colt.

Donal is still in the drawing room, serving tea and shortbread to the depleted group by the fire. Destiny and Branson are upstairs, Nick assumes. The table lamps are lit – though it's still morning, the snow pressing at the window has created a gloomy, twilit atmosphere. It's still falling, and it's beginning to feel personal. Harriet will be out of her mind with worry, he thinks, and nobody's going to be mending phone masts in this blizzard.

'I just can't,' Violet is saying to David. 'I honestly think I'm going to be sick. Thinking of her lying out there in the snow . . .'

'It's horrible, I know,' David says quietly, clearly mindful of Emily, who is behind the couch, playing with an old-fashioned game of bagatelle she found in a cupboard, rattling marbles round the board. She's wearing large, bright yellow head-phones, nodding along to music downloaded on David's phone. Upside down, Nick reads the screen: 'THE VERY BEST OF DISNEY'. Again, it strikes him that David is doing his utmost to protect his daughter. Jingle is sleeping on the rug, purring before the fire like a vibrating cushion.

Gaia must still be with Destiny, he thinks, and feels slightly annoyed. Surely she could loan the dog to Emily just for a little while?

Lorraine and Matilda are looking at a book, heads together like children. Lorraine raises her head.

'*The Secret Garden*!' she says. 'Those lovely old illustrations. I found it in the library when I was looking for something to read to Emily.'

'My daughters loved this story,' says Matilda. She seems fully recovered from the shock of Penelope's death. 'Poor little Mary Lennox, left without a family, forced to travel thousands of miles to a new, unfamiliar country. A lost love and a griev-ing man . . . it's barely a story for children at all, really.'

'Oh, I think all the best children's stories deal with the big stuff of life,' says Violet. 'I once worked with someone who . . .' She pauses. 'Look at this lovely picture of the ivy.'

'Donal,' says Nick as the manager finishes laying out the tea things. He thinks of Lorraine's comment: 'nothing's ever too much trouble'.

The younger man turns and smiles automatically. 'Nick. Tea for you as well?'

'Actually, I was wondering if we could have a quick chat?'

Donal nods, his professional smile falling away. 'Of course. I'll just take the brandy glasses to the kitchen, then I'm all yours.'

'Actually, I'd like to meet Colt too. May I come with you?'

'Sure. He's just prepping some cold stuff for lunch – we've plenty of food in the chest freezers, but . . .' He swallows. 'Well, they're in the outhouse, so, you know. He'd rather not if he doesn't have to . . .'

'Oh God. Yes. Of course.'

Matilda looks up from the book. 'I suppose we should have a chat at some stage, Nick,' she says. 'I don't imagine I've much to offer, but perhaps I'll remember something . . . I suppose one never knows what will turn out to matter later on.' She shakes her head. 'It's so hard to believe.'

Nick is struck afresh by the surreal horror of it all. A brave, ageing widow, always alone at Christmas, and he's planning to quiz her about a brutal murder. 'No rush,' he says. 'Whenever you feel up to it.'

'I'd be happy to try and help in any way,' says Matilda. 'Well, no, not happy – that's a ridiculous word to use. It's just so hard to believe. Here we all are, with the fire and the cat, snow falling and festivities just around the corner – it should be so cosy. A death at Christmas goes against nature itself.'

Nick nods. Her words resonate – 'against nature' is exactly

how he feels about Penelope's death, perhaps because the specific cruelty of the method and the vicious spite behind the dreadful Secret Santa 'gift' are so unfathomable.

He follows Donal across the hall, through a door marked 'Staff Only', down a short, starkly white corridor where a corkboard holds pinned notes and scruffy safety information posters, to the kitchen at the back of the manor. Finally, he's about to meet the mysterious Colt.

10

'All right there, mate?' says Donal. 'You coping?'

A tall, slim man in his mid-twenties turns from the stainless-steel worktop, holding a sharp knife. 'Just about.'

He's unbelievably good-looking, is Nick's first thought. Black hair in short, tight cornrows, huge, amber eyes – he should be on a runway in Milan walking for Prada, not hidden away making cheese sandwiches in snow-bound Yorkshire.

'Colt Alfred. Pleased to meet you.' His accent is pure Yorkshire. 'Sorry I've been stuck down here,' he continues. 'Cheffing's a bit twenty-four-seven, and Donal was saying everyone's so upset about what's happened, I didn't think they needed anyone else popping up for a meet and greet.'

He's the sort of person who's almost impossible to dislike. Charm. Charisma. Colt has that extra ingredient most of us live our entire lives without, Nick realises. He wonders why the man is doing a job where he barely meets anyone.

'Thanks so much for keeping everyone going,' says Nick. 'The food's all great. But don't you need a hand? It's a lot for the two of you to manage.'

Colt smiles, revealing dazzling white, even teeth. 'Nah. I like a challenge. Not under these circumstances, obviously,' he adds quickly. 'But I'm used to it.'

'Are you free now?' Nick asks him. 'I'm trying to get all the information together, so when the police finally get here, we know where everyone was when Penelope was killed.'

He glances up and sees a glass-paned door at the back of the room, evidently leading to the outhouse. Donal catches Nick's eye.

'We moved her, yeah. I don't suppose the police will be happy, but if they don't get here today . . . well, we had to. It wasn't fun,' he adds with a shudder.

'Wrapped her in the duvet,' Colt adds. 'Took her down the back stairs, then I said a little prayer my nan taught me, and . . .' He nods at the door behind him. 'There she is. I'm not loving it, to be honest with you.'

'I can imagine. Thanks for doing such an awful task, guys. I'll help explain to the police if they question it.'

'Nick, there's a few quick things I need to do,' Donal says. 'Can you speak to Colt first, and I'll be back in a bit?'

Nick nods.

'Come on then, DI Nicholas,' Colt says. 'Where do you wanna talk? In the library, with the lead piping?'

'I used to like playing Cluedo at Christmas,' mutters Donal. 'I've gone right off the idea.'

'I think we could talk here,' says Nick.

He nods. 'I need to prep the dining room for lunch. I'll leave you to it.'

Once Donal's gone, Colt throws himself into a kitchen chair, long legs sprawling like a newborn foal's.

'Ask me anything,' he says dramatically.

Nick smiles at him from across the table, and he grins back.

'How long have you worked here?'

Colt gazes up at the ceiling, calculating. 'I'm thinking just over two years. Yeah, two years and three months, in fact.'

'And you don't mind that it's live-in? Seems a bit isolated for a young guy,' Nick adds. 'An old-fashioned manor in the wilds of Yorkshire.'

'Nah, I love it,' Colt says. 'Gets me away from living in Wakey at me mam's, watching her revolving door of dodgy blokes.'

Nick's slightly taken aback by Colt's openness. 'Wakefield? Is that where you were living before?'

'Yeah, couldn't afford to move out. I wasn't interested at school, messed up me GCSEs, then I thought, well, I like cooking – cos Mam never bloody bothers – so I went to catering college, loved it, worked in the airport restaurant at Leeds for a bit, did a bit of private catering for posh types – then this job came up and I got it.'

'Do you not mind being far away from your mates?'

'I'm not thirteen, man,' Colt scoffs. 'Nah. To be honest, I got in a spot of trouble when I was young, bit of robbing, quick dab of this and that . . . I'm glad to get away, keep me nose clean. Literally,' he adds, with a bellow of laughter.

It's almost impossible to suspect him. Colt is entirely likeable and, apparently, entirely authentic. But he has to ask.

'Colt, did you know Penelope or Branson before they arrived here?'

'I didn't even know them after,' says Colt. 'To be honest with you, I didn't meet her while she was alive. Just saw her when I helped Donal . . . you know. Didn't even get a handshake, man.'

'Sorry you had to do that.'

Colt shrugs. 'Yeah. Hope she won't be the vengeful-ghost type, haunting me potatoes.'

Nick laughs, despite everything. 'What about the others? Have you come across any of them before?'

'Don't think so – well, apart from Mrs Mannering. Matilda. She comes every Christmas, so I know her to say hello to. Sad, innit – nice old widow with nobody she can spend Christmas with.'

'It is,' says Nick. 'I suppose she likes the company. Or did, until today. Will you be spending Christmas here?'

'Well, not now, hopefully,' says Colt. 'Don't fancy exchanging gifts with a dead body, thanks. Assuming everyone'll sod off once the police have finished, I'll go to me cousin Tina's in Batley.'

'No girlfriend?'

Colt laughs. 'I'm pure gay, man,' he says. 'Nobody right now, but plenty of fish, innit.'

Nick feels mortally embarrassed. Has he not always been warned never to make assumptions in an interview? Besides which, it's a matter of basic politeness.

'Sorry. I shouldn't have . . .'

'It's fine. No reason you should know. I don't hide it but it's not the kind of hotel where you wear your cropped Pride T-shirt, you know what I mean?'

'Old-fashioned?'

'Oh yeah. Donal fits right in,' adds Colt. 'Mr Silver Service himself.'

Nick detects a note of resentment. 'Are the two of you not mates?'

'We're colleagues. We get along OK – we don't have sleepovers where we giggle over our crushes or anything.'

'How long's he been working here?'

'Bit longer than me. Came from Dublin to take the job, with his Travel and Tourism degree and his shiny manager badge. Nah, he's fine,' Colt adds, seeing Nick's look of curiosity. 'He's just a bit of a suck-up with the guests, can't do enough. I think he's worried he'll lose his job, cos him and Aisling are saving up for a starter home in Keighley. He's OK, man. Not a killer, if that's what you're thinking.'

A thought strikes Nick. 'Did Donal decorate the tree?'

Colt snorts. 'Well, it wasn't me. You think any self-respecting gay guy'd bang together that load of old tut? It was definitely him. You can tell he hates Christmas.'

'Does he? Why?'

'Dunno. Maybe cos Aisling's skiing with poshos, and he's stuck here? But he told me he doesn't bother celebrating – he's happy to work.'

'Colt, did you notice if the star was on the top the other day?'

Colt thinks. 'Nah' he says eventually. 'I actually thought, not only does it look lame-ass as f . . . as anything,' he corrects himself hastily, 'it's not even got a tree topper. Even me mam plonks a plastic angel on the top of her tree.'

'Nearly done.' Nick gives him a reassuring smile.

'Yeah, don't wanna rush you, man, but those cheese sandwiches won't construct themselves.'

'I'm just wondering, with your room being up the stairs just near Penelope's room . . .'

Colt rolls his eyes. 'Chief suspect, innit.'

'No, not at all, but did you hear anything? A door opening maybe, or voices?'

'I wouldn't've heard if I'd been in the same bed. I wear earbuds – "monsoon rain sounds". Go to sleep with 'em in. Picked up the habit to drown out the noise of me mam and me "uncles".'

'Understood,' Nick says, immediately ashamed of his feeble response.

'That's all I got.' Colt shrugs. 'Wish I could tell you more, but most of the time I'm here in the kitchen, or asleep. Or on a run, if we're not snowed in.'

'Has this kind of weather happened before?'

Colt glances at the window, where snow is still coming down. Nick feels a wave of uncomfortable claustrophobia at the thought of the deep, silent drifts stretching for miles around them.

'Never. Rain, yes, gales, yes – but nowt like this. I sodding hate it.' Colt shudders. 'All done with the police interview? Takes me right back, man.' He guffaws.

Nick stands up, a twinge in his back. Beside Colt, he feels profoundly old and dull. 'I'll leave you to it,' he says. 'I want to see how the others are doing.'

The drawing room is beginning to resemble a domestic base camp, with half-finished cups of tea on the coffee table and cardigans draped over chairs. Destiny has come downstairs again and joined the others, and Gaia is bristling on her lap at the sight of Jingle warming himself like a vibrating cushion before the fire. Emily is sitting beside Destiny, tentatively stroking Gaia's left ear.

'Gently,' says Destiny. 'She's very sensitive, she picks up on atmospheres. She knows something deeply traumatic has rent the fabric of this gathering.'

David catches Nick's eye and swiftly looks away.

'I once had a cat who used to stare at an empty chair and miaow,' says Matilda. 'I was never sure if she was seeing a ghost or just hungry.'

'It would have been a spectral presence,' says Destiny with certainty. 'Animals can sense auras, long-gone pain embedded in particular locations – if you're interested, Matilda, a spiritual mentor of mine wrote a book called *Companion Animal Communication on the Auric Plane*, it's excellent.'

Matilda smiles politely. She looks around at the group, the silver teapot and jug on the coffee table, the fire crackling in the hearth. The fallen star has now been removed from the rug. Nick wonders who picked it up.

Violet shudders, looking at where it fell. 'I can't cope with the horror of it.' Tears spring to her eyes and she chokes back a sob. 'I'm so scared. I wish I'd never come here.'

'Why did you come?' asks Nick. It occurs to him that it's unusual for a young woman to choose to spend time alone a few days before Christmas.

'I was supposed to be meeting a . . . friend here for a couple of nights.' Violet takes a shuddering breath. 'I got here first, then of course he . . . he couldn't come because of the snow. I suppose he just turned back and thinks I did the same. But I was early. Idiot that I am, I wanted to get dressed up and be ready for him.'

'Oh, what a crying shame,' breathes Lorraine. 'Still, you can see him as soon as we get out, can't you?'

Violet blinks back the tears. 'It's not quite that simple,' she says awkwardly. 'I don't know when he'll next be able to get away. He's very busy . . .'

A silence falls over the group.

Married, Nick thinks. He won't judge her – she'll find out soon enough that the guy's never going to leave his wife.

'Where's Donal?' David asks.

'He took the star away then he went upstairs to do a quick clean of the bedrooms,' says Lorraine. 'He's a bloke, so expect socks in weird places and hair in the plughole.'

Nick feels a jolt of panic. If Donal's involved in the murder, that means he's enjoying the perfect opportunity to get rid of anything incriminating. He might wash the star – it's no longer on the rug; the murderer's clothes must surely have been stained with blood; the gold wrapping paper must have left remnants behind . . . As Nick's about to go in search of him, Donal appears in the doorway.

'Lunch is served,' he says. 'I'm afraid it's fairly basic, but it should keep the wolf from the door.'

Nick finds it an unfortunate turn of phrase – because the wolf is living amongst them, in this snow-bound manor. And there's a strong possibility that its bloodlust is not yet sated.

11

Branson comes downstairs for lunch, and is immediately overwhelmed with solicitous pats and comforting from the women.
He's evidently been crying; his bright blue eyes are pink, his
cheeks puffy. Lorraine throws her arms round him.

'You sit down, Bran, and we'll get you some food,' she murmurs. 'Can you eat? Is there anything you could fancy?'

'Just a sandwich is fine,' he says, his voice rusty. 'It just
doesn't feel real. Is the phone line working yet?'

Donal, serving drinks, shakes his head. 'I keep trying, I promise you,' he says. 'I hate to say it, but it might be a while yet.'

'And *still* the bloody snow falls.' Violet's voice spirals. 'It's
outrageous that we're trapped in this . . . utter *hell*, miles from
anywhere, with a *killer* in our midst! I literally can't stand it!'

Nick puts a hand on her arm. He can't afford for anyone to
start breaking down. He needs them to help him, and to do
that, they must stay calm. 'I know it's awful,' he says quietly.
'But I think everyone's being so brave, and it's only another
few hours. The snow will stop soon, and—'

'No it won't!' Violet cries. 'It will go on and on and on and
we'll all be trapped here for Christmas, not knowing which
one of us is a *murderer*! Someone else is going to get killed, and
it could be any one of us!'

She bursts into tears and runs from the room. 'I'll go after her,' says Lorraine firmly, but Destiny puts out the hand that isn't clutching the dog. Nick wonders how its legs haven't withered through lack of use.

'Don't,' says Destiny. 'Violet's a person with a chaotic aura, and she needs time to recharge. It's vital that we respect her need for retreat.'

Nick suspects she's right, though he might not have put it quite like that. He finds a seat next to David at the long table. The doctor has loaded his plate with sandwiches and coleslaw, and is cutting Emily's single cheese sandwich into triangles.

'What's the matter with Violet?' Emily asks him.

'She's upset about her friend,' David says quickly. 'She might not be able to see him at Christmas.'

'She can stay here then, and have it with us,' Emily says with the air of someone who's just solved a tricky social conundrum. David turns to Nick and lowers his voice.

'Look,' he says in a tone of urgency, 'I know Violet's a bit hysterical . . .'

Nick has a sudden memory of Harriet in a London pub, flushed with wine and rage. 'All men think women are *hysterical* when we refuse to hide our emotions,' she'd said. 'By "hysterical" you generally mean "telling truths men find uncomfortable".'

God, he wishes she was here – though not as much as he wishes he was there, at home with his wife and Cara, or even mooching around Westfield shopping centre to a soundtrack of jazzed-up carols, looking for the new Robert Harris novel for his father-in-law. He thinks again of the star – where is it now?

'But we do need to get out. I was thinking . . .' David is saying as Emily stares dreamily at the snow, 'what if you and I get a few of the men together, find some spades, and try digging our way out?' He's looking at Nick with the optimism of a zealot, hope glowing in his hazel eyes. 'Violet's right, we can't just stay here, not knowing if someone else will be killed or hurt – we have to at least try.'

Nick tries to marshal a convincing argument. There may be no spades available – they're probably hanging in some snowed-in shed by the kitchen garden; the driveway is at least half a kilometre long, even if they all dig non-stop till nightfall, the snow is still falling and they'll be like seven maids with seven mops . . . he'd far prefer to sit tight, stay together, and wait for a chance to call the police. But David drops his voice to a whisper.

'I can't risk Emily's safety,' he hisses. 'She's everything to me, she's all I have. And if I'm attacked . . . she has nobody. We have to get out.'

Alan sits down across from them, his plate full, a glass of wine in his hand. He has clearly heard part of the conversation.

'Look, I know a bit about cars,' he says, to Nick's utter lack of surprise. Alan strikes him as exactly the kind of man who discusses horsepower over a Sunday roast, and asks other men, 'What are you driving these days?'

'I've been thinking,' Alan goes on. 'What we need is a massive, sturdy door, then we fix it to the bumper of my Land Rover, rev it all the way, and go very slowly down the drive, so it works like a snowplough.'

'That's not a bad idea,' says Nick. 'But where's the Land Rover?'

'Literally parked round the side,' says Alan. 'So we just need to find it and dig it out.'

'What sturdy door?' asks David nervously. 'They're all pretty old – I don't know if the owner would be happy.'

'There's been a murder,' says Nick, exasperated. 'Plus the owner isn't here, whoever they are – they're probably enjoying Christmas in Antigua.'

'That's the plan, then.' Alan looks triumphant. 'I'll get Donal on side, you two find a door – Donal's bound to have a screwdriver lying around somewhere. And we'll need rope, and a knife.'

It sounds unpleasantly like a murder kit, Nick thinks, but he nods. And after that, he'll finally pin the ever-helpful Donal down for a proper chat about where he was last night.

It's mid-afternoon and the light is beginning to fade. Between them, Donal and Colt found two spades and a shovel, and David, Alan and Nick have been doggedly clearing snow ever since. Two hours later they've only just reached the car, parked a few metres from the side porch. It took a while for Alan to locate it – 'Everything looks so different' – and the three of them are cold, soaked through and exhausted. Nick's eyes hurt from the dazzling whiteness around and above and ahead. The door of the small back office is propped against the side porch and, in the absence of any rope, two balls of garden twine sit alongside. Colt had to enter the outhouse to get them and emerged with his head cocked uncomfortably to one side. 'Couldn't look at her.'

It takes a further twenty minutes to clear the car's doors, window and roof, as Alan shouts, 'Watch her paintwork!' and

David wheezes with exertion. Another ten to clear the exhaust pipe of ice. Finally, fumbling in gloved hands, they attempt the intricate process of tying the door to the front bumpers, which, Nick feels, is very similar to threading a needle wearing boxing gloves. All the twine is used up, and it's still listing to the left, but they've poured tepid water over the front doors and windscreen, and soon Alan's inside, attempting to drive directly at the banked snowdrifts. Nick and David watch as he revs the engine and crawls forward, snow scattering in his wake.

'It's working!' David shouts, excited, but as the door presses against the shoulder-high snow, Nick realises that the car has come to a halt. Alan is revving and cursing, but the tyres can't get a purchase on the icy ground.

'We need salt!' shouts David.

'Or an awful lot of Jingle's litter,' adds Nick.

Alan swings open the door, furious, and shakes his head. 'Can't bloody get a grip,' he shouts. 'Not got winter tyres. Shouldn't need them in this bloody country.'

'David and I can push,' Nick suggests, and the two men heave at the back of the vehicle as Alan tries again. For a moment, it seems to work, there's a shifting of snow, blocks falling aside as more thick flakes fall to replace them – but after a few seconds, the car jams again.

'It's impacting the snow,' Nick says. 'I think it's too hard-frozen, it's just turning it into a giant block of ice, rather than clearing it.'

'You're right.' David looks on the verge of tears. 'That's our last hope gone, then.' He puts his hands in their wet woollen gloves over his face. 'I can't believe this.'

Nick puts a hand on his arm. 'David, listen,' he says. 'I suggest we stay together this evening, all of us, and look after Emily and each other.'

'But if the murderer has a key,' David says, 'there's no reason not to kill us in our beds later, while we sleep, like they killed Penelope.'

'Then we should all bring mattresses and bedding down to the drawing room, and sleep there. I don't mind keeping watch – perhaps some of us can take turns.'

'Only one problem, Nick.' Alan has climbed out of the car and is now standing beside them, breathing heavily with frustration. 'Any one of the people keeping watch could be the killer. So how does that help?'

'They'd be a bold killer to try in a room full of people.'

Alan shrugs. 'Depends how desperate they are.'

David emits a small moan.

'Come on.' Nick puts an arm around his shoulders. 'Let's go and warm up, see if we can get a signal anywhere in the house. It's worth a try, at least.'

David nods and allows himself to be led back down the short path they managed to dig out, into the relative warmth and comfort of the back corridor.

Upstairs, Nick hangs his jacket over the radiator to dry and runs the hairdryer over his soaking boots, which has roughly the same effect as breathing on them.

He eats the remaining shortbread on the welcome tray, then heads back down the main staircase. Already the dark is encroaching, snow setting in again for the evening.

Donal is standing in the hall by the reception desk, a glowing phone in his hand. 'Hang on, is yours working?' Sweet relief crashes through Nick. The police, he thinks, then Harriet. He imagines her low, thoughtful voice, a silver chain linking him to home. 'Did you find a signal?'

'Sorry, no. I've just tried all over the manor, but . . .'

For a moment, Nick feels despair.

'Donal, I'm wondering—' he begins, just as David appears on the landing behind him in a hotel-issue dressing gown, his hair wet.

'Nick! Have you seen Emily? Has she been past?'

'No, why, isn't she—'

'She was drawing pictures in our room, and I went for a shower . . .' David's voice breaks. 'I was in there for a while, trying to warm up, and when I came out just now, she wasn't there. She's gone.'

'I'm sure she's not far,' Nick soothes. 'I've been all over the building and I've not seen her – could she be hiding in your room?'

David shakes his head. 'I've looked – under the bed, behind the curtains – she's not there. Someone's taken her!'

12

'Come on, she'll just have gone for a wander, maybe gone to see Gaia.' Nick aims for reassurance, but his words have an irritable undertone, he realises. David seems very highly strung for a family GP – but then, he reminds himself, he's a widower and Emily is all he has.

'But I *told* her,' David insists. 'I told her not to open the door to anyone.'

'That doesn't strictly mean she wasn't allowed to open it for herself,' Donal observes. 'Kids are pretty good at applying logic in their favour.'

'I'll check down here,' says Nick, and David and Donal go to search upstairs. He hears their voices calling her name – she surely can't be far.

In the drawing room, Alan, Lorraine, Violet and Destiny are sitting in various attitudes of dejection around the fire, like a Victorian oil painting entitled *Awaiting Rescue*. Gaia is snuffling up dropped crumbs on the rug, so she's evidently not with Emily. Nick feels a beat of concern.

'What's wrong?' Destiny asks. 'Has something happened?'

She has a set of playing cards spread out on the coffee table. Nick assumes she's playing patience to pass the time, then realises they're arranged in the shape of a cross.

'David can't find Emily. Has she been down here?'

The group exchange alarmed glances.

'No!' says Lorraine. 'I haven't seen her since she was sitting with us about half an hour ago. She went up with David.'

'Should we come and look?' Violet asks. Her voice is quiet; she looks almost translucent with worry. There's nothing left of the confident fashionista.

Nick wonders if she's suffering from shock, or PTSD. Harriet would know.

'I suppose the more the merrier,' Nick says. 'David seems very concerned – though I'm sure she's just exploring.'

'Branson is up there,' says Destiny. 'He went back up after lunch. I've just turned over the King of Swords – a cold, calculating male, someone who is able to entirely separate emotion from action.'

'Oh my God,' says Lorraine, agog. 'Do you think he's got Emily?'

Nick realises that Destiny is using ordinary playing cards as a fortune-telling device, and assumes they must somehow correlate to their meanings in the Tarot deck – which is, in his journalistic opinion, utter nonsense, peddled by the credulous and the grifting for money and attention.

'I really don't think we should be judging a bereaved man based on a pack of cards,' he says evenly.

'No, but Destiny's trained, aren't you? She just did Violet's love life!' Lorraine insists.

'It was so accurate,' Violet breathes. 'Like, she knew that I wear my heart on my sleeve and I've been badly hurt before, because I'm too trusting.'

'Wow, that's so specific,' says Nick. 'I'm going to look for Emily. Anyone coming?'

'I will,' says Lorraine. 'Poor mite. It's no Christmas for a child.'

Nick almost says, 'Are you suggesting that being trapped with a murderer in a house full of panicking adults isn't festive?' He hears Harriet's voice in his head: *Sometimes, Nick, your sarcasm really isn't useful.*

They call Emily's name, hearing the echo of David and Donal trudging around upstairs, doing the same.

'Where's Matilda?' he asks Lorraine as they head to the dining room.

'Went for a lie-down. I think it's all been a bit much.'

There's nobody in the dining room. Donal has finished laying the long table, and in the dim light filtering through the snow, its white tablecloths and hard chairs look cold and unwelcoming. It's a room that needs laughter and candlelight to transform it. Currently, Nick feels like he might never laugh again.

'You try the other corridor,' he says. 'I'll try the kitchens.'

'You don't think she'd have gone outside?' Lorraine frowns. 'If she's anything like our Jade was, she'll be into everything, opening doors, testing the boundaries . . .'

Nick is not yet an experienced father, but Emily doesn't strike him as that sort of child. She seems almost docile. 'She'd come straight back if she did,' he tells Lorraine. 'The drifts are too high, she couldn't get anywhere.' He sincerely hopes he's right, and Emily hasn't attempted to build the igloo she suggested. He shivers, thinking about the weight of collapsed snow on a small body.

'Emily!' he roars.

Nick bursts into the kitchen to find Colt smoking at the table, regardless of several 'No Smoking' stickers in the vicinity.

'Nick!' He stands up and throws his cigarette into the sink in one fluid movement, where it sizzles out.

'Have you seen Emily?'

'No, why? What's up?'

Nick explains and Colt shrugs. 'She might be with Jingle. Kids like animals, don't they?'

That's an excellent suggestion. Now he just needs to find the cat. 'Any idea where . . .?'

'Maybe in Matilda's room,' Colt says. 'I saw the cat coming out of there this morning – he knows which side his bread's buttered.'

Nick turns and races back upstairs to find Donal. He's outside Branson's room, knocking, and seemingly getting no response. David is elsewhere, perhaps searching the floors upstairs.

'Which is Matilda's room?' he asks, urgently.

'Ivy,' says Donal. 'Other end of the corridor, past the stairs.'

He sets off, but Donal calls after him. 'Nick, I can't get an answer from Branson. You don't think . . .'

Nick turns back. Donal is hammering on the door again, calling. There is silence deeper than snowfall from within.

'I'd use your key at this point,' Nick tells him. He braces himself for what they'll find inside. *Please don't let it be Emily . . .*

Donal nods, and produces a jangling set of master keys from his pocket. He sorts through, and slips one into the lock of Rowan, the room where Branson claims to have slept last night.

Donal holds his breath and swings the door open. But the room is empty.

'Where is he?' Donal stares at Nick. 'He surely isn't in Elder? That's where . . . you know. Her blood's still on the sheets; I thought we should leave them for the police.'

Nick, too, is confused. Perhaps a grieving husband might want to feel closer to his dead wife? But surely there'd be no need to sit in the place where she was killed just hours earlier.

'We'd better check.'

Donal leads Nick back to the door of Penelope's room. He'd sooner spend a full Saturday with Harriet at IKEA arguing over bathroom accessories than go back in there, but he can't make Donal go alone. With a barely visible tremor to his wrist, Donal once again unlocks the door and gently pushes it open.

Nick steps in behind him. His eye is drawn instantly to the welter of dark red drying on the white sheets. He looks away. It's evident that Branson isn't here – the door to the small bathroom hangs wide, and nothing has been moved since this morning.

'But he went upstairs,' Donal murmurs, as though raising his voice would disturb the room. 'I saw him go.'

They return to the corridor, shaken. There are now two people missing, and four others looking for them. It strikes Nick as ludicrous: the manor isn't that large – they can't be far away.

As he turns towards Matilda's room – could Branson be there? – he hears a familiar rumbling tone from downstairs, and Lorraine answering. Donal lays a hand on Nick's arm, to still him, and peers over the bannister. He turns back to Nick, his eyes full of baffled suspicion.

'He's downstairs,' Donal whispers. 'That was him. How the hell . . .'

'I guess he came out of his room and went down the back stairs?' Nick hazards. 'Maybe he didn't want to bump into anyone.'

'But he'd have passed me!' Donal insists. 'I've been on this corridor the whole time.'

Nick shakes his head. He hasn't got time to speculate. Branson is alive – and they still need to find Emily.

Much as he doesn't want to disturb an elderly woman having an afternoon nap after a traumatic morning, Nick feels he has no choice. Lorraine clearly hasn't found Emily – and if she's not with Matilda, he's going to have to face the possibility that she's gone outside. He swallows and knocks hard on the door labelled 'Ivy'.

'Yes?'

'Matilda, it's Nick,' he calls, but the panelled door is thick, and she shouts a querulous:

'What? I can't hear!'

He hears her footsteps crossing the polished parquet floor, and the snick of the latch.

The door opens a crack and she peers out. 'Oh, I thought you were David,' she says. 'Come in. Emily and I are just looking at some of my treasures.'

Nick feels a queasy combination of deep relief and profound irritation. 'We've been looking for Emily everywhere,' he manages.

'Oh dear.' Matilda looks upset, her large blue eyes suddenly vulnerable. 'I'm so sorry – I thought David was still helping you men to dig the car out. Did it work?'

Nick shakes his head.

'Ah. Well, worth a try. Emily knocked on my door, you see – I'd told her she could visit me whenever she liked, and I assumed her daddy had said it was allowed. I do apologise.'

She turns back to the room, a smarter, larger version of his own. 'Emily, time to go and find Daddy,' she says. Behind her, Nick sees Emily, entirely unharmed, sitting on the window seat, the table beside her strewn with old photographs and pieces of jewellery.

'As I said, I take my precious things everywhere,' says Matilda.

'Mattie's showed me pictures of all her whole family,' says Emily happily. 'Some of them are more than *eighty years old*! They didn't have phones you could take pictures with and they didn't even have colours!'

'We lived our whole lives in black and white,' says Matilda, smiling, and Emily glances up, amazed, then realises it's a joke and laughs.

Nick backs into the corridor and sees David coming back the other way. He looks pale and he's out of breath.

'Emily's here!' Nick calls quickly. 'It was a misunderstanding; she's been with Matilda!'

David's face collapses with relief. He rushes to the door of Ivy.

'Emily!' he shouts. 'What did I tell you? I warned you – I *told* you not to . . .'

Emily's smile has disappeared. She looks on the verge of tears. 'Sorry, Daddy.'

He shakes his head like a dog, clearing it, and hugs her. 'I was so worried, poppet. I didn't know where you'd gone.'

'I'm sorry, David.' Matilda steps forward. 'I assumed you'd said she could visit.'

'It's not your fault. It's nobody's fault,' he says, his voice shaking. 'I'm just glad she's safe.'

'She's always safe with me.' Matilda smiles at her. 'You're welcome any time, Emily.'

'Can I come and play with your necklaces and see the pictures of your little girls again?'

'Of course you can. Whenever you like.' Sadness crosses Matilda's face. Alone again, thinks Nick. Poor woman.

'Come for a drink,' he suggests. 'Everyone's downstairs.'

'Thank you. I think I shall.' Matilda gathers her old-fashioned black-patent handbag and a blue silk scarf, and follows him.

13

Everyone is once again gathered around the fire. Darkness has fallen outside, but until Donal closes the shutters, it's possible to see the flakes still swirling in the beam of the security lights. Violet crosses the room and draws the curtains.

'I can't bear to see the snow going on and on and on,' she says fretfully. 'It feels like it's been snowing forever.'

Branson is in the chair by the hearth, Gaia perched on his lap. Destiny sits beside him. 'You can tell her anything,' she's saying earnestly. 'She has a very powerful awareness of psychic pain.'

Branson looks as though he's somewhere else entirely. He barely registers Destiny's words, and though the others are discussing increasingly outlandish methods of alerting the police ('Could we climb on the roof and spell out "HELP" with our arms?' Lorraine asks to resounding incredulity), he doesn't focus until Donal enters with the ubiquitous trolley, this time holding a full brandy decanter and matching glasses, and a platter of mince pies.

'Sorry it's all a bit festive,' Donal says. 'It's not really in keeping with the circumstances, I know, but Colt had already made them, so . . .'

'Nothing wrong with a mince pie,' says Alan, nabbing two.

Even Matilda takes an elegant bite, while Emily has one and the glass of squash the ever-thoughtful Donal has brought for her.

As he leaves, Nick stands and follows him from the room.

'I wanted to ask,' he begins, as they draw level in the hall, 'whether you have any views on what's happened?'

Donal pauses. 'I don't know if it's for me to say . . .'

'Oh, come on.' Nick attempts a jocular laugh. 'You've as much right as anyone.'

'I can talk if it's in private,' Donal says cautiously. 'OK, come into the office if you like. I'm just going through the menus for the next couple of days, though it's a bit tricky, not knowing when you'll all be rescued.'

'Us all?' asks Nick. 'You'll be rescued with us, surely? You can't stay here at Christmas with no guests.'

'Ah, no, I actually can,' Donal corrects him as they walk through the chill corridor. 'I've nowhere else to go.'

Nick feels a pulse of discomfort. 'Wouldn't you want to go to family, or friends?'

'Estranged from the family. Friends come and go, don't they? I certainly don't think of foisting myself upon them for Christmas. I'll be fine,' he says. 'Once the Wi-Fi's up and running again.'

'Can I ask why you're estranged?' Nick asks. It's intrusive, but it feels as though it might be important.

Donal opens the door to his office, a small, pale grey room with a desk, shelves of box files, staff rotas pinned up and two hard plastic chairs. There are no home comforts, not even a giant Sports Direct mug for tea or a photo on the desk. Donal appears to have made no mark on the room whatsoever.

'Have a seat.' Donal fiddles with the Venetian blind, then

gives up. 'Never works, this thing. Estranged . . . Oh, lots of reasons. Nothing I particularly want to go into, if that's OK with you. I haven't been back for years. I've got Aisling now,' he adds quickly, as if family members are infinitely replaceable.

'Do you have a photo of her?'

Donal pats his pockets. 'Left my phone in my room. I'll show you later.'

The disquiet Nick feels intensifies.

'Donal, what brought you here? What were you doing before?'

'The job came up, and I was glad to get it. Beautiful place, friendly guests . . .'

And hidden miles away from whatever you left behind, thinks Nick.

'Before, I was working in various jobs. Here and there.' Donal pauses. 'If you don't mind me asking, Nick, how's this relevant?'

'I'm just trying to get a picture of your life,' says Nick. Donal is at his desk, fiddling with a glass paperweight. It looks heavy and he has a sudden vision of Donal's raised arm, the dull thud as he brings it down hard on bone. The paranoia drifting through the manor like smoke is affecting him too, but Nick has to stay calm. If he can't find out why Penelope was killed, and by whom, they're all at risk.

'I could just as easily ask you,' Donal points out. 'You say you're a journalist, but we've no proof of that. You show up out of a blizzard and immediately wheedle your way in, getting on with everyone, asking your questions, stepping in to help. For all I know, your wife and baby don't exist, you've had a bitter grudge against Penelope for years, for reasons unknown, and you decided you'd track her down here and finally bump her off. Good old Nick, friends with everyone, offering to investigate – it can't *possibly* be him, can it?'

Donal glares. Nick knows he's right; without Wi-Fi he has no way of proving his identity – even his driving licence is in the car. 'Look,' he says, eventually, 'I can't prove I didn't do it any more than you can. But think about the facts.' Nick holds up a hand as Donal begins to speak. He remembers the intensity on Lorraine's face as she said, 'I'd keep an eye on that one.'

'One, you know the hotel inside out – you'd know how to get around in the dark, where each room is, and who's sleeping where. The rest of us have never been here before, apart from Matilda.'

'Well, I think we can rule her out,' says Donal grudgingly. 'Penelope could have knocked her out with a gentle tap on the nose.'

Nick almost smiles. 'Two, you have a giant bunch of keys, and can access anyone's room at any time. The rest of us would have had to steal the right key and find the right door in the early hours.'

'Unless Branson did it,' says Donal flatly. 'Has nobody ever told you, Nick, that it's always the husband?'

'Except his story about using the other room checks out,' Nick says. 'His stuff was in there – he said he was looking for one that was unlocked to sleep in.'

'Are you suggesting he couldn't have killed her and then moved rooms?'

'No, but there was no blood on him. When we spoke afterwards, I looked at his nails, his hair – nothing.'

'Because he'd have had a shower after killing her!' Donal says heatedly. 'Honestly, none of this proves a single thing.'

'So who do you think did it?'

Donal finally lets go of the paperweight and leans back. 'Someone I don't entirely trust,' he says. 'Someone I've been watching since they arrived, who doesn't appear to be quite who they say they are. You don't work in customer service for this long without getting a good handle on whether people are truthful.'

'Who?'

Donal stands up. 'I'm not going to tell you tonight,' he says. 'There's something I want to check out – I need to do a bit more sniffing around. There's something I need to find before I can be sure. I was going to look this morning when I was cleaning, but someone came past. But I'll know by morning, and if I'm right, we'll talk then.'

Fury suffuses Nick. 'For God's sake, Donal, there's a killer wandering around! The more I know, the better I can help you! This isn't the time for some solo Famous Five mission.'

'If it was a Famous Five mission, it wouldn't be solo, would it?' Donal relents. 'When I discover it's them, I'll know I can trust you. But until then, I'm saying nothing – except that I'm almost certain it's not Colt. He's never given me the slightest reason to distrust him.'

'I'm happy to hear that,' says Nick, meaning it.

'And now, if you don't mind, I'll get on with the menus for him,' Donal adds. 'Fish pie tonight. There's a load of prawns in the freezer that need using up.'

'Here's hoping it won't be poisoned,' says Nick, trying for a smile, but Donal's expression remains stony as he waves Nick away and returns to his papers.

'Nick!' says Violet as he returns to the drawing room. Branson is still staring blankly at the smouldering logs in the fireplace. 'We've got a plan.'

'Oh?'

'We all know we might be in danger, so we're all going to our rooms at the same time – nine thirty – and jamming furniture against the doors. If anyone tries to break in, we scream, and hopefully someone hears and we catch the killer.'

Nick thinks this sounds like a disastrous plan. The cold, alien mind that would use the festive star as a murder weapon then risk presenting it to a child is not going to be stopped by a rickety Victorian desk.

'What if nobody hears?' asks Alan.

'Then we get the chance to react,' says Violet. 'I don't know about you, but I'm getting a knife from the kitchen and sleeping with it next to me.'

'Hold on,' Nick says, 'don't you think it'd be safer if we're all together? Earlier on, some of us were discussing bringing down mattresses and taking turns to keep watch.'

'Oh, I can't sleep with other people breathing,' says Destiny, horrified. 'It's like torture to me. I have misophonia, I can't cope with certain noises. Snoring makes me feel physically sick.'

'Well, better snoring than screaming, surely,' says David pleasantly. Emily has headphones on again and is leafing through a large book, presumably from the library, showing old-fashioned illustrations of plants and wildlife.

'What do you think, Branson?' Nick asks, and he starts, and half turns his head.

'I want to be by myself,' he says. 'You all do what you want to do, but I'll be in Rowan again. I won't sleep anyway.'

'I must say, the idea of sleeping on just a mattress sounds rather painful at my advanced age . . .' puts in Matilda querulously, and Lorraine agrees:

'Oof, yes, absolute disaster for my neuralgia.'

Nick wants to shake them. *We're at risk of being murdered and you're wittering about back pain.* He breathes in and out slowly. 'We may be able to contact the police tomorrow – this would be for just one night, and it would mean we're all safe. We could have a rota system for the watchers.'

'But, Nick,' Violet speaks up. 'If the murderer's here, they could be the one watching over us in the early hours – ready to strike.'

'That's true.' He has already considered this. 'But it's unlikely they'd do it in a room full of people.'

'Because none of us will get a wink of sleep!' Violet snaps. 'Look, I'm going to bed in my room, with a knife, and the rest of you can take your chances.'

'I am too,' says Matilda, and Alan and Lorraine mutter agreement.

Here we go, Nick thinks. *End of the cosy fireside chats, start of* Lord of the Flies, *every man for himself. That didn't take long.*

Finally, David speaks up. 'I think Nick's idea is good,' he says. 'But if nobody's keen . . .'

There's a painful silence. David glances unhappily at Emily. 'Then let's hope the furniture holds out,' he says eventually.

14

Three days till Christmas Eve

Nick cannot remember a less pleasant night. At two in the morning he's still wide awake, heart bumping noticeably against his ribs, aware of every creak and cough in the snow-bound old manor house. The desk is shoved against his locked door, the chair balanced on top, and he's lifted the wall mirror down and placed it against the door too, hoping that if anyone forces the lock, the glass will shatter and wake him. Though of course, he'll also be providing the intruder with a ready-made weapon. He sighs, rolls to the edge of the tumbled bedsheets and stands up. He wishes he'd borrowed Jingle for the night; at least the cat would be a comforting presence, but after the fish pie – which was delicious and so far, at least, seemingly unpoisoned – Emily bagged him and carted him upstairs like a furry cushion.

Outside, the rising drifts are making monstrous, hump-backed shapes beyond the buried terrace. Maybe in the morning he can find an old TV hidden in the house, or a radio they can at least tune to a news station. The whole country must be at a standstill. For a moment, he worries about Harriet, whether she's able to reach the shops, but of course, London isn't going to be under seven-foot snowdrifts. The city's light dusting has probably melted back to its usual grey chill by now, a simple winter backdrop to noise and life and people, glittering lights and packed buses and tinny Christmas songs. The thought of it is like remembering another planet in a distant solar system. He closes the shutters again and turns back to bed. There's no noise but the occasional clanking of the pipes. He turns off the lamp and waits, tense, for sleep. In its absence, he considers the possibilities. *Who does Donal suspect?* he wonders. And was he probing their personal belongings while they were all eating rich fish pie and exchanging small, sorrowful remarks?

Someone must know who owns this place. Donal was unforthcoming – Nick had vaguely assumed a distant conglomerate, or perhaps a small, local hotel chain. But there's no corporate branding here. Everything feels as though it's appeared organically at some point in Mistletoe Manor's history. Some of the furniture dates back two hundred years or more, as do the books in the library, and there's no evidence of coherent interior design, paint charts and carpet samples – it's as though the house simply evolved on its own.

In the morning, he thinks, he'll press Donal on whose place it actually is, and whether they ever visit. Because if they do, it's not completely out of the question that they might have made it through the snow before it blocked the way in and out – and that they might, for reasons entirely unknown, have committed murder. With the slightly reassuring thought that the killer might not be any of the guests or the staff at all, Nick finally drifts into an uneasy sleep, and dreams about losing Cara in a snowdrift. He can hear her crying, but no matter how much snow he scoops away or how frantically he runs, panting, he never gets closer to where she lies hidden.

He wakes with a choking gasp, and sees it's six thirty. Nick sighs. He may as well get up, to begin another day trapped inside the manor.

He's the first down to breakfast, and is relieved to see that Donal is also up and about, laying the long table and setting out baskets of rolls and pats of butter. The air smells pleasingly of fresh coffee, and the pine scent of the Christmas tree has filled the hall and corridors. Nick might almost feel festive, if it weren't for his awareness of Penelope's body, lying in its frozen shroud behind the kitchen. *I know what you did*. Today, he's determined to find out what she might have done – and why it was devastating enough for someone to kill her.

'Did you find what you were looking for?' he asks Donal, who shakes his head.

'No. But I'll look again later.'

'Are you sure you can't tell me? It would be very helpful.'

''Fraid not. I might be wrong. And I don't trust anyone yet.'

Nick is about to argue, when the sound of hectic panting becomes audible and Destiny arrives with Gaia, whose tongue is lolling from the side of her jaws.

'Morning,' she says. 'I didn't get a wink of sleep, did you? Even my hatha yoga flow session didn't work. Gaia was awake half the night too. She could definitely tell something was wrong.'

Nick wonders whether her mistress thumping about in a series of complex poses might be to blame.

'I hope everyone's OK,' he says. 'I'm not sure I'll relax until we're all assembled for breakfast.'

'Well, Colt's all right,' says Donal. 'I just saw him frying bacon.'

Destiny pulls a face of disgust. So far, Nick thinks, Destiny seems to have no sense of humour whatsoever, and is almost a parody of what Harriet calls 'woo women'. He wants to talk to Destiny next – could she be the person Donal suspects? Turning up and staging a faint, so she'd be brought into the heart of the group, befriending Penelope and borrowing her clothes, meaning she'd get a good look at the layout of her bedroom? None of them really knows anything about each other, as Donal pointed out. She may claim to be a yoga teacher, but for all they know, she could be a KGB spy or an escaped prisoner.

Today, she's back in her draperies: a long, ethnic cardigan over a turtleneck and leggings, with a swoopy black skirt and those tiny ballet shoes. She looks too small to cause anyone harm – but yoga builds core muscles, he remembers Nuala, who ran their antenatal classes, telling them.

'Destiny,' Nick begins, 'I'm trying to get a sense of where everyone was the other night, and their relationship to Penelope, for the police.'

'Is that because you're a "journalist"?' Destiny asks quietly. 'A member of the MSM, who thinks it's fine to hack phones and spread establishment lies about innocent people? I prefer to do my own research, thanks.'

Yes, right down a YouTube rabbit hole where the algorithm feeds you endless conspiracy theories.

'Well, I'm not really that kind of journalist,' he says mildly.

'I've won awards for reporting on social injustice. Anyway, I'd appreciate your thoughts.'

'Fine. But don't think you'll be taking my photo.'

'Why would I need it?' He's genuinely puzzled.

'Because I'm pretty sure I'll find my way into your biased newspaper report on what happened here. I'd rather have my name and face kept out of it.'

'I'm not writing a bloody feature about it!' he says, frustrated. 'I'm trying to stop anyone else being killed!'

She glares, and even Gaia studies him with a vague air of betrayal.

The door opens and admits Alan, Lorraine and David, with Emily trotting in behind him.

'Morning,' says David on a yawn. He looks grey with tiredness. In fact, only Emily seems cheerful.

'Hello, Gaia!' she cries, and throws herself down beside the little dog, scratching its scooped ears. 'Jingle slept on my bed all night!' she confides. 'It was like having a cuddly toy, except Daddy says I'm too old for those now.'

'I didn't exactly say that, poppet.'

'You're never too old for a teddy bear,' says Matilda, overhearing as she enters. She's perfectly coiffed as ever, but there are lilac shadows around her eyes. Today she's wearing a fitted red wool dress, with a sparkling brooch in the shape of a robin pinned to the shoulder.

'You look so Christmassy!' says Emily, in awe.

'Well, I like to dress up a bit for important occasions.' Matilda smiles at her.

'I like dressing up, too,' Emily tells her. 'I dressed as Where's

Wally for school once, but I was the only one, so everyone knew where I was.'

Nick laughs. He looks up as Branson comes in.

'How are you, Bran, my love?' Lorraine asks, pouring tea. 'Any sleep?'

Branson sighs heavily and collapses into a chair. He's wearing the same jumper and jeans as yesterday, and he looks unshowered.

'Not much. Hell, it's all so unreal. She was the sweetest woman, the kindest person. The worst thing is, Pete and her parents still don't know. They're so frail, this will kill them . . . and they're not well off, they wouldn't accept any money from us to make their lives easier . . .' He sighs.

'Awfully difficult,' puts in Matilda from across the table. 'One should never have to suffer privations in old age. Thankfully, my late husband provided for me.'

'What did he do for a living?' asks Nick, interested. Matilda waves a hand.

'Oh, something terribly dull in the City,' she says. 'I was never quite sure what, exactly.'

Nick tries to imagine Harriet not knowing what he does for a living, rather than being subjected to his nightly rants about 'bloody Rob Kershaw and his inability to recognise a good story if it bit him on the arse'. He should rein it in a bit, he thinks guiltily.

Donal silently pours Branson a coffee from the silver pot and slides it towards him.

'I can't imagine what you're going through,' he says gently. 'Are you all right, Destiny?' he adds, glancing at the half-grapefruit on her plate.

'I suppose so,' she says grudgingly. 'Considering.'

'Will there be anyone worried about where you are?' Nick asks.

Destiny shrugs. 'If they are worried, so be it,' she says gnomically.

He thinks again of the outfit she wore as she arrived – the tiny, soaked ballet shoes and the flimsy fabric. *Who doesn't wear a coat and boots to go out in the snow, even if they are teaching a yoga class?*

He's about to ask her, and risk more sulking, when Lorraine asks, 'Where's Violet?' with sudden fear icing her tone. 'We're all here except for her.'

'I can check,' offers Donal. 'She's probably just getting ready.'

Nick feels a sinking sensation in his chest. Surely not another one. Donal is heading for the door when they hear light footsteps in the corridor, and Violet appears, still in her silk dressing gown. There's a murmur of relief.

'Oh my God, the most horrific night.' She addresses the room like an actress commanding a key scene of the play. 'I thought every tiny sound was the murderer coming for me. I finally conked out at dawn, and then I overslept. Sorry if I scared you all.'

'Just glad you're here now!' calls Alan, eyeing her slim figure. Nick glances at Branson, crouched over his coffee, and is surprised to see that the expression on his crumpled face is not so much one of relief, but anger.

During their subdued breakfast, during which Emily secretly feeds Gaia pieces of sausage under the table and Nick silently cheers her on, Violet nods at him, her hands wrapped round a cup of Earl Grey tea.

'Want a chat about my movements?' she asks, almost flir-
tatiously, then sees his face and drops the sparkling-ingénue
act. 'Actually, Nick, I'd like to talk with everyone here,' she
says more soberly. 'It means we're all on the same page.
I don't fancy these leftovers,' she adds, surveying the ravaged
remains of the breakfast buffet. 'Donal, could you bring me a
croissant?'

Slightly taken aback, Donal agrees and hurries off. Nick
wonders who will pay for all this largesse afterwards. He's now
feeling hopeful that after last night's lack of violence, the murderer has achieved his or her aim – and that it was, in fact, all
about Penelope.

Unless you get close to the truth and they come for you, says a
small voice inside him. *You'll be leaving Harriet and Cara forever, because you couldn't leave it alone and wait for the police . . .*
but all the same, he has to try.

The snow is higher still against the long, paned window, the
flakes tracing frosted patterns against the glass. The others sit
quietly, as if waiting for the show to start as Violet sets her cup
down and folds her arms.

'Ready, detective?' she asks.

Nick feels embarrassed. He doesn't want an 'us and them'
atmosphere, with himself cast as the heavy-handed detective,
everyone else the secretive suspects. He'd much rather have
spoken to Violet alone. He's aware, however, that suspicions
are drifting and re-forming like murmurations of starlings, and
it's essential to demonstrate that he's got nothing to hide.

15

'Fire away,' Violet says. 'I mean, I didn't kill Penelope, obviously, but I do understand that you need to talk to us all.'

'Thanks.' Nick feels almost grateful to her, after Destiny's open hostility. 'It must have been so upsetting to open the star.'

'Oh my God.' Violet stares at him with wide grey eyes. 'It was horrific. I keep thinking about it – getting her blood on my hand. I feel it'll never come off, like Lady Macbeth. I've had about nine showers, and it still doesn't feel enough.'

'Hideous.' Lorraine shudders. 'It can't have been any of us, surely?'

'You think someone's hiding in the manor, Lorri?' asks Alan scathingly. 'Creeping about all night and crouching in the laundry basket all day?'

'Oh God, don't.' Lorraine gives a theatrical shudder. 'No, but I mean, there's the chef . . .'

Branson nods. 'I'd like to get a handle on him, for sure.'

Nick fears a lynch mob building and swiftly turns to David. 'What made Emily think of the Secret Santa idea?'

'It's just something we do at work, at our surgery in Durban,' David says.

'*Durban?*' repeats Destiny. 'You don't live in England?'

He shakes his head. 'We moved to South Africa when Emily

was a baby, after . . . Anyway, it's fun. Well, it was. All the surgery staff join in and Emily takes part. We try and match the person with the present . . .'

'So when did the gold parcel arrive on the coffee table, do you think, Lorraine?'

She sighs. 'It must have been when we were all racing about, looking for our gifts, I suppose. I didn't really notice because everyone just threw theirs on to the pile.'

'Any idea where the gold wrapping paper came from?' Nick asks. She shakes her head, and Violet shrugs.

'I asked Donal, but he said it was new to him.'

Has Donal been looking for traces of the wrapping paper in their rooms? Surely the killer wouldn't have been so stupid as to leave any scraps. Did they take the paper the note was written on, too?

Nick suddenly remembers the pen he slipped into his pocket yesterday.

'David,' he says, wary of alerting Emily to adult dissent. She's poking bits of egg under the table and, judging by the sounds emerging, Gaia is grateful. Nick lowers his voice. 'The pen you gave me during the Secret Santa . . .'

David looks alarmed. 'It was Donal's, I think,' he says. 'It was just sitting on his desk, in the hall.'

Nick removes the pen from his jeans and studies it. It's slim, silver, with a rollerball tip. He uncaps it, and makes a stroke on the paper serviette before him.

'Black ink,' he says.

David meets his eye. 'It was in the hall,' he repeats. 'I suppose anyone could have used it the previous night, and put it back.'

114

'Or it was another pen altogether,' says Nick. But this one belongs to Donal, the man who is now smiling professionally as he presents Violet with a croissant, butter and a minuscule pot of jam.

Nick turns to her. 'Did you know any of the guests before you arrived?'

'God, no.' Violet laughs. 'Like I said, I'm only here because I was meant to be spending a couple of days with my . . . well, whatever he is.' She trails off.

'Married?' Destiny asks. Clearly, she lacks Nick's compunction when it comes to embarrassing Violet.

Violet glances around the group, and nods. ''Fraid so. It's hard being a woman who wants a decent man,' she says sadly. 'They're all snapped up by thirty, and single men my own age are total idiots.' She blows gently on the surface of her tea.

Nick notices Lorraine and Alan exchanging a glance, but he can't read its meaning. The others are staring fixedly at their laps, or into their coffee.

Nick waits.

'It's just . . . well, I'll be honest with you, I'm mad about him, and I thought he was about me, but with Christmas coming, he seemed to be cooling off a bit. It's such a familyish time, isn't it? Everyone's safe in their little sparkly nests, pretending like crazy that everything's wonderful. It's tough for the rest of us.'

'So you booked the trip here?'

'Yes. I was desperate to see him before the holidays, and I thought he'd like it. He loves old-timey British stuff, and I know you're all judging me, but honestly, he's not happily married. He just feels guilty and he's not ready to leave her yet. They don't even sleep together any more.'

Nick almost groans. Does Violet not realise what a steaming pile of married-man effluent she's wading through? Perhaps not – she's young, and clearly optimistic.

'So when did you arrive to meet him?'

'The afternoon of the day you got here. Day before yesterday,' Violet says. 'He was supposed to be coming in time for dinner, and staying with me for two nights, but . . .'

The snow, perhaps, thinks Nick. Or, just as likely, he changed his mind.

'I just thought it would be so festive and lovely to be together,' she says. 'Snow, and open fires, and Christmas decorations . . .' She trails off.

'Where are you going for Christmas?'

'My dad's, in Wales,' she says. 'He's OK but my step-siblings are much younger than me. They drive me nuts. So I was sort of relying on having some happy Mistletoe Manor memories to get me through it.' She flashes a crooked smile. 'That turned out well, didn't it?'

Lorraine raises an eyebrow and asks, 'Did you know Penelope at all?'

Violet shakes her head. 'Of course not – I told you, I'd never met any of you. I just thought it looked like a nice, cosy hotel, so I booked.'

'Did you chat to Penelope that evening?'

'Not *about* anything. Just "Hello, where are you from?" type stuff. She mentioned that they'd come from LA, so I asked her about that. She said she'd married Branson and they'd moved there almost straight away after the wedding. She seemed to love it there . . . Said it was "the perfect escape".'

Branson looks away, his expression haunted.

'Escape,' Nick repeats. 'That's interesting.'

'Oh, I think she just meant in the sense of a sunny getaway, you know, not being stuck in freezing old England. God help the poor woman.'

A silence falls as Donal collects plates and stacks cups on the trolley. Nick excuses himself and slips into the hall. He needs a moment to think. He's surprised to find that Violet follows him out.

'I need to ask you something,' she whispers, standing by the cold grate. A draught whispers through the space, and she shivers.

'Of course.'

'Do you think Branson killed her?'

'He seems pretty grief-stricken,' says Nick quietly. 'I'm not sure anyone can act that well. But he certainly had the opportunity.'

'It's always the husband,' says Violet. 'That's what they say, isn't it?'

Nick wonders how many more people will say that to him before they discover the killer – and whether, in this case at least, they might be right.

Only Destiny and Gaia are in the drawing room when he returns from fruitlessly checking his phone signal again. Jingle is perched on the arm of the sofa, rhythmically kneading its worn velvet, but Nick hasn't the heart to stop him. The cat's lamp-like yellow gaze is fixed on the dog, who is lying on the hearthrug with one wary eye half open.

'Where is everyone?'

Destiny waves a vague hand. 'Gone to their rooms, I think.

Lorraine said she was going to pack – she's convinced the police will come today,' she adds scornfully.

'Don't you think they will?'

'Look at it, Nick.' Destiny gestures impatiently to the snowy windowpane. 'I nearly died out there the other night. I was hallucinating. I collapsed. It's ten times deeper now, and they don't even know we're here.'

She's right, he knows. Their best hope is that the snow will stop falling and begin to melt, or that someone will manage to reach the broken phone mast and fix it.

'What were you planning for Christmas?' he asks her. 'I assume you live nearby.'

'I don't do Christmas. It's a capitalist frenzy. Buy, buy, buy, watch TV for days, eat till you're sick, drink till you're unconscious. It actually disgusts me. There's no spirituality, no grace.'

He thinks of the Hogarthian scenes of excess he jostles through on his commute home in December, and accepts that Destiny might have a point.

'Gaia and I usually go on retreat,' Destiny goes on. 'A friend has a cottage up near Hebden, and she's away for the whole month, so we hole up. I practise gratitude, meditate, read. I do some soul-writing, take long, mindful winter walks. It's good for the spirit; you should try it.' She sighs. 'I know you think I'm a credulous idiot, Nick, but trust me, I've been through some dark stuff and my approach to life now is a great deal healthier than the usual Western-world "blot it all out with food, drink and drugs" solution.'

'I know it is,' Nick says. He finds himself feeling a grudging respect for her, despite her lack of humour and her loathing of his profession. 'Look, while you're here,' he continues, 'do you have any thoughts on what happened to Penelope, or why? I'm interested in everyone's perspectives, anything you might have seen or heard.'

'If I knew anything, I'd have said so,' Destiny says. She urgently pats her knee for Gaia to jump up, as though she can't manage a mildly stressful conversation without the little dog on her lap. Jingle watches the crooning and cuddling for a moment, then stalks towards Nick and settles down on his knees. He feels both peculiarly honoured and calmed by the vibrating purr emanating from the cat's warm body.

'Which room are you in?'

'Why?' She glares at him.

'Because I'm trying to work out where everyone was the night Penelope was killed. If you don't want to tell me, I'll ask Donal,' he says, irritated.

'Fine. I'm in Elm. It's on the same corridor as Hawthorn, three doors down, but I didn't hear a thing. I wear ear-plugs at night.'

Nick sighs, inwardly. Another one. 'So the first you knew of her death was . . .'

'Exactly when you knew of it. When Violet unwrapped that disgusting Christmas parcel and you all ran to check on her.'

He nods. 'Am I right in thinking the two of you had never met?'

Destiny rolls her huge brown eyes, and the hand stroking Gaia's head speeds up. 'You know perfectly well that we hadn't. I was soaked through, probably about to come down with pneumonia—'

Nick longs to remind her that pneumonia is caused by a

virus or bacteria, not getting caught in the snow, but can only imagine the ringing accusations of mansplaining that will follow. He nods sympathetically.

'You were teaching a yoga class in this weather?' he asks, thinking about the driving snow, the relentless darkness.

Destiny shrugs. 'It's my main income. A couple of people said they'd try and make it, so . . .'

'Where do you teach?'

She shoots him an irritated glance. 'What does it matter? It's not as if you'd know it.'

Nick nods. 'Just curious. You didn't have a coat or boots on . . .'

'I left home in a hurry,' she says. 'It's not a crime.'

No, thinks Nick. *But it is very peculiar.*

'So, Penelope . . .' he says. He'll come back to Destiny's outfit later.

'Penelope was very kind. I'm shorter than she is – was,' Destiny corrects herself, closing her eyes in sorrow, 'But we were about the same size. I went up to her room, and she got some things out of the wardrobe, I shut myself in the bathroom to put them on, went and hung up my wet things in my own room, and that was it.'

'Did you talk at all?'

'"This might fit. Try this jumper",' says Destiny. 'In-depth communication like that.' She seems determined to be unhelpful.

'You didn't ask her about her stay here, or Christmas plans?'

'She was going to Devon to see her family. But you know that.'

'Can you think of any reason why anyone would want to harm her?'

'Obviously not.' Nick waits for her to say, *But it's always the husband*.

To his surprise, she blinks hard, then says, 'I have my eye on Donal, you know.'

'Any reason?' He expects her to say, *I received an ancestral heart-message*, or, *He makes Gaia's ears twitch when he enters her sacred space*, but Destiny pauses, and says, 'He's too calm. The rest of us are scared to death. Yes, we're all dealing with it in different ways, some are crying, some have shut down, some are seeking comfort in alcohol. You're coping by intellectualising the problem.'

Nick feels momentarily glad that Harriet isn't here, nodding violently: *Because that's what he always bloody does!*

'And,' Destiny goes on, 'everyone's responses are very normal in the face of trauma and threat. Except for Donal's. I haven't seen him shed a tear, or lose his temper, or even look upset. He just carries on like a First World War officer in the trenches, being brave and stoical. I'm telling you, it's not normal.'

'He was a bit irritated with me last night. I asked him a few things and he shut my questions down.'

Destiny raises a perfect black eyebrow. 'Well, he would, wouldn't he?'

'You think I should speak to him again?'

'If you want to find the killer, I think you should speak to all of us, as many times as you need to,' says Destiny. 'I did another spread with the cards when I went upstairs last night. I asked them where we'd find the murderer, and do you know what they said?'

Nick shakes his head. She's going to tell him anyway.

'*Close to home.*'

'But we're all trapped in the same place. Where else would we find them?'

Destiny sighs. 'Mistletoe Manor's not our home, is it? It's Donal's, though.'

'It's Colt's, too.'

'Do you think he did it?'

Nick thinks about the charismatic young chef, his honesty and openness.

'Honestly? No.'

'Well, all we have at the moment is instinct,' says Destiny. 'And mine is that you need to keep a very close eye on Donal. Because whether or not he killed Penelope, I'm certain he's got something to hide.'

16

The others trickle back in gradually, and Nick is surprised to see Emily holding David's hand, her face blotchy with tears.

'What's wrong?' he mouths, and David pulls a regretful expression as he seats himself.

'Go and see Gaia,' he murmurs to his daughter. 'Look, she's on the rug. I bet she'd like to play.'

Reluctantly, Emily crawls over and strokes the dog, still sniffing. David leans in, his voice low.

'I had to tell her,' he says. 'Everyone's so indiscreet, they were all talking about the murder at breakfast – Emily's a bright child. She's been asking questions.'

'You told her Penelope was murdered?'

David shakes his head, horrified. 'No, no – I said she'd died during the night, that we weren't sure how. But I told Emily she should stay close to me, and I suppose she's seen enough on TV to put two and two together. Now she's convinced there's a "bad man" at Mistletoe Manor, and says she won't sleep. You try and do the right thing . . .' He sighs heavily. Nick feels deeply sorry for him.

'Might Matilda be able to help, do you think? They seem to have a bond.'

Nick glances over to the honesty bar, where Matilda is pouring herself a modest glass of sherry. Her scarlet dress glows in the pale, snow-filtered light of the drawing room.

'Maybe.' David rubs a hand across his face. He looks shattered. 'I don't think anything will really help until we can get out of here.'

'Where will you go for Christmas now?'

'Back home, I suppose,' David says. 'If I can get us on a flight. Though it's not much of a Christmas for her, is it? That's why I booked us in here – I thought it might be a bit jollier for Em than being stuck at home with me as usual.'

Nick wonders if David had plans in Britain over Christmas – do they return every year, perhaps to see relations? He's about to ask, but David puts a hand over his face and gives a deep, shuddering sigh. 'Sorry,' he murmurs. 'It's just . . . it's hard to know what to do for the best.'

Nick feels for the guy, as well as Emily. David's doing all he can, and his Christmas is in ruins.

'We'll try and make things OK for her while we're here,' Nick says. 'Play board games. Act normal.'

'That's kind.' David gives him a weak smile. 'Onwards and sideways, eh?'

They both look up as Matilda returns.

'Good morning, Nick,' she says, lifting her small, lead-crystal glass to him. The sherry twinkles amber in the firelight. 'I know one shouldn't drink at my age, but after what's happened . . . needs must. Will you join me?'

'Why not?' Nick stands. 'David?'

'Go on then.' There's a complicit atmosphere of indulgence between them as Nick pours two small glasses. How strange, he thinks, that we're still drawn to our little festive traditions, even under such hideous circumstances.

'Now, Nick.' Matilda leans forward. 'I believe you've been asking all sorts of questions of everyone.'

His heart sinks. Is she about to suggest he's out of line? If so, he's going to have to argue. She smiles at him.

'I'm feeling rather left out,' she says. 'Can I be interviewed, too?'

He laughs with relief. 'Of course. In public or private?'

'We could go into the small sitting room at the back,' suggests Matilda.

'There's a sitting room?' Destiny asks, annoyed. 'I had no idea. It might be perfect for my morning meditation.'

Matilda looks sceptical. 'It's not awfully large. It's rather a nice little room if one needs a retreat from the hurly-burly of the drawing room, though.'

Matilda knows Mistletoe Manor well, Nick realises. She'll be a very useful person to speak to.

'Have you got a few minutes now?' he asks, and she rises stiffly, carrying her sherry, and leads him from the drawing room and back out into the icy hall.

'I wonder why Donal doesn't light the fire in here?' he asks as she shivers at the sudden change in temperature.

'The Yule log,' says Matilda, indicating the large, dry branch in the grate. It looks dusty and etiolated. 'It must only be lit on Christmas Eve. An old tradition, I believe.'

He wonders again why it can't simply be set aside while a normal fire is lit, but she's leading him past the drooping Christmas tree to the other side of the stairs, through a door he'd assumed concealed a large cupboard, and into another red-carpeted corridor. The air smells of faded potpourri and lavender wax, and the old doors here are unpainted, with small, brass-framed labels written in faded, copperplate handwriting: 'Housekeeper's Storeroom', 'Laundering'.

'This is the part of the manor most guests don't know about,' Matilda explains. 'But we are certainly permitted to use the sitting room.'

She opens a door on the left and leads him into a cosy space containing a striped sofa and two sagging green armchairs. The fireplace holds nothing but an embroidered fire-screen, but the radiator in the corner is clanking, and the air is warm. Nick glimpses their faces in the gilt-framed, age-spotted mirror above the mantelpiece as they sit, and wonders who else has been reflected in the century or more since it was hung there.

The light, brocade-papered walls are hung with framed collections of tropical butterflies pinned to black velvet, each one labelled by a spidery, long-dead hand.

'Now,' says Matilda, 'what would you like to know? As I said, I'm afraid I may not be able to tell you a great deal – as you're aware, us elderly ladies do suffer with our hearing.'

'Well.' Nick feels ridiculous, his hulking frame crammed into a dainty armchair, this vulnerable widow who hoped for a quiet Christmas forced to answer his questions like a thuggish suspect. 'I'm sorry your Christmas has been wrecked,' he says.

Matilda smiles. 'When you get to my age, Christmas isn't a great excitement, you know. I'm a bit beyond striped stockings on the mantelpiece and "Has he been?"'

Nick laughs. 'But you were hoping for a pleasant break.'

'Yes, I suppose so.' Matilda thinks for a moment. 'It's Emily

I feel sorry for, really. Children remember every Christmas, don't they? For adults, they all tend to blur into one.'

'I don't suppose any of us will forget this one.'

'No, perhaps not. I suppose you'll want to know if I knew the Mitchells, or if I hold a terrible grudge against Americans or something, won't you?'

'Did you know them?'

Matilda shakes her head. 'I've never met them in my life. This year, I don't know anyone, although of course I've met the staff in previous years. I was surprised to see Donal and Colt still here actually; I thought they might have moved on.'

'Any reason?'

'No, no.' Matilda sips her sherry. 'Just that they're young, and they're stuck out here in the countryside.'

'I had the impression they like it that way,' says Nick. 'So who was here when you arrived?'

'Nobody,' Matilda says promptly. 'I got here first, the day before you all turned up. I rather enjoyed having the place to myself, and of course, it hadn't yet started snowing. I was planning a little walk down the riverbank, perhaps a trip to Haworth and a potter around the Brontë parsonage . . . but it wasn't to be.'

'There were no other guests?'

She shakes her head. 'I imagine the previous people had already gone home for Christmas. And once the snow set in, the rest of the staff did too.'

'Do you know them?'

'Only Carol, the housekeeper. The waiters are an ever-changing bunch.'

'What's she like?' Nick wonders whether Carol, who has

keys to every room and must know the place inside out, might need to be added to his list of suspects. He forms a brief mental picture of Mrs Danvers in Hitchcock's film of *Rebecca*, triumphantly gazing from the upstairs window as she creates havoc.

'Oh, she's a dear little thing. Only in her thirties, mum to twin daughters and a little boy,' Matilda says. 'I see her bobbing about with her cloths and polish, but she doesn't live in, of course, she's down in the village. We were talking about Christmas – she was setting off for Scotland the day I arrived, to spend it with family. I do so hope she arrived safely in all this snow,' she adds fretfully.

Nick mentally crosses Carol off the list. 'How did you meet Penelope?'

'I don't know – I think they were just there at lunch. Yes, that's right – it was before Donal had pushed the tables together, and I was dining on my own. They came in and I said hello, of course. It was just beginning to snow so we talked about the weather – they'd driven from the airport in a hired car, I think.'

She taps her oval, pink-shellacked nails on her knee, trying to remember.

'Yes, Penelope said how warm it was in LA in December, and mentioned that they were going to Devon to see her boy. I said it was a long way in the snow, and she said she wasn't looking forward to the journey. Then Donal came in with menus and so on, and we ate separately, and I suppose they went to their room and the others began to turn up through the afternoon.'

'Did you overhear what they were talking about at lunchtime?'

She gives him a quizzical look. 'I'm not in the habit of eaves-dropping, young man. I was reading my novel.'

Nick sighs inwardly. 'I assume you didn't hear anything that night?'

'Not a thing. I usually have a small nightcap at around ten, and I sleep like the de—' She stops. 'I'm sure you know what I mean.'

'When you were finding your Secret Santa gift, did you see anyone else?'

'I saw Branson coming out of a room,' she says. 'I assumed it was his own, but it's not where Penelope was found.'

'Yes, he explained that they sleep in separate rooms because of his snoring. He was in Rowan.'

Matilda widens her pale eyes. 'Oh no, he wasn't,' she says. 'He was coming out of Laburnum. That's on quite a different corridor – it overlooks the gardens.'

Nick stares at her. 'Did he have anything with him? Anyone?'

'Not that I could see. But he was glancing about, as though he'd prefer not to be seen. When he saw me coming, he seemed quite normal.'

'Perhaps he was just looking for Violet's gift.'

'Yes, perhaps he was,' says Matilda, but she sets the remains of her sherry aside, and her expression is unusually troubled.

Lunch is a subdued meal, with quiches and salads laid out for them. 'Not very festive, is it?' Lorraine grumbles, piling coleslaw on to her plate. 'You want massive stews and pies at Christmas, not flaming picky bits.'

Nick wonders if the food currently consists of whatever ensures Colt doesn't have to visit the outhouse again. He can't blame him, if so.

'Now then, Nick,' says Alan, stabbing a fork in the air, 'we've been wondering about a telly. None of us have one in our rooms, but it's hard to believe a place this size hasn't got a single one.'

'I was thinking the same,' Nick agrees. 'Perhaps I can have a look round after lunch, see if Donal has any suggestions. Even a radio might be useful.'

'Good man.' Alan nods, satisfied. 'This snow can't go on for much longer.'

'I mean, it *can*,' says Destiny, pouring herself a glass of water. 'Climate crisis is happening right now, Mother Earth is crying in pain as we burn and pillage . . .'

'You don't believe in that, do you?' Violet asks scornfully. 'It's long been proven that climate change is a myth. Weather is a natural cycle; it's not this great disaster everyone seems to—'

'Oh, really? Then how do you explain the vast numbers of climate refugees, burning deserts, biblical floods?' Destiny snaps. 'How do you explain the disastrous forest fires across Australia and California?'

'Funny, I've been to California quite recently,' says Violet. 'Everything looked perfectly fine to me.'

'Ladies!' David leans across, distressed. 'We can't start falling out; we have to pull together. It's the only way we'll get through this. Can we simply agree to differ?'

'It's hard to agree to differ with an idiot,' says Violet under her breath, but Gaia barks shrilly as Donal returns with a platter of sliced Christmas cake, and Destiny doesn't hear her. They turn from each other, and talk moves on to where Lorraine and Alan's daughter will think they are, how worried she'll be, and how they'll make it up to her and the kiddies when they finally reach her house. It seems to involve a lot of expensive gifts.

Matilda is at the far end, reading her novel. *Marking Time* by Elizabeth Jane Howard – Nick's mother-in-law loves her books. He wonders if Harriet will go to her parents' if he's not back by Christmas Day. But he will be, of course. He can't allow fear to creep in.

As he chomps through the cake, having picked off the marzipan (*You're like a child*, says Harriet in his head. *So* fussy), Nick is aware of something niggling at him. Something about Violet . . .

California. She was in California 'quite recently'. He must ask her why she was there. Could she possibly have known Penelope after all, he wonders – and could Penelope have hurt her in some way? *I know what you did.*

17

More than twenty-four hours since the body was found, and he feels no further on in his investigations. Perhaps he should back down, Nick thinks gloomily, let someone else have a try.

But first, he'll turn the place upside down and find a TV. He's on his way from the dining room, about to begin the search, when Donal pokes his head out of the office and beckons to him.

'Listen,' says Donal in a low voice, 'I might have found something.'

Nick stops, his heart thumping. 'What?'

Donal glances behind Nick, to where Lorraine has bent to stroke Jingle. 'Can't say now,' he says. 'Meet me in the library in twenty minutes.'

'OK. Donal, are there any televisions in the place?'

Donal pulls a face. 'Never seen one. Another thing the owner doesn't like, apparently. Me and Colt just watch films and stuff on our phones.'

'Mind if I have a look round, see if there's a radio or something?'

'Be my guest. But I doubt it.'

Donal retreats into the office, and Nick trudges upstairs. Should he have agreed to meet Donal alone? If he's the killer, the library is tucked away enough to muffle a shout or scream. Perhaps Nick should enlist David to come with him – but he won't want to leave Emily and put himself at risk. He feels cowardly for even considering that the slight young man, who has only ever shown him consideration, could be plotting his murder – but despite Destiny's questionable take on spirituality, her reading of him seems accurate. Donal does appear to be wearing a mask of bland politeness at all times. Even in the face of murder.

Upstairs, Nick tries a few door handles, but all the guest rooms are now locked. Hardly surprising, with a killer roaming the manor. The unoccupied rooms he looks into are empty of anything but their slightly dusty furniture, though each, he notes, has a painting over the bed featuring mistletoe.

The others have once again gathered around the drawing-room fire, so he should have free rein to search further. Nick passes Penelope's room, and sees the door that must lead to Colt's room and perhaps other staff quarters. It's unlocked, and opens on to a narrow flight of polished, uncarpeted oak stairs.

He treads quietly upwards, and emerges on the second floor of the manor, which is clearly not designed for guests. The corridor is laid with cheap, grey office carpet, there's a naked bulb in the harsh overhead light and, unlike the lavish landscapes and portraits which line the guest areas, here the white walls are bare.

With a stab of guilt, Nick tries the handle of the room nearest the stairs, which he guesses belongs to Colt. It opens on to a small, square room, containing a single bed with a blue-striped duvet. There's a 1960s French film poster Blu-Tacked to the wall, and on the desk beneath the window is an iPad, a couple of phone chargers, a half-empty can of Red Bull and a scatter of toiletries. In the bin, there's a crumpled cigarette packet and a handful of receipts. Nick picks one out and smooths it, but it's only from the local garage a few days ago, for crisps and soft drinks. Quickly, wondering what he expected, he tosses it back.

There's no thick paper or envelopes, and certainly no traces of gold wrapping paper. In the little chest of drawers, there are a few clean chefs' whites and checked trousers, a spare pair of kitchen Crocs underneath, and a tangle of boxers, jeans and T-shirts in the laundry bag shoved behind it. There's no trace of blood – it's a neat, minimal bedroom belonging to someone whose life is largely lived elsewhere in the building. Nick feels a wash of hot shame and leaves quickly, clicking the door shut behind him.

The next door leads to a cleaner's closet, stacked with mops and bulk supplies, and another further down must be Donal's room, Nick realises, as the door is firmly locked. The last door, at the end of the corridor, opens on to a storeroom.

Labelled boxes and moth-proof bags – 'Cushions', 'Old towels' – are stacked high against the windowless walls, looking very much as if they've been there for years. There are a couple of broken chairs, a rolled Persian rug and, he notices, an old, splintered tea-chest labelled 'Christmas decs and costumes'.

Nick lifts the lid away and peers in. Coils of dulled silver tinsel, a few dusty baubles too heavy to hang on the tree, and a couple of costumes that look as though they were made for a long-ago nativity play: one with feathered wings and a silver-foil halo. Whatever the killer wore to stab Penelope, he or she didn't hide it up here. And there are no televisions or radios, either. Sighing, Nick replaces the crate's lid and returns to the back stairs.

As he opens the door to the guest corridor, he stops. Some-one is walking away, towards the other end. The light is dim, but he can see it's a man – thick-set, tall. Branson.

Nick watches as the American turns the corner at the end, passing Rowan without a glance. Nick hurries after him, treading as lightly as possible on the parquet, practising an expression of friendly surprise, should Branson turn and spot him. At the end of the corridor, Nick stops and flattens himself against the wall, feeling ludicrous, like a child playing cops and robbers. He peers round the corner. There's now no sign of the other man, so Nick heads down the corridor, checking the doors. Outside Laburnum, he pauses and leans towards the panelled door. He can hear voices inside – Branson's gravelly rumble, and a higher-pitched tone, which sounds upset.

The door is too thick to make out the words, or who the person is – but it's definitely a woman. Nick feels adrenalin buzzing through his veins. As far as he's aware, Branson and Penelope arrived alone – but suppose Branson knew some-one who was already here? Suppose they committed murder together? He pulls back sharply as footsteps approach the door on the other side, and he dashes to the corner, turning it just as he hears the door open, and Branson saying, 'I'll see you later. Try not to worry.'

Nick gallops down the main stairs two at a time, eager to reach the hall before Branson spots him, and strolls casually into the drawing room. Only Alan and David are by the fire, talking quietly.

'Lorraine's barely slept,' Alan says. 'I sent her up for a nap, but she's scared to be on her own. I'll go and check on her in a minute.'

David nods. Emily is on the rug, reading an Enid Blyton book, her ever-present headphones once again clamped over her ears. She looks up and removes them as Nick sits down, leaving them round her neck like a tiny DJ. Nick smiles at her.

'Did you go to boarding school, Nick?' she asks. 'I'm reading about Malory Towers, and I want to go to one when I'm a bit bigger.'

'I went to a day school,' he tells her. 'My dad was the Latin teacher.'

Her eyes widen. 'Was your mum one too?'

'No,' he says. 'I'm afraid my mum . . .' He glances at David. 'Well, she di . . . passed away, when I was little.'

'Mine did too,' says Emily. 'I'm a half of an orphan.'

She returns cheerfully to her book, and David smiles sadly at Nick. 'She doesn't remember her,' he tells him. 'Sometimes I think that's for the best, but then again . . .'

'I'm sorry.' The journalist in Nick wants to know how she died, but he can't bring himself to ask. Probably cancer, like his own mother, Gwen. She died when he was nine – only a little older than Emily. The difference is, he does remember her. He had assumed David was divorced, and only had Emily for the holidays. Now, he realises just how close they must be.

'Getting anywhere with your investigations?' asks David, and Nick wonders whether to mention Branson. He decides against it, reminding himself that nobody can be trusted.

Branson himself arrives, and raises a hand. 'Still snowing,' he observes pointlessly.

'How are you getting on?' Alan asks brusquely, evidently hoping that Branson will say, *Fine, no need to discuss it any further.*

'Terrible. I'm not sleeping. Every time I close my eyes I see her there. I can't . . .' He sighs and glances at Nick. 'I just went to see Violet. She said if I needed to talk . . . I tried, but it doesn't help. Until we catch the bastard that did it, nothing helps.'

Nick feels both relieved and frustrated. He thought . . . he doesn't know what he thought. Violet was just being kind, trying to help a stranger in unfathomable pain. She was also, perhaps, being foolish – because for all she knows, Branson could have killed his wife after all and be acting up a storm of grief. Although Matilda saw him too, coming out of Laburnum – Violet's room – perhaps Branson simply needs a friend.

'She's got a counselling qualification, you know,' Branson says now.

'Who?' Alan asks, irritably nudging Jingle away with his gold snaffle loafer. Nick finds it hard to trust people who dislike cats, and pats the sofa beside him. Jingle leaps up, and crackles an appreciative purr as Nick strokes his head.

'Violet. She said she could listen without offering advice, and that's what I thought I needed, but . . . nothing works.' His voice breaks on a sob, and Nick puts an awkward hand on his shoulder.

'I'll fetch you a brandy . . .' mutters Alan, heaving himself upright. 'It's five o'clock somewhere.'

Donal. Nick looks at his watch – it's after two; he's late for their meeting. He removes his hand from Branson's heaving shoulder. 'I'll be five minutes,' he says. 'I just need to . . . David, could you . . .?'

David slides on to the sofa beside Branson, and murmurs, 'It's terribly hard, mate, I know,' as Nick apologetically hurries from the drawing room.

There's nobody in the hall, and no sounds of life elsewhere. The tree drops a cascade of dry needles as he passes – he wonders why it's already dying, when the hall is so cold. The bottom branches are almost bare – even the tree lights are off, Nick notes.

Nick pushes open the door of the library, hopeful that Donal has waited and will be sitting in a wing-backed chair, ready to tell all. But it's immediately clear that he's not here – the room is chilly, empty of life. The snow is now so high at the window that the filtered light is grey and murky, like the bottom of a winter pond.

Cursing himself, Nick turns to go and look for Donal, and sees Matilda making her way slowly downstairs. She lifts a hand in greeting and he hurries to help her down.

'I'm fine,' she says. 'It's these blasted shoes – shiny soles. We used to run a cheese grater over new shoe soles to roughen them, but all these little tricks have been forgotten now, haven't they? It's all instant gratification, throw them away and buy a new pair.'

Nick has been subjected to several similar rants from Harriet on her occasional eco-missions ('Plastic toys, Nick, *really*?') and knows simply to nod.

'Have you seen Violet?' Matilda asks as she reaches the hall and orients herself towards the drawing room. 'I wanted to ask her something.'

Nick explains what Branson has revealed.

'Oh, I see!' Matilda's eyes shine with unexpected tears. 'What a relief. My goodness. I was awfully worried that something was amiss, with him creeping about in different bedrooms.'

'Yes, it seems Violet's just being a Good Samaritan,' Nick agrees. 'Mystery solved.'

'Well, one mystery, anyway,' says Matilda drily. 'We still have a murderer to catch.'

She pats his arm and makes her way slowly to the drawing room, pulling her cardigan tight against the chill as Nick heads in the other direction towards the kitchen, to find Donal.

He's about to push open the door when he hears raised voices.

18

'I'm not saying that, though, am I?' A tone of irritation from Donal.

'It sounds very much like you're saying exactly that. If you don't trust me, say so to my face.'

'What if I don't? How does saying it to your face help?'

'At least you could be honest and say you think I murdered a woman in her bed. Say that you think you've spent two years working next to a bloody psycho.'

Nick freezes, listening.

'I don't!' Donal slams something down on a surface with a hard smack. 'But we've got a bunch of terrified guests about to turn on each other, we're stuck here with no phones, and someone's killing people. All I'm saying is, you know where everything is, you've got a dodgy past, you hate posh people . . .'

'You think I killed Penelope because she's *posh*?' Colt's voice spirals in disbelief.

'I don't even know! I don't know *you*,' Donal shouts. 'I work with you every day, and I don't know anything about you.'

'And I don't know anything about you apart from that you've got a so-called fiancée nobody's ever seen, and you're the most uptight bloke I've ever met. Maybe you killed

Penelope! Maybe you were having an affair with her! I don't *know*, do I?'

There's the sound of glass smashing and Colt shouting, 'What the hell . . .?'

Donal shoulders his way out of the kitchen and storms past Nick. There are pink spots high on his cheeks and his eyes are blazing.

Nick tries to speak, but Donal doesn't stop to hear whatever he's about to say. His feet pound up the stairs, and soon, distantly and far above them, Nick hears the sound of a heavy door being violently slammed.

He peers tentatively into the kitchen.

'Colt,' he says. 'I'm sorry, I overheard some of it. I wasn't eavesdropping, I was coming to talk to Donal.'

'Good luck with that.' Colt is breathing heavily. At his feet, the shards of a glass jug shine like scattered ice.

'Are you OK?'

Colt shrugs and fetches the kitchen broom from the corner. 'Not really. Is anyone OK right now?'

'Do you really think he killed her?'

Colt sighs. 'I think . . . I don't know. It could have been Donal; it could have been you. It could have been that bloody French bulldog.'

'More likely Jingle,' says Nick, aiming for brief levity. Colt half smiles.

'Nah, man. He's a good cat. Listen, I need to clear this up and start on dinner prep. Let me know if you need anything.'

'I will. Thanks, Colt.'

The younger man nods, and turns back to the shattered glass.

*

Gradually, the others gather once again around the fire. Violet slips in beside Branson, briefly laying a hand on his knee. 'Any better?' she asks him, and he shudders something between a shrug and a head-shake.

David moves up so Destiny can take her usual place. 'What have you been up to?' he asks her conversationally.

'Meditating. Asking for spirit guidance. Walking Gaia up and down the corridors. Trying not to go mad.'

'I suppose we wouldn't know if we did,' David remarks. 'The thing with madness is, you generally don't realise you're mad.'

'Oh, we're all mad as a box of toads in my family, and we know it all right,' says Lorraine happily. 'Don't we, Alan?' She turns to the others. 'He always says me and my sisters are absolutely berserk when we get together.'

Alan smiles tightly. 'I don't say that.'

'You *do*! You say you've never known anything like it cos your ex-wife was so quiet . . .'

'That's *enough*, Lorraine.'

Nick sees him shoot her a glare so chilling, Lorraine stops speaking, and swallows. 'Sorry,' she whispers.

So Alan has an ex-wife. Nick wonders how he and Lorraine met, what their story is. Beyond Lorraine's cheerful chatter about Christmas at Jade's house, he knows very little about them, and he hasn't yet spoken to Alan alone. He wonders quite how their marriage works – this is the first sign that they aren't an entirely united front. That Alan might be hiding a cruel streak beneath the golf-club bonhomie.

*

The afternoon inches by. Nick plays a couple of games of Scrabble with Matilda and Violet, letting Emily help by suggesting small words he could use. As a result, he loses badly.

Branson tells Alan and Lorraine about life in Malibu – 'You never need to think, *What will I wear today?* because it's always sunny,' he says. 'Penny loved it so much, I always wondered why she didn't move somewhere warm years before I met her.'

'Her son and parents, I suppose,' says Lorraine. 'I'd never have dragged our Jade abroad when she was little.'

'And they still don't know she's dead . . .' Branson puts a hand over his face again, and Lorraine clutches his elbow in sympathy.

Talk turns again to the note.

'Who has neat writing?' wonders Lorraine. She gazes at the paper, which remains on the table before them. 'It's kind of disguised, you can tell, but if we had a graphologist . . .'

'A what?' Branson asks.

'Someone who studies handwriting,' Destiny puts in. 'It's a very interesting method of—'

'They have a whole page on it in *Soul Secrets Magazine*,' says Lorraine. 'I love it – "Real-life women tell their spooky stories".'

'It's nonsense,' says Alan impatiently. 'It's all made up.'

'It is not!' Lorraine bristles. 'They have actual *photographs*, Alan.'

Nick wonders whether it would be even vaguely useful to compare everyone's handwriting, and concludes that it wouldn't. Almost anyone can write in neat capitals if they need to.

'What could she have done?' Lorraine asks again, and Violet shakes her head.

'An affair? A vengeful ex-husband, maybe?'

Branson glares. 'That was *not* why her last marriage ended, Vi.'

Branson, of course, would want to believe that Penelope was blameless. Nick wonders if Violet's hit on something.

'Her ex,' he says. 'What do you know about him, Branson?'

The American sighs. 'Not a lot. "Irreconcilable differences". Still has a good relationship with Peter. Does something woke – social-work type of thing.'

'So he and Penny didn't speak at all?'

'Nope. Not that I know about.'

Nick has a wild thought. 'Could he be here . . . one of the group . . .?'

'Only if it's you,' says Lorraine. 'Because it's not Alan, and David's a GP with a daughter.'

Branson shakes his head. 'Nah,' he says. 'She'd have told me. Why would she keep it secret if someone she knew so well was here?'

He's right, Nick thinks. *It would be madness to pretend*. He glances across at Violet, and is surprised by her expression. She has been upset all day, of course – but now she looks despairing.

David and Destiny are holding a murmured conversation, which seems to be about the crossover between natural remedies and what Destiny refers to as 'big pharma placebos'. David is being remarkably patient, Nick thinks. Or perhaps he agrees with Destiny that the West is slowly poisoning itself thanks to its refusal to wake up and embrace the earth's true bounty.

More likely, Nick assumes, he's not fully listening, but

admiring her exquisite face and lithe limbs as she sits cross-legged, Gaia snoring in the nest of her lap.

Curious, Nick tunes into their conversation.

'I used to study medicine,' Destiny is telling David. 'I went to Edinburgh, I was going to be a doctor, a paediatrician. And then in my third year, I got ill and I nearly died, and not one doctor knew how to help me.'

'What was the illness?' David asks gently.

'ME,' says Destiny. 'I was so burnt out and exhausted, I couldn't walk – I could barely speak. My mum and dad were beside themselves, my boyfriend left me. One – male – doctor told me I was "malingering".'

She waits for David's horror, and he obliges. 'So what happened?' he asks.

'I realised mainstream medicine wasn't going to help me,' she tells him. 'I did my own research. I started doing chair yoga, and I'd be exhausted after ten minutes, but I carried on. I looked up natural cures, and once I could get up, I began foraging in the local woods for berries and fungi, real alternatives to big pharma, which is only interested in perpetuating ill health so it can charge a fortune for its so-called cures. My medicine cabinet is available to all, for nothing. I learned how to cure myself, and I trained as a yoga teacher, naturopath and shaman. That was eight years ago, and I haven't been ill since.'

David nods slowly. 'You must think I'm a bit of a nightmare, then!' he says awkwardly.

She shakes her head solemnly. 'No. I think you have the potential to do great good. But you must learn to harness nature's power,' she says. 'When we get out of here, I could teach you – show you what I've learned, start you on a path that will change your life for good. There are so many wonderful tinctures, life-giving berries you can find, even in the depths of winter.'

David is clearly mesmerised by her beauty, thinks Nick. Normally, he's pretty sure any doctor would be mounting a passionate defence of Western medicine, but David's just nodding along, smiling into her huge brown eyes.

The light outside has gone altogether by four o'clock, and Donal comes in to close the shutters and draw the curtains.

'Can I get a tea, mate?' calls Alan, and everyone clamours their own drinks orders.

Donal comes across to note them down. He's no longer flushed. There's no trace of the rage Nick saw when he whirled from the kitchen earlier, as he smiles and blandly enquires after everyone, whether they've had a nap, who won Scrabble, if they need fresh towels.

For a moment, Nick envisages Donal as a spider on the moulded plaster ceiling gazing down on everyone as they go about their business, studying their routes, ticking down the hours as he waits for the moment to trap them in his intricate web. David's right, he thinks bitterly, you don't know when you're going mad.

'Dinner will be a little later tonight,' Donal tells the group. 'David, we can do something earlier for Emily if you'd rather she didn't have to wait?'

David smiles at him. 'Very kind of you. I think she'd prefer to eat with everyone else, would you, poppet?'

She nods, attention still on her book.

Donal catches Nick's eye. 'Quick word when I've served the drinks?'

At last, thinks Nick. Maybe, finally, he can discover what Donal's found, and how it might in any way be relevant to catching the murderer.

They meet in the small sitting room where he spoke to Matilda. 'Not to be paranoid,' says Donal, turning the brass key, 'but I'm going to lock the door.'

Nick experiences a moment of disquiet. Is it really wise to be in this hidden little enclave, with no way out and a potential murderer standing in front of him? He scans the room quickly – a poker in the fireplace, a heavy Chinese vase on the coffee table, the mounted butterflies in glass frames that could shatter if he brought one down hard enough on the edge of the coffee table—

Donal offers a twisted smile. 'You're thinking about how to fend me off, aren't you?'

'I'd be fairly stupid if I wasn't.'

Donal sighs and seats himself in the stuffed armchair nearest to the hearth. He's lit a small fire, and it smoulders in the grate, fizzling occasionally as snowflakes drift down the chimney.

'You don't have to worry, Nick.' He throws his hands up like a cheerleader. 'Look, no weapons. I just don't want anyone barging in and overhearing us.'

'Go on, then. What have you found out?'

Donal leans forward. 'When I was cleaning, I had a good look around,' he says. 'I also let myself into the rooms that don't have an occupant right now, not counting Rowan, the one Branson's been sleeping in. They're Ash, Yew, Briar and

Sycamore. Ash, Briar and Sycamore were empty, but I saw something in Yew.'

Nick smiles at Donal's unwitting play on words, but Donal goes on, 'I looked under the bed and behind the curtains, in the drawers – but it was hidden inside the mini-bar.'

'What was?'

Donal reaches in to the pocket of his black trousers and pulls out a small piece of paper. At first, Nick thinks it's a note, something like the one Penelope received, but this paper is thinner, and torn at the edges. Donal places it on the coffee table and turns it over. The wrapping paper shines gold in the firelight.

'Wow.'

'I know,' says Donal. The paper is a perfect match for the shining metallic wrapping of the Christmas star, but on this piece, there's no trace of blood.

'Anything else?'

Donal shakes his head. 'Just this. I guess they thought nobody'd look in there.'

'Was Yew locked?'

Donal nods.

'Who has keys?'

'Nobody but me.' Donal sighs. 'They're always with me, on me, around me . . . the guest keys are in the hall desk drawer, and that's always locked.'

'So somebody stole your keys and returned them.'

'When? Nick, I keep them on my belt; I sleep with the door locked.'

'Was it locked the first night? When Penelope was killed?'

Donal closes his eyes. 'I don't know. It didn't occur to me

that I'd need to . . . maybe not. But who'd risk coming into my room, which is tiny?'

Nick's about to say 'I know', remembering Colt's cramped quarters, but manages to catch himself.

'I mean, they'd have been standing right by my head,' Donal goes on. 'I'd have heard them clanking around.'

'You don't wear earbuds like Colt?'

'No, never. If anything goes wrong overnight, or the fire alarm goes off, I'm the first port of call.'

'Then they must have stolen the guest key.'

'Nope. I checked as soon as I came back down. It's there.'

'They put it back then.'

'And locked the drawer with my keys?'

'Ah.'

They stare at each other.

'Someone who's been here before?' Nick tries. 'Maybe they made a copy?'

'Nobody *has* been here before, except Matilda, every Christmas for God knows how long. Apart from that . . .' Donal shrugs. 'I know you overheard Colt. If you suspect me too, better say so now.'

Nick pauses. He doesn't – unless Donal producing the wrapping paper is a double bluff. It would certainly mean that suspicion swings away from him, after Colt's questions and Lorraine's certainty that he's guilty. But Donal told him he'd found something before the row in the kitchen, he remembers.

'I have to believe you're innocent,' Nick says eventually. 'Like you have to believe that I am.'

Donal nods. 'Exactly. Faith, isn't it? No proof, just belief.'

'Have you told anyone else about the paper?'

'Not yet. Listen, I've got to go – but why don't we meet after dinner in the upstairs corridor when they're all in the drawing room again, and have a look for bloodstained clothes? The killer had to be wearing something, and it has to be hidden somewhere.'

'Unless they were naked,' says Nick. 'Which puts Branson back in the frame, seeing as he could have been in bed next to her.'

'Branson's always been in the frame,' says Donal. 'I've long been a believer in the Occam's razor theory. Very often, it's the most obvious solution that's staring us in the face.'

19

It's a long time until dinner. People head upstairs to get ready in couples, afraid to be alone. Nick assumes that by 'getting ready' they mean brushing their hair, perhaps putting on shoes rather than slippers – nobody is bothering to change for the evening now, it would be like hosting a cabaret in a mausoleum. He sits on the edge of his bed, stroking Jingle who has followed him upstairs, staring at the useless screen of his phone.

It's just three nights until Christmas Eve, he realises. He has never in his life felt less festive, including the year his mother died and he and his dad visited the grandparents with the ticking clock and bullying board games. He can feel the lump in his throat even, recalling the cheap pack of floury mince pies, still in their red plastic tray as his grandmother handed them round, the thick silence as they sat through a repeat of *Morecambe and Wise*. He wonders what Harriet's doing. Cursing him? Calling the police?

In his room, he sits on the bed and glumly appraises the situation.

He needs to talk to Alan, to Branson again, to David. He needs to work out the puzzle of the room keys – unless Donal is mistaken and the room was unlocked all along. Or, he reminds himself, Donal is simply lying, as Colt believes, aiming to confuse and misdirect.

Nick remembers a magician at a childhood party he once attended. He flourished his magic wand, asked the children to reach behind his ear for pound coins, bedazzled them with glittering patter. Only Nick kept his eyes fixed on the man's sleeve, and the white glint of the card he'd pushed inside his cuff. Only Nick was disappointed to realise that his instincts had been right, and real magic didn't exist. Who is now performing that sleight of hand, directing attention entirely the wrong way?

He hears a door closing on the floor above, the creak of footsteps echoing through the old building. The heating pipes cough and clank. He needs to come up with a theory fast, before somebody else is attacked. But deep down, Nick dares to ask himself, does he not think they're all pretty safe now? In his heart, isn't he convinced that *I know what you did* safely marks Penelope as the sole victim of the grudge that led to her murder?

He should tell the others about the wrapping paper, he decides. Look for signs of guilt – micro-expressions, the sudden shock of discovery. He's seen that once before, with Candice, the girlfriend he had at university. She had been distant, her laugh brittle, her touch lacklustre for weeks. Nick tried to get to the bottom of it, wondering about depression or unwritten essays. 'It's like you're having an affair,' he joked. Her eyes flashed shock, and though she denied it, he knew. Like all good clichés, it turned out to be her tutor.

What he needs to do, he thinks now, is to find out as much as he can about Penelope. He needs to stop tiptoeing around

Branson's apparent grief and dig into what the hell she might have done. Whatever it was, she didn't deserve to die. But finding out will surely lead straight to her killer. *California*, he thinks. *Violet*.

He has to navigate his way out of this snow-bound maze before Christmas, get back to his wife and baby – and to do so, he needs to overcome his natural social instinct to respect other people's boundaries, and channel the award-winning investigative reporter who's happy to trample straight through them.

With fresh resolve beating in his blood, Nick showers, checks fruitlessly for phone signal, reminds himself to find the laundry room and wash his limp, exhausted clothes tomorrow – did Donal look in there for the bloodstained clothes? Of course he did . . . unless Donal did it . . . Thinking, wondering, assessing, Nick makes his way back down to the dining room.

The aroma of rich beef stew is so thick, he could scoop the air with a spoon. Nick tries to engineer a seat beside Branson to begin his gentle interrogation, but finds himself kettled between David and Destiny, and opposite Alan. The stew is already on the table, in two vast tureens set on trivets, with a dish of fluffy mashed potatoes between them. Gaia is of course on Destiny's lap, frantically sniffing the air, her tiny paws like a rabbit's feet scrabbling at the tablecloth.

'I wonder where my meal is?' Destiny says loudly. 'It's funny how the one vegan is always an afterthought, isn't it?'

Lorraine makes sympathetic noises. 'We haven't seen Donal yet,' she says. 'I'm sure he's gone to get it.'

'Well, I look forward to my dry bread roll,' says Destiny.

'It seems quite unfair,' says David. 'Of all of us, you're the one who cares most about the planet; yet, as you say, you get served last.'

Destiny smiles graciously in acknowledgement. 'Thank you. I can't tell you how poor the offerings are when I'm travelling in the UK – the vegan concept hasn't reached Britain's service stations, I can tell you that. Ultra-processed garbage wherever you look, fizzy drinks, vacuum-packed meat that's barely passed safety checks . . .' She carries on in this vein as David nods sympathetically and Lorraine covertly casts longing looks at the stew.

'Of course, India's an entirely different story,' Destiny is saying now, warming to her theme. Gaia's torso has breached the tabletop, and Nick wonders if he should say something before she plunges head-first into the tureen. 'The freshest plant-based foods, pulses, legumes, the most incredible thalis . . .'

'Our Jade got horrible food poisoning in Goa from some ulcerated chicken,' Lorraine says. 'She wasn't off the loo for a week.'

Destiny stops speaking. 'Thank you for that mental image, Lorraine,' she says, pushing back her chair. 'I'm going to look for my food before I starve to death.'

Nick wonders why Destiny seems to spend so much time travelling around the country. It's not as though yoga teachers teach a class in every city – his only experience of yoga is Harriet pulling on ancient Sweaty Betty leggings and groaning about her hips, but she always seems to go to the same class with the same teacher.

Destiny is gone a long time. When Lorraine has finally given in and ladled out the stew in her absence, Destiny returns, holding a bowl of plain pasta with garlic and olive oil. It smells better than it looks.

'There's no sign of Donal,' she says, a small frown creasing her smooth brow. 'I've been round to the kitchen, but that chef, Colt, says he didn't come down for dinner service. He told me he hasn't seen him since before we all went upstairs.'

Nick feels a jolt of alarm. David sets down his fork.

'Are you all right Destiny?' he asks. 'You look a bit pale.'

David's right. Destiny has collapsed back into her chair and pushed her bowl away. Her curtain of thick black hair obscures her face.

'He's always here, isn't he?' she says quietly. 'He'd never miss the dinner service. I think something's happened.'

'No need to be melodramatic . . .' Alan begins.

Emily looks at Destiny with wide eyes. 'Like what sort of thing?'

'He's perhaps had a nap and overslept,' says Nick quickly. Emily's a very sweet child, but this entire situation would be a great deal easier to navigate without her presence. Although, he remembers, Donal doesn't oversleep. He always sets his alarm.

'He's perhaps died, like Penelope did,' says Emily through a piece of beef. 'Someone has perhaps killed him. He's perhaps—'

'Don't be silly, poppet,' says David. 'I'm sure Donal is fine.'

Nick has made short work of the stew. He pushes his chair back. 'I'll go and check. I'm sure there's nothing to worry about.'

'I could come too,' says Lorraine anxiously.

'Maybe we should all form a conga line,' snaps Alan. 'Just let the man leave, Lorraine.'

155

'I forgot my book,' says Violet, overhearing. 'I'll come up and get it. Hang on, Nick, I don't like being alone upstairs.'

He waits, annoyed, as she gathers her Gucci handbag and shoves in a couple more mouthfuls of stew.

'Do you actually think something's happened?' she demands as they leave. 'What if he's not OK? What if he's . . . you know.'

'I'm sure he's fine,' Nick says shortly, although he's aware of a buzzing in his bloodstream that can only be driven by fear of what he might discover.

'Wait for me by the stairs, please,' Violet calls, disappearing round the corner to Laburnum.

Nick glances up and down the corridor. It's empty and there's no sound of footsteps above him. *It's fine. Donal was angry after his row with Colt. Maybe he's trying to show us how hard he works, how much we'd struggle without him.*

He makes his way past Penelope's room, veering away instinctively as if the door itself is electrified, and opens the door on to the back stairs that lead to the staff bedrooms.

'Oh, there you are!' Violet calls as she rounds the corner. 'Hang on, I'm just—' She stops. Nick isn't moving.

'Don't come any nearer,' he says, his voice emerging in a whisper.

'Why? What's wrong?' Violet ignores him, running past the main staircase to find out what he's seen.

Nick pushes her back. 'Don't!'

Both of them stand together, a few steps beneath the body, gazing, speechless. Donal is lying twisted, his legs at an unnatural angle on the steep stairs. His face is grey, his eyes wide

156

open. And around his neck is the string of fairy lights that was on the tree, the wires pulled into a fatal garrotte.

Nick isn't sure if it's shock, revulsion, or a dim awareness that the scene should be preserved for the police, but his legs are propelling him backwards, and Violet seems to be experiencing a similar force. She leans on the balustrade overlooking the main hall, gasping for breath. Nick looks down on Donal's polished desk, its ordered pens and jotter, and feels a wave of profound sorrow for the young man. Whatever he was hiding, he wasn't a killer.

'They're going to murder all of us, aren't they?' Violet's voice spirals into shrill panic. 'Whoever it is, they won't rest until we're all dead, all just corpses in their sick game!' Her words break on a sob, and then she's in Nick's arms, her face buried in his chest, wailing with fear and grief.

'Nick! What the hell?'

David is looking up at them, his pleasant, ordinary face washed with confusion. 'I thought the cat was hurt – I didn't want Emily to hear . . .'

Nick looks over Violet's heaving shoulder.

'Donal,' he says, and David blanches, then sprints up the stairs.

'Where?'

'Attic stairs. Just found him.'

David runs past them and flings open the door, then stops dead. Like Nick, he understands immediately that there's no chance of reviving Donal, that he's been dead for some time.

David murmurs something Nick can't hear – an expression

of grief, or perhaps despair, then he sinks to his knees on the staircase and presses his fingers pointlessly to Donal's neck. He shakes his head.

'How long?'

'It's pretty cold up here but his skin's still retaining a trace of heat. One, two hours at most.'

'So when we went up to get ready for dinner?'

David nods. 'Most likely.'

As he speaks, Nick realises that was obviously when the murderer struck – before dinner, when, for the first time that day, they were all distracted, showering, atomised in their separate spaces. 'Not yet,' Donal said when Nick asked if he'd told anyone. Perhaps he had since confided in another member of the group – and this was the result.

Violet is still ululating wildly, deranged with fear and shock.

'Come on,' says Nick. 'Can you make it downstairs?'

She shakes her head against his chest, and he leans in so she can hear him. Her long, shining hair smells of vanilla, the scent of innocence, and he thinks of how young she is, and how fragile.

'Shall I take you to your room? I can get Lorraine, or Matilda . . .?'

'No . . . no . . .' She takes a great, shuddering breath. 'I need to see Branson. He's the only one who . . . who . . .'

She collapses again, into his arms.

'I'll go,' murmurs David. 'We'll need to tell the others.'

Nick shakes his head. 'Not yet. Wait till dinner's over. I need to think.'

David nods, and a few moments later returns with Branson. Once in the hall, Branson hears Violet's sobs, and takes the stairs at speed. 'My God,' he says. 'Honey, come here. What's happened?'

Like a cat, she peels away from Nick, leaving a chill damp patch on his chest, and attaches herself to Branson, clinging to him. He strokes her back, soothing and murmuring. As her sobs subside, she manages to croak, 'Donal's dead,' and the instantaneous shock on Branson's face persuades Nick, for a moment at least, that while he might be keeping other secrets, he surely can't be the killer.

20

'She needs to lie down,' Branson manages as Violet clings to him. 'I'll take her . . .'

'Thanks.' Nick turns to David. 'Can we move him – the body? Colt's room is just up there . . .'

'I'll examine him first. Though it looks like a straightforward strangulation,' David adds sombrely. 'You can see the petechiae and the subconjunctival haemorrhage . . . Sorry.' He's noted Nick's blank expression. 'Burst blood vessels in the eyes and on the skin, congruent with asphyxia. At first glance, he's otherwise uninjured, so I'd say the killer surprised him from behind as he went down the stairs, with the fairy lights – holding the wire taut. There's no sign of a fight, though of course I'll check his fingernails and look for bruising.'

David, Nick realises, has gone straight into professional mode in the face of trauma: perhaps as a defence mechanism, or maybe simply because of his long experience in medicine. 'You get a bit immune,' a university friend of his once told him, in her fourth year of training to be a doctor. 'The bodies kind of don't bother you after a while.'

As if he's spoken out loud, David adds, 'I must seem rather cold. I assure you, Nick, I'm utterly horrified.' He blinks. 'And scared, shocked, sad . . . he's so bloody young. But I suppose

I feel bringing the murderer to justice is all we can do now. So most of all, I feel angry.'

Nick nods. 'So do I.'

Now, he's determined to find out who has ended two lives — someone who sleeps and eats alongside them; who lurks within their frightened little group like a shark in a coral reef, waiting to strike. There's no more time to waste.

Telling the others is even worse than Nick imagined. They're huddled like penned sheep around the drawing-room fire, knowing something is wrong, fearful of hearing the truth.

He takes a deep breath, and scans the pale, upturned faces.

'I'm so sorry to tell you all, but Donal is dead,' he begins, and his next words are drowned out by gasps of horror.

'He can't be!' Lorraine cries. 'He can't, can he, Alan? I only saw him just before teatime! He was fine!'

People always say this, Nick thinks. At the beginning of his career, working on the local paper, he interviewed several bereaved spouses and devastated parents who had lost loved ones suddenly. They all, without fail, expressed their shock that 'It was just a normal morning', that 'We only saw him an hour before it happened', as if those marked for sudden death carry a sign, as if they should have known what was coming.

'Are you saying he's been killed?' demands Alan, his face stippled pink and white with distress.

David, just behind Nick, says, 'I'm afraid so. About an hour ago, I think. So dreadful.' He looks at Emily, who is sitting by Matilda, Jingle on her lap.

'Is he murdered, Daddy?' she asks. 'Will we all get murdered?'

David rushes past Nick, tears gleaming in his eyes, and gathers her to him. Jingle leaps off Emily's knee and streaks away.

'Daddy! He'd just sat on me! I was stroking him!'

Nick is glad to see that Emily's hierarchy of concerns is still as an eight-year-old's should be. Destiny and Lorraine are hugging, and Nick sees shudders running through the younger woman like electric currents. Destiny is crying great, silent sobs, her open mouth a black hole of grief as Lorraine shakes her head and murmurs, rubbing Destiny's slender back as if she's a fretful baby.

Alan stands. 'This can't go on,' he announces. 'It's absolute madness. People are being offed left, right and centre. Thing is, Nick, how do we know you're not the killer? You're so helpful, aren't you? Interviewing everyone, poking about, always first on the scene to find a body. Believe me, I've seen enough thrillers to know that makes you the chief suspect.'

'Don't be ridiculous.' David turns from Emily, and Nick is surprised by the cold fury in his tone. 'Grow up, Alan, Nick hasn't shown the slightest sign that he's the murderer – he's putting himself in danger to help us!'

'So you say,' Alan mutters, subsiding into his chair again. 'But we don't know, do we? That's my point. It could be you, David, or Violet, or . . . or anyone!'

Matilda clutches the arms of her chair. 'It's impossible to imagine that it was any of us,' she whispers. Nick silently agrees.

Lorraine says nervously, 'Where's Violet?'

'With Branson,' Nick tells her, sudden fear flashing through him. What was he thinking? Leaving Violet to the man who may, for all he knows, have killed his wife – and now Donal.

He turns and races upstairs, pelts down the corridor and bangs hard on the door of Laburnum.

'Violet!'

'Who is it?'

Relief courses through him at the sound of her voice.

'It's Nick. Are you OK?'

'Yes.' She sounds shaken, but very much alive.

'Is Branson there?'

'Yes, he's been looking after me,' she calls.

'I'm here.' There's a click and the rattle of a door-chain being drawn back. Branson peers round the door, keeping it half closed so Nick can't see inside the room.

'She's lying down,' he explains. 'It was such a shock . . .'

'Of course.' Nick feels foolish. 'I just wanted to check she's all right. Do you want to come and get a drink?'

Branson glances behind him. 'I'll wait till this one feels up to coming back down,' he says quietly. 'She's only just quit the hysterics.'

It's rather a blunt way to put it. Nick thinks again of Harriet's views on 'hysteria', but this isn't the time for a feminist lecture, so he nods and retreats downstairs, where, to his alarm, he sees that Destiny is still sobbing in great gasps, almost unable to breathe with distress.

David is looking anxiously at Matilda, and Lorraine is now sitting with her arm around the yoga teacher, rocking and shushing, while Alan hovers nervously, proffering a glass of brandy.

Lorraine waves it away. 'She doesn't *drink*, Alan. Debbie, love, you'll make yourself poorly,' she murmurs. 'Try and get your breath.'

She looks up and shoots a worried glance at Nick. 'She won't stop,' Lorraine mouths. 'She's beside herself.'

'David, have you got any sedatives with you?' Nick asks.

David nods. 'I sometimes take sleeping pills,' he says, 'but not when I'm alone with Emily, in case she needs me. They might still be in my case – hang on.'

He disappears to his room. It occurs to Nick to hope that the pills are sealed in their blister pack. If not, Destiny probably shouldn't risk it.

The lack of trust creeping through their small group is like a toxic mist, one in which everyone is isolated and nobody dares to reach a comforting hand through the poisonous murk.

Donal was surely murdered because he knew something, Nick realises. There was no note this time, no 'I know what you did'. Just a quick, brutal killing – and one, for some sickening reason, that's again related to Christmas.

David returns and sits down again before he presses two pills from a sealed pink pack. Nick feels a wash of relief.

'Here,' the doctor holds them out to Destiny. 'These will help.'

She shakes her head. 'I'm not taking those,' she manages between sobs, and pushes his hand away.

'Look, it's nothing dangerous . . .'

'Everything's dangerous,' she hisses. 'And I don't take big pharma crap.'

'I'll help you upstairs—' Lorraine begins, but Destiny shakes her head again, more violently.

'Not alone. I'm staying here.'

'OK, love,' Lorraine agrees. 'We'll pop you down on the couch.'

She fetches the green chenille throw from the arm of Matilda's chair and tucks it over Destiny.

'Emily, let's go upstairs,' says David, who has apparently had enough of devastated women. 'We can play Guess Who? – I brought it with us.'

Emily looks reluctant. 'I don't really want to be upstairs,' she says in a small voice. 'The murderer might be there.'

Nick feels a jolt of horror for the small girl. Here with her dad for Christmas, expecting snowmen and games and jollity . . . she's so small, he thinks, looking at her in her jeans and pink-striped jumper. His heart aches for both Emily and David.

'Look,' Nick says. 'Why don't we all stay here in the drawing room tonight? The men can fetch mattresses and bedding from upstairs, and we can all sleep in here. After Donal . . .' He sighs. 'Well, it seems a good idea to stick together.'

Lorraine nods. 'I agree,' she says, and to Nick's surprise, Alan adds:

'Makes sense.'

'David?'

'Sure.' He glances down at Emily. 'I'd feel better having company, and I think she would, too.'

'Can Jingle and Gaia stay with us?'

The little dog is huddled next to Destiny, who has finally sobbed herself to sleep unsedated, her hand slackening in Lorraine's reassuring grip.

'I expect so,' David tells her, trying to smile. He looks anguished. Nick thinks of trying to protect Cara from something like this without Harriet to comfort her, and his heart clenches.

'Right,' Nick says, trying to sound positive and bright, for Emily's sake. 'I'll get Branson, and Colt . . .'

As he speaks the chef's name, it belatedly occurs to him that he's been entirely focused on the guests. Colt doesn't yet know of Donal's fate – and there's no indication of whether the chef has met a similar grisly end. Nick bolts from the room.

The kitchen is empty, and Nick's heart speeds up as he glances around – the surfaces are wiped down, the cooking equipment is all put away, and the red-tiled floor gleams, a couple of wet patches testifying to a recent mopping. Where is Colt? He's about to steel himself to check the outhouse, where Penelope's shrouded body lies, but as he steps forward, the door behind him opens and Colt appears, jumping in surprise as he sees Nick.

'Whoa!' Colt says, a hand to his chest. 'You scared me, man! What's up?'

A powerful reek of cigarette smoke accompanies him as he passes Nick and sits down at the kitchen table.

'Still no sign of Donal down here,' he begins. 'Have you seen—'

Nick holds up a hand, and Colt stops speaking, evidently alarmed by the expression on his face.

'I've really bad news,' Nick tells him. He takes a breath. 'There's no easy way to say this, Colt, but Donal . . . he's been, well . . .'

Colt stares at him. 'Killed?'

Nick nods, and Colt raises his hands to cover his face and gives a long, horrified groan.

'It's gonna look like I did it,' Colt mumbles through his

fingers. 'We had the row, that was the last time I . . . oh Jesus. It wasn't me. Nick, I swear, I didn't kill him.'

Nick feels heaviness settle in his chest. He likes Colt; the idea of him being led away in handcuffs pains him. He seems like a young man who's overcome a lot, found a good job, worked hard . . . and yet, Colt was almost certainly the last person to speak to his dead colleague. And they had been arguing.

21

'Colt, listen, where were you between about five and six?' asks Nick. 'Did anyone see you?'

Colt drops his arms and leans forward, gazing down at the shining tabletop.

'I was making dinner for all of you,' he says. 'Braising beef, chopping carrots, frying onions. I went down to the wine cellar to get a bottle at about five thirty, to add to the stew.'

'You don't keep wine in the kitchen?'

'Nah. The occasional thirsty guest . . .' Colt sighs. 'I've got a key to the cellar. Donal was happy to let me have it cos I don't drink.'

'Why not?'

Colt eyes him. 'Because I used to drink and it didn't go well.'

Nick doesn't pursue it. 'Did anyone see you, or come into the kitchen?'

Despairingly, Colt shakes his head. 'No. I was just getting on with it. It's one of them dishes you have to stir, keep an eye on. I served it, I was just clearing up, then bloody Destiny barges in, demanding pasta and whatnot. I'd forgotten about her, if I'm honest.'

'What time?'

Colt shakes his head. 'Dunno. During dinner. She stayed the

whole time I cooked it, telling me what to do though.' He rolls his eyes.

Perhaps Destiny is blameless, then, Nick thinks. Unless you counted bossiness.

'Did you hear anything around five?'

Colt shakes his head. 'Nothing. I had my earbuds in.' He pauses. 'How did he die?'

Nick tells him, and Colt winces. 'Man. Are you gonna tell me I need to bring another body down? It'll be a bloody morgue out there.'

'No, I'll do it. Maybe David or Alan can help.'

'Thanks, mate. I owe you.' Colt lights a cigarette and drags painfully hard on the filter. He releases a stream of smoke, taking care, unlike Branson, to aim it away from Nick.

'Can you think of any reason why Donal might have been killed?'

Colt shrugs. 'No. But like I told him, I wasn't certain he's who he says – said – he is. He was quiet. He didn't want to talk.'

'Did you ever hear him talking to Aisling – his girlfriend?'

Colt shakes his head. 'Never. That's why I wondered . . . Oh, I dunno. Ignore me.'

Nick doesn't want to ignore him – right now, Colt's recollections are his best hope. 'Wondered . . . ?'

'If she exists at all. But why would he make her up?'

Nick has a shrewd idea of why, as he thinks about the uneasy dynamic between Donal and Colt, the tension that hovered earlier. But he's not going to tell Colt.

'Did Donal mention how he felt about Penelope's death?' he asks instead.

Colt looks blank. 'Upset. Obviously. He was the manager, he's not going to go, *Brilliant, a murder in Christmas week, must get that up on the website,* is he?'

'I really mean, did he suggest who he had in mind as the murderer?'

'Yes. Me. As you probably heard.'

'Nobody else he mentioned?'

Colt slowly shakes his head. 'I guess it's me in handcuffs when the Feds finally show up.'

'The police? You're no more in the frame than anyone else as far as I'm concerned.'

Colt looks him up and down. 'Maybe as far as you're concerned. But not as far as the poshos are. That lot out there, with their big jobs and their money and their proper vowels, they'll all agree it were me. Who else?'

Nick hopes he's wrong, but he's aware, from his years at the *Globe*, that young men with troubled pasts, men who look like Colt, are often the first suspects – even when subsequent events prove them entirely innocent.

'I'm doing my utmost to find the person who's doing this,' Nick says.

Colt shakes his head. 'I reckon you can rule out Emily. Other than that, I don't trust a single bloody one of 'em. To be honest, Nick, you seem like a nice enough bloke, but I don't even trust you.'

'Fair enough.' Nick stands as Colt lights another cigarette. 'I wouldn't, either. But if you want to join us all sleeping in the drawing room, we're going to stick together overnight and hope the police make it tomorrow.'

Colt half smiles and shakes his head. 'Knock yourselves out, lock yourselves in,' he says. 'I'll take my chances in my own room overnight.'

Nick is about to tell him where Donal's body was found, but thinks better of it. Dreading the prospect, he bids Colt goodnight, and goes in search of David and Alan to aid him in the grim task of carrying Donal to his temporary resting place beside Penelope.

Back in the drawing room, Violet and Branson are sitting staring into the fire, Destiny is still asleep, and Lorraine and Alan are bickering quietly. Matilda is playing a slow-moving game of Snap! with Emily, while David looks on, his deeply troubled expression adding ten years to his face.

'Donal had found a bit of the paper the star was wrapped in,' Nick says as he takes a seat. 'It was hidden in one of the unused bedrooms. Did he tell any of you?'

The others turn to him, shaking their heads, murmuring denials.

'So we're no closer then,' says Matilda. Nick appreciates that 'we'. It makes him feel briefly less alone.

'The killer can't have been Donal,' observes Violet. 'So who else has keys?'

'Nobody.' Nick sighs. 'Or nobody that we know of. We only have Donal's word on that. Colt may have some, I suppose. Or, of course, the room might have been unlocked.'

Branson nods. 'The one I slept in that first night . . . Rowan. That was unlocked.'

Violet glances at him. 'Look,' she says. 'Is it wise to let everyone in on everything? The murderer will know exactly what we know. Surely that will help them?'

'Well, I trust Nick,' says Lorraine. 'He's got a baby girl he needs to get back to.'

Alan glares at her. 'He might still be a murderer, Lorraine,' he says. 'We don't even know if this so-called baby girl exists.'

Nick feels a flash of hot fury, thinking of Cara's gummy grin, her bright, trusting gaze.

'She bloody does,' he says. 'And I assure you, she's just as real as *your Jade*. I'm trying to solve this mess to keep us all safe, and because I'm desperate to get home to my family for Christmas.'

Alan shrugs theatrically. 'Fill your boots then, Sherlock. But don't blame me when you get whacked over the head with a bloody snow-globe.'

'Or tied up with tinsel,' says Matilda almost gaily. She remembers what's happened, and claps a hand over her mouth. 'Gosh, I'm so sorry. I do apologise.'

'It's fine,' Lorraine says. 'You've got to laugh, Mattie, or we'd never stop crying.'

'You haven't actually.' Violet glares from her perch by the fire. In Donal's absence, Branson has been tending to the flames. 'You don't have to laugh at all. Two people are dead, one of us will almost certainly be next, and there's no way out. Forgive me if I don't find myself giggling.'

Violet glowers, and turns back to Branson, whispering something in his ear. He nods solemnly.

They're so at ease in each other's company. They seem to have formed a bond very quickly. *California . . .*

Nick is about to speak, when Alan turns to him. 'The lad's body, then. Who's going to move it?'

Nick indicates David. 'I suppose the three of us could . . .' he begins.

David swallows. 'Must I?'

'None of us *wants* to!' Alan says with some force, and Nick silently agrees.

'Perhaps you could take photos of his position, David,' he suggests. 'Make sure we don't destroy any evidence as we move him.'

The GP sighs. 'All right. I just feel so bloody claustrophobic. It's the horror of not knowing who I can trust – even leaving Emily in here . . . Well, you're both fathers, you'll know how I feel.'

Branson overhears. 'I'll help,' he says. 'I'm OK with a body when it's not my own wife. My old dad was a cop, so I got used to the idea of death pretty fast.'

'I'm sorry,' David says, 'was he . . .?'

Branson half laughs. 'No, he's fine, living in a retirement condo in Fort Lauderdale with his third wife, Pammy-Lou. I just mean I'm not afraid of seeing a corpse.'

All four of them trudge upstairs, and hesitate before the door to the back stairs. After a heavy moment, Nick grasps the handle and swings it open. On some childish plane of magical thinking, he's hoping the body has disappeared – that Donal is playing a trick and now he's in his room, packing to escape . . . but of course he's still there, as is the murder weapon, wrapped tightly around his throat.

Alan makes an involuntary sound of distress, David shakes his head, and Branson mutters, 'I hope they electrocute the animal who did this.'

Between them, they lift the semi-rigid corpse and begin to

manoeuvre it down the stairs towards the kitchen. As they progress in their ghastly funeral cortège, Nick fights down his horror, slips a hand into Donal's jacket, closes his fingers over the cold bunch of keys and drops them into his trouser pocket. 'Careful there, Nick,' says Branson, oblivious, and Nick apologises and places a gentle, steering hand under Donal's back as they carry the young man's slight body through the corridor towards the frozen outhouse.

The shower isn't hot enough. Nick has risked a return to his room and feels the need to scald away the horror of the day, the shock and sadness, the anger, the terrible claustrophobia and exhaustion of never knowing whom to trust and whom to suspect. Once out, he opens the bedroom shutter a crack and, with a sudden thrill, realises that the constant, dizzy whirl of flakes has finally ceased. A white sliver of moon like a pared nail hangs in the sky. Might it begin to melt tomorrow? Might they finally make it back to civilisation, to professional help, to the forces of law and order?

It's hard to imagine the world beyond their snow-bound island. He knows it's out there, but they might as well be floating in space.

Fully dressed, Nick reaches into his pocket and touches the metallic chill of the keys again – he feels a strange sense that he's stolen a talisman from Donal, a source of energy and strength. *Fanciful idiot.* He extracts the bunch and studies them. There are a couple of large iron keys that must be for the main door of the manor, and a series – he counts – of twelve smaller ones, then a scatter of oddly-shaped keys that are presumably for various laundry cupboards, sheds, windows . . .

He walks, swiftly, to the end of the corridor past the main stairs, and takes a breath before once again opening the door to the back stairs. There's no trace of the dead man, but all the same, he keeps to the edges of the stair treads, mindful that he risks trampling on a crime scene. The knowledge that the snow has stopped falling has given him hope – this may be their final night here, and his last chance to uncover the killer. If he fails, the deaths might continue – and he'll be trapped here for Christmas, at the mercy of a vengeful lunatic. *Not as vengeful as I'll be if you don't make it home,* says Harriet in his head. Nick almost smiles.

On the top landing, he surveys the corridor. The stark light-bulb burns pointless energy – Donal must have left it on, which might suggest he was ambushed before descending the stairs – or that he was killed in the bedroom, and the killer moved the body. David didn't find anything obvious; there are no marks on the walls or floor. Until forensics gets here, they have no idea where Donal died.

Nick passes Colt's door, and makes his way swiftly down the corridor. He tries a key, which twists then sticks in the lock. Six more do the same, but the seventh clicks round. Nick turns the handle and enters Donal's room.

Like Colt's bedroom, there's a single bed and a small desk, but that's where the similarity ends. Donal's bedlinen is a sombre grey cotton, the duvet tucked tightly into the mattress; there are no pictures or photographs on the walls, and the desk contains nothing but a black notepad, neatly aligned with the corner, and a small metal lamp. A quick glance in the drawers shows folded work shirts and trousers and a couple of more casual outfits. Wherever Donal kept his personal items, it wasn't here.

There's no sign of disarray, no indication of a struggle. Nick glances under the bed before leaving, and sees the glow of a lock screen. Sighing with relief, he extends a hand to reach the phone, detaches it from the charger it's plugged into and leans against the desk as he studies it. The screen shows an image of Mistletoe Manor in summer, a sight so incongruous it takes Nick a moment to recognise the building. There are trees in leaf, emerald lawns sweeping down to the river, the manor's old sandstone glowing golden in the evening sun.

He taps the screen, but nothing happens. *Passcode.*

The excitement drains from his body. Donal's birthday? No idea. He was about twenty-eight . . . Nick tries *1996*, *1997*, *1998* . . . the phone remains locked. The year he won the Cork Irish dancing trophy? He types in *2011*, feeling foolish. Nothing.

He looks again at the screen, where the manor's windows glow orange in the sun, and the vast front door gleams black. Above it is a sandstone lintel. Nick narrows his eyes, willing what he seeks to be visible. And there it is – a number carved over the door, one he couldn't possibly have seen on his blasted, snow-blown arrival. The date the manor was built.

Nick types slowly, knowing another mistake will lock him out for good – *1712*.

The screen springs to life and fills with apps, and despite everything, Nick finds himself grinning. He begins with Instagram, but is disappointed to see that Donal never posts, he only likes other people's pictures.

He follows a handful of men around his age, his mates, Nick assumes, as several are from Dublin, and a few male celebrities – actors and singers. He scrolls on, but finds nothing notable, and no messages.

Facebook? Donal is logged out, and Nick's heart sinks. He's got no chance of guessing the password this time. Most guys Donal's age only use it to keep in touch with family – it's probably just memes from Irish aunties, he tells himself. He scrolls to the Photos app. This, surely, will yield something – Donal's fiancée Aisling, perhaps.

Nick leaps in shock as the door creaks open. Heart hammering, he snatches up the metal lamp and holds it before him, poised to strike. In his confusion and panic, it's a moment before he registers the tinkle of a small bell and realises that the intruder isn't the killer he's looking for. Jingle jumps on to Donal's bed and sinuously kneads the duvet, purring like a motorbike engine on a cold morning.

'You little *tosser* . . .' Nick attempts to regulate his breathing, and turns back to open the Photos app, absently scratching the cat's head. What he sees on the screen almost makes him drop the phone.

Jingle gazes at him impassively, his eyes the luminous gold of a harvest moon. Nick doesn't want it to be true, but Donal's photographs appear to be showing him – in plain sight, high definition, full colour – a watertight motivation for the killer. Someone who had the means, the motive, the opportunity . . . Nick closes his eyes.

If it's not the husband, he thinks bitterly, it's almost certainly the last person you'd ever want it to be. Slipping the phone into his pocket, he leaves the room and slowly makes his way downstairs, towards the reckoning.

22

'Hello again.' Colt is still there, a mug of tea in his hand, apparently staring into space. 'Need a snack?'

Nick pulls out a chair opposite Colt and sits down. 'I know why you did it,' he says, evenly.

'What?' Colt's expression is a blank page. *He's good*, thinks Nick. *Almost convincing.*

'I know why you killed Donal. And I'm assuming you killed Penelope too, but I'm less certain of the reason for that. Maybe you can explain.'

It strikes Nick that Colt could very easily grab a long knife from the block on the worktop and kill him, too. He should have asked David or Branson to come with him – though even as the thought crosses his mind, he dismisses it. None of them would be a match for this coiled, athletic young man. Colt hasn't moved. He's rigid in his chair, radiating shock and contempt.

'Because I'm mixed race,' he says eventually. 'Because I'm working class. I get it. *Oh, he's a black lad, none too bright, was in trouble with the police. Must be a murderer.* I genuinely thought you were a bit better than that, Nick.'

'That's not why!' Nick feels a wave of horror at the accusation. 'Look.'

He thumbs through Donal's phone, finds the Photos app, and pushes it across to Colt. 'Explain that.'

Colt stares down at a picture of himself, taken unawares. It shows him in side profile, stirring a pan, sweat beading on his brow in the steam.

'I don't get it . . .'

'Scroll on.'

Photo after photo, all taken when Colt is looking away from the camera, all focusing on the curve of his lips, the light catching his amber eyes, the taut muscles of his arms as he lifts a pan. Some show him laughing, others serious, all taken quickly, surreptitiously. There's one of Colt sitting up in bed, bare-chested, surprised, taken from the doorway of his room from a low angle.

Colt is still, only his thumb moving as he looks through the endless stream of images, some dating back to the beginning of his time at the manor. The last shows Colt earlier today, turning, half smiling at Donal from the stove. It was taken minutes before Nick walked in on their row.

'You knew he was obsessed with you, didn't you?' Nick says. 'You'd had enough, after he thought you might be the murderer. You wanted him gone.'

Colt slowly drags his eyes from the small, glowing screen and meets Nick's gaze.

'Are you kidding me?'

Nick waits.

'This is . . . What the actual . . . How would I have known?' Colt shoves the phone back towards Nick. 'If I'd *known*, I'd have said, *Sorry, mate, you're not my type, but let's get you on Grindr and find you a nice bloke*. I'd have helped him, not *killed* him.'

'Come on,' says Nick. 'You said yourself that you didn't get on — you saw the pictures, and after Donal's accusation, you snapped.'

'One problem,' says Colt tightly. 'If he was so obsessed with me, why would he accuse me of murder?'

'Maybe that's why he was so upset,' suggests Nick. 'Thinking the man he loved had done that.'

'Jesus Christ.' Colt puts his long fingers to his temples and breathes heavily. 'I had no idea. I thought he was engaged to bloody Aisling. I didn't know he was sneaking around like a flaming paparazzi. I never saw his phone!'

'You never once caught him taking a picture of you?'

'Once. Last summer. I was getting some sun on the terrace, had my T-shirt off. I opened my eyes and he was taking a photo. I asked what the hell he was doing — he said he was taking candid snaps round the manor for social media. I told him to delete it.' Colt heaves a sigh. 'Guess he didn't.'

Nick assesses him. Colt looks exhausted, puzzled, sad. He doesn't look guilty, or caught out.

'There are no photos of anyone who might be Aisling,' Nick says quietly.

'I don't reckon Aisling exists,' Colt says. 'I always wondered. She never visited; he just used to drop her into conversation. Looks like she was his cover story. Poor guy. That'll be why his family didn't speak to him.'

'Because he was gay?'

Colt nods. 'He once mentioned that his parents are very strict Catholics. Doesn't take a genius, does it?'

'Why not come out once he'd left, though?'

Colt's look is steady. 'You don't know much about shame,

do you, Nick? In your nice, straight, middle-class world, with your good media job and your wife and baby. I bet you think you're an ally, and you see a Pride march go past, and think, *Ooh, good for them,* and you smile supportively at rainbow flags. You don't know what it's like to be young and scared and working class, when all the lads you know use "poof" as a massive diss, and your family can't even imagine that a son of theirs might not be "normal". We don't all live in a bubble, mate.' He shakes his head. 'I wish he'd told me, though.'

Nick is feeling an unpleasant, creeping sensation of shame right now.

'You really didn't know?'

Colt just looks at him.

Nick pauses in the hall, sick at heart. Yes, Colt could be lying – but Nick doesn't think so. When he first saw those obsessive, meticulous pictures, he'd been so sure that Colt had found out, that he'd been horrified and enraged by Donal's stalker-like behaviour. He hadn't reckoned on compassion and understanding. He's back to square one, only now he feels like a judgemental fool as well as a hopeless detective. He needs a drink.

In the drawing room, Emily is asleep on the sofa next to Lorraine, tucked under the chenille throw. Nick heads to the sideboard and pours himself a small whisky. Without Donal to check and replenish, the decanter is running low.

'I'll take one of those, Nick, if you don't mind,' says Branson.

'Ooh, one for me, too,' calls Lorraine.

For God's sake. Two people lie dead in the freezing night, and everyone's behaving as if they're at a cocktail party. A shaft of steel enters Nick's soul. He's had enough.

'I've spoken to Colt,' he announces. Will he tell the others what was on Donal's phone? *It's not relevant.* He believes Colt. Which means someone in this room, right now, murdered Donal and is sitting cosily by the fire.

'Well?' demands Alan. 'Did he kill Donal?'

'I don't think so,' Nick says. 'Were any of you together during the period before dinner? Can anyone vouch for one another?'

There's a silence.

'I was in my room, trying to meditate,' says Destiny. 'I was chanting – I didn't hear anything.'

'I was having a snooze,' admits Matilda. 'The thought that poor Donal was being . . . so close to my room . . .' She blinks away tears.

'We were just pottering,' says Lorraine helpfully. 'I was writing some cards, and Alan was doing his nose hairs in the sink. He's got one of those little whirly electric things that plucks them out.'

Violet snorts and turns it into a cough, as Alan snaps, 'For God's sake, Lorraine! And anyway,' he adds spitefully, 'you went out to look for a magnifying mirror.'

'Oh, I knocked on Vi's door to borrow one, because I couldn't see to do my eyebrows,' admits Lorraine. 'But you didn't answer, Vi – I thought you must be asleep.'

'Or somewhere else,' says Destiny, raising an eyebrow. Violet glares at her.

'I was having a nap. With headphones in.'

Odd, thinks Nick, that Violet is so nervous – and yet would

happily block her hearing and remain alone in her room, with a killer on the loose.

'Emily and I were playing Guess Who?' says David. 'She's a whizz at remembering the faces.' Emily is placing stickers into a colourful album, the headphones firmly back on. Nick isn't going to rip them off and ask the poor child to confirm her father's whereabouts.

'Where were you, Branson?' Destiny asks. Gaia's ears lift as though the dog, too, expects an answer.

'I was in my room,' he says. 'I mean, Rowan, the one I was in when I snored. I was . . . I needed to move all our stuff out of the . . . where she was . . .'

'Not with Violet, then?' presses Destiny.

Nick waits, intrigued.

'Because as I came downstairs, I thought I saw you leaving Laburnum. Violet's room. And it's the oddest thing, but I saw Violet peering out, too, and she was only wearing her robe. And then she kissed you.'

'He just came to . . .' Violet casts a hopeless look at Branson, who is crimson.

'Why are you lying to us all?' asks Destiny calmly. 'It's obvious.'

'Lying about what?' Lorraine's head jerks up like a meerkat. 'What does she mean, Vi?'

'Nothing! She's just guessing!'

The little group hangs in suspended animation, like an icicle trembling before it snaps and falls.

23

'It's not how it looks.' Violet is employing the greatest affair cliché of all time. She looks intensely rattled. 'We're not having an affair, we just get on well.'

Branson turns to her, his expression melancholy. 'Listen, babe,' he says. 'I think we need to tell the truth. It'll look worse for us if we lie.'

'Lie about what?' Violet gabbles. 'I never met you in my life before—'

'Vi. Give it up.'

'I knew it.' Destiny settles back, a proprietary hand on Gaia's head.

'Are you saying you're a . . . a *couple*?' Alan demands, outrage quivering in his tone.

Nick waits as Branson sinks his head into his hands and lets out a long, broken groan.

'We've been so stupid,' Branson murmurs. 'Now you're all going to think we killed her . . .'

'Branson! Why are you doing this?' Violet's voice is high and fearful; she's almost keening with distress. 'Nick, don't listen, he's not in his right mind, he—'

'Yeah, I am.' Branson sits up. 'I can't do it any more. Since Penny died, I've realised – I was just a stupid, ageing, easily flattered guy.' He turns to Violet. 'I'm sorry, babe. I can't keep lying. I'm done.'

Blindly, Violet pushes back her chair and runs from the room. In the ensuing silence they hear her footsteps racing upstairs, accompanied by harsh sobs. Lorraine calls, 'Vi! Come back!' But there is only the distant sound of a slamming door.

Branson releases a long breath and lights a cigarette, ignoring the tutting and flapping from the women. 'First of all,' he says, 'neither of us killed Penny. I need to make that clear.'

Well, you would say that, wouldn't you?

Out loud, Nick simply says, 'I'm listening.'

'Violet met Penny through work,' Branson begins, his voice shaking. 'Penny had been at Inkwell Publishing for years, and when Violet joined the publicity department, they worked together a little. They got on, despite the age gap, and Penny invited her to a few dinner parties – she and her ex did a lot of entertaining. When Penny met me and moved to California, they stayed in touch, and the summer before last, Violet said she was doing a US road trip with a friend and could she come visit us?' Branson pauses.

'I can see all too well where this is going,' mutters Alan, and Lorraine nods.

'Turned out the friend was a boyfriend, and they broke up somewhere around Baton Rouge. He flew home and she decided to carry on. Penny was real happy to see her and the three of us hung out for a few days . . .'

He swallows. *I bet you did,* thinks Nick, reminding himself that it isn't a journalist's place to judge. It strikes him that it is, however, a detective's.

'Go on.'

'This is . . . I'm ashamed. It's not who I am. I love – I loved my wife. Well, I guess you can figure out what happened. One night Penny went to bed and Violet and I stayed up talking. We were a little bombed, and Vi . . . well, she wanted to swim in the ocean. I said it wasn't safe to go alone and she talked me into going down to the shore with her, and then . . .' He swallows. 'Skinny dipping . . .'

'And one thing led to another?' puts in Lorraine.

Branson nods. 'You got it. Yeah . . . in the pool house.' He closes his eyes, regret etched on his craggy features. 'We had a few stolen moments after that, but Violet had to leave after a few days. I thought I'd put it behind me . . . I'd never done anything like that before: I was just so flattered, a beautiful young girl like her . . .'

'You're not the first. Or the last,' says Nick.

'Well, that's the truth,' snaps Destiny.

'No. But it gets worse,' Branson goes on. 'I got an email from Violet a week later. She said I had to come over to the UK and see her. She wouldn't tell me why, and I thought she must be pregnant. Guys, I could hardly think straight with fear. I'd messed up so bad. If Penny found out, I was toast.' Branson shakes his head, remembering.

'And rightly so,' says Matilda stiffly. Branson nods.

'I invented some business trip, and flew to London. Violet met me at the airport. She said she had a plan. She wanted a relationship – she said I didn't have to leave Penny, she didn't want marriage, but she did want regular transatlantic visits and gifts and sex. She told me she was done with men her own age.'

'And of course, you said, *No, I'm happily married, it was a one-off*,' says Destiny sarcastically.

Branson looks wretched. 'I wish I had. I was weak.'

'So what happened then?' Lorraine looks beadily at him.

'We met up, maybe every couple of months. I'd pay for her flights, put her up in a luxury hotel, visit her, buy dinner . . . Sometimes I'd fly to London.'

'You were her sugar daddy,' states Destiny.

'If that's what you want to call it. I got kind of fond of her. She made me laugh, she's fun, she's so . . . alive.'

He trails off. 'I felt bad about Penny, of course I did, but we were still happy – it was like a completely separate life when I was with Violet.'

How convenient, thinks Nick.

'You didn't worry she'd up her demands? Start asking for more money?'

'No. The arrangement was beneficial to both of us.'

Matilda gives a delicate shudder.

'I set up a little account for her.' Branson shrugs. 'I think she mostly spends it on clothes.'

That explains Violet's wardrobe of designer garments on a publishing salary.

'So the reason Violet's here . . .?' prompts Lorraine.

'Because I told her we were coming to the UK, let slip the name of the place. I was so stupid, but I never thought she'd risk it.'

'What exactly was she risking?' Nick asks.

Branson heaves a sigh. 'She wanted me to leave Penny. She'd got bored of our arrangement. She wanted more – a proper relationship.'

'So she just turned up?' Destiny sounds sceptical. 'But Penny would have recognised her!'

'She did,' says Branson. 'Obviously. She thought it was all a great big coincidence, and was happy to see her. Violet spun her story about being in love with a married man, and begged her not to say we all knew each other. She said she was embarrassed and she was just going to leave the next day. Penny bought it . . . she was so damn trusting.'

'So that night . . .?'

Branson sighs heavily. 'Yeah. I was with Violet, while she begged me to leave Penny. I don't often snore. I just slipped out when Penny fell asleep. I knew she'd still be asleep when I got back first thing. Violet likes me to stay the night with her . . .'

'Did you say you would? Leave, I mean?' asks Nick. Because if Branson said no . . . He thinks of Violet's passionate feelings that she wears so close to the surface. Her sudden tempers.

'No. I said I loved my wife. And we agreed to carry on as we were.'

'So you're each other's alibis.'

Branson nods. 'You're going to ask if Violet could have done it in a rage when I refused to leave Penny. But why the note? What did Penny do? Absolutely nothing. It was us who did something unforgivable, not her.' He blinks back tears.

Nick notes the past tense. Perhaps Branson really has come to his senses.

'Bedding your mistress the day after your wife dies?' mutters Alan. 'Yes, I'd say that's pretty unforgivable.'

'People do all kinds of things when they're grieving,' says Lorraine flatly.

'If she killed Penelope, maybe she hoped you could be together all the time,' Destiny offers. 'That way, she'd get the whole California-wife lifestyle, not just the mistress's trinkets. She has a very strong motive.'

Not for the first time, Nick wonders whether Destiny is really as woo-woo as she seems.

Branson nods. 'I know, but . . . I guess you'll say it could have been jealousy, but Violet was distraught when Penny was found. And devastated about Donal. I just don't think she's that great of an actress.'

Except she pretended to be Penelope's friend for eighteen months, Nick thinks. *And she was back in bed with you this afternoon.*

He wonders if he's finally found their killer.

'Well!' Matilda sets her drink down with a click. 'That's enough revelations for one evening. I think I'll toddle off to bed.'

'Oh no, Matilda, you mustn't!' Lorraine leans forward. 'We have no idea how safe you'll be up there alone. Stay with everyone else, down here.'

Matilda sighs. 'I'm afraid at my age, one needs certain comforts. I hardly think sleeping on a mattress on the floor, with people snoring around me . . .'

'Lorraine's right,' David puts in. 'Tell her, Alan – she can't go wandering off.'

'I shall lock the door!' Matilda insists. 'And besides, why would I be a target? It's clear that the killer had a grudge against Penelope, and Donal knew too much.'

She's right, Nick thinks. The note for Penelope, the sudden death of Donal, soon after telling Nick what he'd found . . . which means Nick is next in line. The more he discovers, the more danger he's in.

'I'll be staying down here,' Branson says firmly. 'Come on, Mattie, we'll all sleep better knowing you're safe.'

'Fine,' says Matilda crossly. 'I can see I won't hear the end of it if I don't give in. But somebody large will have to bring a mattress down – they're all doubles.'

Nick, Alan, Branson and David form a group of removal men, lifting the mattresses down from the spare rooms. As they heft and manoeuvre, the women hurry to their rooms to collect up night things, leaving the doors open, and Nick takes the opportunity to peer inside.

Matilda's room is exactly as it was the first time he looked in, when they found Emily there. It smells faintly of perfume, and there's a warm red dressing gown hanging on the back of the door. He sees her pictures, the ones she showed to Emily, still spread out on the table, the album open to show two little girls building a sandcastle. Judging by the wide-shouldered, pastel fashions and Matilda's sweep of curly hair, it looks like the eighties. They're all smiling at the person behind the camera: her husband, Nick assumes. 'JoJo, Kate and Mattie, '83' is written in a careful hand beneath the photograph. Nick hadn't even been born. He hopes he'll be taking pictures of Cara on beaches in years to come, though of course they'll probably be on his phone.

He thinks again of poor, obsessed Donal. What lies we tell about ourselves, in order to feel accepted.

Nick follows Alan and Lorraine to their room to help carry Lorraine's armfuls of pillows. They go ahead, trailing bedding, and Nick is last to leave. Lorraine has a great many sequinned clothes and high-heeled shoes spilling from a pink,

190

hard-shell suitcase, and Alan has used the trouser press and laid out a shoe-polishing kit. Nick smiles to himself. A series of half-wrapped presents are on the desk, a World's Best Golfer mug and a sparkly 'festive lip gloss' set. There are a couple of long rolls of wrapping paper tucked away to the side. He looks more closely.

One, which has already been used, is dark blue with 'Merry Xmas!' in a repeating pattern of gold cursive. The other – Nick's heart bangs against his ribs. The other is a dull gold, with a section already cut out. It's roughly the amount you'd need to wrap a Christmas star.

24

'I don't know!' Lorraine looks on the verge of tears. 'I haven't looked at it!'

Lorraine is sitting on the stairs, as if she can't hold up her own weight. Instructions and the sound of scraping furniture drift from the drawing room. The others are all heavily occupied.

'Nick, I swear on our Jade's life, I'd never!' she wails.

'Explain again what happened when you arrived.'

Lorraine takes a snivelling gulp, and reiterates what she's just told him.

'We saw the hotel sign, and the snow was getting properly bad, so I said to Alan we should try and get a room just for the night – I didn't want to get stuck on the motorway in it, and for once he agreed with me. So it was about three o'clock and it was coming down hard. Donal said they had a free room, and I told Alan to get the stuff from the car while I got settled in . . .'

Nick feels a brief flash of sympathy for Alan.

'He brought up our suitcases first, and he'd left some of the bags in the hall to bring up next. That was the presents for the kiddies, and some bits for Jade's husband Carl and her cousin Jenny that I still needed to wrap, cos I didn't want to leave them in the car and I thought I'd get them done that evening, though I wasn't sure the lip glosses were quite right for Jen once I looked at them properly – she's a *quiet* dresser, if you know what I mean. Our Jade's all about the drama, but Jen's more of an M & S girl . . .'

Nick nods, trying not to seethe with impatience. If she doesn't get on with it, someone will emerge and find them on the stairs, and Lorraine's confession will be stopped in its tracks. He reminds himself that nervous interviewees need careful handling. 'Tease it out, Nicholas,' his old editor used to say. 'Never rush 'em. Bit by bit, like flags from a magician's top hat. That's how you get your story.'

'So the wrapping . . .' he prompts.

'Yeah, so.' She takes a deep breath and wipes away a hovering tear. Her mascara has run into the lines around her eyes. She doesn't look anything like Nick's idea of a killer.

'When Alan brought up the suitcases, I couldn't find my phone charger. I thought he'd left it in the car and it was getting dark and he was saying he wasn't going to get it, so I had a bit of a go at him . . .'

Nick nods. He can imagine the 'go'.

'So I reckon we were in our room for about half an hour, arguing and looking for the bloody charger, and all the time we were doing that, the present bags and wrapping were in the hall.'

'So you honestly think someone came along, snipped off a piece of gold paper and then used it later to wrap the star, when at that point they didn't even know there'd be a Secret Santa game?'

Lorraine shrugs mutinously. 'I don't know, do I? I'm just telling you what happened.'

'Because it looks very much as if you wrapped the star. The missing paper's exactly the right size.'

'Well, guess what, I didn't, because I'm not a bloody psychopath. And' – she narrows her eyes – 'when we got here, one of the first things I said to Alan was, "Oh, look, there's no topper on the tree." Ask him, he'll back me up. I thought it looked a bit depressing. So wherever the star was, it had already been taken.'

'So who was already here when you arrived?' Nick knows, or thinks he does, but he wants to hear Lorraine's recollection.

'Matilda was.' Lorraine thinks. 'Penelope and Branson. Donal, obviously. Colt, I suppose he must have been here, though I didn't see him. Violet . . .' She thinks. 'And then just David and Emily. That was it.'

'By the time I arrived, the bags had been taken upstairs,' says Nick.

'Yeah, Alan brought them up. I'd found the charger in my make-up bag, and we went down for a drink a bit before you turned up. And then Destiny fell inside.'

'Yes.' He studies her face.

'Nick, you can't think it was me or Alan. Why would we kill Penelope? I've never met the woman in my life, and nor has he. It's madness to think we could.'

'It's hard to imagine it was any of us,' he says. 'But it wasn't Donal. You were very keen for me to think it was.'

'I thought he'd done it!' she exclaims. 'He seemed dodgy. Secretive. Too nice. I don't trust people who won't show their real feelings. You never know what they'll do next.' She looks away and Nick has the sense that she's remembering someone else.

'That's all I can tell you,' Lorraine says. 'When the police get here, you can tell them all about it, but I swear to God if I go to prison and don't get to see my grandkids grow up because of some bloody wrapping paper from Sainsbury's, I will find you and I will kill you.'

Nick raises his eyebrows.

'I won't, obviously,' Lorraine snaps. 'It's what Liam Neeson says in *Taken*.'

She lifts herself from the stair, dusts down her sweatshirt, which reads 'Jingle all the way!' in embroidered candy canes, and returns to the drawing room.

Nick sighs. He can't believe that Lorraine is a killer. Alan? *I know what you did*. It all comes back to that terrible note. He has to speak to Violet – and find out more about Penelope's past.

Twenty minutes later, as many mattresses as will fit are all arranged in two rows, the furniture is pushed to the corner of the room and the bed-mates agreed.

There is no sign of Violet, and she's refusing to answer the door. A muffled 'Go 'way' is the only response to repeated knocking, Branson reports. It's not as if she's going anywhere, Nick reasons. They can wait.

Destiny is on the sofa, and David and Nick are sharing a mattress, so Emily will share with Matilda. Branson is alone on the end, and Alan is already asleep, his snuffling snores almost comforting. Nick wonders if he'll grind his teeth.

'I'm gonna lock the door,' says Branson. He turns the large key in the lock, as Lorraine murmurs:

'What if Colt has a key?'

'I don't think he . . .' begins Nick, but Branson nods.

'Good call. Here, help me push the credenza in front of the door, Nick.'

'Excuse me!' Matilda argues. 'My ancient bladder is not what it was. I may need to pay a visit during the night. I can't be shoving sideboards to and fro.'

'If you do need to go anywhere in the night, I'll come with you,' says David firmly. 'Nobody wanders about on their own.'

Branson backs down, grumbling, and Nick tucks the duvet around himself, aware of soft breathing around him. He wonders if they should have asked Colt more insistently to join them – but if he isn't the murderer, it occurs to Nick, then the killer is locked in here with them. And if so, he or she is unlikely to kill anyone tonight, when they're all huddled together. Besides which, he still has Donal's keys shoved firmly under the mattress, in case he needs them.

It takes him a long time to fall asleep, and when he does, he dreams of tree ornaments, smashed and strewn and covered in blood in a dense, snowy forest. There's a presence flitting behind the trees, dark and ephemeral, and Nick knows he has to find and capture it, but he can't get there, and his feet are trapped deep in ice, there's a bell ringing all around him . . . He blinks awake to find early-morning light filtering into the room, and Jingle standing on his chest, apparently ready for his breakfast. Nick glances round, reassured to see that everyone is safe, duvets rhythmically rising and falling with their sleeping breath. But as he looks to his left, past David, he sees that only Emily is in the bed she is sharing with Matilda. The older woman has gone – and the door to the drawing room is wide open.

Nick climbs out of the duvet, and is marginally relieved to see that Matilda's red dressing gown has disappeared, so she hasn't been taken against her will. But an old lady, alone in the manor . . . People begin to stir around him, and Gaia, tucked beneath Destiny's thick tumble of hair, gives a small bark and struggles upright.

'Oh my gosh, I did not sleep a wink,' says Lorraine on a vast yawn. 'Your *snoring*, Alan . . . it's like a pack of feral hogs.'

'And good morning to you,' he mutters. Nick almost laughs, but he's all too aware that he must tackle Violet. He can't imagine her killing anyone — but isn't that what everyone says about murderers?

He was once sent to interview the neighbours of a violent killer after his conviction, and all of them said the same. 'Always had a friendly "good morning" for you . . . He helped me start my car once . . . I can't believe it . . .' Nobody ever believes it, and yet, here they are.

'Does anyone know where Matilda's gone?' Nick asks.

Destiny sits upright on the sofa.

'*Gone?*' she repeats, horrified. She swings her toned legs from the cushions and stands, pulling the throw tightly around herself. 'When? Where has she gone?'

'Probably to her room,' murmurs David, half-awake. 'Someone should check . . .'

Nick, used to being woken at dawn by a new baby, is already dressed. He heads for the door, calling, 'I'm sure she's fine.'

He hurries to Matilda's bedroom and knocks. There's no response. The other doors . . . all are locked. Matilda doesn't have a key to any of them. Worried, Nick glances at the back stairs — she surely wouldn't have gone up there?

The hall clock chimes eight, and he suddenly remembers something she told him. He jogs back down the main staircase, turns right through the small door, and almost runs into the little sitting room with the green armchairs and pinned butterflies. And there on the sofa, neatly wrapped in the chenille throw, is Matilda, fast asleep, her reading glasses set on top of the book beside her.

Nick collapses against the door with relief, and she turns and half sits up under the blanket.

'Oh, goodness,' she says. 'Nick. Has something happened?'

Without her careful make-up, her hair unbrushed, she looks small and vulnerable, and her alarmed expression tugs at his heart.

'I'm so sorry I scared you.' He smiles at her. 'We didn't know where you'd gone, and we panicked.'

'Oh!' A hand flies to her mouth. 'I didn't think . . . I just crept out at about three. I know what David said . . .' she adds, seeing his expression. 'But I couldn't bear any more of Alan's snoring, and Emily was thrashing about like an otter . . . I do need my own space at night. I did try to say so, but I was shouted down,' she adds rather peevishly.

'You must have left the door open,' he says. 'Jingle wandered in.'

'I'm sure I closed it.' She looks puzzled. 'I distinctly remember hoping the click wouldn't wake anybody . . .'

'Perhaps someone else went out too,' suggests Nick. *Or someone came in.*

He leaves Matilda, and heads to the dining room, where Colt is laying out platters for hot food.

'Morning,' Colt says. 'Did you see the snow's stopped? Thought I'd do sausages and eggs to celebrate our imminent escape.'

Nick is pierced by another arrow of guilt. 'Great,' he says warmly. 'I'll round up the others.'

All the talk over the sausages is of the weather. The shutters have been thrown open, and weak sunlight pours in. After days of darkness and spinning, relentless blizzards, it feels like the coming of spring – although so far, Nick notes, there's no sign of any thaw.

Icicles still hang from the gutters, and the drifts pressing against the panes have acquired the prismatic shimmer of thick ice, powder hardening into impenetrable cliffs of frozen crystals. Despite the excited chatter around him, he's not so sure there's a way out yet – but perhaps the phone mast might be fixed today? Now the snow has stopped, it might be easier to find out. After breakfast, Nick hurries back down to the kitchen.

'Colt,' he says, 'is there a way to get on the roof?'

The chef turns. 'There is, actually. But I might not recommend it when it's covered in ice.'

'Tell me anyway.'

'Your funeral,' says Colt; then pauses. 'Sorry, man. You go right to the bottom of the corridor Laburnum and Ash are on, open the fire door at the end, and there's an exit that leads to a fire escape. Climb up that, and you can get on to a flat bit at the back, but you have to lift yourself over the ledge. It's a great view, but one slip and you're toast. Why do you want to go up there?'

'See if I can get a signal, now the snow's stopped. I might even be able to see the mast, check if anyone's out there fixing it.'

'Good luck.' Colt glances behind him at the door to the outhouse. 'Get the Feds out here before anyone else drops dead.'

25

Two days till Christmas Eve

The fire-exit door is frozen shut. It takes Nick several minutes of rattling and kicking to dislodge enough ice to shove it open a crack. The snow has banked around it, covering the steps and railings, and he spends a further hour kicking great heaps of ice and snow down to the courtyard beneath. By the time he's created a way up the steps, he's roasting in his jacket and hat, and breathing heavily, but he doesn't care. Being outdoors, breathing fresh air after days of stifling, old-fashioned rooms and choking woodsmoke, is like a drug coursing through his sluggish blood, lifting his dour mood. He fills his lungs with freezing, azure air and watches the steam curl from his mouth as he lets the long breath go. They should move to the countryside, he thinks euphorically. He, Harriet and Cara, a cottage with acres of space for her to play in as she grows up . . . Nick swears as his foot slips on a patch of ice and he grabs the frozen railing. *Focus.*

He swings himself up the icy steps, looking only upwards, kicking mounds of snow through the gaps as he climbs. When he reaches the ledge at the perimeter of the vast, snow-blanketed roof, his heart sinks. It's impossible to tell whether he's climbing on to a flat area; the snow is too deep. He'll fall into a drift, and if there's ice beneath, he could simply slide over the lip of the roof and meet his death fifty feet below.

He uses his arms to knock a thick cap of snow from the ledge, and pulls himself on to it. From the angle of the roof, he guesses the walled edge is around two feet high. There's nothing else to hold on to. Slowly, Nick reaches one foot down into the snow, battling the fear that he'll get stuck up here – only Colt knows where he's gone.

He feels a solid, flat surface beneath his boot, and experiences a wave of relief that there's a narrow walkway to stand on before the roof slopes upwards. Nick lowers himself, holding on to the ledge; then, finally, when he knows he's stable enough, he reaches into his pocket and extracts his phone, hardly daring to hope that the screen will show 4G access.

But as he opens the lock screen, and Cara's tiny face disappears, his mood plummets. No bars, no signal . . . it was all for nothing, and he still has to get back down to spend yet another day with the inmates of this murderous, luxury prison.

He looks over the edge. The whiteness is blinding. The formal garden directly beneath lies under several feet of snow, the back gate a tight row of iron rails poking out behind a walled kitchen garden. Beyond lie fields and woods, and further away the hint of a road. Telegraph wires hang like hammocks under their burden of snow, and on a hill in the far distance, rising above the white treetops, Nick can make out something resembling a telephone mast, but there's no human life visible, no waiting trucks, no men working, ant-like, in boots and hard hats.

Sighing, he prepares to climb back down from his fruitless attempt. Nick holds on to the ledge and peers over to where he can see the roof of a small shed against the hedge, about thirty feet from the back porch. There's something beside it, a black stick . . . He narrows his eyes. It's a spade, he realises. As his vision adjusts to the blinding snow, he focuses on its handle, and tracking his gaze further, he sees the displaced snow, shoved aside in chaotic mounds. Finally, he makes out the footprints, large and heavy. They're leading directly to the house.

After a lengthy hot shower that fails to heat his frozen core, Nick dresses once again and returns downstairs. Lorraine is hovering in the hallway, despite its unpleasant chill.

'There you are!' Clearly, she's been waiting for him for some time. 'I've been wondering where you'd got to.'

Nick feels a flash of annoyance. He wanted to go straight to the back porch, study the footprints, find out who's been creeping around out there.

'What's up?'

'Apart from two dead bodies and being trapped with a killer?' Lorraine snaps. 'I need a word, Nick. I do know it might be you, I understand that you might stab me, but I have to talk to somebody.'

Nick's irritation drains away and is instantly replaced by curiosity. 'I assure you, I will not stab you, Lorraine. Library again?'

'No, all those old books creep me out. There's a little room I found when we were all looking for Emily the other day – we'll go there.'

He follows her down the corridor Matilda showed him, and Lorraine glances theatrically around herself before opening a door on to a small room bathed in winter sunlight. It has old-fashioned, floral wallpaper and cushioned white wicker furniture. A pretty Georgian desk stands in the window; there's a scatter of dog-eared paperback thrillers on a shelf and a cat basket for Jingle beside the sofa.

'It must have been Donal's sitting room,' Nick says, surprised. 'It's so much nicer than the other rooms.'

'More homely,' agrees Lorraine. 'Still no telly, mind you.'

She sits opposite him, plucking nervously at the fabric of her black trousers.

'What's going on?' Nick asks. 'Are you suspicious of someone?'

She nods, and looks away. 'It's hard . . .' she begins, and swallows. 'I don't like to point the finger.'

'It doesn't mean they're guilty,' he says gently. 'But anything odd – well, I'd really like to know.'

'That's why I wanted to talk to you,' she says. 'The thing is, the person I'm suspicious of . . . Oh, bloody hell.' She takes a long breath. 'It's Alan.'

Nick stares. 'Why?'

'I woke up about four,' she says. 'I couldn't hear Alan snoring, and I panicked for a second, thinking he was dead. I turned over, and he wasn't next to me – I thought he'd gone to the loo, you know middle-aged men and their wonky prostates . . .'

Nick nods encouragingly, though the thought makes him wince.

'But I lay there for a good fifteen minutes, and he didn't come back. I was about to get up and go and look for him, though I don't mind telling you, I was terrified I'd find him hanging from a piece of tinsel or heaven knows what, and then I heard him coming back in. He got in next to me, and – oh my

God, Nick – he was freezing. Like a block of ice. It wasn't just "been to the loo" cold, it was like he'd been outside for hours.'

'Did you ask him . . .'

'Of course I did!' Lorraine shakes her head. 'I asked him first thing this morning and he said he'd just been for a pee. That's the problem – I don't believe him. So what was he doing?'

She stares at Nick, challenge in her eyes.

'Are you generally close? Would he tell you if he was in trouble, or upset?'

Lorraine sighs and looks at her long, lacquered nails. 'Yes and no. I mean, we get on, mostly, but . . . it's never been completely equal. I was the company receptionist when we met and he was the boss,' she says. 'It was twenty-five years ago, but I reckon on some level he always thinks of me as "sexy little Lorraine" with my head full of fluff. He always thought I should be grateful that he took on our Jade when she was four. It pees me off, actually.'

'Did Alan have any children when you met?'

Lorraine nods. 'Him and his wife, Liz, had two boys. Anyway . . .'

So it had begun as an affair. Nick doesn't press her. 'Might he have wanted something from the car?'

'Well, if he did, why didn't he tell me? That's not suspicious!'

Lorraine's right. He thinks of the footsteps, the spade in the snow. What was Alan doing, attempting to dig his way out in the freezing dark of the early hours? And why wouldn't he tell his own wife? Suddenly, boring, tetchy Alan is looking like his number-one suspect.

26

He finds Alan on his way downstairs, toothpaste flecks on his shirt. He's whistling between his teeth, a tune Nick recognises as Fleetwood Mac's 'You Can Go Your Own Way'.

Alan looks uneasy as Nick raises a hand to halt his progress. 'I'm heading back to the drawing room. Matilda and I were about to teach Emily to play Monopoly.'

'That's kind of you both. It won't take a sec—'

'I see the Great Detective is on the warpath,' says Alan sourly. 'What is it now? Poison in the Christmas pudding?'

'No, but two people are dead,' Nick points out. 'It's helpful if we can all try to support each other in finding out who killed them.'

Oh my God, Nick, you're so pompous sometimes, says Harriet in his head. He knows he is. Right now, he doesn't care.

Alan stands by the sparse Christmas tree, half hidden by its branches. His stiffened, military posture reminds Nick of a nutcracker doll.

'Fire away.'

'You went outside last night,' Nick says. It's a statement, not a question. 'You left by the back porch, and used a spade to dig your way out in the moonlight, and then you realised it was too hard to escape, and you came back, freezing cold, in the early hours. Then you told your wife you'd just been to the loo. I'm wondering why.'

Alan is shaking his head, a performatively amused smile on his face. 'My goodness,' he says. 'I've always heard you journalists are good at making things up. You've surpassed yourself, Nick.'

'In what way?' He lets the pop at journalism go; he's used to it.

'I didn't "leave by the back porch", or "use a spade" to do anything,' he says, huffing a patronising little laugh. 'If you must know, I have prostate trouble, and I'd forgotten my pills — I went to our room to get them but I didn't want Lorraine to know, because she's beside herself with fear that I'll be killed if I leave her side. So I said I'd just been to the loo by the stairs. It's icy in this hall, and I was only wearing cotton pyjamas. It's hardly surprising I was chilly when I went back to bed.'

'So who was digging themselves out, then thought better of it?'

Alan shrugs. 'I have no idea. But I can assure you, it wasn't me. Now, if you'll excuse me, I've a hotel to build on Park Lane. And we can only hope it's better appointed than this one.'

He turns and strides past the tree towards the drawing room, where Nick can hear Emily's high voice excitably asking questions, and Matilda's gentle replies. There's nobody in the hall now, and Nick glances at the empty upstairs landing and makes a decision.

Outside Oak, Alan and Lorraine's room, he hesitates. If he's caught, he suspects the atmosphere will degenerate swiftly from suspicious tension to civil war. He hasn't asked Alan about the wrapping paper yet, because first, he needs to know how good a liar he is. Nick tries each key until one slides the lock back, and lets himself in.

It looks just as it did last night, although some of the clothing mountain has been tidied away. The shutters are open and light is falling on the desk, where the roll of gold paper is still propped alongside. He looks more closely. The rip is neat enough, he realises – but the edges aren't cut, they're torn, as though someone was in a hurry and couldn't find scissors. Nick has often done it himself rather than rummage through the kitchen drawer: folded a crease and then carefully ripped along it. Harriet laughs at his amateurish Christmas-wrapping attempts, next to her exquisite little origami parcels, decorated with pine cones and ribbons. Homesickness squeezes his heart.

He checks the drawers, but there's only a hairdryer and a regulation sewing kit alongside a Gideon Bible, rather than the thick envelopes and writing paper he hoped to find. The pen on the desk has a bright pink flamingo topper and writes in gold ink.

The bedside drawers yield nothing more than a couple of pill blister packs. The label of one suggests Alan is at least telling the truth about his prostate issues; the other is Lorraine's and, as far as Nick can remember, carries the name of pills that treat high blood pressure.

He looks in the wardrobe, trying not to rattle the hangers, avoiding his own glance in the long mirror. He isn't enjoying creeping around, spying on his fellow guests and staff, no matter what Alan believes about journalists. Lorraine's silver high heels are thrown in, straps tangled around a pair of Alan's slippers in a cartoonish old-man tartan, which Nick reflects were almost certainly a gift. Nobody would choose to relax wearing those. He bends and rummages behind the shoes at the front, and that's when he finds what he's looking for.

Outside, the sky is clouding over again, and the pale sun has been snuffed out. The icy gardens no longer sparkle; they lie bleak and cheerless under their heavy blanket of snow, and it takes Nick a moment to orient himself towards where he saw the footprints. As he steps from the back porch, he sees there's a narrow path leading between high banks of snow, one that wavers, and is in places blocked with small avalanches. It ends with the abandoned spade.

Nick fumbles his phone from his pocket and studies the photograph he took of the sole of Alan's still-damp boot. He bends, steadying himself, and holds it beside the nearest footprint. Neat ridges, a small rectangle where the brand name is stamped, concentric circles on the heel. A perfect match.

Alan lied. And Nick is determined to find out why, before anyone else is murdered.

Violet reappears at lunchtime. She's wan, subdued, as though the light has drained from her. Huddled in a black cashmere polo neck and baggy trousers, she seats herself at the far end of the dining table, away from the others. Branson studiously ignores her presence. He still looks wretched – grief has turned his handsome, ageing face to a rigid mask.

Lorraine moves to sit beside Violet. 'Come on, love,' Nick hears her murmur. 'You're not the first to fall for a married man. Nobody's judging.'

Violet swallows. 'Everyone's judging,' she says. 'The worst thing is, they all think I had a motive. But I'd never – I couldn't ever—'

She seems to be on the verge of tears, and Nick looks away as Lorraine pats Violet's thin wrist.

Colt has left out tureens of vegetable soup and a pile of bread rolls.

'Something I can eat at last,' says Destiny, ladling out a large bowl for herself. David smiles at her.

'That's a relief. It must be very difficult when you're away from home.'

'It is,' she agrees. 'I cannot wait to get back there and process this trauma through bodywork.'

'Give yourself a respray while you're at it,' chortles Alan, and she shoots him a contemptuous glance. Nick looks at him, his weathered pink face and tidy salt-and-pepper moustache. He looks like a bank manager waiting to collect his pension. If he's the killer, could it be driven by financial need? Branson and Penelope are very rich – what if Alan and Lorraine somehow know Penelope's son, and hatched a plot around life insurance? Was Alan trying to get to the shed to hide the evidence that Donal had found – and, as he evidently failed, where is it now?

Nick is so deep in thought, he jumps when Violet's voice rises.

'I can't! I just can't!'

'Come on, we're all in the same boat,' says Branson with some annoyance, and Matilda says:

'Oh dear, perhaps just try a roll . . .'

'What's wrong?' Nick asks.

Violet has pushed her bowl away and is eyeing it warily, as though it might be alive.

'Violet won't eat the soup,' says Lorraine, sotto voce. 'She thinks it might be poisoned.'

'Why?' David sounds frightened. Emily, Nick notices, stops eating and sets her spoon down.

'No reason!' Branson says, but Violet interrupts.

'No reason except people are being killed, we don't know anything about Colt but he's cooking all our food, and, frankly, I'm not prepared to risk dying for the sake of some soup!'

'Daddy, will it make me poorly?' Emily quavers, and David puts his arm around her.

'I'm quite sure it won't, darling,' he says, firmly. 'But to be on the safe side, why don't I go and find something for you and Violet to eat that we know is OK?'

Nick wants to ask David if it's wise to give credence to Emily's fears, or to fuel Violet's growing paranoia, but on the other hand, Colt is still a suspect. As David leaves the room, and Emily surreptitiously drops her bread roll on the floor, immediately to be gobbled up by Gaia, Nick finishes his own soup, hoping he's not being entirely foolish. The others don't seem worried, there's talk of a Monopoly championship this afternoon, and hopes remain high that somehow, someone will manage to contact the police today.

'Has it ever snowed like this before around here?' asks Nick to distract himself. Violet pours Matilda a glass of wine and refills her own.

'I just about remember the great freeze of 1947,' says Matilda, taking a delicate bite from one of the mince pies that Colt has left on the sideboard. 'I was only two, but my goodness, the bitter cold. The snow lasted for months – all of February and most of March, I believe. The drifts were twenty feet high in places. My mother used to go to the shops on a sledge, with me tucked up on her lap in a blanket.'

'Really?' Emily is entranced. 'I would *love* to do that!'

Matilda continues to reminisce about sweet rationing and frost patterns on the windowpanes, and everyone listens. It seems so innocent, the roomful of guests rapt at an old woman's memories, and he's almost shocked when David returns carrying two plates and sets them before Violet and Emily.

'Oven chips and fish fingers,' he says. 'Best I could do, but they were new packets, so . . .'

'Did Colt object?' Nick asks.

David raises an eyebrow. 'He wasn't delighted. But desperate times call for desperate measures.'

Emily is now happily eating her lunch, and Violet manages a watery smile. 'Thank you so much, David,' she says. 'Or should I say Dr . . . what's your surname?'

'Foley,' he supplies. 'Of Irish origin, I believe. Though I was born in Harrogate.'

'Oh, you're local?'

Nick is surprised. There's no hint of Yorkshire in David's polite vowels.

'Yes, but I was packed off to boarding school at eight, then straight to a medical degree, worked at Bart's for a decade, then Emily and I have been in South Africa for a few years.'

'Since my mummy died,' says Emily through a mouthful of fish finger.

David lowers his voice. 'I was offered the job at a new clinic, and it was a fresh start for both of us. Where we live is pretty safe, a gated community. Emily had a nanny until she started school, and now she has a lovely childminder, Blessing.'

'I love Blessing,' Emily agrees. 'She plays with me in the garden and she doesn't mind doing football.'

Nick smiles at her. 'Good woman.'

Lorraine is earwigging. 'No family still in the UK? That's sad.'

David blinks. 'Not really,' he says firmly. 'It's been just the two of us for a long time.'

'Well, I bet you're a super single dad,' Lorraine says. 'Whatever made you come here for Christmas? You could have had a lovely, sunny time in South Africa and avoided all this!'

David smiles wearily. 'I wanted to show Em where I grew up,' he says. 'In retrospect, I imagine she could have got by without knowing.'

It's when lunch is cleared away and they're beginning to stand up to return to the drawing room that it happens. A glass crashes to the floor and explodes into fragments, and Nick turns to see Matilda half collapsed in her chair. She is breathing heavily, her eyes rolling back.

'Matilda!' shrieks Violet, and Branson shoves back his chair and rushes to her side.

There is consternation, exclamations – David is loosening the bow at Matilda's throat, taking her pulse, and Lorraine sweeps Emily from the room, crying, 'Let's find Jingle!'

'Is she . . .?' begins Nick, and David glances up.

'She's breathing,' he says. 'Help me lift her.'

Between them, they lift Matilda, who murmurs, 'My room.'

Branson and Alan carry her up, Nick unlocks her door with the key she fishes from her handbag, and they stagger in, gently lowering her to the mattress.

'What's happening?' David asks. 'Can you describe your symptoms?'

'Sick. Dizzy.' Matilda tries to sit up, but falls back against the pillows. 'My throat, burning . . . I don't know what . . .' She trails off, her speech slurring, and her eyelids flutter closed.

'Is it a stroke?' Nick turns to David, and he shakes his head.

'I don't think so.' He lowers his voice. 'She's showing some pretty classic signs of poisoning.'

27

'Poison? My God!' Branson shouts. Matilda's eyes flicker open.

'Shhh.' Nick herds him back to the corridor. 'Let's try not to upset her further.'

Alan looks stricken. 'But who would . . . she's an old lady!' he manages, furiously.

Downstairs, Nick can hear Destiny and Lorraine, their voices spiralling in fear, and Destiny's next words float up as they climb the stairs: '. . . need to cleanse the manor.'

'Cleanse the manor!' scoffs Alan. 'Get rid of that bloody chef, more like, that's what's needed! He's the murderer, it's plain as day.'

'Hold on,' says Nick. 'We're all fine, aren't we? And Matilda ate what we ate – so if it's poison, it's been administered some other way.'

'Her drink?' Alan suggests. 'Who poured it?'

None of them can remember.

'She's fallen unconscious,' David calls, worried. 'Someone needs to sit with her, make sure she doesn't vomit and choke.'

'Can't you do something?' Branson demands. 'You're a doctor, aren't you? Don't you have some kind of antidote in your damn kit?'

'I don't know what the poison is, and have no way of testing,'

David says patiently. 'I don't have my "kit" with me. I can only make a guess that it's some kind of natural toxin. Her symptoms are similar to nightshade poisoning. I've seen it once or twice.'

'She'll die!' exclaims Lorraine, arriving in the doorway. 'She'll die, while we all sit and watch!'

David ignores her. 'We'll need salt water: it's an emetic. I'll give it to her when she comes round. I can't administer it while she's unconscious.'

Lorraine and Destiny hurry back downstairs to make some in the kitchen.

What if she doesn't come round? Nick wonders. Who would target somebody as vulnerable as Matilda, and why? He glances at the painting above Matilda's bed. Like the dark oil of the hawthorn in his own room, it shows an ivy-covered tree trunk bound with spiny clumps of mistletoe, the white berries shining against the dark leaves.

'Excuse me a minute.' Nick hurries from the room, down the stairs and towards the library, where he flicks on the lights and scans the shelves. Soon, he exhausts the modern volumes and moves on to the dusty sets of gold-leaf-trimmed, leather-bound volumes kept behind glass. Finally, he spots what he's looking for. He removes *Plantae Venenatae* from the shelf, for once grateful that his father got him through Latin GCSE, and turns to 'Viscum'.

'Purging, a burning pain of the throat, visions, fainting, unconsciousness, convulsions, death.'

Nick slams the book shut, pushes it back into place, and runs back upstairs.

Destiny is chanting. Nick can hear her as he reaches the hall.

216

'*I command any negativity, low vibrational energy and non-benevolent beings within this space to leave and go towards the light,*' she intones loudly. '*You are not welcome in this house . . .*' As she walks towards the stairs, she tinkles a small bell ahead of her, waving her arms. '*Be free, leave us now, begone, low beings of the ether and demonic thoughtforms . . .*'

'Is that Jingle's collar bell she's wafting about?' Lorraine asks Violet as they stand watching.

Violet's mouth twitches. 'Looks like it.'

Emily stands back, making the most of her chance to cuddle Gaia while her owner is occupied.

Destiny has reached the landing. 'Chant with me!' she calls down to the watching guests below. 'Form a circle of light!'

'I think I should check on Matilda,' Nick says apologetically, edging past Lorraine.

'Oh, Alan's still up there,' she says, in a low voice. 'Him and Branson stayed with David. I don't think Alan trusts him. We don't even know he's actually a doctor.'

Nick stops. David's certainty about times of death, his gentle bedside manner . . . could it all be lies? His mind races, but he sees Emily, standing with the dog, and he bends towards her.

'Emily, do you know the name of the hospital your daddy works at?'

'Yes,' she says promptly. 'Blessing wrote it down on the fridge. It's the Mediclinic something or other, in Durban.'

He feels relief wash over him, but he has to be sure. 'Have you ever visited him there, while he's at work?'

She nods proudly. 'Quite a lot, actually. The nurses all know my name and they give me colouring things while he's on a shift if Blessing has to go home early. They're very nice to me.'

Nick turns to Lorraine. 'Looks like we needn't worry on that score.'

She shrugs petulantly. 'Right now, I'm worried about everyone, Nick.'

Destiny is moving slowly down the landing, ringing the tiny bell. '*I banish all the low energies of the earth and call upon—*'

The door of Matilda's room flies open and Branson emerges.

'Can you knock it off? There's a senior lady unconscious in here!'

'I'm cleansing the building!'

'Well, go cleanse somewhere else! She's sick, she needs quiet!'

'Fine!' Destiny snaps. 'Don't come crying to me when your space is full of negative energy.'

'My wife being killed in our bed is negative energy,' he shouts. 'Take your stupid play-acting and shove it!'

'How dare—' begins Destiny, but Branson has slammed the door in her face.

'I'm going to check he's OK,' Violet mutters, and sprints upstairs, almost shoving Destiny aside in her rush to reach him.

The veneer of social politeness is dropping away as fear and paranoia stalk the manor. Soon, Nick thinks, they'll all be turning on one another like rats in a maze.

He attempts to smile reassuringly at Emily, but she only gazes back at him, her eyes huge, clutching the little dog to herself as if she'll never let it go.

'One of us should probably stay with her,' David is saying as Nick taps on Matilda's door and is admitted. She's still unconscious, her frail chest slowly rising and falling. 'If we only knew what she's ingested . . .'

'I think I do know,' Nick says. 'Mistletoe berries. It's entirely in keeping with the killer's "festive" theme, however sick. I looked it up in the library – there's no cure, but she'd need a pretty large dose for it to be fatal.'

'Good God,' says Alan, disgusted. 'Trying to poison an eighty-year-old woman – they're not right in the head!'

'Where would they get the berries?' Branson asks.

Nick thinks of the footsteps in the snow, the oak trees with balls of mistletoe held aloft in their branches like nests.

'There's plenty around here, if anyone made it outside.'

'You did,' says Alan, a mean twist to his small mouth. 'You went out earlier, to check the phone signal, or so you claimed.'

And so did you, thinks Nick. *The difference is, I'm not lying about it.*

David volunteers to sit with Matilda for a while.

'I'll come and take over in an hour,' Nick promises.

Downstairs, Destiny has finished her ceremony, and is brooding in a wing-backed chair with Gaia, looking into the fire. *Nature's cure* . . . Nick remembers Destiny's enthusiasm for foraging berries. Surely not . . . Making life harder for herself doesn't make her a killer.

The group feels incomplete without Matilda, Nick thinks. Perhaps they're all in need of a mother figure, someone safe to cling to when the lights go out.

Branson is standing at the honesty bar, tremors running through his hand as he pours a large brandy into a crystal balloon glass. The older man looks exhausted, his handsome face almost grey with strain and grief.

But murderers are under strain, too . . . Nick reminds himself.

'One for you?' Branson asks. Nick nods, though it seems in bad taste to toast anything, even one another.

'Branson, I've a couple of things I need to know,' he says quietly. 'The note Penelope opened . . .'

'"I know what you did",' says Branson, heavily.

'Yes. Do you have any idea at all what it means? It may seem intrusive, but now Matilda's been poisoned, and I'm very eager that we all get out of here alive. If there's anything – an affair Penelope had, or something she did . . . now's the time to tell me.'

Branson nods. 'I wish I knew, Nick. I've been over it a million times in my mind. We were happy. When I met her, as I told you, she just said she'd had a tough time recently. I never met her ex, Sebastian, but I assumed he'd been a poor husband.'

'Her son, Peter – has he mentioned anything about his dad?'

Branson shakes his head. 'I only met him briefly at the wedding. He was pleasant enough, seemed pretty fond of his mom. He didn't mention his father.'

'He's never been to stay with you?'

'Penny always said he was too busy. She came back a couple of times to visit him. He FaceTimed her sometimes. There never seemed to be any issues there. Jesus, Nick, I can't believe he still doesn't know. It's a bad dream.'

'Branson, do you think Violet could have killed Penelope?'

He stares incredulously. 'Well, no. I was with her all night. I . . . I mean, I fell asleep, but . . .'

'So in theory, she could easily have slipped out, hurried down to Penelope's room, and murdered her.'

'She wouldn't – I know it sounds crazy, but she *liked* Penny. She used to say our relationship had nothing to do with their friendship . . .'

Nick looks steadily at him. 'She's the only one here, apart from you, who had a motive,' he says, quietly.

'But if I knew she'd killed my wife, I'd never stay with her – I'd hand her over to the police!'

'But you don't know. And you're defending her.'

'Why would she write that goddamn note?' Branson demands. 'I swear, if I had any idea what it meant, I'd say so right now. It wasn't her. Violet's not a killer, I'd stake my life on it.'

You might need to, Nick thinks.

An hour later, David emerges from Matilda's room. 'Still unconscious,' he says. He looks worried. 'Breathing OK, pulse normal, but she won't wake.'

'I'll sit with her.'

'Maybe outside the door,' he suggests. He looks embarrassed. 'It's just . . . Nick, if she doesn't make it, I'd hate for you to be accused of anything.'

'I might be anyway. I could easily let myself in. I took Donal's keys,' he confesses. 'I thought I'd better keep them safe.'

'Give them to me then,' David says. 'If she makes a sound, coughs, anything like that, you call me and I run up with them. That way, I'll know you couldn't have harmed her.'

'But if she stops breathing . . .'

'If she does and you're there, you'll be accused of murder.'

He's right, Nick realises. The atmosphere is foetid with suspicion. He agrees, fetches a chair from his room and places it outside Matilda's door. He feels like a medieval guard, watching over the dying queen.

'Call if you need me,' says David. He returns downstairs – Nick imagines he's looking forward to spending some time with Emily.

As the afternoon wears on, Nick gazes down the landing towards the brittle branches of the Christmas tree, mentally sorting through the suspects, racking his brains over why someone would want to harm Matilda. Is she getting too close to guessing the killer? Her mind is sharp, and she's always at the heart of fireside conversation – has one of them said too much, let something slip? She knows the hotel inside out, too – maybe she's been poking around, looking for evidence. He thinks about Violet. She's tall, young and strong – it's possible she could have committed both murders if she took the victims by surprise. That first night she was sparkling with energy, whisking them all into playing games – was that the result of pumping adrenalin, knowing she was going to commit murder that night? Or was she simply feeling excited, knowing her secret boyfriend was watching her – perhaps wanting her?

And then there's Alan. He lied about being out there in the darkness, digging while everyone slept. His ex-wife . . . Nick has assumed Alan simply left her for Lorraine and she's still happily living her best life without him somewhere. It now occurs to him that she may have died. And if she did – were the circumstances entirely natural? Branson . . . it makes sense that he might have murdered his wife so he could marry his mistress – even killed Donal, for getting too close to the truth. But Matilda?

Nick rubs his face and heaves a long sigh. He allows himself to think about Harriet. He's imagining her arms around him, her thick tangle of hair brushing his cheek, when he's jerked upright by the sound of violent coughing from Matilda's room. It sounds as though she's choking.

Heart thumping, Nick automatically reaches into his pocket for the keys, then he remembers. 'David!'

There's no reply to his shout. Why did he agree to hand them over? There isn't time to run downstairs, Matilda is gasping and spluttering on the other side of the door.

'I'm coming in!' he calls, then he lifts his foot and kicks hard alongside the lock. The door is solid, panelled oak. It was built to last. He kicks again and feels a shooting pain sear through his ankle. This time, the lock splinters and, after a final, agonising kick, the door flies open.

28

Matilda is slumped against the pillows, wheezing. The violent choking has stopped, but she's still comatose. Her eyes are closed and she shows no awareness that someone's just kicked her bedroom door in.

Nick hurries to her side, hoping she won't wake up and scream at the sight of him.

He lifts her fragile wrist from the bedspread and measures her pulse. To his relief, it seems steady. Her breathing is gradually quieting, and her cheeks have a little colour. Nick lets out a long breath.

'Matilda,' he whispers. He wants her to turn on to her side, so she won't choke again. 'Mattie.'

There's no response. Nick gives her shoulder a light shake, but Matilda remains unconscious. Is she in a coma? He wonders if he should fetch David, and turns to see him hovering in the doorway. 'My God, Nick, I'm so sorry,' he says. 'I didn't hear you shout – a few of us heard you kicking the door, though. Is she . . .?'

'She's still here,' Nick says. The adrenalin hit has drained away, leaving him shaken.

'Look, go and have a breather,' David suggests. 'I'll stay here, check her vitals, and take my chances that she'll survive.'

'If she doesn't . . .'

'She will.' David is firm. 'Go on, you look done in. I'll leave the door open.'

David hands Nick the keys, and settles in the small, striped armchair across from the bed, and Nick returns the chair he's been sitting in to his own room. As he's about to leave, he hears a small movement around the corner leading to Laburnum, Violet's room. Jingle, he thinks, waiting to see the cat appear. He could do with the comfort of stroking him.

Nick waits, puzzled, but the noise comes no closer. He wonders if the cat has simply settled down in the corridor. He creeps to the door and peers round. There's no sign of Jingle. As he scans the shadows, a door opens further down and Violet steps out backwards, still speaking to somebody inside.

Branson? Nick flattens himself against the wall, straining to hear, but her whispers are low, and the replies equally muted. He hurries back to his room in time to slip inside before Violet passes. Nick waits for a moment after she's gone, and is rewarded by the click of a bedroom door and footsteps. He's expecting to see Branson's bulk hurrying towards the stairs. Instead, Nick sees that Violet's companion is much smaller and slimmer than the American.

As he watches through the spy hole, light catches the passer-by's profile – and Nick is startled to see that it's Destiny.

Downstairs, despite his puzzlement, and his concern for Matilda, Nick makes his way to the small sitting room with the butterflies, sinks on to the chaise, and falls asleep almost instantly, dreaming of Harriet. She's calling, 'It's easy, Nick, you're just not looking the right way!' but he's on a bicycle and it's wobbling along an icy towpath. He's gaining speed, going faster and faster until the scenery is a blur and Harriet's shouts are distant cries, he's ringing his bicycle bell frantically, then he hits a bump and shoots upright, gasping, before he plunges into the water.

Jingle is sitting on his chest again, violently licking his paws as his bell tinkles. Destiny has clearly given his collar back.

'What time is it?' Nick asks the cat, who only gazes at him, a gnomic creature from a different plane. The fire has died, and while the shutters are open, outside it's now dark, and the room is cold. Evening again. The day after tomorrow will be Christmas Eve, and Nick can't contemplate not being home by then. If he has to, he thinks fiercely, he'll walk back to London.

In the hall, where the tree looks more melancholy than ever, merely an echo of festivity with its drooping branches and sparse decorations, Nick is relieved to hear the low hum of talk drifting from the dining room. Nothing disastrous has occurred in his absence and, according to the clock above Donal's desk, as he still thinks of it, it's just after five.

He wonders whether to check first on Matilda, but as he stands irresolute in the hall, David appears, holding Emily's hand.

'Hello, Nick,' she says. 'I got to hold Gaia while Destiny had a bath.'

'And now we're going to the library to find a jigsaw.' David smiles down at her.

Nick wonders how much he can say in front of Emily.

'Is Matilda . . .?'

'Up and about,' says David to Nick's surprise. 'Much recovered – she's in the drawing room; she wants to thank you.'

'Here he is,' Violet calls as Nick enters the room.

Heads turn and Matilda half rises from her chair. She looks frail but improved, her hair brushed and styled into its usual chic white bob, a touch of make-up, her dress a smart royal blue with a brooch in the shape of a glittering snowflake.

'I'm so glad you've recovered,' says Nick, relief coursing through him at the sight of her.

'Mostly thanks to you.' Matilda smiles, reaching for him and clasping his wrist in her warm, papery hand. 'David told me you broke in when I was choking. I've no memory of it, I'm afraid, but I can't thank you enough.'

'It's nothing.' Nick feels embarrassed. 'Besides, you were OK, thankfully. I just checked on you and then David came up.'

'But you see, I might not have been.'

Violet compresses her lips. 'I'm not prepared to risk eating another thing that man cooks,' she says. 'I was already suspicious, but now . . .'

Destiny nods. 'We don't want to be poisoned,' she says. 'And we're starting to think the murderer might be Colt.'

Having held a summit meeting earlier, Violet and Destiny explain they are 'scared'.

'We went over everything,' Violet says. 'And we both think it can't be anyone else. You need to tell him, Nick. We're doing our own cooking from now on.'

The two of them seem to have gone from sceptical enmity to supportive sisterhood in an afternoon. Perhaps because they're of a similar age, they're finally finding comfort in one another, he thinks. Adversity creates strange bedfellows.

Nick makes his way to the kitchen with a heart as heavy as his footsteps, longing for a reprieve. He knows everyone is a suspect, he's aware that anyone can be convincing when it comes to avoiding a lifetime behind bars – but he simply cannot imagine Colt writing that note, folding the paper, sealing the expensive envelope and delivering it to his victim. No more can he envisage the chef carefully detaching the Christmas star from its branch and tiptoeing to Penelope's room, or using something as camply ludicrous as a string of fairy lights to strangle his colleague. Everything Nick knows about Colt suggests he's fair, humorous, decent. *But he was in trouble with the police,* says a small voice in his mind. *He had a difficult upbringing* . . . Petty crime, he reminds himself, is not the same as a calculated programme of murder.

Taking a deep breath, Nick steels himself and taps lightly on the door of the kitchen.

There's nobody there. The door to the outhouse is closed, and Nick remembers with a shudder the two bodies that lie just beyond. Quickly, he opens the huge catering fridge and scans the contents, running his eye over drawers of vegetables, shelves of carefully wrapped meat and cheese. He turns to the larder, studies the rows of labelled spices, tins, jars . . .

'What are you doing?'

Nick starts violently and a jar of chilli flakes drops from his fingers and smashes on the tiles.

'Great,' says Colt, from the doorway. 'It took me fifteen minutes to clear up all the broken glass in the dining room. Thrilled to start again.'

'I'll clean it up.'

'Nah, you won't. I'm on it. But I'm wondering why you're fossicking through my cupboards.'

'I . . . Matilda was poisoned. She's been ill all afternoon.'

Colt looks stunned. 'What do you mean, "poisoned"? Everything I cook is fresh, I've got certificates for food hygiene coming out my ears . . .'

'No.' Nick longs to escape. 'We think it was deliberate. Probably mistletoe berries.'

'Jesus! Is she all right?'

'Thankfully, yes. But now . . . well, some of the others are refusing to eat food you've cooked for dinner. They're scared.'

Colt deflates, pulling out a chair and throwing himself into it.

'You all think I did it.'

'You prepared the lunch.'

'And you all ate it. So why weren't you poisoned too, Nick? Could it be that whatever was up with her is nothing to do with what Mrs Mannering ate?' Colt closes his eyes and takes a long breath. 'You know what? If I was a psycho, would I be so bloody daft as to poison someone?' His voice rises. 'Do you really think I'd be sending food out of the kitchen that might kill one of you? Because it'd be pointing straight back to me, wouldn't it, Nick?'

'I agree with you,' he says. Colt looks broken, on the verge of tears. 'But Lorraine and Violet are insisting they cook their own food, Matilda won't eat—'

Colt radiates righteous fury. 'Tell you what, the minute the Feds get here, they've got free rein to search my kitchen, my bedroom, my boxer shorts and my bank account. Good luck to 'em. And when they've done that, and found nothing, I'm off.

I'm going abroad,' he adds. 'Why'm I even staying in this cold, miserable country? I'll get a job in Spain. I might go to Bali. But I'm not sticking around this bloody morgue to be accused of murdering old ladies.'

Nick opens his mouth to speak, but finds he has no answer.

Colt rips at the waist ties of his white apron, and chucks it on the floor.

'Kitchen's all yours,' he says. 'Knock yourselves out. And good luck finding the bastard, because while you're all trembling with fear about a bacon roll, they're probably planning the next murder.'

He shoulders past Nick, out of the kitchen, and strides down the corridor.

Nick sags against the door frame. He'd feel exactly the same in Colt's position. He makes his way back to the dining room, and tells the others they're free to use the kitchen to make dinner.

'Thanks, Nick.' Violet beams, and Destiny gives him a grateful nod.

'The thing is,' he adds, shame over Colt's treatment coursing through him, 'you still don't even know if you can trust each other.'

They're interrupted by a slam that sounds like the front door – but it can't be, Nick thinks, it's pitch-black, the snow is several feet deep or more on the porch, there's no getting past the drifts that encircle the manor.

He hurries to the hall, followed by Branson, Lorraine and Alan, and flings open the huge door.

A few feet away, illuminated by the porch light, Colt is digging with the spade Nick last saw by the outhouse. He's kicked and shoved his way into the drift by the door, and he's now a frenzy of activity, chopping at the frozen banks, flinging chunks of impacted snow as ice showers behind him. Nick's heart sinks.

'Colt,' he calls. 'Mate. Look, you can't make it – it's night, it's miles to the gate. Come on, we can talk about this.'

Colt swears and keeps digging. He's young, fit, athletic – but even he is already tiring. The relentless push and lift of heavy snow will be making his muscles burn, thinks Nick; he's got maybe another half-hour in him, panting with exertion in the freezing air, and then he'll be forced to give up.

Nick turns to the others. 'Give us a minute,' he says apologetically. 'I need to speak to him.'

'There's nothing you can say that we can't hear . . .' snaps Alan, but Branson puts a hand on his arm.

'Come on,' he says. 'Nick's right. The guy can't make it.'

Reluctantly, Alan and Lorraine turn back inside.

'Colt,' Nick says again. 'Please. You'll die of exposure and exhaustion out here. I promise if you come back, I'll support you. I don't think you killed anyone.'

'Why not?' Colt's voice is a ragged shout. 'Everyone else does. Why would you believe me?'

'I just do.'

Nick's old editor flashes through his mind. 'Never trust your instincts. Trust the facts.' Is he being an idiot, because Colt is so likeable? None of them seems like a killer, he reminds himself – but somebody is.

'Look, I just don't want you to get hypothermia . . .'

Colt turns to face Nick. 'Better than being stuck with that bunch of hypocrites. *Ooh, the chef, he's so scary,*' he mimics. '*He's big and black and from Yorkshire, he might be a murderer.*'

His voice cracks. 'I'm scared too!' he bellows. 'I don't want to be killed by some lunatic with a festive grudge! I don't want to be found with tinsel stuffed down my throat or a poisoned chocolate Santa in my hand! I'm young, I want to bloody live my life!'

He throws down the spade, shoulders heaving with emotion.

'I know you're right. I know I can't escape. But it was worth a try to get away from this bunch of . . .' His voice peters out, his hands hanging empty at his sides. 'Sod it.' Colt kicks the spade aside and strides back towards Nick. 'I'm going for a hot shower. They can all make their own food now, the ungrateful bastards.'

Nick turns and watches Colt take the stairs two at a time. The door to the attic stairs slams after him, and a moment later, Nick hears the hiss and boom of the old pipes as water begins to run.

Now they not only have a murderer in their midst – they're a cook down, too. A wave of despair crashes over him. How long will it be until rescue arrives?

29

Outside the drawing-room window, snow is falling heavily again, to general despair. 'I thought it had stopped!' cries Violet, slamming the shutters together. 'It's like a curse!'

'It seems it'll just go on forever,' agrees David. 'I planned to find somewhere else for me and Emily to spend Christmas, but it's getting so close now – I may have to just look for a flight home as soon as we get Wi-Fi. Still no sign of it.'

'Though I expect the police will want to speak to us all,' murmurs Matilda, 'so that might hold things up a bit.'

David shakes his head. He looks exhausted. Nick wonders what long-term effects these terrible few days will have on them all. He remembers Matilda earlier, saying 'the snow lasted for months . . .' and shudders. They'll get out soon, he thinks. They must.

The drawing-room hearth is dead and wood is running low. Nick lays a small fire in the cold grate and crouches over it, blowing gently on the flames. He's reminded of his father: old-fashioned and emotionally austere, but he cared about his family. Nick remembers how he'd always rise first in winter and light a fire, so it would be warm when he and his mum got up. When Nick was twelve, his dad taught him to do it himself. He also taught him the art of reasoned argument. Not much of that around here, he thinks wearily. But when in doubt, logic is always the best route. The first rule of journalism, he remembers: *Who, what, where, when, why?*

Never mind how the killer does it, or what they're using as weapons, Nick tells himself, *it's time to think about why.*

He stares into the small, licking flames, considering. Nick is still convinced that the initial motivation was to punish Penelope, and that the ritual nature of the method, its sinister twist on Christmas joy, is serving some deep psychological purpose for the murderer.

He turns to Branson, who is miserably stacking and restacking the draughts from a set Emily found in the library.

'Listen,' he says quietly, 'could Penelope have upset someone at Christmas in the past? Had an affair, maybe, when she was with her ex?'

Branson looks horrified. 'I can't see Penny ever doing that. She was loyal to a fault.'

'But if she did,' chips in Destiny, eavesdropping, 'maybe the man she had an affair with was furious when she ended it. Or perhaps his wife found out.' She gazes around the group. 'It could be one of us.'

'It couldn't,' says Branson. 'You're the only single woman here, and obviously, she'd have recognised the man she had an affair with.'

'What about Nick?' Violet says. 'Perhaps he—'

'I'm happily married and twenty years younger,' says Nick. 'I assure you, it's not me. Look, it begins with Penelope,' he says. 'Unlike me, Destiny or Lorraine and Alan, she was expected to be here, on the way to Devon.'

It occurs to him that if she grew up in Harrogate, the family must have moved at some point. It was a long way to go. Could they have been escaping some scandal? Or maybe they just wanted to retire somewhere warmer. *That's the trouble,* he thinks. Everything and nothing is suspicious.

I know what you did.

Perhaps whatever Penelope did happened before she met Branson, and the American doesn't even know about it. If only Nick knew the identity of Penelope's ex-husband. Did she leave him for Branson? In which case, he'd have reason to be angry. But to wait six years, lure her to a hotel and murder her in a blizzard? Could he have paid one of the others to do it? Nick wonders. He tries to imagine David, gentle dad and worried GP, stabbing Penelope for money, and almost laughs. Destiny was on the way to teach a yoga class, as far as they know. Could all her woo be an act? Might she and Penelope have known each other from long ago?

There's a general assumption here that everyone is exactly who they claim to be. But without Google, it's impossible to be sure. All they have is instinct – and as every decent journalist knows, that can be a poor substitute for knowledge.

Nick looks around at the other men. David, whose wife, as far as they know, is long dead – and Emily clearly had no prior knowledge of Penelope, or any of the guests. Besides, they've both been in South Africa for years. There's no obvious connection there. Donal, far too young, and evidently gay. Colt – the idea is ludicrous. Alan? He's been with Lorraine for well over twenty years, and it's hard to imagine elegant, upper-class Penelope having an affair with him. Unless Alan was in love with her, a secret stalker . . . but how would they even have met?

Alan catches his eye. 'Before you ask, Penelope wasn't my type,' he says stiffly. 'Lorraine is. She always has been.'

He's rewarded with a beaming smile from his wife.

'It surely comes back to Violet,' says Destiny, ignoring them. 'You had more reason than anyone to want Penelope out of the way. Or Branson, maybe you killed her. Maybe the note was a decoy and you'd simply had enough of her.'

'But why kill her here, surrounded by fellow guests, trapped by snow?' asks Nick reasonably. 'If Branson wanted to murder his wife, a massive, isolated house on the beach offers plenty more ways of making it look like an accident than stabbing her with a Christmas star in front of witnesses.'

'And I didn't want to murder her,' Branson says heavily. 'That's the real issue. I loved her. I'd never have left her for Violet.'

Nick looks up as Violet's eyes redden. 'Well, that's the truth, at least,' she mutters.

He considers the women and their possible motives. Destiny – could Penelope have consulted her about an astrological reading? But she'd been living in Malibu for the past five years. Destiny is a yoga teacher in Yorkshire. Matilda? Supposing Penelope was one of her two daughters, who somehow betrayed her mother? He's about to frame a question, when he realises they'd only be in their forties. Penelope was older. A secret love-child, then, or maybe she had an affair with Matilda's husband, who . . . *Oh, for God's sake.* Nick heaves a sigh of frustration. He's veering into the territory of Lorraine's TV dramas. Soon, he'll have Penelope disguised as her own estranged daughter, abseiling down the chimney with a pistol in her teeth. Besides, the idea of an eighty-year-old woman strangling a fit young man with a string of fairy lights is entirely absurd.

As for Lorraine – she seems the most straightforward of all of them, incapable of dissembling. But the wrapping paper was in her room. And he can imagine Lorraine losing her temper. What he can't envisage, however, is her engaging in the cold, clinical planning required to wrap a Christmas star and let a small child watch as it's unwrapped, dripping blood.

Nick looks at the little group, huddled around the cave fire again as tigers stalk beyond, and is once again gripped by claustrophobia. The fug of bedding, cigarettes, woodsmoke and stale alcohol sits in his lungs like a toxic gas. He stands and makes his way back upstairs again, to check for a signal.

'I know it's him,' Destiny is saying, importantly, as he returns hopelessly to the fireside, his phone having proven as dead as ever. 'The Tarot told us so, and we were fools not to heed its warning.'

Nick wonders why only fortune tellers use words like 'heed'.

'It just said a tall dark man,' says Lorraine irritably. 'It didn't say anything about a chef.'

'There isn't a *cookery* card in the Tarot's Major Arcana,' snaps Destiny. 'It told me enough. I know what Colt is.'

Nick feels a wave of fury. 'You don't know any more than we do,' he says. 'Just because Matilda was poisoned—'

'Oh, come on!' Violet rounds on him, two pink spots on her cheeks. 'Who else would poison Mattie? It's not me and I can tell you for a fact it's not Destiny. Alan and Lorraine, highly unlikely. Branson, why would he? David and Emily, I hardly think so. So that just leaves you, Nick. You and Colt. Which would you rather?'

Nick shakes his head. 'Think what you like. I can't stop you.'

'Nick.' Branson moves across to sit beside him. 'Can I have a word?'

'Sure.' Nick glances around, but the others are now in a gesticulating huddle, discussing their theories.

Branson lowers his voice. 'It's just . . . we're all under suspicion, I get that, but I'm beginning to home in on a particular person, and I wondered if I could get your thoughts.'

Nick waits.

'Alan,' whispers Branson. 'I'm starting to think he might be the killer.' He taps a cigarette against his perfectly white teeth.

Nick pours himself a glass of wine from the open bottle. *Another one, Nick?* enquires Harriet in his head. *Just this once, yes, actually,* he tells his imaginary wife firmly. *I bloody need it.*

'What's made you suspicious?' he asks. As far as he's aware, Branson knows nothing about Alan's doomed escape bid.

'Lorraine was talking about Alan's ex-wife, and she said she was "difficult".'

'Well, ex-wives often are. And ex-husbands,' Nick adds, thinking of Penelope's.

'No, but the way she said it – as if the ex was no longer around, and then she kind of caught herself and gave Alan a look, as if she'd spoken out of turn.'

'Did he say anything?'

'No, but he clocked it. Listening to Destiny, it made me wonder if he's violent with Lorraine.'

Nick thinks of bubbly, motherly Lorraine, her sarcastic little digs at her ill-tempered husband, her genuine smile when he was flattering earlier. 'I don't get that sense,' he says, 'but it's worth keeping in mind.'

'But most of all,' Branson goes on, finally lighting his cigarette, 'he's always hanging around, without ever doing anything. Lurking like a goddamn pike in the reeds. You can see all of us are barely holding it together. I'm sick to my stomach with grief, Destiny's obviously terrified, Violet's having panic attacks, David's shaking with fear but he's putting on a brave face for Emily, old Matilda's been poisoned and she's still keeping cheerful, you're doing all you can to get to the bottom of it all . . . and what's he doing?'

Nick considers. 'Might Penelope have known Alan in some capacity?'

'How? She left Harrogate in her teens, Nick – she lived in London before she met me. She'd never been to Mistletoe Manor in her life, and God knows, I wish we'd never set foot in the place. I'm certain they'd never met.'

Nick nods slowly. He wants Branson to be right, he realises. Dull, pompous Alan, with his mean little put-downs of his wife and his transparent obsession with status cars. *Could* he have known of Penelope in some way? Might she have known his ex-wife?

He escapes the kangaroo court of the drawing room and makes his way to the kitchen for a cup of tea. Alan is already there, fussily making a pot with loose leaves, a strainer, and a teacup and saucer.

'Expecting guests?'

'I prefer to drink tea that's fresh,' says Alan. 'I am the tea-maker in our house. Lorraine likes those horrible flavoured coffees – caramel syrup, sprinkled chocolate. She's obsessed

239

with something called Pumpkin Spice that smells like an air freshener.'

Nick smiles, despite everything. 'There's something I need to ask you about,' he says.

Alan shrugs irritably, but pulls out a kitchen chair, hitching his trouser up before crossing his legs. Nick hasn't witnessed anyone do that since his father used to pull up the knee of his suit trousers 'to preserve the fabric' as he sat down.

The silence thickens. Nick feels as if he's summoned the older man to an HR meeting about time-keeping. He smiles, in an attempt to defuse the tension.

'I see it's snowing again,' says Alan.

'Yes. Bad news for all of us,' agrees Nick. 'Alan, tell me something.' He leans forward; he's had enough small talk. 'Now the others aren't here, did you know Penelope?'

'What? No! Obviously not. Lorraine and I weren't even planning to stay here – how would I—'

'No, I mean years ago. Back before she knew Branson, when she still lived in England.'

'Still no. For goodness' sake, we'd hardly have been each other's type of person – some upper-class publishing type and a self-made businessman? I like Dick Francis books and Newcastle United, what on earth would we have in common?'

Fair point, thinks Nick. 'I thought perhaps your ex-wife might have known her.'

He waits.

Alan blanches at the reference. 'Liz? Why would she have known her? Liz and I grew up together near Gateshead; we certainly weren't mixing with high society.'

'Really?'

A flash of anger. 'Really. People like you have no idea. I had nothing but the clothes I stood up in, I was dyslexic, which nobody bothered to discover till I was grown up, I had no O levels, nothing. I got where I am through hard bloody graft, not from picking up an Oxbridge degree in Ottolenghi Dinner Party Studies like you.'

'English at Bristol,' says Nick calmly. 'Do you stay in touch with Liz?'

Alan's face suggests a punch is imminent. Nick involuntarily braces as the man shoves back his chair.

'No. Because I can't. And it's not something I talk about, particularly not to you, *Hercule Harrow*. Or was it Eton?'

'Neither,' says Nick after a tense pause. 'Alan – when you were trying to dig your way out, what were you going to do about Lorraine? Just leave her here, with a killer?'

Alan half rises in his seat, as though elevated by shock. *Your performative nonsense won't work on me*, thinks Nick.

'Do you honestly think I'd abandon my wife?' he blusters. 'You don't know anything about me, you have no right—'

'You're correct. I don't know anything about you. Look,' Nick says. 'I checked. Your boots were wet. You'd been out in the snow.'

Alan sighs heavily. 'Fine. I had. And rest assured, my only intention was to seek help and rescue Lorraine and everyone else! I had a burst of adrenalin, I thought . . . I used to be a runner,' he adds. 'I was athletic, I told myself I could still do it. Be a hero, save you all.' He gives a bitter laugh. 'I almost froze to death. I came in and got back into my pyjamas and got into bed and cuddled Lorraine. Some hero.'

'None of us are heroes, Alan,' Nick says. 'It's not Hollywood. We're just scared people, trying to stay alive till we're rescued.'

Alan nods. 'I didn't even manage to bring the spade back,' he says. 'My arms were too bloody tired to carry it.'

'We could have helped you.'

'I don't know who the murderer is, do I? I was hardly going to invite him out with me into the middle of a snowdrift.'

'Him?'

'Well, it's most likely, don't you think?'

'Me, David, Branson, Colt. One of us, then?'

Alan shrugs. 'Why not? I know it's not Lorraine, and it's not Emily or Matilda. I doubt it's a yoga teacher or a pretty young airhead, either.'

'I don't think Violet's an airhead,' says Nick. Alan has evidently missed Harriet's Feminism 101 tutorial.

'Well, I doubt she's a killer.'

Alan returns the teaspoon to its saucer, and sinks into a chair.

A thought strikes Nick. 'The gold wrapping paper?' he says. 'It was in your room.'

Alan shrugs. 'I honestly don't know. But I can tell you, Nick, neither me nor Lorraine would ever do that to a child. I've been a dad and a stepfather; I have grandkids. Killing people is bad of course. But letting an excited little girl watch someone unwrap that star, dripping blood?' He shakes his head. 'That's not bad. It's evil.'

30

Matilda, Lorraine and David are still in the drawing room. Nobody seems to have started on dinner. Destiny is sipping from a steaming mug as she strokes Gaia's ears. Emily smiles at Nick from her perch by the fire. Jingle is on her lap.

'I watched every pour,' says Matilda to him as he and Alan join them. 'It's quite safe.'

Nick allows David to pour him a glass of brandy and is glad of its fragrant warmth. There's a coldness inside him like a lump of ice.

'Where are Violet and Branson?'

'Violet has gone for a bath,' says Matilda. 'Branson wanted some time alone, I think.'

'That makes a change,' says Destiny bitterly. Nick wonders if she has a personal reason to resent men who cheat – or Branson in particular.

'Destiny, could I—' he begins.

'Why am I in the firing line?' she interrupts.

She's holding a herbal infusion, and it perfumes the warm air with sickly fruit. Nick loathes the reek of herbal tea. Harriet keeps hers in a closed tin 'because you're so weird about it'. He can't understand why the dust from a hedgerow is preferable to a strong cup of Yorkshire Gold.

'You're not, no more than anyone else. I just want to ask you a few things. We haven't really talked.'

She glares. 'I'm still struggling to understand why you've been appointed judge, jury and executioner . . .' She trails off. 'For all we know . . .'

'Yes, I know, I'm just as likely as you are to be the killer.'

Lorraine looks up. 'We could all be the killer, Dest. May as well answer the questions.'

'Fine. Goddess help me.'

Nick tries to smile supportively at Destiny. 'I'm just wondering where you're from,' he says. 'It's hard to tell, from your accent.'

'Yorkshire. Which is why I live here.'

'Countryside? City?'

She sighs. 'Sheffield. But now I live about two miles from here, with Gaia. Happy?'

'I have to ask about relationships . . .'

'No, you don't, actually.' Destiny puts a hand over Gaia's ears, as if to protect her child from hearing an argument.

'I'm not sure that's relevant,' murmurs David. 'Surely Destiny's relationships are her own business?'

Nick sighs. 'Look, could you just tell us?' He cuts to the chase: 'Did you know Penelope or Branson before you came here?'

Destiny closes her eyes in weary contempt. 'How would I have known them?'

'I don't know, Destiny. I'm asking whether you did.'

Matilda is watching, her eyes fixed on Destiny's face.

Destiny sighs. 'No. I didn't. I have a very small circle of trusted friends, mentors and shamans. Penelope and Branson were total strangers to me. I wish they still were. I don't tend to socialise with rich, corporate types.'

Something strikes Nick. He braces himself.

'You trained as a doctor . . .' She nods grimly. 'Do you agree with David on when Penelope and Donal were killed? Does he strike you as honest?'

Heads shoot up.

'I'm sorry, David,' Nick says. 'I have to ask.'

David shrugs and nods simultaneously. He won't meet Nick's eye.

'*David?*' Destiny stares at him, startled out of her aggravation. 'He's the most . . . OK, I don't like traditional medicine, and I think the grifters behind big pharma should be in prison, but . . .' She shakes her head. 'You're a good father, David. You'll do anything for that little girl. You'd never risk losing her. And you're a good listener,' she adds, the unspoken implication being *unlike you*, *Nick*.

'Have you confided in David about something?' Nick asks Destiny. He hates feeling like a bully, pushing and pressing, but he has to know.

David flushes a hot pink.

'Not particularly.' Destiny glares at Nick. Her eyes are like a songbird's, black and bright.

'Are you sure?' Nick takes a deep breath. 'Look, all of you, this is life or death. It's vital we know what secrets people have been keeping. It's the only way we're going to find out what's been happening, and why two innocent people are dead.'

'I suppose you could tell the others,' David says to Destiny. 'I think they'd understand—'

'It isn't about being *understood*,' Destiny hisses. 'It's a question of privacy.'

Lorraine leans forward. 'Tell us, Debbie, love,' she says with

245

the caring rapaciousness of all unstoppable gossips. 'Better out than in.'

Destiny heaves a shuddering sigh. 'Fine. Obviously, you'll all go on at me till I do. I wasn't on my way to yoga when I arrived.'

'Oh?' says Matilda, her brow creasing into a frown. 'But you were dressed in such flimsy clothes, those little ballet shoes—'

'That was because I was at home, cooking dinner,' Destiny says. 'And my ex, Mac, came round. It was a horrible break-up; I hadn't seen him for months . . .'

Nick feels something cold slither through his stomach.

'I thought he was over it,' she says. 'He said he needed to pick up some stuff from the spare room that he'd left behind. I didn't want to let him in, and he was angry,' Destiny goes on. 'He was angry a lot.'

'How long had you been together?' asks Lorraine.

'Two years. Till I ended it because he was so controlling.' Destiny takes a long breath. 'But he'd never hurt me before.'

The group is silent, horrified.

'You don't have to tell us any more.' Nick feels sickened at how hard he's pushed her to talk about it.

'It's OK. David knows already.' Destiny shrugs. 'So I let him in and Mac shoved me against the stove. He had his hands tight round my neck. Donal being strangled . . . well, it made me realise how close I'd come. That's why I fell apart.'

'Oh God,' murmurs Lorraine. 'Then what happened?'

'I couldn't breathe, I was trying to reach the rice pan to throw it at him . . . then Gaia bit his ankle, and he let go for a second, and I just grabbed the car keys and Gaia, ran to the car and drove away in the snow. I didn't know what to do.'

The firelight shines on her perfect face as Destiny pushes back her hair, and Nick sees the vivid lilac bruising beneath her ear.

'I drove and drove, but I was running out of petrol and I didn't have any money. I couldn't go back. I saw footprints in the snow – they must have been yours, Nick – and I thought they might lead to a house where I could shelter. And that's how I ended up here . . .'

Lorraine has her arm around Destiny's small shoulders. She looks on the verge of tears. 'I wish you'd said, love,' she murmurs.

'What good would it have done? I only told David because he's a doctor and I was worried about the damage to my neck.'

And he's a good listener, unlike me, thinks Nick, ashamed.

'So are you really a yoga teacher?' asks Alan.

'Alan!' snaps Lorraine.

Destiny half smiles. 'Yes,' she says. 'Everything else I've told you is true. I am going to a cottage alone for Christmas – he never liked me coming to his family's, because "they're a bit funny about Asians", apparently.'

'My God,' David murmurs. 'Destiny, I don't know where Emily and I will go after all this, but come with us. Seriously. We'd love to have you, and we'll work out a plan for your future.'

'Thank you.'

Nick looks at them, smiling into each other's eyes, and wonders where they'll go from here. If it might be together.

31

Dinner is a salad, featuring half-cooked ribbons of slimy courgette and a scattering of raw macadamia nuts, assembled by Destiny and served by Violet, who came downstairs with her wet hair pinned up. She seems to have decided to behave like a polite guest on a pleasant weekend break, sitting in the corner with a book. Branson arrives with red eyes, avoiding Violet's glance, and pours a brandy so large Nick worries he'll choke.

He misses Colt's cooking with a visceral longing. There's still no sign of the chef as Nick pokes unhappily at the tepid vegetable matter on his plate, and he has a sudden mental image of the young man lying lifeless on his bed.

Lorraine forks at a large, pale nut. 'Is there any meat, Debs?'

'No.' Destiny is irritated. 'Obviously not, I'm vegan. I'm hardly going to be chopping up corpses . . .' She realises what she's said. 'Anyway, I got the recipe ages ago from the Beansprout Lady on TikTok. You should try her fermented pine-nut cheese: it's a revelation.'

Branson pushes his untouched plate away. 'What did Alan say?' he murmurs to Nick.

Nick tells him. 'I still can't think of a motive,' he says. 'Or at least, it's not yet possible to guess.' A thought strikes him.

'Alan,' he calls down the table. 'What's your business? You haven't said.'

Alan looks both irritated and proud. 'Software security,' he says promptly. 'There's not much Pinner Consulting doesn't know about computing safety.'

'Thanks.'

Nick turns back to Branson. 'Tell me everything you remember about the competition you won to stay here.'

Branson pulls a face. 'Mind if I smoke?'

Nick shrugs, and Branson shakes his lighter. 'Getting low on fluid,' he says with a sigh. 'It was Penny, really. She was the one who entered.'

'But you told me she didn't enter, she just found out she'd won. From a group?'

'Oh yeah, you're right. That's true.' Branson exhales an acrid stream of smoke. 'So, she was in this nostalgia group about growing up in Harrogate, and sometime back in October I guess it was, she came and found me in my study and said, "Hey, guess what, we've won a trip." She said she'd had a message from some admin person to say she'd been chosen for a two-night stay at Mistletoe Manor. Penny checked it out and it seemed legit, and we thought, *Hell, we're going to the UK for Christmas anyway* . . .' Branson shakes his head, and falls silent.

'Might you have access to Penny's computer?'

'She didn't bring it.'

Nick's heart sinks.

'She did bring her phone though. I just . . . After what happened, I put it in the bedside drawer. I couldn't look at it.'

'Do you know her passcode?'

'Sure. It's our wedding anniversary.' Branson looks away,

clearly unwilling to meet the judgement he fears he'll see in Nick's eyes. 'I'll go get it.'

Branson returns, clutching an iPhone. The screensaver is a picture of Penelope and Branson, running on the beach with a golden Labrador. They look like an advert for midlife vitamin supplements. He deftly taps the screen and hands it to Nick.

'Here's the screenshots I took, in case it was a scam.'

The first photo is the group page: 'We grew up in Harrogate and Surrounds'. There are over eight hundred people in the group, and none of the names are familiar. Nick scrolls through a few screenshots – most of the posts are from older members, black-and-white pictures of terraced houses and ragged children with lengthy, misspelled captions about playing in the street till dusk and a farthing for an ice lolly. It doesn't seem the sort of thing the sophisticated Penelope would have enjoyed. The next photo reveals the message he's looking for.

Congratulations, Penelope! You've won a trip for two to beautiful Mistletoe Manor!

The message goes on to explain that she's been randomly selected from the group, that all she has to do is email admin@ harrogatememories.com for the details. The message sender is simply 'Harrogate Memories', and there's a shot of the email too, a reiteration of the Facebook message, offering a two-night stay with dinner – *must be taken in the week before Christmas*.

That's hardly normal, is it? Nick wonders. Most places are full before Christmas; the last thing they want is competition winners clogging the place up, costing them money. The final messages are obviously an afterthought, Branson ensuring 'everything's legit' as he puts it.

The image is of a private message to Penelope. *Hi! Saw your profile and thought our new group might be of interest! Would love it if you'd join!*

Penelope had typed a jolly *No problemo!* beneath. She must have clicked the link and joined on 5 October. She won the prize on the fourteenth. The group was launched last September.

Someone was very keen to get Penelope to Mistletoe Manor this week. *Whoever the admin is,* thinks Nick, as he hands the phone back to Branson, *they're here with us right now, sleeping alongside us, eating with us, crying and commiserating even as they plan their next move.* He has to find them, before someone else is murdered.

Nick feels he's had enough wine. It's making his head feel muggy and humid, and he needs to be sharp. As he crosses the hall after dinner, he opens the vast front door to let some air into the building and disperse the fug of Branson's cigarettes. The snow is still relentlessly falling. It feels both cruel and personal, as though the weather is enacting a cosmic punishment. *Get a grip, Nick. You're not Destiny.* He's increasingly aware of how fragile mental health can become, when humans are trapped and under great stress. Nick turns as Lorraine appears behind him.

'Bloody brass monkeys,' she says. 'Get that door shut!'

'Sorry.' Reluctantly, Nick closes the door, and Lorraine follows him back into the freezing hall.

'God, that tree's had it,' she says, looking at the drooping pine. 'It's like the opposite of Christmas.'

He looks at the space where the fairy lights used to be. 'Lorraine, I need to check something with you.'

The smile drops from her face. 'Go on.'

'Did something happen to Liz?'

'Liz?' She freezes, like a cat before a snake.

'Alan's ex-wife. I wondered if . . .'

'No. We don't talk about . . . It's got absolutely nothing to do with – no!' Lorraine turns and almost runs back to the drawing room, her breath coming in short, panicky gasps. Nick is left in the hall gazing after her, as the clock chimes away another hour of this dark day.

Nick returns to his room to make a cup of tea – *No wonder you don't sleep well, you're awash with caffeine,* says Harriet in his head – and is startled by a sudden scratching at the base of the door. He cracks it open, and Jingle saunters in, jumping neatly on to the bed where he settles down and launches a purr like a stick rattling on railings. Nick is enormously pleased to see him, not least because the cat is currently the only individual in the entire manor he can trust. He may have a few interview techniques, but that's all he's got. He can't detain anyone, or arrest them, or charge them. All he can do is ask questions. He sighs. He has another unpleasant task ahead.

Up the attic stairs, Colt's door is firmly closed, and Nick knocks gently.

'Colt?'

'Yeah, man.'

Nick is flooded with relief to hear his voice. 'Just wanted to check you're OK. Do you need anything?'

'Nah. I'm good.'

'Food? A drink?'

'Nope. Got what I need.'

Nick hesitates, reluctant to abandon the younger man, or let him believe he's still the prime suspect.

'Might have a lead, Colt,' he says through the door. 'I need to do a bit more digging. For what it's worth, I don't think it was you.'

A pause.

'Cheers. It wasn't.'

'No. Well . . . bye, then.'

There is silence behind the door. Nick heads downstairs, convinced he could have handled the brief conversation a great deal better.

If they can all just get through the night, tomorrow, surely, they'll make it out of Mistletoe Manor. He has to find the killer, and get home in time for Cara's first Christmas. He misses his tiny daughter with a visceral homesickness.

Nick thinks with yearning of their flat, the innocent scent of Cara's baby wipes mingling with the soothing warmth of Harriet's birthday-present Feu de Bois Diptyque candle. This is different from time spent away working. Then, he knows when he's coming back, he can FaceTime, he can tell Harriet all about his day and listen to stories of hers . . . but this, snow-bound and fearful, feels like being in a diving bell on the bottom of the ocean, unsure how long the oxygen will last.

With a stab of guilt, Nick remembers Harriet's disappointment as he headed off. 'The week before Christmas, Nick! I'll have to do everything on my own.'

He'd been brusque and thoughtless. 'It's *work*, Harri. It's not like I'm choosing to abandon you.'

She'd shrugged, Cara in her arms as she watched him throw clothes into a bag.

'You love getting away, though, don't you?' she asked.

'Makes you appreciate us all the more. Whereas I never get the chance to appreciate our home life because I'm always here.'

'Only till the end of maternity leave.'

Harriet sighed. 'If I have a job to go back to.'

Oh, stop moaning, Nick recalls thinking fiercely. *I'm doing my best, can't you see that?*

It occurs to him now that he's entirely failed to notice Harriet doing her best, for months. He'll make it up to her, he promises himself. If he ever gets out of here.

In his bedroom, Nick unplugs his phone from the charger and takes it over to the window. He opens the shutters, and pushes up the sash. Snowflakes swirl into the room, melting against his skin.

He leans from the window in the freezing air, holding the phone up as high as he can reach. Surely by now, the mast has been mended? The main roads must have been gritted too: this isn't *The Day After Tomorrow*. He peers at the small, glowing screen, struggling to see amid the whirling snow. Is that . . .?

He brings it to his face to check, and his body floods with adrenalin. One bar of signal.

Nick dials, but even as he does so, the bar drops away. There isn't enough for a call. He tries texting 999, but nothing happens. He waves the phone frantically into the frozen night, praying to the gods of technology. Nothing.

Call the police. Get them to come to Mistletoe Manor, on York-shire Moors. I'm OK but we need help NOW. Urgent. N x.

He presses send, watching the symbol spin. He imagines Harriet lit by the soft glow of the Christmas tree. She'll be in front of the TV watching one of their old favourites, perhaps *Slow Horses*, or *Shetland*. Fictional murders. So entertaining.

In his mind, she hears the soft ding of an arriving message, she scans the screen, then dials 999, rising from the sofa clutching her glass of Merlot as she gives the location . . . How long will it take the police to get through? They'll have access to a snow-plough. By midnight, this could all be over. Nick draws his numb hand back into the room and looks at the screen again, his heart thudding with hope.

No bars. His desperate message remains unsent.

Nick makes his way downstairs. Branson, who is sitting alone in an armchair, catches Nick's eye with a complicit half-smile. He seems less grief- stricken now he's offloaded his suspicions. Or is he simply tired of pretending?

Destiny is brushing her long, shining hair. She smiles at Emily. 'What will you do till bedtime?'

'I want to explore, but Daddy says he has to come with me,' grumbles Emily. 'It's boring being with grown-ups all the time.'

Sensible David, thinks Nick.

'I want to look for clues,' adds Emily.

'Clues?'

'To the murders.'

'Emily!' David looks stricken.

'Daddy, I know about murders. I read books. Anyway, Bless-ing told me ages ago her cousin was killed in a car-jacking. The men had on masks and they got out guns and they shot him right in the head and blood went everywhere . . .'

'Blessing should never have told you!' David sounds angry and Emily shrinks back.

'Sorry, Daddy. She didn't mean to.'

'You're too little to know about things like that.'

'I'm not. I'm nine quite soon.' Emily's bottom lip quivers and she stares unblinkingly at the fire.

Destiny puts a gentle hand on her arm. 'It's all right, love,' she says. 'It's not your fault.' She turns to David. 'You've done an amazing job of protecting her, David, but she's right. She's got to face reality.'

'She's eight years old!' Nick hasn't seen David truly upset before. His whole body is rigid with distress, and his hand is shaking as he holds Emily's toothbrush. 'She's been through enough. Losing her mother, moving to South Africa . . .'

'Emily,' Matilda leans forward, 'why don't we go and look at more of my photos? I know you enjoy sorting them out.' She glances up. 'If that's all right, David.'

'If you'd like to, Em.'

She nods, and Matilda takes her hand, leading the small girl away from talk of murder and mayhem.

Half an hour later, they're back.

'Auntie Mattie showed me more photos of her little girls, Joanna and Catherine,' gabbles Emily. 'She calls Joanna JoJo. And we talked about her husband and about the clothes people wore in the olden days . . .'

'Well, not entirely the olden days.' Matilda laughs, sitting down. 'It was the 1980s not the 1880s.'

'No, but they had really great toys,' Emily enthuses. She tells Violet, 'There was a photo of Christmas morning and JoJo was holding a Girl's World – it's like a big doll's head you can do make-up on and style its hair.'

'Oh, I had one of those!' Lorraine laughs. 'Me and my sister were always squabbling over it, and once she scribbled on its cheek with a green felt-tip! Our mum went mad about that . . .'

'I wish I had a sister to play with, though,' says Emily. 'Like JoJo and Catherine. They were good friends, Auntie Mattie says.'

'Where are your daughters now, Mattie?' Lorraine asks, still smiling.

Matilda sighs, and glances at Emily as Violet distracts her with her own memories of the coveted Barbie jeep she once unwrapped as a little girl.

'A long way away,' Matilda tells Lorraine. 'That's why my photos are so important. I do miss them so, especially at this time of year.'

'Grandchildren?'

'Yes. I'm a very proud granny.'

'Aaah.' Lorraine puts her head on one side. 'Can't you visit? Mind you, plane fares are astronomical now, aren't they?'

Matilda nods. 'Yes, and I'm not as young as I was. It's all such a dreadful faff.'

'You're not wrong. Last time we went to Faliraki . . .' Lorraine is off on an anecdote. Nick wonders why these beloved daughters don't visit their aged mother at Christmas. Then again, there's no understanding other people's families. He remembers his own dismal festive visits to the grandparents. Perhaps to Matilda's grandchildren it would feel just as bad: the ticking clock and the careful doling out of gritty mince pies. No wonder they'd rather stay in Brisbane or New York or wherever they are. Right now, he'd give a great deal to be several thousand miles away from here, too.

'You look terrible, Nick,' says Destiny, seeing his

expression. 'Want me to run through some yoga basics? In fact, we all should – including you, Emily. It'll help you feel calm when everyone's being a worry-bucket. Including your old dad.' Destiny smiles winningly at David, and he smiles grudgingly back.

'That's very kind, Destiny.'

'I'll give it a go,' says Branson unexpectedly. 'Penny was big into yoga. I wish I'd paid more attention.'

'I'll give it another whirl,' agrees Lorraine. 'Can't hurt.'

Matilda and Alan play gin rummy by the fire, occasionally looking over as Destiny shows them how to release the breath, shake out the tension, essay a sun salutation . . . Nick has joined in for want of an excuse, but he finds the exercise, however mild, is surprisingly helpful. He tunes out Destiny's intonations about cleansing goddess breaths, and just follows her movements. Harriet would never believe it, he thinks as he contorts himself into a downward dog. He may never tell her.

'Destiny, that was wonderful,' says David afterwards. He looks almost healthy, his cheeks flushed from movement. 'I always advise exercise for my patients, but I must suggest more of them try yoga . . .'

Destiny looks delighted. 'It's so good holistically,' she murmurs, gazing into David's eyes. Nick wonders again if there could be something developing there, but surely David isn't Destiny's type? He's so fretful and ordinary-looking. Then again . . . perhaps she needs someone she can boss about. And perhaps he likes to be bossed.

He watches them for a moment as they stand together, chatting enthusiastically about the joy of exercise while Emily arranges stuffed toys on her designated bed. Matilda looks up from her playing cards as Destiny laughs at something David says, and puts a hand on his arm. David smiles into her eyes. What a cosy scene they must make, Nick thinks, the snow falling outside and the little group at the fireside, engaged in their old-fashioned pursuits. It doesn't change the fact that somebody in this manor is a murderer.

32

'I think I'm ready for bed,' says Matilda, covering a yawn with her hand. It's almost ten, Emily is drooping, and Branson is staring silently into the fire as Violet concentrates on her book. Nick pretends not to see the tears snaking down her pale cheeks. Is it grief that her love affair with Branson is over – or guilt? Nick feels as close as he's ever come to despair. It will stop snowing eventually, they're not in Narnia, but what else will have happened by then? How close will he be to a confession from the murderer? Because right now, he feels he's never been further away.

He helps David arrange the mattresses and bedding in the drawing room while the others change and wash. The lack of deaths since Donal's strangling has led to a false sense of security, Nick suspects. The general consensus seems to be *Donal knew too much – the rest of us know nothing, so we're safe*. Nick is the obvious counterpoint to that reassuring belief, and Branson and Violet know it. So do Alan and Lorraine, and Colt, too. All his key suspects, sharpening their knives . . . but he can't give up now.

If Violet's sleeping nearby he can at least watch over her and Branson. He isn't planning to close his eyes tonight. She finally settles into bed alongside Destiny, turning away from Nick and David, her face buried in the pillow. Gaia spins three times and settles into the gap between their still bodies. Nick's rather sad that there's no sign of Jingle; he has begun to find the cat's presence a great comfort. David is awake alongside him, though Emily's eyes have fluttered closed.

Matilda has consented to stay downstairs tonight, after her 'funny turn' as she refers to the poisoning. 'I doubt I shall sleep particularly well,' she says, wrapped in her red woollen dressing gown, her face shining with cold cream. 'Still, safety in numbers, I suppose.'

'You OK?' Nick asks David quietly.

'Not really. It's not so much what's already happened, it's not knowing what's coming next.' David swallows. 'If I lost Emily, I'd die. I'd have nothing to live for.'

Nick wants to say something reassuring, but he understands. If Harriet were gone, and it was just him and Cara . . .

'You won't lose her,' he says eventually, and David gives him a sad smile.

'I'll do anything to keep her safe. Whatever it takes.'

'I'd feel the same way.'

In this spirit of mutual understanding they fall silent, though Nick remains uncomfortably aware of the breathing, the coughs, the whispers in the darkness. Somebody knocks over a glass of water with a crash and swears, and a lamp is switched on while it's mopped with a pillowcase. The fire is burning down, and the outside chill is creeping into the drawing room. Nick tries to read on his Kindle app for a while – an airport thriller – but he can't focus. He finds himself obsessively checking the phone signal, and scrolling to the still-unsent message he had hoped would save them. The slow hours crawl by.

*

He's still awake at 1 a.m., and the fire has died altogether. It's freezing in the room, and it occurs to Nick that the firewood basket is empty and he's no idea if there's any more. That was Donal's job. He feels a stab of sadness, thinking of the polite, unhappy young man whose remains are still lying just behind the kitchen. He shifts as quietly as possible to a sitting position, intending to go and fetch a blanket from his bedroom. He may be killed en route, but he's prepared to risk it for a little warmth.

'Nick!'

The whisper comes from the next bed, and he turns to see Destiny half-sitting, a waterfall of hair over her face.

'I can't sleep,' she hisses. 'It's so cold. I've been meditating on a soul journey in the desert, but I can't stop shivering.'

Lorraine stirs. 'Can't sleep either. I'm going back to our room. At least it's got a radiator. Wake up, Alan, I'm not going on my own.'

Matilda glides past, her face a pale moon in the darkness. 'I shall lock my door and take my chances,' she murmurs. 'That mattress is like a box of eggs.'

'Look,' says Nick. 'Shouldn't we all stay put, where we're safe? I can bring down more bedding.'

'It's the energy in here,' says Destiny. She gives a small shudder. 'It's so toxic.'

'Probably Branson's fags,' says Alan.

Destiny ignores him, gathering Gaia and her duvet. 'I'm off, and I'm locking my door. Goodnight.'

David and Emily are still here, as are Violet and Branson, albeit in separate beds. With those two under his surveillance, Nick feels reasonably certain that the others will be safe.

He fetches the chenille throw from the sofa and rolls over in the makeshift bed, determined to stay awake until dawn.

It's still dark. Around him, sleeping bodies breathe steadily. Violet coughs in her sleep. Nick must have drifted off for a moment or two, reassured by the silence, warmed by the extra blankets. He glances at his watch – 3.45 a.m. Hours of night yet to endure.

What woke him? He stares into the darkness. Nick sits up, checking that Branson's bulk is still in bed. He's in the same position he was in when Nick fell asleep just a couple of minutes ago, on his back, like a crashed skydiver. The fire is long dead, but he can still smell the smouldering wood, a nauseating reek of acrid smoke. It seems stronger than before – perhaps the darkness has sharpened his senses . . . He sniffs the air again, suddenly alert.

It isn't coming from the hearth, it's coming from the hall. Nick's first thought is that someone has lit the fire out there – but it's not Christmas Eve yet, it's not time for the Yule log to be lit. He pulls on his jeans and uses the torch on his phone to pick his way to the entrance hall. There's nothing in the vast fireplace, but out here, the smell is stronger, even more unpleasant. Has someone lit a fire in one of the bedrooms? Nick looks up the stairs, and as he does so, his breath stops in his throat. Thick, grey smoke is curling from the corridor where he sleeps. The corridor which now appears to be on fire and where, he realises, Destiny is currently locked in her room.

'Fire!' Nick's bellow could be heard three fields away. 'Wake up! Fire!'

He looks around and sees the old-fashioned dinner gong,

half hidden behind the Christmas tree. He grasps the mallet and whacks it as hard as he can against the brass disc, causing a reverberation that booms through the building.

Branson and David come stumbling out of the drawing room, half dressed. Nick points to the smoke now obscuring the dim corridor upstairs with an impenetrable fog.

'What's happening?' Violet shrieks.

'Fire! Get Emily wrapped in a duvet and outside. Now!' Nick has never seen David so urgently commanding.

'Come on.' Nick beckons the two men. 'We have to get everyone out.'

Already, Lorraine and Alan have appeared on the landing, exclaiming in horror. Lorraine almost falls downstairs in her haste to escape, and Alan isn't far behind, rushing down like the coward he is, as Nick, David and Branson race up.

'You fetch Colt and Matilda,' Nick shouts to the others. 'I'll get Destiny.'

He turns, pulling his T-shirt up over his mouth, and plunges into the thick gouts of smoke pouring down the landing. It's impossible to know where he is in the fog, but he can hear crackling as he nears the source of the fire, and there's an ominous orange glow.

'Destiny!' he yells, but the shout is lost as he chokes. He crouches low, his breath rasping. Nick straightens and grasps the door handle. The brass sears his palm and he snatches his hand away, swearing. He steps back and aims a violent kick at the lock, but the Georgian door is solid hardwood. It holds firm against his efforts, and he almost sobs with frustration. Nick digs into his jeans pocket and finds the keys. It's impossible to see anything, his eyes are streaming and his breath is coming in short gasps. He tries inserting one, but he can't get his burning hand close enough to turn the key.

'Mind out!'

Colt shoves him aside, and karate-kicks the lock with all his strength. Something splinters, the door flies open and a sheet of bright flame billows towards them.

Nick races to the window and flings up the sash. The conflagration is raging by the bed, and the desk and chair are engulfed by flames. He once interviewed a fire service chief who told him that cold air helps to dampen a fire. As the snow gusts into the bedroom and smoke pours out into the night, he hopes to God the guy was right. He turns to see the silhouette of Colt, his arms bare, dragging at something heavy . . .

'Help me!' he yells through the smoke, and Nick gropes blindly through the dark, choking fog. Destiny is lying in the bed, unmoving. He grasps her legs as Colt lifts her under the arms, and together they stumble from the room, slamming the door behind them in an attempt to contain the fire.

'Water,' Nick gasps, as they lay Destiny in the dark corridor that's still thick with smoke. 'For the fire.'

'Bathroom,' shouts Colt and, as he turns, David looms through the haze, his face smeared with soot, leading Matilda who is coughing violently but alive. Freezing air pours from the open front door of the manor, and as the smoke dissipates, Nick sees the huddle on the step, their faces turned towards him in anguish like a Biblical painting.

'Look after Destiny,' he tells David, and he and Colt sprint back to Destiny's room where the fire is still raging and has reached the bed, turning the blankets to glowing lace, devouring the pillows. If the manor burns down . . . Nick can't think about that. They'd find a way to survive, he tells himself. They'd have to. He turns on both basin and bath taps, and rips off his T-shirt, soaking it and tying it over his face. Colt does the same, then Nick snatches up the metal waste bin and fills it, running to chuck it over the bed. Colt has disappeared but as Nick fills the bin, again and again, he returns carrying a bulky red fire extinguisher.

'No effing idea how to make it work,' Colt shouts, and Nick grabs it from him, squeezes the handle and sprays foam at the dressing table, as Colt takes over water duties. He chucks and refills, chucks and refills, and it seems they're getting nowhere. The carpet is smouldering, and Colt grabs the shower attachment over the bath and aims it, spraying an arc of water into the room. It won't reach the furniture, but the carpet flames sizzle and die. Nick feels a burst of hope, aiming the foam at every fresh outbreak of flame, every glowing ember.

After what feels like hours, but is probably only minutes, between them they extinguish the last licking tongue of fire. Both of them are panting, choking inside the damp cloth around their faces.

'Destiny,' Nick whispers hoarsely, and they stumble back down the corridor.

Branson and David have carried her downstairs, and she's lying in the soot-stained bedclothes she was wrapped in when they found her.

The front door is still open, and Violet is crouched on the step in the snow, hugging Emily, as Lorraine sobs into Alan's chest and he robotically pats her shoulder. The smoke is hanging in a swathe at the ceiling like morning mist, though the worst of it has drifted into the night through the open doors and windows. The temperature inside must be below freezing.

'Is she . . .' begins Nick, pulling down his face covering and gasping a lungful of fresh air. David shakes his head.

'I tried everything,' he says dully. 'Everything. But the smoke inhalation . . . she's so small.' A tear runs down his cheek, a bright trail through the soot. 'I tried so hard, Nick.'

33

Silently, they gaze at Destiny's little body, the cascade of hair obscuring her smoke-blackened face. A sudden sob lurches through Nick. For a moment, he puts his head in his hands, steadying his breath. He feels a hand on his arm. Colt.

'We did our best,' he murmurs. 'You were a hero, mate.'

'No more than you were.'

'Where's Gaia?' Lorraine suddenly cries. 'The dog, where is she?'

The group falls silent in shared horror. 'I'm sorry, Lorraine,' begins Branson. 'She must have been—'

He's interrupted by Matilda, emerging from the drawing room wrapped in a blanket and clutching something to her chest.

'She's all right,' she says quietly. 'I found her. She was hiding under the sofa.'

'But how did she . . .' Nick begins, as Colt says:

'But the door was locked.'

'She must have run out when you kicked it down,' says Branson. 'The smoke and the confusion – she saw her chance and she escaped. Emily . . .' He raises his voice slightly, and the child turns from Violet's embrace. Nick sees that she's trembling with cold and shock. 'Can you cuddle Gaia, please?' Branson asks her. 'She needs a friend right now.'

Emily nods, and takes the small, sooty dog from Matilda. She sits on the step, hugging the little creature as though she'll never let her go. David joins his daughter and pulls her to his chest.

It's so cold. Nick looks at the empty hearth in the hall, and something jolts in his brain. He turns and runs up the stairs, back to Destiny's room. Nick snaps on the overhead light. The room resembles the set of a horror movie, one wall charred beyond recognition, wallpaper hanging in strips, and the bed blackened and soaked. Only the painting of an elm tree over the bed remains untouched, the mistletoe berries shining from its branches like stars on the darkest night. Nick shivers convulsively as he searches, scanning the carpet, wondering where he'll find it, whether there'll be any trace left. And here it is, half-kicked under the bed in their frenzy to rescue Destiny – a damp, carbonised lump, almost unrecognisable. The festive symbol of good company and good cheer. Nick looks at the charred remains of the Yule log and feels only despair.

What's the end game? he wonders. Is the killer simply a psychopath, enjoying wielding the power of life and death? Was Penelope the intended target and the others collateral, owing to their suspicions? But if that's the case why is he, Nick, still here? He's made no secret of his amateurish sleuthing. Or does each victim represent something to the killer? Then there's the insane Christmas theme to the killings . . .

Harriet likes to apply psychology when she's discussing their friends' relationships and Nick is tuning in and out. 'Sam's emotionally unavailable because of his absent father,' she'll say, or, 'Izzy was an eldest child – that's why she takes responsibility for everything, it's classic.'

What's the psychology here? Someone who is desperate to

make a point. A bid for attention – but not for themselves. For their message. Someone, he thinks, who hates Christmas, who has perhaps suffered a terrible loss or life blow at this time of year, who for some reason blamed Penelope. Someone who's unobtrusive, helpful, who can steal keys without being seen, who is strong enough to kill a fit young man and whose conscience is frozen over with hatred, or vengeance. Someone who plans long in advance, a spider spinning a web to draw the victims close enough to kill.

The smoke has drifted away into the frozen night. Colt has gone to check the damage to the other upstairs rooms, and for now, Destiny's body has been gently carried to the back office, the door locked. 'I said a prayer for her,' Branson offers. It doesn't seem much for a young woman's life.

Nick's in the library with the others. It's the only room that doesn't reek of smoke. Matilda has insisted on returning to bed. 'I can't bear it,' she said, her voice quavering. 'I need to be on my own for a while. That poor girl . . .' Lorraine took her upstairs. She reported back that the radiators were all on, and it was 'warming up a bit', though Nick wonders if they'll find Matilda blue from hypothermia by morning.

'I just think, Nick, this person won't stop till we're all dead,' Lorraine says now. In her shock and grief, she's adopted a hectoring tone, as though Nick has personally sanctioned the killing spree. 'Little Destiny! All she's ever done wrong is be a bit annoying. And the fire could have killed every one of us if you'd not woken up.'

He's aware of the truth of Lorraine's words, but equally, he feels strongly that Destiny was the intended target, the Yule log another carefully chosen weapon in the killer's twisted, festive war.

Violet is in shock. She's pressing her hands together, rocking back and forth, pale as milk and breathing stertorously. Branson is avoiding her yearning, wide-eyed gaze. Alan and Lorraine have pulled their chairs together in a rare show of unity.

'Can any of you remember the last time you saw the Yule log in the grate?' Nick asks.

Branson closes his eyes. 'I think yesterday morning. I was heading upstairs and saw the log there. I thought: *Why are we waiting for some crazy-ass tradition when people are being killed and we're freezing? Just light the goddamn fire.*'

'Somebody did,' says Violet. She gives a high little laugh, and he shoots her a look of irritable concern.

'Now I'm thinking about it, I'm pretty sure it wasn't there last night,' Nick says. 'So the killer evidently planned it all in advance.'

'But how did Destiny not wake up?' Alan demands. 'How did the killer even have a key to her room?'

'I think she was sedated,' says Nick. 'David, do you know what happened to the sedatives you offered Destiny?'

David is sitting on an armchair beside the one Emily is now sleeping in, holding his daughter's limp hand. Gaia is lying across Emily's lap, sooty and wide-eyed.

'No.' David's voice shakes. 'I think I put them in my bedside drawer. I can check.'

'Nick has Donal's keys,' says Alan suddenly. 'They're in his pocket. He carries them everywhere. Like a jailer,' he adds, his tone bitter. 'Why are we all listening to this bloke when he could well be the killer?'

'He tried to save her,' says Colt coldly. 'We both did.'

'That's what you claim,' mutters Alan.

'Look, Alan.' Nick gathers his strength. 'We're all under suspicion until the police get here. Not one of us trusts the others. We just have to accept that. I don't see what else we can do.'

David meets Nick's gaze with a wretched expression. 'I can't believe it,' he whispers. 'I can't believe somebody would do that.'

'Any ideas who it might have been?'

David shakes his head. 'I really liked her, Nick,' he murmurs. 'I know she was a bit woo-woo, but we had so much else in common. I thought, when we got out, I'd ask her to dinner . . .' He blinks back tears. 'I thought perhaps she liked me, too.'

'I'm so sorry. David, could you check for those pills? I think we need to know if Destiny was sedated.'

Reluctantly David releases Emily's hand. 'I'll look.'

When he returns, he looks distraught. 'Nick, they're gone. The whole pack is empty. Someone was in my room. They've taken them and left the packet.'

'Any other meds gone?'

'No. Just the sedatives. I haven't looked at them since yesterday.'

David could be lying of course, but Nick doesn't think he is. Besides, he's certain that David couldn't have left their shared mattress, sedated Destiny and set the fire before returning in the handful of minutes Nick was asleep.

'Who has access to your bedroom?'

David shakes his head. 'Only someone with a key.' He gives a small, uneasy smile. 'I guess that would be you.'

'Yes.' Nick sighs. 'But I know I didn't do it. So someone else must have one, too.'

The air is still thick with an oily, acrid mist, despite the open windows. Nick feels he'll never get the reek from his nostrils, that it will follow him wherever he goes after this. If he ever gets out.

The others are quiet, though Violet is lying down, crying quietly into her pillow, an empty space in the bed beside her. Nick almost wishes Branson would comfort her, but he's across the room, an inert lump beneath the bedclothes. Colt has gone back to his own room, and Matilda is barricaded into hers.

Nick stares at the moulded ceiling through the smoky haze, running over events in his mind. At six, unable to lie still beside a lightly snoring David any longer, he tiptoes from the room and makes his way upstairs. He soon finds what he's looking for: a round plastic shell on the ceiling, near the corner leading to Violet's room. He can't reach it, but he doesn't need to. Nick can see already that the smoke alarm has been smashed, its wires dangling uselessly beneath the casing.

He's certain David didn't kill Destiny; he was right beside him. That brings him back, once again, to Lorraine, Alan and Colt. He's discounting Matilda and Emily, too old and too young; neither of them would be physically capable of stabbing Penelope or strangling Donal. Besides, the idea of either one being a killer is absurd. Is he allowing Colt's charm and charisma to override his suspicions? Is he afraid of being racist, or classist, a typical London liberal, bending over backwards to exonerate the man with least to lose? As Jingle looks on with mild contempt, he makes a decision. As of now, nobody's off the hook.

By seven, they're all dressed. Nobody has slept, and a pall of exhausted disbelief hangs over them, along with the remnants of the smoke.

'I'll sort out the breakfast,' says Nick.

'Can't eat,' whispers Lorraine. 'We have to get out of here today,' she adds shakily. 'I can't do this any more.'

Violet turns red-rimmed eyes to her. 'None of us can. I don't trust a single morsel of food or drink in this place, I'd rather starve.'

Nick thinks again of Matilda's poisoning. In the melee of the fire and another death, it's been overlooked. But that was the one murder attempt that failed, another one with the killer's sick, festive hallmark. It wouldn't hurt to have one more look . . .

In the kitchen, Nick goes through the spice cupboard again, feels behind the tins, rummages amongst and into the packets. Of course, there's nothing to say the evidence would be in the kitchen. It's a wild goose chase, he knows that. He thinks of the paintings in each room, the berries glowing white above the beds. Berries. *For God's sake, Nick,* says Harriet's voice. *You don't keep berries in the cupboard if you want to preserve them. You keep them in the fridge.* And that's where he finds it, a small phial the size of a test tube, hidden in the recess behind the boxes of Christmas cheese.

Nick palms the glass container and draws it out to examine under the harsh overhead kitchen light. There are five mistletoe berries, neatly aligned like peas in their pod. There's a space where the missing sixth should be.

34

One day till Christmas Eve

'I've never seen this in my life, man.'

Colt stands by the sofa in the drawing room, a specimen in a glass case as eight faces stare at him.

'They were in the fridge, at the back.'

'Right, so anyone who has access to the kitchen could have put them there. Which is literally everyone, including you.'

Colt's right, he knows, but like Donal, Nick has always been a believer in the Occam's razor theory. The most obvious solution is generally correct.

'Colt, it doesn't look great.'

'I don't give a crap what it *looks like*.' Colt meets his gaze, hurt and anger in his eyes. 'I have no reason to kill any of you! You think I want to be trapped in this pit, watching folk get picked off like rabbits? You think I want to be suspected by a bunch of posh assholes who think they're better than me because of my funny Yorkshire accent and my skin colour?'

'Now, hang on a minute—' begins Alan.

'That's not why—' Nick interrupts, and Colt snorts.

'Isn't it?'

'Colt, it's because of several things.' Nick holds up his hand

and checks off his points. 'One, you know the manor really well. You may have copied the keys or have access to—'

'Except I didn't.'

'Two,' Nick goes on, 'it'd require someone strong to stab Penelope like that. She was tall and muscular, and if she'd fought back . . .'

'So that's you, David, Branson, Alan . . .'

'I'm half your size!' Alan shouts furiously.

Colt shrugs. 'You're still a bloke. Just about.'

'Three, Donal's death. It would have been easy for you to follow him down the stairs and then garrotte him with the wire. He was obsessed with you.'

'He was obsessed . . . What?' Lorraine repeats, astounded, and Nick remembers that he's kept Donal's secret – perhaps in a bid to offer the tragic young man some dignity in death.

'He was gay,' says Colt. 'He liked me, apparently.'

'Well, maybe you were revolted by that,' says Violet. 'Perhaps you couldn't cope with a gay man working alongside—'

'I'm gay too, love,' says Colt. 'So I doubt it was that.'

'Perhaps he was competition,' says Branson triumphantly. 'Or perhaps you were ashamed of your feelings . . .'

'What, I felt so uncomfortable with my own sexuality that I immediately had to murder anyone who fancied me? Get to . . .' Colt swears, disgusted.

'You did tell me you hate Christmas,' Nick says. 'The killer obviously does, too. And then there's Destiny—'

'Nick.' Colt leans forward, fury in his expression. Nick is uncomfortably aware that Colt is younger, fitter and bigger than he is. 'Do you honestly think I killed three people because I don't like Christmas? Even the effing Grinch didn't go that far.'

Lorraine snorts and Nick almost smiles. He wishes he didn't like Colt so much.

'Matilda was poisoned though,' he says. 'And you were cooking that day.'

'Like I said before – why would I poison an old lady?' Colt shakes his head and glares around the group. 'You know what? I've had enough. I'm out of here.'

Nick is barely standing before he hears Colt's boots banging a tattoo on the parquet. There's a pause – has he gone to the kitchen? – and then, a few moments later, the echoing slam of the vast front door.

Branson and David leap to their feet as Violet cries, 'He'll freeze out there!' and Alan mutters:

'There goes the murderer.'

'We don't know that—' starts Nick, but Matilda holds up a hand.

'Perhaps we do, Nick,' she says. 'Colt's got boundless opportunity, he's been alone while we've all been together . . . For every murder, he can't account for where he was. And the berries . . . one of them was used to try and poison me.'

David takes the tube from Nick and examines it. 'They really are mistletoe berries. My God.' He looks at Nick. 'Some-one who hates the manor and everyone in it,' he says quietly. 'Someone filled with rage and resentment.' He shakes his head, blinking back the sudden glint of tears.

'Colt was in trouble with the police when he was younger,' Nick says reluctantly. 'He's not had an easy life.'

David stands and makes his way to the hall, and opens the door to the pre-dawn darkness. Nick and the others follow, drawn by the brightening cold beyond the smoke-choked manor house.

Colt has the spade again and he's already several yards away, cutting out a path for himself with speed and grace. All the same, it will take him hours. Colt is wearing a cheap padded bomber jacket, and has no hat or gloves.

'Guy's gonna freeze to death,' says Branson. Nick silently agrees. Colt is digging in the direction of the woods to their left rather than towards the drive and the gates. Does he know a shorter route to the road? Or is he planning to hide there, and evade the police when they finally show up?

David nods. 'Hypothermia will set in when he stops exercising his muscles, and his core temperature drops. It can happen fast, and if he lies down in the snow . . .'

They fall silent.

'We have to get him back,' says Nick.

'But if he's the killer' – Branson puts a meaty hand on Nick's arm – 'and we're pretty sure he is . . . he's now angrier than a polecat. Particularly with you.'

Nick has an uncomfortable feeling that Branson is right. If Colt really has planned it all, Nick is almost certainly his next victim, because he's the only one getting in the way. *Occam's razor.*

The alternative is leaving Colt to die out there.

'We have to get him back.' Nick turns to the others. Alan has joined them in the hall, and Lorraine, too, is peering out, shivering in the cold air.

'I'll go,' Alan says unexpectedly. 'I'm a business owner; I know how to reason with cocky young lads.'

Nick doubts any of the 'cocky young lads' on Alan's payroll are murderers, but he smiles slightly. 'Go for it.'

'I'll need boots.'

'There's some wellies in the cupboard under the stairs,' says Lorraine. 'I think they keep them for guests.'

Booted, Alan pulls on his expensive-looking wool coat and sets out after Colt. 'Don't follow me,' he tells Nick, Branson and David quietly, 'but when I get him back, you three must overpower him, then we'll lock him in one of the bedrooms, keep an eye on him.'

Nick feels a shudder of revulsion. How has it come to this? Bringing Colt down, locking him up like an animal . . . who do they think they are? There's no arrest, no charge, yet they've appointed themselves judge and jury.

'Look . . .' he begins, but it's too late. Alan is wading through the narrow channel through the drift of snow towards Colt, raising his voice.

'Hey!' he calls. 'It's no use, you know. The police are coming!'

Colt ignores him. He's digging robotically, a relentless rhythm of bending and straightening, cutting and throwing snow behind him. A spray of ice catches Alan in the face.

'Oi! You can't get away!' Alan is gaining on him, slithering and stumbling. 'Come back to the house, mate, and we'll let the police sort it.'

'I'm not your *mate*.'

'Fine, but look, you'll die out here.'

'Not as fast as you will.' Colt's straightened up; he's holding the spade in both hands, a weapon.

'Come on, there's no need for this.' Alan holds his hands up and backs away, almost falling on a discarded lump of snow.

'There's every need. Get away from me.'

'Look, I just think . . .'

'I don't give a crap what you think, little man. Scared . . . little . . . man.'

With each word, Colt jabs the spade towards Alan's chest and he whimpers in fright.

'Colt, I'm sorry,' Nick calls. 'Please don't do this, you'll die out here.'

'Nick's right,' Branson shouts. 'The police will get here soon, and then they can investigate properly . . .'

'Sooner die in the snow than die in prison for something I never did.' Colt violently jabs the spade again, and Alan skips backwards, hurrying to the safety of the porch.

'If anyone else fancies a go . . .' Colt raises the spade.

'Oh, Colt, come back, love,' shouts Lorraine. She's standing on the doorstep in her jeans and silver ankle boots, arms wrapped around her fluffy reindeer-appliqué jumper as she shivers. 'We can sort this out. There's no need to be like this.'

'Is there not?' Colt's bitter laugh floats back to them through the still air. They watch as he digs on, miles to go, the woods a distant smudge of black and white.

Nick feels a sick grief that he's caused this. As long as he lives, Colt's despair will remain on his conscience — whether the young man is the killer or not.

Matilda's appearance when they finally assemble in the dining room is reassuringly normal. She's dressed as smartly as usual, in a cream cashmere dress with a holly-leaf brooch. Her hair is brushed and curled, and her diamond earrings are clipped on. Only her expression gives away her distress.

'I barely slept,' she murmurs. 'One just goes over and over it. Senseless. Vicious. Poor little Deborah.' Her blue eyes dampen and she fishes a cotton handkerchief from her patent-leather bag. 'I'm sorry . . .'

Matilda sinks into the armchair by the fire, and sobs. Violet rushes to her side and cradles her, and Lorraine crouches beside her.

'It's too much for a woman of your age,' Lorraine murmurs. 'You've been so brave, Mattie, but everyone has their breaking point.'

'I think I've reached it.' Matilda gives a watery smile.

Nick looks around at the group's pinched, exhausted faces and soot-stained clothes. His own jeans are stiff with dirt and smoke.

'Not long till we're rescued now,' he says hopelessly. 'We just have to get through the last few hours until the police come.'

'Oh, the police, the police!' shrieks Violet. 'I feel as if I'm in some awful play where everyone waits for rescue, day after day, and nobody ever comes!'

She sinks on to the couch, sobbing. This time, Branson puts an arm around her and keeps it there.

Nick feels the claustrophobia of despair grip him. *What would Harriet suggest?* He stands. Her calm voice in his head instructs him simply to go and make a pot of tea.

Crossing the icy hall to the kitchen, its deep red walls now stained black from last night's smoke, Nick pauses. He opens the front door, expecting a further gust of snowflakes, another icy blast.

He stands on the step in wonder. The drifts are still high, the drive still buried under an avalanche and the trees still bending under their burden of snow. But the air is changing. Now the temperature is cold, but no longer arctic. All around him, he can hear the drip and tinkle of melting ice falling from the gutters. As he watches, a chunk of snow slides from the roof and crashes through the drift beneath. The sky is chalk blue, and a hard white sun is rising over the woods.

He breathes out slowly, leaving a plume of steam hanging in the fresh morning air. For the first time in days, Nick feels hope.

Hardly daring to try, he raises his phone to see if he can get a signal, but there's nothing. Still, if the thaw has begun, by the end of the day they could try the car again. Back inside, he heads upstairs. Nobody picked up the keys he dropped, so he retrieves them. If they don't want them . . . Jingle emerges from beneath the Christmas tree, where he's been playing with a fallen bauble, and follows him up. The air in the bedroom carries the tang of smoked kippers, although the window's been open all night. Nick leans out, allowing the weak sun to bathe his face.

He lets the cat nest in the pillows while he showers, scrubbing off the smoke and grime, watching black water swirl down the plughole.

'We need to eat,' Lorraine says as they assemble downstairs. 'No wonder we're all beside ourselves. Maybe there's some sealed bread in the freezer, for toast.'

'I don't feel hungry,' says Matilda.

'I don't either.' Emily is wearing a green corduroy skirt, red tights and a white jumper. There's something of the Christmas elf about her and Nick is forcibly struck by the terrible incongruity of a child forced into bearing witness to this very particular hell.

Perhaps Matilda feels the same, because she touches Emily's round cheek and says, 'Would you like to bring Gaia, and come to look at my photographs again?'

Emily nods. 'Yes, please.'

'Emily, you really should have some breakfast . . .' David begins, but she shrugs him off.

'I will later,' she says. 'I want to see the little girls in the pictures again.'

David gazes helplessly after his daughter like a man abandoned.

Nick, too, watches her go, holding hands with Matilda as they slowly make their way upstairs.

Drinking his coffee, Nick feels a sick wash of guilt for the suspicions he's harboured. *Was Destiny really a yoga teacher?* For God's sake. He'd almost rather trust everyone here than allow that level of toxic paranoia to overwhelm him again. Unfortunately, he can't. Because someone here killed Penelope; someone strangled Donal; someone poisoned Matilda; and someone rendered Destiny unconscious and then locked her in a room on fire.

35

The manor is beginning to feel like a European town hall clock, little human-shaped automatons emerging from their slots as the hour chimes, then sliding back in. Nothing ever changes, apart from the number of wooden figures.

Everyone's now back in the drawing room – 'the bloody drawing room' as Nick has begun to think of it. If he makes it out alive, this room will haunt his nightmares. The tired brocade walls, the endless symphony of the fire spitting and cracking, the hushed murmur of grief and the thick, intimate scent of other people's bedsheets . . . he almost envies Colt the fresh air and the piercing cold, the chance to move fast under that far white sun.

With his thoughts running on such grim lines, Nick is pleased to see Jingle winding his way round the sofa. The cat jumps on to his lap, stretching luxuriously as Nick strokes his spine. He'll miss this little animal.

Gaia is watching from her position on Emily's knee. The little girl seems to have taken over her care, feeding her by the fire. David has already taken the dog to 'do her business' by the porch. What will happen to her, he wonders, when David and Emily return to South Africa?

As Jingle plucks threads from his jeans, the room keys in his pocket prod painfully into his hip. He hasn't used them much, Nick thinks. He's read enough police reports to know that every contact leaves a trace and most killers aren't organised enough to hide or destroy every shred of evidence. It was Colt, surely, even if they don't yet know his motive – though Nick still suspects that Penelope was the target, that she had somehow harmed the young man. The others were simply drifting too close to the truth for comfort.

Colt might come back and finish you off, says a small, cowardly voice in his mind. *Shouldn't you lie low until the police can be alerted?*

But Colt would be mad to come back. He said himself that he'd rather die.

No harm checking for evidence, Nick decides. If he does find something in Colt's room, at least they'll know for sure that they're safe now. Perhaps then they can finally begin to trust one another.

Nick is heading back upstairs, his heart heavy, when he hears Emily's voice behind him. 'Wait for me,' she says. 'I want to see what you're doing.' He wonders where David has gone, and whether it's wise for Emily to accompany him on his spying mission, poking around the smoke-damaged bedrooms and searching for evidence of murderous intentions.

'Where's your dad?'

'Gone to take Gaia for another wee-wee. I said, "Can we keep her?" and he said no but I'm going to keep asking until he gives in.'

Emily smiles winningly. She's so little, Nick thinks. How will she ever get over all this?

'Are you looking for murder weapons?' Emily asks conversationally. 'I can help – I'm really good at finding stuff.'

Alarm bells jangle in Nick's head. *This is so inappropriate . . .*

'Look, I think you'd better go back and wait for your daddy,' he says firmly. As Emily's face falls, Matilda emerges from the drawing room, her book beneath her arm.

'Nick!' She beams at him. 'I think congratulations are in order.'

'Are they?' He's confused.

'You found the baddie,' she says with a glance towards Emily, who is now leaning over the bannister, fiddling with a drooping string of silver bells on the tree. 'You sent him away, I believe.'

'Oh!' Nick tries to smile. 'Let's hope he was the right baddie.'

'Dear, he tried to poison me. If you and David hadn't sat with me . . . Now I know I can trust you all, I want to apologise. For my doubts, for not appreciating your kindness . . . and I'd like to thank you for your determination in uncovering what's happened.'

Nick feels embarrassed. 'Thanks, but it's only because I'm so desperate to get home . . . and we still can't know the reasons behind what he did.'

'Ours not to reason why,' says Matilda firmly. 'As long as we know who. Look, Emily, shall we go up to my room and have a biscuit? I've some special Christmas shortbread with chocolate on it.' She turns to Nick. 'I always bring a big tin for the staff. But as there's no one left . . .'

'Yes, please,' says Emily politely. 'Can Nick come too?'

'I think the least he deserves is a biscuit or two.' Matilda twinkles at him, and with some relief, he gives in. After this, he's going to try the police again.

Matilda's room smells pleasantly of roses, in contrast to the lingering reek of smoke elsewhere. Her photograph albums are neatly stacked on the table, a small pile of paperbacks by the bed. It's hard to imagine that this bedroom was the scene of a near-fatal poisoning yesterday, or that Matilda was so desperately unwell. She looks more relaxed than she has since that first night when they were all together, Violet cheerfully proposing a game, their only concern how quickly the snowstorm would pass.

Matilda opens the biscuit tin and flicks on the kettle. 'I've found the secret source of teabags,' she says in a confiding tone. 'The housekeeper's cupboard, on the next corridor. Discovered it years ago.' She winks, and Nick laughs.

Emily is pulling the top photograph album towards her, opening it like a picture book while Matilda makes the tea.

'I like this one,' she says. She turns the leather album so that Nick can see. It's a snapshot of JoJo and Catherine, he assumes, playing on a swing while a much younger Matilda and her husband look on. The girls are wearing old-fashioned smocked dresses and T-bar sandals. Nick remembers being a small child in the late eighties – his playmates were more likely to wear dungarees and Transformers T-shirts than this sort of Ladybird-book get-up.

'Lovely,' he says politely. Emily turns the page as Matilda brings over two mugs of tea and a scarlet biscuit tin in the shape of a nutcracker doll.

'Oh, that was a day at the seaside.' Matilda smiles. 'We went to Scarborough for JoJo's birthday. I remember Catherine made her a card with a bucket and spade drawn on and we all joked that it looked like a plant pot.' Her voice suddenly wavers and she blinks back tears.

'Don't cry, Auntie Mattie!' Emily looks alarmed, and Matilda manages a weak smile.

'I'm all right, darling,' she says. 'I just miss them being little, that's all. Make the most of childhood while you can; you'll be grown up soon enough.'

'Can I see the Christmas one again?'

'Of course.' Matilda leafs through the pages and stops at a larger photograph of the two sisters kneeling by the tree on Christmas Day. They're a little older here, wearing matching tartan dressing gowns and surrounded by a sea of wrapping paper. Nick thinks suddenly of the gold paper in Lorraine and Alan's room. Did Colt really rip a section from the roll as it stood in the hall on the day they arrived? It was such a precise and peculiar thing for a young man to do, no matter how angry he was. And why hide the remains in an unused bedroom? He could have burned it, or shredded it at the bottom of the kitchen bin.

'They were six and eight here,' says Matilda, her polished fingernail tracing the page. 'Catherine adored Christmas.'

'She looks a bit like me,' says Emily, pointing at the elder of the two. 'She's got curly hair like mine, and brown eyes.'

'So she has.' Matilda smiles. 'Perhaps you like drawing, too. Catherine loved art.'

'I do like drawing.' Emily nods. 'I like drawing animals. One day, Daddy's going to take me on a safari.'

'How wonderful!' Matilda claps her hands. 'A bit dangerous though perhaps – all those lions and tigers!'

'You don't see tigers on a safari drive,' Emily says scornfully. 'They live in the jungle. And you ride in a jeep with a ranger: it's completely safe.'

Nick suppresses a smile. Perhaps Emily isn't so similar to Matilda's perfect children after all.

After some speculation on how fast the snow will melt, it occurs to Nick to ask where Matilda will go, if they make it out by Christmas Day.

'Oh, I hadn't thought.' She shrugs. 'I suppose I may stay put.'

'Here?' Nick can't keep the horror from his voice. 'On your own?'

'Well, now that I've nothing to fear . . .' She shrugs. It sounds desperately bleak. Nick almost invites her to London, then imagines Harriet's face after his long absence if he turns up to their two-bedroom shoebox flat with a lonely widow in tow. He'll think about it, he decides.

He leaves Matilda and Emily discussing what children used to get for Christmas in the 1940s. 'An orange,' Matilda says, 'and sometimes a little doll or a book.' Emily pulls an expression of horror that makes them both laugh.

Back in the corridor, he pauses. The keys weigh heavy. Should he have one last look, see if he can find more evidence to link Colt directly to the crimes? There's something niggling at him. Why would Colt have a key to all the rooms? He's the chef, not the manager. If he'd taken them into the nearest town to obtain copies, wouldn't Donal have noticed that they were missing? Perhaps if he took them one at a time . . . but these are distinctive, old-fashioned keys to the rooms, they're not bog-standard Yale keys that would pass through the shop unnoticed.

Of course, he could have claimed to be the manager, taken them from Donal's drawer . . . but he'd have had to steal the drawer key, too, unless Donal's great passion compelled him to hand it over. None of it seems likely, or possible. Nick crosses to the landing window and looks out across the long gardens. There's no sign of Colt. He can see the small channel he's cut, leading away, but there's no dark figure crumpled in the snow, no spade . . . the narrow gully simply ends. He must have doubled back, Nick realises, a sick dread creeping through him. *So where is he now?*

If Colt does have keys, he could be anywhere in the manor. Nick has to find him.

He begins in the attic rooms. The storeroom remains untouched since the last time he looked, and Donal's bedroom is a stark, lonely shrine. There are no photos of Aisling, Nick notes – because she doesn't exist.

The other rooms are empty, the cleaner's cupboard is locked, and Colt's own room is exactly as he left it. Nick heads to the guest bedroom corridor, closing the door to the back stairs behind him. Matilda and Emily are safe for now; he doubts Colt will target them anyway. Colt's motive nags away at his mind like a twinging molar. Could Penelope have once let him down somehow? Promised him something and failed to deliver? Does Colt know her son, Peter? But even if he does, the sinister Christmas connection to the killings suggests a much more labyrinthine motive than any Nick can come up with for the cheerful, straight-talking chef. He has to assume it's all an act – and Colt has been concealing a past far darker than a few minor tangles with the law.

The unused bedrooms are all empty; the bathrooms and wardrobes conceal nothing but dust. Destiny's room is a blackened shell, the reek of damp bedding and smoke driving him back to the corridor after a glance into the bathroom and under the bed.

Lorraine and Alan's room is neater than Nick remembers, but otherwise unremarkable. He takes a cursory look in the drawers, finding nothing but medication and the Gideon Bible left by some long-ago guest, and there's little beneath the bed but a pair of discarded lacy knickers. Nick feels a tremor of revulsion at his intrusion into these strangers' intimate lives. He'll quickly look in Violet's room, and Branson's, then let the others know – they can search downstairs together.

Violet's suitcase is still spilling designer labels and now he knows why. Almost reflexively, he flicks open the bedside drawers to check before leaving. He stops.

Branson's lighter is in the drawer, with a packet of his cigarettes. Perhaps they haven't stopped sleeping together after all. On the other side of the bed is Violet's drawer. It contains a bottle of lavender 'pillow spray', and a Louis Vuitton purse holding various credit cards. But something else is sticking out at the back: a black and orange cardboard box. Nick pulls on the corner then swears softly as he realises what he's holding.

Sick doubt courses through him. Whoever set the fire in Destiny's room had already drugged her with David's sedatives. Violet is tall, young and strong. She, of all of them, had most reason to want Penelope out of the picture, and she was here before the snow began to fall in earnest, Nick realises. She'd have had time to collect a few berries and then, when she and Destiny took over cooking duties, it would have been easy to hide them in the fridge. As for Matilda's poisoning . . . Violet could easily have slipped a crushed berry into the dark wine.

In his mind's eye he can see her now, carrying the heavy Yule log upstairs, tapping on Destiny's door, offering to make her a herbal tea . . . *I can't sleep either*. And as Destiny passes out, she lights the wood, watching until it burns fast and hard, lets herself out, and runs back downstairs. Perhaps it was Violet returning that woke him up. With help, the blaze would have taken just a few moments to go from smouldering firewood to a sheet of flame. Of course the killer used an accelerant. Nick gazes at the half-empty packet of firelighters in his hand.

At the end of the corridor, the door to the fire escape is closed and there are no footprints leading up the steps. Nick opens the door for a moment, scanning the garden and the fields behind the house for signs of Colt. He peers more closely. Leading alongside the walled kitchen garden is a rough channel cut through the drifts, while a dome of snow has been shoved from the top of the seven-foot-high wall. A large planter has been dragged beneath. He can't see the snow in the kitchen garden, but the boundary wall has a similar gap in its covering of snow, and beyond, in the far distance, Nick sees a minuscule silhouette, bending and straightening, moving slowly towards the line of trees. Colt must have decided the fastest route is at the back. Nick feels his heart lift. Alive. Free. Colt doesn't know, however, that he's been exonerated – or that Nick will now carry a lifetime of guilt on his account.

36

'Christmas Eve tomorrow.' Lorraine heaves a sigh. 'Jade'll be doing her nut. She'll think we're dead.'

They're sitting on the sofa staring at the fire again. Nick braved the outhouse and was rewarded with a stack of firewood. Being in close proximity to the three victims was almost worth it for the warmth now bathing the drawing room. Nick finds he can't look at the flames, however. What they can do is seared into his mind.

Beside him, Violet and Branson are drinking coffee and doing the crossword in an old newspaper. Whatever the status of their relationship, they have a noticeable ease in each other's company. David sits opposite, staring at his book, although he doesn't seem to be reading. Emily and Matilda are in her room again, Nick presumes.

'Does anyone fancy a cup of tea?' he asks. He needs a moment to think before he tackles Violet.

Violet and Branson nod towards their steaming coffee cups, though David looks up, smiling. 'Yes, please. I'll come and help you.'

As they cross the hall, David glances at the tree and shudders. 'Thank God he's gone,' he murmurs. 'I can't tell you what a relief it is to know that Emily's safe now. That we all are.'

Nick wonders if he's chosen the right confidant in David, but in truth, he can think of nobody else. Branson is too close to Violet, Lorraine and Alan too volatile, Matilda too trusting.

'Listen,' Nick says under the noise of rushing water as he fills the huge kettle. 'I think we might have been wrong. I've found new evidence, and, David . . . I don't think Colt is the killer.'

Colour drains from David's face and he puts a steadying hand on the steel worktop.

'What do you mean?' His voice emerges in a whisper.

'I found something in Violet's room.'

For a moment, David seems unable to speak. Nick wonders if he's in shock.

'But we . . . Colt's the murderer. We had to let him go, Nick, he threatened us . . .'

'We'd just accused him of killing three people and the attempted murder of another. We were going to lock him up. I can't blame him, can you?'

Nick sits at the kitchen table, remembering Colt sprawled in the opposite chair. How hopelessly short-sighted they've been.

'What did you find?' David has recovered himself. He sits opposite, ready to listen, and Nick tells him everything, running through his reasoning as he talks.

'Oh God.' David shakes his head. 'If I'd thought for a second that those sedatives . . .'

'I know. It's not your fault.'

'I still feel awful though. So Branson and Violet . . . he's still sleeping with her? After what she's done?'

'I don't think he knows.'

David nods thoughtfully 'But why Destiny? I guess she

thought Donal knew too much, but Destiny knew nothing more than the rest of us. Some silly card readings . . .'

Nick shrugs. 'Maybe she had suspicions and confided in someone she believed was her friend. Violet must have thought she was getting too close to the truth.'

But wasn't Violet in bed when he woke up? Nick tries to remember: the smell of smoke, the sleeping bodies around him . . . yes, he heard her cough. Perhaps he'd been asleep longer than he thought. The noise that woke him could, after all, have been Violet hurrying back to bed, her lungs burning, unable to catch her breath . . .

David stares fixedly at the light overhead, holding back tears. 'Beneath her alternative wafty stuff, Destiny had a sharp mind. You don't get into medical school without one,' he says. 'I was beginning to like her a great deal.'

'So now what?' asks Nick. 'Citizen's arrest?'

David shakes his head. He points out of the window at the dripping gutters. 'Snow's still melting,' he says. 'In a few hours, we can try Alan's car again. If we make it to the road this time, we can find a way to call the police. In the meantime, I'll stick close to Violet. Nick, could you check Emily's OK? I . . . It sounds silly but I'd rather she stayed away from the drawing room. At least I know she's safe with Matilda.'

'Of course. Then I think I'll ask Lorraine to help me make lunch. Just to be on the safe side.'

He can hear Emily and Matilda talking as he approaches the door. He taps lightly.

'Come in,' calls Matilda, 'it's open.' With the vanishing of Colt, all fear has gone. Matilda believes they're safe, and so does Emily. Nick's heart feels leaden. He can't tell them. Not until the police get here.

Emily is now sitting at the desk, drawing in a notebook, explaining to Matilda what she's doing. 'This is the rhinoceros. Can you say how to spell that please? It's a bit difficult . . .'

'Hello,' says Nick. 'Your dad sent me up to check you're OK. It'll be lunchtime soon.'

'Can I have a ham sandwich?' Emily is carefully drawing the rhino's eye. It's good for her age. Nick thinks again of Cara and wonders what she'll one day excel at. His heart squeezes.

'I think so.'

Emily hums as she draws. Nick recognises it as a song from *The Muppet Christmas Carol* and smiles.

'All's well, as you can see,' says Matilda. 'It's so lovely to have a child around, amid all this misery.'

Not for the child, Nick thinks. He wonders where her own grandchildren are right now. Nick decides he knows Matilda well enough to ask.

'Where are your daughters living exactly? You said they were far away.'

Matilda pauses, her hand resting on a posed picture of Catherine aged around twelve. She was a beautiful child, with long, shining brown hair and a wide grin.

'Catherine is. JoJo lives in Manchester.'

'Oh! But that's not far away at all.' Nick is puzzled. 'Can't you go over for Christmas?'

Matilda shakes her head. 'I'm afraid we fell out badly, a few years ago. I've tried, but . . .'

'I'm so sorry.' He imagines the pain of a grown-up Cara deliberately choosing not to see him. It's unbearable. He longs to bring Matilda some comfort. 'What about Catherine?' he asks tentatively. 'Are you in touch?'

She swallows, her faded blue eyes bright with tears. 'We lost her,' she says quietly. 'It was a long time ago, but . . . I always feel it was my fault. If only I'd known what she was planning, I'd have . . .' She takes a shuddering breath. 'I'd have done things very differently.'

The most terrible loss of all. Nick knows that now. Once, he thought losing Harriet would be the worst thing that could happen to him. Now, the idea of Cara ever being that unhappy, of knowing he's failed his daughter . . . He briefly lays a hand over Matilda's delicate fingers.

'God, I'm so sorry. I'd never have asked if I'd known.'

'I know.' She nods. 'I don't talk about it often, because it makes people feel so terribly awkward. I'm glad you asked.'

'Asked what?' Emily looks up from her picture, which now includes a giraffe with a comically quizzical expression.

'What time lunch will be served.' Matilda smiles at her. 'I'm starving, aren't you?'

Nick and Lorraine manage to rustle up pasta with marinara sauce and a great deal of cheese for lunch. Stores are running low, although the food for Christmas Day remains in the chest freezer in the outbuilding, right beside the bodies. Nick hopes profoundly that there will be no need to go in there yet again and fetch it. Now there are so few of them left, they should be able to eke out the food in the fridge until they can escape.

As he promised earlier, David is sticking closely to Violet, although Branson seems more distant. Does he suspect his mistress of murder, too? Or is he simply tiring of her now the illicit thrill has gone, to be replaced by guilt?

'We'll dig the car out again,' Alan says through a mouthful of Matilda's shortbread. She's generously brought her tin of biscuits down. 'Maybe the old girl can make it up the drive this time.'

As he and Branson discuss horsepower and traction, Nick glances out of the window. The sun has disappeared behind a bank of cloud the colour of a fading bruise and, to his horror, thick flakes are falling once again.

'Look,' he murmurs, nudging David and nodding at the icy panes. David blinks at the scene, unwilling to register what's happening.

'Colt,' he says eventually. 'Do you think . . .?'

Nick closes his eyes. 'I hope so,' he says. Colt's surely made it to the road by now, but if he hasn't, his thin jacket will be soaked through. His body temperature will drop like a stone, and in a couple of hours, darkness will fall.

'Alan,' says Nick, 'Shall we try the car now?'

The engine won't start. 'Snow in the tail-pipe,' suggests Branson, and Alan gives him a scathing look.

'Try hitting it,' calls Lorraine encouragingly from the porch. David is still with Violet in the dining room. He can't shadow her all afternoon, Nick thinks; at some point, they're going to have to let the others know that Colt is most likely innocent and Violet is not. He needs to speak to Branson first so he has all possible information before he accuses her.

I know what you did.

What had Penelope done to Violet? Something work-related?

Or was it a veiled reference to her marrying Branson for money?

They've dug the car out again, but it's not moving. 'Engine's frozen,' says Alan. 'I'll need to get it started and leave it running.'

'Then the battery could die,' says Branson. 'Can you pop the hood? I'll take a look.'

'Actually, the battery's at the back in a Discovery.'

Somehow, Alan manages to sound obnoxious even when he's simply relaying facts. Branson trudges through the displaced snow to have a look.

'It's gone.'

'What?'

'The battery's gone.'

Alan almost falls out of the car in his hurry. 'Don't be bloody ridiculous, it can't have *gone*.'

Nick peers over Branson's shoulder and sees a gaping space where the battery should be, ripped-out wires dangling. Alan is speechless.

'Looks like we're not going anywhere until we can get out on foot.' Branson looks distressed. 'Guess that was Colt's final revenge, huh?'

Alan kicks the bumper violently, and falls sideways into a snowdrift. Branson fishes him out.

'Where is it, though?' wonders Nick. 'It's a pretty big thing to hide.'

They look around at the vast snowdrifts, stretching for miles on all sides.

'I guess we'll find out when it melts,' says Branson.

Back inside, the rooms seem even smaller, the snow falling

outside ever thicker. Lorraine is leading a desultory game of seated charades by the fire.

David, Matilda and Emily are trying to guess, while Violet scrolls through her phone settings. 'Why isn't the emergency call option working?' she mutters, jabbing at the screen. If by some miracle they do get out today, there's a good chance Violet will vanish before the police can reach her. She has plenty of money, a network of well-connected friends. Nick has to confront her – but first, he must speak to Branson.

They're in the library, mainly because Nick likes it there. The air feels clearer, the light sharper than inside the dim, fuggy drawing room.

'Must have left my lighter upstairs,' Branson says. 'Give me a second, I'll get it.'

'It's in the bedside drawer.' Branson stares at him and Nick shrugs. 'I looked. That's what I want to speak to you about.'

Branson returns to his chair. 'Guess I'll cope without a smoke,' he says slowly. 'I hope you're not accusing me, Nick.'

'Not of murder, no. I *am* accusing you of turning a blind eye to your murderous girlfriend. You must have suspected.'

Shock flares in Branson's eyes. 'You're not serious.'

Nick has had enough. He leans forward and speaks clearly. 'Branson, out of everyone here, Violet has the most obvious reason to want Penelope out of the way. This situation provided the perfect opportunity – she could hardly do it when it was just the three of you at the house in California. This way, she has a whole set of ready-made suspects to blame. Violet's tall; she's young and strong. She's clever, and she's in love with you.'

'Yes, but a passionate affair isn't the same as—'

'Passion is what *leads* to murder. Love, hate, desperation.'

'I could have stopped it,' Branson says hopelessly. 'I could have confessed to my wife, and I didn't. I have to live with that shame.'

Yes, you do, thinks Nick.

'Also,' Nick continues, 'the facts are staring us in the face. It was Violet who unwrapped the star and kicked the whole thing off. Violet arrived here early enough to collect the berries. Violet volunteered to use the kitchen and hid them there to implicate Colt. Violet poured Matilda's wine.'

A light sheen of sweat coats Branson's brow, despite the temperature. 'Donal . . .' he begins weakly.

'Donal knew something. She had to get him out of the way. With Destiny, I think she was talking about her suspicions – Violet knew it wouldn't be long before Destiny worked it out. I think Violet ran up there, set the fire, and if I hadn't woken she'd have waited a little longer, then raised the alarm. And,' Nick finishes, 'I found a pack of firelighters in her bedside drawer.'

Branson looks shell-shocked. 'Why poison Matilda?'

'Again, perhaps she was beginning to suspect. We don't know if she said anything to Violet. Matilda now thinks it was Colt, so Violet will assume she's safe.'

Branson holds Nick's gaze. 'My God,' he murmurs, his face a mask of distress. 'My God.'

'So should we . . .'

'Wait.' Branson holds a hand up. 'Listen, Nick. There's something you really need to know.'

37

'It's worse than I told you.' Branson rubs his face. 'I'm so ashamed, Nick. I feel sure Penny's death is my fault. I was so weak, so pathetic. Another stupid, ageing man, flattered into deceiving the wife he loves. Loved.' He draws a long breath.

'Tell me what's happened.'

'I really could use a cigarette.'

Nick waits while Branson goes upstairs. He hears Lorraine asking him something as he returns, and the rumble of Branson's reply. Thankfully, she doesn't follow him back to the library.

'Lorraine's trying the police on her cell again,' says Branson. 'Doubt it'll work.'

He subsides into the wing chair.

'All right, look. Violet talked me into having an affair . . .' He sees Nick's expression. 'OK, I was happy to do it. But that's not enough for her. She told me that first night here that she wants to marry me. She wants . . .' Branson pauses, blinking. 'She wants to move to Malibu, live in our house, be my wife. She wants to be Penny.'

'What did you say?'

'I said no! Of course I did — I never had any intention of marrying her, it'd be like eating chocolate for every meal for the rest of your life. I wanted Penny, I loved Penny. Violet was just . . . fun. Flattering. But maybe . . . maybe my refusal tipped her into this . . . horror.' He covers his face with his hands. 'My God, Nick. How has it ever come to this?'

Nick falls silent for a moment.

'The evidence against her is stacked very high. Look, Branson, we need to tell the others. Otherwise, I'm afraid she's going to follow Colt and disappear – or worse, get rid of someone else.' *Like me.*

Branson nods. Together, they leave the library and head for the drawing room again, where their depleted little group is huddled round the fire.

This will be the last time, thinks Nick. *Soon, this will all be over.*

'David, could you and Emily take Gaia for a little walk?' Nick asks. 'Branson and I need to speak to Violet about . . . grown-up stuff.'

'Sure.' David holds a hand out to Emily. 'Come on, poppet.'

'I want to stay!'

'No. You're coming with me.' It's the first time Nick's heard David raise his voice even slightly. Emily immediately subsides and leaves the room with him, holding Gaia's lead. Perhaps David isn't quite the pushover Nick once thought.

'What's up?' Violet peers up, smiling winningly at Branson. 'Lorraine says she thinks her text might have gone, don't you? She's got some app that means you hardly need any signal . . .'

'Violet,' Branson says.

Matilda, Alan and Lorraine look at him.

'We know,' he says heavily. 'To quote your own note, honey, "I know what you did."'

'*What?*' Violet leaps to her feet. 'You can't mean what I think you do?' The hot pink flush is back, high on her cheekbones, and she's breathing fast, her chest hitching.

Lorraine turns to Alan. 'What does he mean?'

'How should I know?' He shrugs irritably. 'We all know Colt was the killer.'

'He wasn't.' Nick speaks quietly but firmly. 'Violet, there are firelighters in your bedside drawer.'

'There are *what?*'

'Good Lord!' cries Matilda. 'Whatever would you need those for . . .' She trails off as realisation strikes. The air in the drawing room still carries the faint tang of stale smoke.

'They're not mine! Someone planted them there, obviously.' Violet seems close to panic. 'I've never lit a fire in my life – I wouldn't know how!'

That's almost believable, thinks Nick – but anyone can learn.

'Besides, where would I get them?'

'Plenty of stores in the housekeeper's cupboard,' Nick says. 'It's not far from your room, is it? Never locked.'

'Are you suggesting I *killed people*?' Violet emits an eerie wail of grief and panic. 'Why? Why would I do something so evil?'

'You aren't above cheating on your friend,' says Branson. 'That's pretty evil.'

'Oh, don't you dare!' Violet rounds on him. 'You weren't complaining in the pool house, were you? Or any of the other times! You were just looking for an excuse because Penelope was so bloody boring!'

'Don't speak about my wife like that!' bellows Branson.

Violet gives a bitter little laugh. 'Oh, *now* you love her. Now she's dead and can't nag you and irritate you and use you for money . . .'

'That's a bit rich,' mutters Nick.

'Penelope didn't do any of those things,' says Branson. 'You, however . . .'

'Hold on.' Lorraine is holding a hand up, her eyes round with horror. 'Are you saying Violet killed Penelope? And murdered Donal and Destiny, and tried to poison Matilda? But it was Colt! He ran off – he tried to kill Alan . . .'

'He brandished a spade threateningly,' corrects Nick. 'He didn't try to kill him. Lorraine, the evidence against Violet cannot be ignored now that we've found the firelighters.'

He goes through it again – the wrapped star, the poured wine, the fire . . .

'And you tried to talk me into marrying you,' Branson tells her. 'I'd sooner marry a rattlesnake. Tell the police what you like. I'm done.'

Violet's face crumples. 'I didn't kill anyone!' she screams. 'I didn't!'

'Oh, my dear.' Matilda's face is impassive in the firelight. 'I'm afraid it looks very much as though you did.'

Violet has barricaded herself into the bedroom, sobbing hysterically, and Nick has locked the door from the outside. Branson has the only other key to the room. He has retrieved his things and moved to Rowan, the room where he claimed he'd been sleeping on the night Penelope was murdered. David has returned, although Matilda has taken Emily to the library to play Monopoly again. Looking in to check on their whereabouts, Nick thought what a charming scene they made, their heads bent over the board, laughing as they chose the dog and the top hat as counters. If only Matilda could have a relationship like that with her real grandchildren.

'How did you not hear her leave though, Branson?' Lorraine asks now as they sit, shaken, around the fire. 'That night, I mean — how did you sleep through her literally murdering your wife?'

'Lorraine!' snaps Alan. 'That's enough!'

Nick silently vows once again to be a better husband to Harriet when he gets back.

'No, it's a fair question.' Branson looks distraught. 'I sleep deeply. Violet knows that.'

'It's so bloody cold.' Lorraine shudders. 'Psychopathic. Knowing she planned it all for months before.'

'Months?' Branson looks puzzled.

'You didn't win any competition, did you, pet?' Lorraine sighs. 'Violet set that group up; she must've done. She targeted Penelope to make sure you'd come. I assume she knew you'd be in England this particular week?'

David nods. 'I'm afraid she's right. It's the obvious explanation. Though I don't know why she chose this hotel.'

Branson groans. 'It's my fault. All of it.'

'No,' Nick says. 'It's Violet's fault. Nobody else's. Did she hate Christmas?' he asks Branson. 'The killer clearly does.'

'Not that I know of,' Branson says miserably. 'Last year she made a huge fuss because I was spending it with Penny in Hawaii. She said, "Christmas is the best time of year and I can't even see you," or something like that.'

'Christmas can be pretty miserable when you're a mistress,' Lorraine puts in quietly.

'Lorraine! For God's sake, must we?' Alan glares.

'I'm only saying.' She shrugs. 'It *was* lonely.'

Branson glances up, as though he hasn't registered the significance of Lorraine's admission at all. 'I tell you who did hate Christmas,' he says, almost to himself. 'Penny. She loathed the whole thing, always wanted to get away. That's why we went to Waikoloa. She hated snow, too.'

'Why?' Nick asks. There's something just out of reach, something he needs to grasp. *What am I missing?* 'Branson, why did she hate Christmas?'

Branson shrugs. 'She never told me. She said she didn't want to talk about it. I assumed it was something to do with her ex.'

'So how come you came back this year?' Lorraine asks.

'She wanted to see her boy,' Branson says. 'Pete. She missed him.'

'I can't imagine moving to America and not seeing our Jade,' says Lorraine.

Nick thinks of Cara. He'd go to the ends of the earth to be near her. As it is, he can't even get out of this house.

'Did your text send?' he asks Lorraine, remembering.

'Don't think so.' She checks, without enthusiasm. 'Wait, it says sent. I had half a bar of signal if I hung out of the bedroom and leaned to the left.'

There are gasps, exclamations. The collective energy shifts in an instant from grim acceptance to optimism, a dark room suddenly illuminated.

Lorraine looks at Nick, her eyes shining. 'Do you think they got it? I sent one to Jade too. She's sensible; she'd call the police if it reached her.'

'I hope they did.' Nick smiles at Lorraine. They're among the last ones standing and he feels a warmth towards her that's been lacking until now. She's a decent woman, he thinks. Brash, but kind. Maybe tonight, thanks to her, they'll all be saved.

'Better start thinking about dinner,' says Lorraine.

'I'll give you a hand,' says Alan unexpectedly. Nick watches them go. Relationships can be so complicated. What did Penelope do – and to whom? Until he discovers exactly what that note means, he can't be entirely sure this is over.

Tonight, Nick is glad of the wine. It's helping to keep his mind off what's happened to Colt, and where he might be. The temperature has dropped again. The drifts will be sealed with a hard shell of ice by morning.

David isn't hungry. He pushes the shepherd's pie around his plate. Nick hears his grandmother's long-ago voice in his head: 'Eat up, Nicholas, you're not bonsai gardening.'

'Are you OK?' he asks. David looks up.

'Yeah. Well, no. It's taken a bit of a toll, hasn't it? I'm just wondering what to do about all this when we get home. Counselling for this one?' He glances at Emily, who is feeding a spoonful of pie to Gaia.

'Wouldn't hurt. It's a lot to process.' It occurs to Nick that he's never used the word 'process' in this context before. Even now, it feels uncomfortable.

David closes his eyes. 'God, Nick, I don't think I can stand much more of this. I need to get my little girl away from all the horror. Go back home, where she's safe.'

'Not long now,' Nick says. 'Lorraine may have contacted the police. She had half a bar of signal, remember.'

David shakes his head. 'They really can't come soon enough.'

The small talk is all done. The sickening awareness that the killer is locked in her room and Colt, falsely accused, is somewhere out there in the frozen darkness casts a pall over any attempts at conversation.

'I reckon we'll sleep in our own room tonight,' says Lorraine when the dinner things have been cleared away. 'Now we know we're safe.'

'Oh yes,' says Matilda fervently. 'One does so long for a little privacy.'

'I'll put this one to bed and have a hot bath, I think,' David agrees. 'Been another long and terrible day, here at Miserable Manor.'

'You OK with that, Branson?' Nick asks. 'Will you feel safe alone?'

'Safer than I'd be with Violet,' says Branson with a sad smile. 'I'll lock my door.'

'What if she sets another fire?' asks David suddenly. He looks pale, clammy. 'That could see us all off.'

'She won't.' Branson shakes his head. 'I took the firelighters and the lighter away. She can't get out.'

Nick feels a shudder of revulsion. It's as though Violet is a wild animal, or a woman in a Victorian freak show, kept behind bars. But the others are right, she is a criminal, and she is dangerous. If only she'd tell him what she meant by that note. It's the last piece of the puzzle – and it still doesn't quite fit.

38

It's a relief to be back in his bedroom, with only Jingle for company. Nick feels absurdly flattered that the cat has chosen him, and makes a space by his knees for Jingle to settle down.

The deep, rhythmic purr is reassuring, but Nick can't sleep. The heating wheezes and bangs and, when the group parted on the landing, there had been no response to Lorraine's desperate texts. Perhaps they hadn't sent at all. Reflexively, Nick checks his own phone signal. Nothing. In a few hours it will be Christmas Eve.

If Colt has survived, if Nick ever finds him again, he'll do anything to alleviate the terrible guilt he feels. If Colt has died out there in the snow, he'll carry that burden wherever he goes. The fear and misery of the last few days is crashing in on Nick.

Someone raps hard on the door. He starts upright, and Jingle mews in fright and streaks under the bed. Nick turns on the lamp, his heart thudding.

'Who is it?'

'It's me.' The voice is tearful. 'Lorraine. Nick, can you open the door?'

She almost falls into the room.

'It's Alan,' she manages, clutching on to Nick. His heart plummets. Not another death, surely. Not when it all seemed to be over.

'Where is he?'

'That's the thing,' Lorraine wails. 'He's gone. I woke up, and his side of the bed was empty.'

'Lorraine, get your breath. He's probably gone for a nightcap downstairs. Maybe he couldn't sleep.'

'No.' She shakes her head. 'I checked. There's no sign of him. He was upset when we went to bed. Nick, I think he's left. He's gone out in the snow, and . . .' Her words are muffled by tears.

'We'll find him.' Nick pulls on his jeans, levers on his boots. By the time he's dressed for the outdoors, Lorraine is calmer, huddled in the desk chair wearing her hotel dressing gown.

'How long ago did you fall asleep?' Nick asks.

'I don't know! Two hours? He could be dead in the snow by now. Or what if he's been killed?'

'Violet's locked in—'

'*If* it was her,' Lorraine mutters. 'Truth is, Nick, I don't trust anyone any more. I don't think I ever will again.'

'Stay in your room in case he comes back,' Nick says. 'I'll go and search.'

She nods. Her eyes are wide with panic and, without her usual careful make-up, she looks pale and vulnerable. Briefly, he puts his arm around her. 'I'll find him, I promise.'

Nick sets off towards the stairs, Jingle trotting in his wake. For the rest of his life, he thinks, he'll dream about these red-carpeted stairs – up and down, fire and snow, death and sorrow, and the ever-present, vegetal scent of the dying tree. As he reaches for the bannister, he hears a noise. Nick pauses. It's a male voice, but it's not David's measured tones, or Branson's low rumble. It sounds desperate. Nick stands immobile, straining to listen.

'It was us.'

The voice seems to be coming from the end of the corridor: Matilda's room.

Surely Alan isn't confessing? Is Matilda safe?

He hurries to the door, tiptoeing as lightly as he does when Cara has just fallen asleep. He thinks of the agonising, soft tread to her bedroom door, the tinkle of her animal mobile, the paralysing dread that any second, she'll open one big blue eye and wail. What he'd give to be there now, lifting his daughter's sleepy little body, cradling her to his chest.

He listens. He hears the murmur of Matilda's voice. She doesn't sound afraid, he realises, just sad.

'It was us,' Alan says again. 'Me and Lorraine.'

'Surely you can't think—' Matilda says.

'You're not listening!' His voice rises. 'Me and Lorraine killed her, and not an hour goes by that I don't wish I could go back and undo it.'

Nick freezes. Inside the room, there's silence.

'I know how you feel,' Matilda says eventually. 'My daughter died, and I think about her every hour too.'

'I'm so sorry.' Alan pauses. 'Was she a child when . . .'

'No. No, she was quite grown up. I'll show you.'

There's a rustle and snap as Matilda opens a clasp. 'There. I keep this one hidden away in my purse. I don't often like to look at more recent pictures; it's easier to look at the old albums and remember her as a child. Seeing her as an adult reminds me too much of what happened.'

'She was beautiful,' Alan says. 'I'm sorry.'

'Grief is a terrible thing, Alan. It will eat you whole and leave nothing behind if you let it.'

There's a noise behind Nick, and he turns, expecting to see Jingle. But Lorraine is standing a little way down the corridor, listening, her face stiff with shock.

'The thing is, Matilda,' Alan says, muffled, 'it's hard to think of me and Lorraine as anything other than murderers.'

'Alan!' Lorraine screams, shoving Nick aside as she beats on the door. 'Alan, you promised! You swore to me you'd never – you *swore*!'

Inside, there's a thick silence.

'I think you'd better let her in,' says Matilda, and Nick hears the sound of a turning key.

'Nick!' Alan's face is haunted. He's holding a tumbler of whisky. Matilda is in her dressing gown, sitting in the desk chair, and the lamp by the bed is switched on.

'I'm sorry,' Nick says. 'Lorraine was worried. She thought you'd gone outside. I'm afraid I heard some of your conversation.'

'A conversation you literally promised me you'd *never have with anyone*,' Lorraine sobs.

'Look, Alan, it sounded as though you were confessing.' Nick closes the door behind him. His heart is thumping. 'Are you saying you and Lorraine are the murderers?'

Matilda gasps. 'Oh no! Not at all!' Just as Alan says:

'Not here. Not these victims.'

'Oh, for God's sake, Alan! I told you to see a therapist!'

Lorraine shouts. 'You bottle it all up inside, and now look! You've exploded like a bloody piñata!'

Nick subsides on to the corner of the bed. 'I don't want to interrupt a good marital row,' he says, 'but could one of you tell me what this is all about?'

Gradually, they piece it together.

'We had an affair,' Lorraine says.

'Liz . . . my wife,' adds Alan. 'She found out.'

'Very sad,' murmurs Matilda.

'Alan left her and their two boys and moved in with me and little Jade,' Lorraine says. 'It wasn't Liz's fault, she'd done nothing wrong, we just fell in love.'

'OK . . .' This is not an unfamiliar story of human failing, and Nick can't work out where murder comes into it.

'Liz was devastated,' says Alan. 'Signed off work with depression, stopped looking after herself.'

'Phoned him up night and day,' adds Lorraine. 'Then one night, about three months after we got together, she phoned and said she'd taken an overdose.'

'I mean, she'd said it before,' Alan adds. 'She'd said it loads of times, and she never had, she just wanted me to go back home and look after her.'

'And that night . . .' Lorraine presses her hands hard against her chest. 'It's so awful, Nick, honestly – that night, I'd invited the girls from work round so they could meet Alan. He was a handsome beggar back then, they were all excited and I didn't want to cancel.'

'So I didn't go,' says Alan heavily. 'I turned the phone off and I ignored Liz's calls.' He stops, swallowing hard.

'When nobody heard from her for a few days . . .' Lorraine supplies. 'Well. They went round and they found her there.'

Now Nick understands.

'Never saw my lads again. They stayed with Liz's parents, wouldn't answer my calls . . . I love Lorraine and we stayed together through it all,' says Alan, 'but the guilt . . . it's been torture for both of us, all these years. We always said we wouldn't tell anyone. I couldn't bear Jade to know, and people would judge us too hard.'

'I'm not sure they would,' says Matilda gently. 'What you did was done out of desperation. It wasn't malicious.'

'We as good as murdered her,' says Alan. 'Lorraine, I'm sorry I told Matilda. I just . . . These deaths, one after the other, they've brought it all back. Violet having an affair with Branson . . . So many echoes of what happened. I couldn't sleep and I went down for a nightcap. Matilda was having one too. She asked if I wanted to talk and it just came out.'

Lorraine lays her hand on his arm. 'It's all right, pet,' she says. 'I get it. Maybe when we get back home after Christmas, we can go and see someone together. You know, talk about it, finally. Try and put it all to rest.'

Alan nods. 'I think that's a good idea.'

Slowly, holding on to each other, they make their way back to bed.

'I think they'll be all right,' says Matilda, watching them go, and Nick nods. Surprisingly, he agrees.

39

Christmas Eve

He's woken by a scream. Shrill and piercing, it's coming from the hall.

He almost falls out of bed, pulling on jeans, sprinting to the door, twisting the key in the lock, racing towards the stairs. *Someone's dying. But Violet was locked in . . .* He pulls up short as, disorientated, he takes in the scene before him.

Early-morning sun is filtering through the fanlight, illuminating the entrance hall. Matilda is lying on the parquet floor, her eyes closed. Gaia is nosing tentatively at her side. There is nobody nearby except Emily. The little girl is standing on the stairs in a shaft of sunlight, wearing a Christmas angel costume with feathered wings and a tinsel halo.

'Uncle Nick,' she says in a small, trembling voice. 'I called out to Auntie Matilda and she screamed and fell down.' She looks up at him. 'I think she might be dead.'

Nick hurries past her and presses his fingers to Matilda's neck. Relief floods his body as he registers a steady pulse. She's fainted — not a cardiac arrest, or a stroke, then. Not another murder.

As he takes her wrist, she stirs and her eyelids flutter.

'Catherine,' she whispers.

'No, it's Nick.'

'Catherine was here.' Matilda's eyes flicker open and focus on his face. 'Where is she? Where's my little girl?'

She struggles to sit up, and Nick catches her as she sways.

'Did you bang your head?'

'No . . . I don't think so.'

'Then I'm going to carry you to the drawing room. Ready?'

He bends and scoops Matilda into his arms. Today she's wearing a black velvet dress and a diamond and emerald brooch. She's so frail beneath the smart frocks and the careful make-up. She weighs so little. Gently, he carries her through and lays her on the long, velvet sofa. The fire is dead, but the sunlight is warming the room, gilding the brass fender and reflecting in the mirrors. The snow has stopped.

'It was her,' Matilda says fretfully. 'It was my little girl; she's come back to me at last.'

'I'm going to get the doctor,' says Nick. He leans out into the hall as Matilda murmurs to herself.

'Emily!' he calls. 'Auntie Mattie had a fright, that's all. She's OK. Could you get your daddy now?'

Emily nods, tinsel halo bobbing, and he hears her small feet disappearing down the corridor, swiftly followed by the click of Gaia's tiny claws on the parquet.

Matilda gazes up at him like a child. 'I thought, my little Catherine . . .' She closes her eyes again. 'It was Emily. I see that now.'

'I think she dressed up, because it's Christmas Eve.'

'Yes, I know it is. I'd never forget Christmas Eve.'

David bursts into the drawing room. 'Emily said Matilda fell? What happened?'

'She passed out. She's had a shock.'

'What kind of . . .'

'Sorry, Daddy.' Emily trails into the drawing room, wings drooping, her face downcast. 'I didn't know it was bad – I just wanted to be a Christmas angel. I was looking for treasure upstairs and I found a box that said Christmas decs and costumes . . .'

'It wasn't bad, darling.'

'I think Auntie Mattie mistook you for someone else,' Nick tells her, gently. He turns to David and mouths, 'Catherine.'

David swallows. 'Oh dear,' he murmurs. 'Upsetting.'

As David bends to Matilda to check her breathing, and Emily disappears upstairs to change – 'Probably for the best, poppet' – something snags at Nick's mind.

While nobody's watching, he slips back to the hall, where Matilda's old-fashioned black patent-leather bag lies abandoned on the wooden floor.

Glancing up the stairs, he checks nobody's coming down the corridor, and he softly unsnaps the clasp and looks inside. Face powder, a bottle of Rive Gauche perfume, a pen, a large, dark green leather purse. Nick checks he can still hear the murmur of David's voice from the drawing room, and opens it.

A set of bank cards . . . he notes a Coutts black card. Nick knows from his newspaper's finance desk that only the very rich are given access to these. Matilda must be a millionaire. He feels a jolt of unease. Why does she come here every year, to this run-down, shabby hotel with its skeleton staff? Why not spend Christmas in the Maldives, or at Claridge's?

He needs to see Catherine's face. There she is, tucked into the pocket. A small, glossy colour photograph, showing a remarkably beautiful woman in her early forties – she lived much longer than Nick imagined: he'd assumed she died young, by suicide. This woman looks strong, powerful and confident, her long brown hair tumbling over her shoulders, and a hint of humour in her huge hazel eyes. Charisma burns from the photograph, and Nick feels a pang of sorrow that such a vibrant life is gone forever. As he gazes at Catherine's face, he feels that unease again, a tug of familiarity. Has he met her? He'd surely remember. Silently, he extracts his phone from his pocket and snaps a picture of the photograph. As he tucks it back into the purse, his fingers touch thinner paper. He draws it out to find he's holding a faded newspaper clipping. Nick is about to unfold it when he hears swift footsteps approaching down the corridor, and Emily's voice calling, 'Daddy?'

Nick replaces the clipping, closes the bag, and brings it through to Matilda.

'Oh, Nick, thank you,' she says, and he feels pierced by guilt.

'I feel so silly . . . I thought . . . my daughter had a similar costume to Emily's, and for a moment, in the sunlight . . .'

'It's all right,' he tells her. 'It's completely understandable.'

Emily skids to a stop at the door. 'Is she OK now?'

Matilda sits up and smiles at her. 'I'm fine, Emily,' she says. 'It was a silly mistake, not your fault at all.'

Emily smiles tentatively. 'I just wanted to dress up, cos it's Christmas Eve.'

'Perhaps we can play a festive game later,' says David. He looks exhausted, his eyes red-rimmed.

'Oh, I think there've been enough games,' says Matilda. Her tone is cool, and Nick wonders if she's talking about more than Monopoly and charades.

As he stands to make a pot of tea, the sound of shouting floats from upstairs.

'I think that's Auntie Violet,' says Emily conversationally.

Nick hurries to the hall and hears distant bellowing. '. . . so stupid,' Branson yells. 'A rich, middle-aged man and you used me like . . .' He moves away and Nick can't hear his next words.

Violet screams, 'You were happy enough!'

'Not now I know you're a goddamn serial killer!'

There's a crash, Branson swears, and Violet screams, 'I'm not! I'm not, I'm not! Why won't you believe me? I never killed anyone!'

'That note,' Branson shouts. 'You wanna tell me what that was about? What did Penny ever do to you?'

'Nothing!' Violet screeches. '*And I didn't write it because I didn't kill her!*'

A door slams and seconds later Branson appears, taking the stairs two at a time.

'Sorry about that,' he mutters, striding past. 'Goddamn madwoman.'

Branson disappears in the direction of the dining room. 'No breakfast?' he calls, disappointed, seeing the empty table.

'Afraid not yet,' Nick tells him. 'I'll see what's in the fridge.'

As Nick rummages through foil-wrapped packages, he thinks of Colt and winces in guilty pain. The sun is shining, the sky is a crystalline winter blue and the snow is beginning to melt – but it's hard to imagine that Colt survived the night, unless he found shelter by dusk. The murders were committed by Violet, the evidence is irrefutable – *unless someone put the firelighters in her drawer*. But nobody other than he and Branson has a key, and he's almost certain Branson is innocent.

He longs for the police to arrive. If only Lorraine's text had made it. Now, they'll be here until Christmas Day itself or beyond, waiting for the snow to melt. He can't think about Harriet and Cara. Instead, as Nick fries bacon and cracks eggs into Colt's enormous, well-seasoned iron frying pan, Catherine's face floats in his mind. Where has he seen it before? If only he'd had time to read that clipping. Perhaps it's none of his business . . . but until he knows for sure how and when Catherine died, his memory will scratch at him like claws on a closed door.

Lorraine appears as he's plating up, and offers to take breakfast to Violet. 'I'll just tap on the door and stand back,' she says. 'Give me your key so I can lock her in again.'

'No.' Nick shakes his head. 'I'd like to speak to her. I'll take it up, if you can serve the others.'

'She might attack you . . .'

'She's not a Minotaur. I'll take my chances.' Nick picks up the plate and a mug of tea and heads upstairs.

He taps lightly on the door.

'What?' calls Violet rudely.

'It's Nick. I've got your breakfast.'

'Oh, I thought you were Branson.'

He unlocks the door.

'Thanks,' she says grudgingly.

'May I come in?'

She shrugs, and steps aside. Nick perches on the desk chair as Violet sits on the bed and ploughs into her breakfast. She's still wearing her silk robe. Nick wonders what she'll do, now her funding source has dried up.

'Violet,' he begins, 'are you quite sure Branson didn't plant those firelighters?'

'Yes.' Violet nods soberly. 'I am. The truth is, Nick, he bloody adored Penelope. I knew he'd never leave her, he was only with me because he was worried about losing his looks, and I flattered him. That first time in the pool house, he was really drunk, and I could see he regretted it right away. But I couldn't bear to let him go. I was so lonely.'

'Why? You're young and pretty and vivacious . . .' Nick feels like a maiden aunt, jollying her along.

Violet shrugs. 'Always felt like an outsider. I'm not posh really, I just learned to sound it when I went to uni. I changed my name too: I was born Valerie. Little Val Evans whose dad owns the chip shop. I was clever and I got into publishing PR after I graduated. I soon realised they're all called Saskia and Phoebe and go to their family estates in Berkshire for Christmas. I go to my dad's council house in Merthyr Tydfil. Mum lives in Spain; we don't get on.'

Nick wonders why she's telling him all this. Violet looks up from her toast.

'I've lost Branson. Everyone thinks I'm a murderer. I'm scared to death I'll go to prison for something I haven't done, so I want you to know the truth, even if you don't believe me.'

Nick nods. 'Go on.'

'I could tell Branson was getting cold feet, but he was terrified of me telling Penny if he dumped me.'

'He told me he liked you.'

'Stockholm Syndrome.' Violet half smiles. 'When you become attached to your captors. I made sure he got everything he needed physically, but I was no match for Penny emotionally and intellectually. So I booked into Mistletoe Manor, knowing they'd both be here. I claimed it was a coincidence, and Penny believed me. Branson knew it wasn't, of course.' Violet pauses. 'I thought we could sneak around, and I'd show him what he was missing.

'The worst thing is, Nick, I liked her. She was so kind to me; we really were good friends. Despite the age gap, when I started at that job, she was my only friend. But then . . . something happened.'

'What do you mean?'

'It was years ago. I'd seen her at the office Christmas party, and she was fine. But then she didn't reply to any of my messages over that Christmas, and when I saw her again in the new year, she looked . . . different. Older. She just said, "Something happened," but she wouldn't tell me anything else. Soon after that, she met Branson and married him at a registry office with two witnesses off the street. She didn't invite a single person she knew. And next thing I heard, they'd moved to California and I didn't have any friends left at all. Still don't.'

Nick leans forward. 'What do you think happened?'

'I don't know. We kept in touch a bit on Facebook, and I invited myself to stay when I visited the US. And . . . well, you know what happened with Branson. I fell in love with him, and he didn't fall in love with me. Nick, I know I've behaved appallingly, but I swear I didn't kill anyone. I had no idea what was in that parcel when I unwrapped it. I was asleep when someone started that fire.'

'But nobody else has keys to your room,' says Nick. 'The firelighters . . .'

'I know. That's what's going to put me in prison, isn't it?' She stares at him, desperation in her eyes. 'But I'm innocent. At least, I'm innocent of murder.'

'Did you write that note to Penelope?'

'No!' Violet almost sobs with frustration. 'I wouldn't say "I know what you did", because that's just it. I *don't* know what she did. Nobody knows – apart from the killer.'

40

Back in his room, where Jingle has covered his pillow in a light dusting of fur, Nick takes the phone from his pocket and scrolls to the Photos app. Catherine looks back at him, wryly amused, beautiful, alive. He could swear he's seen her before . . . was she famous? Harriet would know. She has a mental map of who's starred in what, going back decades. They'll be watching a police procedural drama and Harriet will point at some constable with two lines of dialogue and say, 'That indie film we saw at the Curzon three years ago! He was the brother!' Nick has no such power of recall for faces.

He could ask Matilda, but she's already had a shock today. He doesn't want to compound her grief, and besides, he remembers, he's not supposed to have seen the photo at all. Sighing, he slips the phone back into his pocket and heads downstairs.

The small group is gathered around the fire, discussing a way out.

'Now the snow's melting,' says Alan, 'we could try and make it to the gate. Flag down a car.'

'The drifts are feet high still,' Lorraine argues. 'I want to get to our Jade's by tomorrow more than anything, but I don't want us to die of cold.'

'Lorraine's right,' says Matilda. She's holding a steaming

cup of tea and nibbling a shortbread biscuit. 'Best sit tight now, and wait for the police.'

'Yes, but they still don't know!' Branson is frustrated. 'They can't come if they don't know what's happened!'

'Perhaps we can try another text . . .' David ventures. 'They must be busy. I suppose the roads are still icy, and it's Christmas Eve so they're probably dealing with accidents . . .' He trails off, and Nick sees a micro-expression flash across his face – it looks like sudden pain. Is David ill? He doesn't want to probe in front of Emily.

'David, can I borrow you for a second?'

Nick grimaces at his own choice of words, subconsciously absorbed from his old news editor. In Mark Niven's case, they almost always heralded a bollocking. Nick was only on news for a year or so, thankfully. It wasn't for him; he's much happier on investigative features, where he's been for the past six years. *Six years* . . . Nick can't move. It's as though someone has drawn back a muffling black curtain, and the view has opened up before him, changing everything.

He knows where he's seen Catherine's face.

They sit in the library. 'It's Christmas Eve,' says Nick. 'I know it's early, but do you fancy a whisky? I found the secret supply in the kitchen cupboard.'

David smiles. 'Not much to celebrate,' he says sadly. 'Still stuck here, Violet a murderer, three people dead. Four, if you count poor Colt.'

'I wasn't thinking of celebrating so much as toasting our ongoing survival,' says Nick.

'Actually' – David looks away – 'I don't really drink spirits.'

'Fair enough. I'll stick to tea for now.'

Nick leans back in his wing chair. He's sat in it so often the last few days, the cushions have moulded to his shape. He'll almost miss it when they leave.

'David, I need to ask you something.'

He looks up. 'Fire away.'

'Emily's mum . . . your wife. You never said exactly how she died, and I wondered . . .'

David's expression is puzzled. 'I'm not sure what that has to do with anything.'

'Humour me. I'm just curious.'

David sighs. 'I said it was an illness because Emily was there. She's always believed her mum was poorly and didn't get better. She was too little to remember what happened.'

'She wasn't ill?'

'No. She was perfectly healthy. That's what makes it so awful.'

David blinks, and his long fingers beat a tattoo on the arms of the wing-backed chair. The silence extends.

'Can you tell me?'

'If I must. I can't say I enjoy talking about it, and look, Nick, you mustn't tell Emily. I mean it.' David's mild brown eyes look almost fierce.

Nick nods. *Come on, just tell me.*

'Well.' David rubs the bridge of his nose. 'She died in a car crash. The other driver's fault.'

'I'm so sorry.'

'Thank you. She was an older mum; we'd gone through IVF. Emily was our miracle baby, as they call it. The thing was, she could have died too. Emily was in the back of the car. She was thrown clear and the police found her when they were called to the scene of the crash. She was still strapped into her car seat, lying in the snow, in the dark. If she hadn't been wearing her little padded snowsuit . . .'

Tears spill down David's face and he raises a hand to wipe them away. 'You see why I don't like talking about it?'

Nick does. He sees, too, why David is so protective of his only child.

'She was only two,' David says. 'I never know whether it's good or bad that she doesn't remember her mother.'

'Don't you have any photos up?'

David shakes his head. 'Too painful. I loved her so much. It's easier just to focus on Emily, do everything I can to keep her safe.'

'That's why you moved abroad?'

David nods. 'Too many memories here.'

'I'm bloody sorry that happened, David. It's very tough.'

He smiles, weakly. 'I've got my little girl, though,' he says. 'She's what matters now.'

MUM OF ONE DIES IN CHRISTMAS EVE CRASH

A Harrogate woman has died following a car crash on Christmas Eve. Katy Foley, 41, was travelling home with her daughter, 2, in the back seat.

According to an eyewitness, her Toyota Yaris was run off the road during the blizzard by a black Mercedes, which was 'veering all over the place', then drove away at speed.

Foley died at the scene. Her daughter was found unhurt, after being thrown clear of the vehicle.

The crash was reported to local police shortly before 6.30 p.m.

Sergeant Bill Ackerman said: 'We are investigating the circumstances of this tragic incident and are keen to hear from any witnesses.'

He appealed for anyone with information or dashcam footage to contact North Yorkshire police.

It came in over the wires on Boxing Day that year, and Mark told him to write it up in the middle of a long, tedious shift, between a short filler on dwindling mince pie sales and something on a 'snowmageddon weather-bomb' hitting the North. Nick had wondered about the woman in the supplied photograph, had been struck by the loveliness of her face. He'd bashed out a quick piece, spared a brief thought for the little daughter, and moved on. Soon after, he transferred to features.

Alone in the library, after David's departure, Nick takes out his phone and looks again at Katy Foley. It's her. David's wife, Emily's mum . . . and Matilda's daughter. Catherine.

For a moment, he is overwhelmed. Nick closes his eyes, and presses the heels of his hands against the sockets, until he can only see crimson shapes dancing frenetically in the darkness. He'd prefer to remain like this until the police come, but he can't. He has to deal with it. He has to run upstairs and let Violet know that they were wrong about her.

David has returned to the drawing room, unaware of his revelation. Nick moves slowly to the window, his movements clumsy with shock, like somebody stumbling away from an accident. Outside, the sun is warming the snow, and the gutters are running with clear water, the drifts collapsing into themselves.

Very soon, they'll be able to wade down the drive to civilisation. It's time to bring it to a close.

As he returns to the drawing room, where it all began, Lorraine is holding up her phone in triumph.

'Nick!' she shouts. 'It got through! The police are coming!'

The others are exclaiming, cheering, high-fiving.

Branson looks weak with relief. 'Thank God,' he murmurs, 'thank God, now my poor wife can be treated with respect.'

If you'd respected her enough not to sneak off to Violet's room . . . Nick thinks, but he catches himself. He's made mistakes far worse than foolish infidelity. He's sent an innocent man to his death, launched a witch hunt, got it all wrong . . . but now, finally, he knows he's right.

Nick steps forward. 'Listen,' he begins, just as Lorraine cries:

'Listen!'

Far in the distance, they can hear a familiar sound – rhythmic, eerie. As they stand in silence, it grows in volume. Sirens. The police are on their way, and soon, at last, they'll be rescued.

Nick doesn't have long. He holds up a hand. 'Can someone go and fetch Violet? Quickly.'

'I'll go.' Lorraine looks worried. 'Hang on, will I be safe?'

'I promise,' says Nick. 'Violet hasn't killed anyone.'

There's an outcry. 'But you said . . .!' 'The firelighters!' 'She did!'

'No,' he tells them. 'She didn't.'

'What is this?' Alan sounds tense. 'You've not come up with some cock-eyed new theory just before the police arrive, surely? If you don't think it was Violet, leave it to the police, for heaven's sake. You've been wrong every time so far. Much as you'd expect from a so-called journalist.'

Nick doesn't dignify that remark with a reply.

When Lorraine returns with Violet, who looks washed out and red-eyed, her hair greasy and tied back, they take their seats around the fire. Nick is interested to see that once again everyone has taken the seat they chose that first night. It feels as though months have passed since then.

The sirens have reached the gate, and their slow whoop is a reminder that this is their last hour together. Soon, they'll be parted, interviewed, driven away . . . it's essential that everyone understands what really happened, before they tell their stories.

A ring of expectant faces turn to Nick. 'Go on, then,' says Alan. 'Spit it out.'

He stands as they sit. He needs the room to pace and think as he talks.

'Penelope didn't drive,' he says. 'It seemed odd, she was so competent, she lived in LA – everyone there drives. Something had happened, years ago. Violet told me that, and so did Branson. Until today, I didn't know it had taken place at Christmas. I thought it was something that happened *to* her. In fact, it was something she did that happened to someone else.'

'I've no idea what you're talking about.' Matilda's face is almost translucent, and as she reaches for her teacup, her hand is shaking.

'It's the anniversary of your daughter's death, isn't it?' Nick asks her. 'Christmas Eve.'

He turns to Emily, who is regarding him, wide-eyed, Gaia on her lap. 'Could you take Gaia to the porch?' he asks her. 'Put a coat on. Now the snow's melting, she might like to go out . . .'

'I don't want to. Daddy, I want to stay.'

David looks at her. 'No, darling, Uncle Nick's right. Go on. Don't go far.'

Grumbling – 'I'm never allowed to hear *anything*' – she stomps off, Gaia trotting behind her.

Nick takes a deep breath. '"I know what you did." You could say that to any one of us, and it would strike home. We've all got things we're not proud of, things in our past that keep us awake at night. But in Penelope's case, she knew exactly what it meant. She killed somebody on Christmas Eve, leaving a child motherless, and she fled the scene.'

'*What?*'

Branson is staring at him. 'This is . . . What the hell, Nick? What are you talking about?'

'She never told you,' Nick says. 'I assume she was too ashamed. But here's the truth. Penelope killed Catherine Foley, six years ago, in a blizzard on Christmas Eve. It was a hit and run – she didn't stop to see what she'd done. She only found out later.'

Violet's face is a mask of horror. Matilda is squeezing her hands together so tightly, the knuckles gleam like unearthed bones.

'Are you saying Penelope killed my Catherine?' Her voice trembles.

'Oh, come on.' Nick is surprised by the rage in his own voice. 'You know she did.'

'Catherine was David's wife, too,' says Matilda. 'Perhaps he was the killer, seeking revenge. Don't you think a doctor is a more likely murderer than an old lady?'

Lorraine has been watching, rigid with shock. 'Your daughter was David's *wife*? You've known each other all along?'

'Emily's your granddaughter.' Branson gets there first. He stares wildly at the older woman, breathing hard, attempting to make sense of it.

'Come on, Matilda,' says Nick. Her gaze locks on to his, blue as the empty winter sky. 'It's time to tell the truth. You owe us that.'

'I owe you nothing.'

She tries to stand, but Alan places a firm hand on her shoulder and pushes her back into the chair. 'I confided in you,' he says flatly. 'I told you things nobody but me and Lorraine know. If I'd had the slightest idea . . .'

Violet emits a strangled sob. 'You all blamed me,' she says. 'I thought I was going to prison. I thought my life was over.'

'I'm so sorry.' Nick means it. She's done bad things – but she's not a killer.

Branson stands. He's big; he towers over Matilda.

'So who was it?' he says slowly. 'Was it you? Or David?'

'I'm eighty years old! Do you honestly think I could stab a woman like Penelope? Or strangle a fit young man?' She quails in her chair. 'I'm as horrified as you are!'

Their faces turn to David. He is clutching the arm of the sofa with one hand, the other is over his face. His shoulders are shaking.

'Oh, you're pathetic!' Matilda snaps. 'Look at yourself. You were never good enough for Catherine.'

'Tell them!' David's voice is a wail of despair. 'Tell them the truth! Nick knows, he's going to tell the police – it's all over, Matilda.'

41

There is a thick silence. The sirens have stopped now, but in the distance, at the bottom of the drive, there are voices, shouts, the sound of a diesel engine throbbing into life.

Matilda takes a long breath, and smooths down the skirt of her dress. She looks at them all in turn before she speaks.

'Catherine was killed six years ago today,' she begins. 'Every year since, I've come here, to Mistletoe Manor. I don't celebrate in my heart, but I honour her memory. She loved Christmas. When she was a little girl it was her favourite time of year. JoJo adored her summer birthday but not my little Catherine – she wanted jingle bells and presents and snow. She was a little dancing elf, with her dark curls and her big eyes . . .'

Violet sighs loudly.

'I'll tell the truth in my own way,' Matilda says coldly. 'Earlier this year, I met an old friend of Penelope's at a party in Harrogate. People like me to attend their functions because I'm rich. After his City career, my late husband owned various properties across Yorkshire. When he died, they came to me, with a great deal of money.'

She pauses. The group is rapt, listening.

'This friend told me something I hadn't known. And that was when I decided that something must be done.'

'Stop speaking in riddles,' snaps Branson. 'Did you kill my wife?'

'No,' says Matilda. 'I assure you I did not.'

David looks up, his face a mask of anguish. 'You as good as did.'

'Let me speak.' Matilda is calm as the throbbing engine of an approaching snowplough carries on the still air. 'The police told us that it was Peter who killed Catherine. Penelope's son. He was only seventeen, a new driver; he hadn't been drinking. When they tracked the car down, he confessed to everything. He told the police that he'd skidded on a patch of ice in the blizzard, that he hadn't seen what happened to the other car, the snow was coming down too hard. He said he'd panicked and sped home and his mother told him to go to the police. They were just on their way to the station to report it. Exemplary behaviour.'

Matilda nods in mock admiration as the others exchange puzzled glances.

'So he went to jail?' Branson asks. It's clear this is news to him.

'No, he didn't, would you believe? He was initially charged with causing death by dangerous driving, then it was commuted to leaving the scene of an accident, because the weather was deemed to be a mitigating factor, along with his age. His parents paid for the very best lawyers, naturally, and in the end, he was given a twelve-month suspended sentence and a large fine, which they also paid. He was disqualified from driving for five years. So, he'll soon be behind the wheel again.'

She offers the group a tight, brittle smile. 'All's well that ends well. Of course, I was distraught, as was David, but I tried to live with my grief. Then I went to that party, in September this year. The woman I met there, Susan, had no idea of my connection to Penelope's family. It was a party for the law firm my husband had always used, and Susan was one of the partners' second wives. I sat next to her at dinner and the talk turned to miscarriages of justice. She'd had a few glasses of champagne, and I remember exactly what she said. "A woman was killed in a car crash on Christmas Eve a few years ago," she told me, "and the teenage driver was arrested and charged. It was my old schoolfriend's son." My whole body turned cold. Was she going to claim that he was innocent – that my darling daughter's death was just an unfortunate accident? But she carried on. She said, "I went to see my old friend soon after it happened, and she broke down. She told me the truth, that it was she who had been driving, but she was over the limit. That she didn't see the junction, not just because of the snow but because she was drunk. She was driving home from some Christmas party, and she'd been laying into the mulled wine" – that's what she said, *laying into*,' Matilda repeats. 'Knowing she'd be getting into her car, after dark, in a snowstorm.'

Matilda pauses. Nobody speaks.

'The woman told me her friend had run Catherine's little car off the road and panicked. And rather than coming clean, and risking prison' – Matilda draws a deep breath – 'she persuaded her son to take the blame, knowing he was at home, sober, promising he'd get the best lawyers and he wouldn't go to prison. I asked, "What was her name?" But of course, I already knew.

'I asked Susan how she lived with that knowledge, as the wife of a lawyer and as a human being with, one presumes, a moral compass. She said it tortured her, she wished she'd never found out . . . but Penelope and her husband broke up, under the strain of the lie. He wasn't supportive of throwing their teenage son to the wolves, oddly enough – and very soon afterwards, she met someone else and fled to America, to "start again".'

Matilda's eyes flash. 'How *lovely* for her, starting all over again in a Malibu mansion with a brand-new, adoring husband. Catherine didn't get that chance. She was driving here to Mistletoe Manor, to surprise me. We always stayed here at Christmas, though I wasn't expecting her until Christmas morning. But her life was snatched from her in seconds, her baby left without a mother, her mother left without a daughter. And her husband . . .'

David's face is buried in his hands.

'So when you found out the truth, you set up the Facebook group?' Nick asks.

Matilda nods. 'Yes. I may be old, but I'm not incapable. I knew Penelope grew up in the area, and I hoped she'd take advantage of the so-called prize. I was lucky other people joined to make it appear legitimate – there's a lot of old folk who enjoy pointless nostalgia. "Eee, we used to play on bombsites . . . Go-karts made from orange crates . . . Folks was poor but honest . . ."' she mocks. 'Once she'd joined, it was easy. I was going to offer to pay for the flights too, but Branson's terribly rich, aren't you? Dear Penny didn't even ask.' She glances up at him. His face is purple with anger.

'But why didn't she recognise you?' Violet asks. 'Why didn't she know you were Catherine's mother?'

'I'd never met her. I didn't go to court for the sentencing.

I was . . . well, for a year or so, I was inconsolable. I could barely get out of bed, and JoJo was useless.'

'That's not fair,' begins David fiercely. 'She has a family, miles away. She couldn't drop everything to be with you night and day.'

'Couldn't she? As for you.' She turns to David, icy contempt radiating from her. 'Taking *my granddaughter* thousands of miles away. Allowing me no contact. She was all I had left.'

'You know why I took her away.' David's voice shakes. 'You wanted custody. You claimed I wasn't fit to care for her.'

'Well, you weren't! Working all hours, drinking . . .'

'I wasn't *drinking*!' David explodes. 'A few glasses of wine every night! I was never in any way a danger to her! Not like you were, obsessing over your dead daughter, trying to dress *my child* up in Catherine's old baby clothes! It was wrong—'

'I was grieving!' Matilda snaps. 'And then before the year was out, off you went, never coming back, always too busy to let me visit . . . I didn't even know your address!'

'Because I didn't trust you! And I was right not to. You'd have tried to kidnap her.'

'Why did you come back this Christmas?' Nick asks David. The noise of the snowplough cuts through the air as it grinds slowly towards the porch.

'I thought Emily should see where her mum's family is from. I wanted her to meet JoJo's boys, get to know her cousins. And I thought enough time had passed that Matilda might be more mentally stable, able to build a relationship with Emily. But I didn't want Emily to know she was her grandmother in case I was wrong and she hadn't changed. I came back on the basis that Matilda wouldn't tell her just yet.'

'And I kept my side of the bargain,' says Matilda.

'Yes. I just didn't understand the bargain I was making,' says David bitterly.

Violet fixes Matilda with a steady gaze. 'So what exactly did you do next?'

'I hadn't allowed for the snow,' Matilda says thoughtfully. 'That was a surprise. But it was lucky, in the end, that there were more suspects than I'd anticipated. Nick, Lorraine and Alan, Destiny . . . all these extra people turning up.'

'How did you kill her? At your age?' Branson asks.

'I'm getting to that,' says Matilda implacably. 'David played his part very well, not a hint of recognition towards me.'

'That was easy,' mutters David. 'I didn't want to look at you at all.'

'Emily's Secret Santa game,' says Nick. 'How could you know she'd suggest that?'

'Oh, I didn't.' Matilda smiles. 'I was simply going to wrap it and ensure the star was found somewhere that day. But her suggestion added an extra layer of festive theatricality, don't you think?'

The others exchange glances. Lorraine's expression is one of frozen disbelief; Alan looks queasy with horror; Branson is shaking his head, unable to speak.

'Oh, you're all so horrified,' Matilda says scornfully. 'But think harder. Have you ever lost someone due to the actions of someone else? Didn't you want to harm the person who took the one you love? Wipe them from the earth? Look at you, Branson. I can see the hatred radiating from you. Well, that's how I feel. But you only lost your wife of a few years. I lost the precious daughter I'd loved for over forty years, I lost my granddaughter as a result, and I lost the love of my other daughter and grandchildren because the rage and grief sent me mad.'

She gazes imperiously around the group. 'I wonder if any of you can look into your heart of hearts, and tell me you wouldn't feel the same.'

'I wouldn't *kill* someone . . .' begins Lorraine.

'No,' agrees Matilda. 'You'd just stand back and let her kill herself.'

'What about Donal?' Nick asks in the ensuing silence, broken only by the noise of the encroaching snowplough. 'Why did he have to die? He was only young. He'd done nothing wrong.'

'Because he suspected.' Matilda shrugged. 'Collateral damage, I'm afraid. He was asking questions, poking about. He found the wrapping paper scrap – I'd taken the paper from Lorraine's luggage. It was so shiny, I thought it would be perfect. I wrapped up the star and was going to burn the rest in the drawing room when I placed it on the table. But then I saw Destiny leaving her room, and I couldn't risk being seen,' she says calmly. It's as though she's explaining a small professional error to an exacting boss. 'I opened the nearest door and I hid it in there, thinking I'd go back for it. I knew Donal must have found it, because he had the keys. He knew I'd lost my daughter at Christmas. He was a bright boy; he'd soon have added it all up.'

'Why didn't you kill me?' Nick asks steadily. 'I was "poking about" too.'

Matilda shrugs and pulls a face that's almost flirtatious. 'I rather liked you. And you were getting nowhere. Besides, Donal knew something you didn't.'

'Do enlighten us,' says Violet. She's curled into a tight ball, rage emanating from her.

'He knew that I'm the owner,' says Matilda. 'Mistletoe Manor is mine. How it didn't occur to any of you . . . there were enough clues.'

The puzzle pieces finally click into place, and Nick wants to slap himself. Someone else had keys. Someone else knew the layout of the manor. Someone had access to the phone lines, which, he now realises, were not down due to the storm, but because they'd been cut. And someone turned off the Wi-Fi.

'But hold on.' Lorraine sits upright. 'The mistletoe berry poisoning . . . You were so ill!'

Nick's heart sinks. He's been so stupid. What was it his old editor used to say? 'Don't listen to what they're telling you, Nick. Listen to what they're not telling you.'

42

Matilda twinkles, as though she's played a delightfully naughty practical joke on them all. 'It's not hard to fake a few symptoms. When you're my age, people automatically assume you're at death's door. I used to do a bit of am-dram, you know. The Harrogate Troubadours. I quite enjoyed acting "being poisoned".'

'You put the berries in the fridge,' says Nick. 'You let us believe it was Colt, and watched us drive him away from his home and his job.'

Matilda shrugs. 'Needs must. I couldn't have you suspecting me, or our quiet little doctor.'

There's a noise in the hall. Emily has come back in from outside.

'Em, poppet,' calls David, a slight shake in his voice, 'can you take Gaia into the library? I'll be there soon.'

'But . . .'

'Now!'

Her footsteps hurry away, accompanied by Gaia's clicking claws. Jingle strolls into the drawing room and makes for Nick's lap. He wonders if he's ever felt so pleased to see anything. He strokes the cat as questions crowd his mind.

'Why Destiny?' he asks eventually. 'She had nothing to do

with Mistletoe Manor, or you, or Catherine. Why did she have to die?'

A sob shakes David's shoulders, and Violet blinks away tears.

'Because of David,' says Matilda. 'He was beginning to get close to her and I couldn't risk it. He really is the weak link in all of this. My dear late husband used to say, "As soon as you delegate, you're putting your trust in someone less committed than you are." He was so right.' She sighs. 'I could see that David was under immense mental strain, that it was only a matter of time before he crumbled and confessed the truth to somebody. Deborah – I refuse to call her that ridiculous, made-up name – was the obvious choice. She was an ex-doctor, very attractive – she looked like a rather low-rent version of my beautiful Catherine. I could see he was drawn to her. Weren't you?' she suddenly snaps at David.

'Yes.' He nods. 'Because as well as being beautiful, she was good. You wouldn't understand that.'

'Why the fire?' Alan is pale with shock. 'Why so brutal?'

'It had to be something I could manage myself.' Matilda shrugs. 'The Yule log was my own tradition – every year, we'd light it at six o'clock on Christmas Eve to honour Catherine's memory. This year, I thought it would be fitting to use it to start the fire. It was terribly heavy, but I managed it. The adrenalin, I suppose.'

They stare at her, dumb with horror. 'In what way *fitting*?' asks Violet eventually.

'It continued the Christmas theme,' says Matilda. 'Catherine loved the festive blaze. We'd all gather round the fire, toasting crumpets, telling jokes. Such a pretty little girl . . .'

She really is insane, thinks Nick. What do you do with somebody like this? Would she live out her days in a secure psychiatric hospital, rather than prison?

'I knew David had sedatives with him,' Matilda goes on. 'I stole them from his bedside table, and I crushed up four or five, then I tapped on Deborah's door in the early hours. I told her I couldn't sleep because I was frightened, and I asked if she'd share a cup of herbal tea with me.

'She agreed; she was kind like that.' Matilda smiles fondly, as if remembering a particularly special friend. 'I'd already brought the Yule log upstairs with me, and I smashed the smoke alarm with it. I was afraid you'd all wake up, but I was going to say I was sleepwalking. A hackneyed excuse, I know, but in the end, I didn't need it.

'Deborah passed out very quickly, and I carried in the log – firelighters from the cupboard, too: it's a treasure trove. I made sure it was left unlocked, so anyone could access it. Then I lit the wood, left, and locked her door behind me.'

Matilda looks at Nick. 'Shame you woke up. I was hoping to leave the blaze a little longer, but the job was done, so it didn't really matter.'

'And then you put the firelighters in my bedside drawer,' says Violet.

'Yes. I wasn't sure they'd be found, so I was going to come up with some reason to look in there – a stolen necklace, perhaps, one of my diamond brooches missing . . . but Nick got there first. A very useful stooge.'

The worst thing is, she's right, thinks Nick. He has aided and abetted Matilda at every turn; suspecting everyone but her, blaming Colt, accusing Violet . . . He wonders if another

344

career would suit him better. 'Third village idiot' in a Jacobean play, perhaps.

'What would you have done if the snow hadn't trapped us?' Nick asks. 'Killed Penelope, of course, but then what?'

'Oh.' Matilda gives a little one-shouldered shrug. 'I'd have made my accusations and gone home. Then it would have been up to the police to make their arrests.'

'Accusations?' asks Branson. He can barely speak with the pain of betrayal and loss. He must know now that Penelope targeted him, a rich bachelor who could marry her and whisk her far from the English legal system – just in case anyone ever wondered why she'd allowed a seventeen-year-old who had only recently passed his test to drive home alone in a blizzard. Branson had betrayed his wife – but she had betrayed him first.

'She means me. She was going to accuse me.' David finally removes his hands from his face. He appears to have aged by several years during the course of Matilda's revelations. His entire body shakes. Nick sees Lorraine instinctively reach out her hand to comfort him, then swiftly withdraw it. 'I can't lose Emily,' David says, tears thick in his voice. 'She's everything to me.'

'Oh dear.' Matilda gives a little laugh. 'I'm afraid you already have. So, David.' She smiles brightly at him. 'Will you tell them all the final part, or shall I?'

'The police will be here soon,' says Violet, nodding to the window. The vehicle is almost outside. 'Tell us.'

'I had no choice,' begins David. 'I never wanted to do it.'

'Oh, the classic excuse of weak men and women everywhere,' says Matilda. She adopts a high, wheedling tone. '*It wasn't my fault. She made me do it.*'

'Shut up,' he says. 'I'll tell it in my own way. At least allow me that.'

She shrugs, and sits back. Her diamond and emerald brooch sparkles in the light, and Nick realises it's supposed to be a sprig of mistletoe – Matilda's final statement of allegiance to the house and its memories.

'Matilda invited Emily and me for Christmas,' David says. 'She wrote to the hospital where I work, and she said she didn't have long left to live, and she yearned to see her granddaughter before it was too late. She guilt-tripped me and I gave in. Look at her,' he adds bitterly. 'There's nothing wrong with her. She's like a cockroach.'

'Go on,' says Nick. David takes a long, quivering breath.

'When I arrived, she was all sweetness. I thought she'd begun to move on at last. She wanted to spend time with Emily, get to know her – we planned to drive over to Manchester, meet the cousins and see JoJo . . . I thought it might all be OK. But the night we arrived, Matilda made sure Donal was out of the way, and then she told me her plan.'

David pauses. 'I was almost physically sick. I'm a doctor, my whole life has been about making people better, saving their lives, not . . .' He convulses.

'Not what?' asks Alan coldly.

'Not murder!' David cries. 'Matilda blackmailed me. She told me that she wants full custody of Emily – and I knew why. So she could pretend that my daughter was Catherine reincarnated, so she could dress her up like a doll and play old-fashioned games, and teach her to be just the same, and woe betide Emily if she ever reveals a hint of her own personality, rather than her mother's! I won't let that happen, I'd rather die.

She's everything I have and I'm her *father*,' David spits. 'You had your chance at parenthood; your daughters grew up with you, in a happy, stable, rich family. Yet you want to take Emily's childhood away from me.'

Lorraine clears her throat. 'I'm not hearing much about what Emily wants here,' she says, disgusted. 'It's all about you two, dividing her up like a bloody cake.'

David blinks. 'You're right,' he says. 'But it was my love for Emily that drove me to this point. Matilda told me that she was too frail to kill Penelope – so I had to do it.'

There are gasps. Branson turns to look at the smaller man, hatred in his eyes.

'She said that if I didn't, she'd tell the police I was an abusive father and that I'd hurt Katy during our marriage,' David goes on. 'She'd fabricated letters and emails supposedly from my wife – *David blames me for the IVF not working, he's been hitting me again, Mummy, I don't know what to do* . . . She showed them to me. Matilda is vicious,' he hisses. 'She had it all planned. I was so afraid, I knew how convincing she could be. I knew she could stop me taking Emily home, that she'd weave a pack of lies and before I knew it, social services would be involved, and Matilda would be stepping in, with her millions and her big house. I'd lose Em. I couldn't take that risk.'

'So you killed Penelope.'

David nods, his eyes squeezed shut. 'It was the worst thing I've ever had to do,' he whispers. 'She pulled off her eye-mask and she looked at me . . .'

Nick thinks of Penelope's terrified, staring eyes, the fear she must have experienced as she died.

'Who wrote the note?' asks Violet.

'I did.' Matilda smiles, as though accepting praise. 'The fountain pen's in my handbag; I know you were looking for it, Nick. I wanted her to know she wasn't safe, I wanted her to feel a fraction of the fear that I felt when the police knocked on the door that night.'

'You didn't go straight to the police?' Alan demands.

'We were trapped! She'd cut the phone lines – there was no going to the police,' David insists.

All that hopeless checking and wondering when they'd be fixed . . . Nick feels another wave of rage.

'You could have warned Penny, given her the chance to tell me, so we could get away,' says Branson.

'Except you weren't there,' David says. 'You were with your mistress.'

'How did you know he wouldn't be there, in bed with Penny?' Violet whispers.

'I didn't,' David admits. 'I mildly sedated his drink earlier on, thinking he'd be knocked out.'

'So that's why you couldn't manage to . . .' murmurs Violet, and Branson flashes her a look of fury.

'Then Matilda gave me the star and she told me to use that as a weapon. I gave it back to her afterwards . . .' David weeps again. 'I had no idea she'd wrap it like that, so Emily would see it . . .'

'I thought she'd be playing with the dog,' Matilda says. 'That's why I gave her the lead – it was Pixie's, Catherine's little puppy when she was a child. She loved that dog.'

Nick tries to follow the dark labyrinth of Matilda's mind, and fails.

'Besides, I took the star away again afterwards.' Matilda

shrugs. 'I wrapped it in a jumper in my wardrobe, so you didn't even have to look at it.'

'Donal,' says Nick. 'You killed him, too.'

David nods. 'She upped the threats, she said if I didn't, she'd tell you all that she'd seen me hurting Emily. I knew she meant it.'

'So,' says Branson, 'she made you use the fairy lights on Donal?'

David nods. 'All part of her sick game. *Festive deaths.* Because without Katy, nobody's allowed to be happy at Christmas.'

'So what did you do?' Lorraine's lips are white; her words emerge in a whisper.

'I waited in the cupboard on the upstairs landing until I heard Donal come out of his room, and then I just followed him and I . . . It was quick,' he adds. 'There was the element of surprise, so . . .'

'Oh, well done,' says Nick. 'Good for you. At least he didn't suffer.'

'I didn't mean . . .'

'And you knew about what she'd done to Colt, with the berries? Or was that you as well?' Nick asks.

David shakes his head. 'No! I mean, I guessed, but . . .'

'But of course, you couldn't say anything.' Lorraine gives him a twisted little smile. 'Poor you, David, forced into this awful position.'

'I was!'

Lorraine looks away, revolted by his self-pity.

'What was the endgame, Matilda?' Nick asks. The snow-plough is now throbbing just feet from the front porch. They can hear the collapsing snow as it pushes through the melting drifts. 'What did you want, in the end?'

Matilda smiles. 'It was simple. I wanted Penelope to be punished. I wanted a relationship with my granddaughter. I realised I could kill two birds with one stone. David's so blinded by his love for Emily, I knew he'd do what I wanted. It was his only hope of keeping her.'

David looks at her. 'Job done, then,' he says, in a half-whisper. 'Job done.'

Somebody is pounding on the door. 'Police! Open up!'

Nick runs to admit them, and a team of armed officers race in, a sea of dark stab vests and helmets.

'Someone get Emily!' David shouts. 'She'll be scared!'

'There's a child?' One of the men turns urgently to Nick.

'Yes, she's fine, she's in the library—' Two of them race down the corridor as he points, followed by Lorraine and Violet.

'We know who did it,' Nick tells the officers. He points at Matilda and David, who have been frogmarched into the hall by Branson and Alan. 'They've confessed.'

'Not much use if it's verbal,' one says.

Nick takes his small Dictaphone recorder out of his pocket, its red light still glowing.

'I suppose journalists are still useful for something,' he says quietly, handing it over.

David is sobbing as he's handcuffed, begging to see Emily.

'David, no,' Nick says. 'Don't let her see you like this. Maybe she can visit you when things have settled down.'

Nick watches as the trembling doctor is led away to the cars that have followed the snowplough up the drive, blue lights silently whirling over the snow. David's sobs carry in the still air as car radios crackle with instructions.

A female police officer is reading Matilda her rights. She is blinking as though she doesn't quite understand, affecting shock and bemusement. She doesn't yet know about the recording, now in the possession of the North Yorkshire Police.

Nick looks down the corridor. Alan is leading a small phalanx of officers towards the kitchen. Three bodies, all frozen. They'll need the ambulances that are currently crawling up the drive.

'Please,' Matilda cries, a broken plea. 'My photographs – you can handcuff me, but before you take me away, I must have my pictures.'

An officer nods at his junior, and she takes Matilda's arm. 'Come on then,' she says. 'Quick as you can.'

Clearly, they have judged this elegant, frightened old woman poses no flight risk. Nick isn't so sure.

Upstairs, doors are being flung open, there are barks of '*Clear!*', thudding, booted feet. As Nick stands in the hall, waiting to give his statement, Emily emerges from the corridor. She's holding hands with Lorraine, who has tears running down her cheeks. Emily's eyes are dry, her expression pinched with shock and confusion. Violet is following, holding Gaia.

'What will happen to Emily?' Nick asks as an officer gently ushers the three of them into a police car.

Lorraine turns. 'I'm going to find JoJo, Nick,' she calls. 'She's her auntie. She'll know what to do.'

Nick nods, his heart aching for Emily. Perhaps, finally, somebody will consider what's best for her. He hopes she can keep Gaia, wherever she goes. As the car slowly pulls away and disappears down the drive, he steps on to the porch again.

There's a commotion coming from a room upstairs. A female

voice shouts, 'Get down!' and as he looks towards the noise, a sash window at the end of the corridor is flung up. To his horror, Matilda teeters on the sill. The ground beneath her is impacted snow, flattened by the plough. She holds on to the frame with both hands, swaying. In her black dress, she reminds him of a spider dangling from a thread.

'Matilda, no!' yells Nick. He's already skidding and slithering towards the scene, arms outstretched to catch her. He can hear the female PC gabbling into her radio.

Matilda jumps.

She's lying face down, her limbs making a snow angel on the lawn. The whirring blue lights give the blood trickling from her head a surreal, purple sheen. Nick watches as an officer takes her pulse, tries again, looks up at his colleague, shakes his head.

She got away with it, then. She was never going to prison. That was obvious from the moment she began to speak, revealing what he should have known from the beginning. He sees it now, like a projector spooling film through his mind.

Christmas Eve. Katy, driving through the snow to Mistletoe Manor, that cosy hotel of her mother's where they always celebrate the holidays as a family. Perhaps Matilda no longer wants to host at home, now her husband is gone, and this offers the solution. Katy decides to go straight there before the weather sets in, rather than wait until morning. Her husband will come after work; they'll all be together. The snowstorm worsens as Katy peers at the road, windscreen wipers battling the relentless snow.

Nick sees Matilda decorating the tree, the box of Nativity

costumes and baubles beside her. The fire blazes in the hearth, and Matilda smiles, thinking of her newest grandchild, little Emily. They'll lift her up when she arrives tomorrow, and help her to place the pointed star right at the top of the tree.

There's a knock and Matilda hurries to answer, snow blowing in as she opens the huge door. Two police officers stand on the step. Their hats are held in their hands and before they speak, she knows.

She'll never celebrate Christmas again.

It's mid-afternoon when Nick is released from questioning, and the low sun is glowing orange over the manor. Before he calls Harriet, he shakes Branson's hand.

'You'll go back to America?'

'Not yet. First I'm heading to Devon. It'll be tough, but I'd rather they hear it from me.' He swallows. 'I'd like to offer Pete my support. Look after him a little, now his mom's gone.'

'Good of you.'

'I've got a lot of making-up to do.'

The others are at the police station. Once the police are happy with their statements, Lorraine and Alan will finally head to Jade's. They should make it in time for dinner, if they can hire a car. The officer driving Alan didn't look thrilled by the enormous bag of children's presents stuffed into the boot. Nick assumes that Violet will head back to her flat in London. It's all over with Branson. *Perhaps she'll rethink her life*, Nick muses. *Do some good in the world*.

He won't keep in touch with any of them. They were never friends, just strangers thrown together in the most appalling circumstances. It's too late to develop trust now. There's just one person he'll contact after Christmas. Someone to whom he owes a heartfelt apology.

'He came into the station this morning,' the sergeant taking his statement told Nick. 'He was frozen solid; we were worried he had hypothermia. That's why we came straight here. He told us what had happened.'

'You didn't get a text from Lorraine Pinner?'

The sergeant shrugged and shook her head. 'Don't think so.'

'Do you know where he's gone for Christmas?'

'Yeah, his cousin came and picked him up. He's gone there for a bit.'

Nick nodded. He can find the address. He's a journalist.

Epilogue

There is no snow left in London. Nick gazes down at the street where fairy lights glow in each front window and festive wreaths decorate the doors. The pavements are cold and grey, the small gardens bare and brown under the streetlamps. His heart lifts at the sight of the familiar scene. Down the road, he can hear carol singers approaching, chorusing a ragged 'Good King Wenceslas'.

'It melted almost as soon as it arrived.' Harriet has her arms around his waist. She's barely let go since he got here, though she's finally stopped crying.

'I thought you were dead,' she kept saying. 'I got your voice-mail, but I couldn't hear the name of the hotel – it cut out. The police didn't want to know; they said they were too busy dealing with "emergencies".'

'I'd say three murders is probably an emergency.' Nick tries to smile at her, but finds his voice is shaking.

Harriet breaks away and pours him a glass of wine from the open bottle on the table. It glows crimson in the candlelight.

Everything he's longed for is here. The battered sofa, the scent of home, the little Christmas tree, bushy and fresh, with its spangled decorations and soft white lights. Harriet has lit tall church candles in the fireplace, and there's a pie in the oven.

Most of all, his wife, and their daughter. Harriet's beautiful, tired face, her long dark hair held back by a red bow for Christmas Eve, her familiar perfume. And Cara. On the long drive back, after a jump-start from the friendly sergeant, Nick feared his baby might have forgotten him, but she crowed with delight, reaching her arms to him in her Christmas-pudding Babygro.

'She missed you even more than I did,' said Harriet. 'She's been an absolute madam all week.'

'That's my girl.' Nick danced Cara round the room as she shrieked with excitement. Now, their baby is finally asleep in her cot, the coloured lights of the mobile twirling over her face.

'We should eat,' says Harriet. 'I've been so worried, I've been living on toast all week. Let's sit down and you can tell me everything, from the first moment you arrived at Mistletoe Manor.'

As he crosses to the table with its holly-patterned cloth, Nick glances at the perfectly wrapped parcels under the tree and is struck by a terrible thought.

'Harriet,' he says. 'I'm so sorry. I haven't got you a present . . .'

Harriet turns, laughing. 'Oh, I think you'll find you have.'

The newcomer is sitting proudly on the sofa. Nick and Harriet watch as he lifts his head and surveys his new home, before settling on to the cushions with an expression that clearly says, 'Yes. This will do nicely.'

'I think Jingle will fit in with us very well,' Harriet says. 'As long as he doesn't fight with the orange cat at number twenty-four.'

'He won't. He's a good cat.'

As Nick sits at their little kitchen table, he looks again at the tree, with its beloved, battered angel perched on the topmost branch.

Next year, he'll help Cara put it up there. And again, he thinks, every year after that, for all their Christmases to come.

Acknowledgements

Many thanks and much gratitude to Charlotte Osment, Susannah Hamilton and Richenda Todd. Thanks to the Century editorial, design and marketing teams, who have made the process of writing this book both enjoyable and smooth. (Any lack of smoothness is entirely down to me.)

As ever, gratitude to the SCM for making me laugh every day, and a big, blood-stained thank you to crime queens Erin Kelly, Andreina Cordani and Catherine Cooper for the endless support.

Thanks most of all to Wolf, Andy, Mum, Dad, Joan and David, for ensuring my Christmases have never remotely resembled the one in this book.